JOAQUIN FUERTES

THE FUERTES CARTEL COLLECTION 1-3

CHIQUITA DENNIE

LATEST RELEASES FROM CHIQUITA DENNIE

The Early Years-A Prequel Short Story

Antonio and Sabrina: Struck in Love 1, 2, 3,4,5

Heart of Stone, Book 1 (Emery & Jackson)

Heart Of Stone Book 1.5 Emery &Jackson A Valentine's Day Short

Janice and Carlo: Captivated By His Love

Heart of Stone, Book 2 (Jordan and Damon)

Temptation

Heart of Stone, Book 3 (Angela and Brent)

Cocky Catcher

Bossy Billionaire

Bottoms Up Heart of Stone, Book 3.5(Jessica and Joseph Short

Love Shorts: A Collection of Short Stories

Joaquin Fuertes (The Fuertes Cartel Book 1)

Exposed (Salvation Society Novel)

Joaquin Fuertes (The Fuertes Cartel Book 2)

Refuel (A Driven World Novel)

Pressure (A Driven World Novel)

Until Serena (HEA World Novel)

Antonio and Sabrina: Struck in Love 5

Heart of Stone, Book 4 (Jessica and Joseph)
She's All I Need
Red Light District (A Fantasy Romance Short)
Something Gained (A Romantic Comedy Book 1)
Aydin-TN Security Book 1
Upcoming Releases (2022/2023):
Dare To Love
The Carrington Cartel Book 1
Something Earned (A Romantic Comedy Book 2)
The Carrington Cartel Book 2

This book is dedicated to the readers that have been with me since day one.
The support means a lot and you've helped me to follow my dreams.

AUTHOR INSPIRATION

Show up every day like it's your time to shine.

——Chiquita Dennie

INTRODUCTION

Are you signed up for my newsletter?

Join today and find out all the latest in new releases, contests, giveaways, sneak peeks and more.

www.chiquitadennie.com

DISCLAIMER

This work of fiction contains dark themes, kidnapping, torture, strong language, and explicit sexual content and is only intended for mature readers. This story may contain unconventional situations, language, and sexual encounters that may offend some readers. If you're looking for sweet, fluffy romance, I would recommend another book. This book is for mature readers (18+).

SYNOPSIS

Sofia is a world-famous actress and singer on Broadway. Being on the stage has been a lifelong dream. Living in New York, her life is a non-stop roller coaster of parties, magazine shoots, and more. Once her friendship with Sabrina Washington became public, any and everything was put on notice.

Joaquin is a quiet deadly force. He's known in the illegal business as Ghost. Someone that shows up only when the client needs to disappear. The second he bumps into Sofia after a meeting at the restaurant, her beauty causes his heart to beat faster. He reminds himself to not fall in love, only continue working in the shadows to keep his clients' businesses out of the spotlight.

Will these two opposites see the storm that is brewing staring right there in front of them? Or will a split second of losing your breath cause you to lose control and wreak destruction when that foundation is broken?

PREVIOUSLY...STRUCK IN LOVE 4

As the son of Joaquin Fuertes, the longest-running Mayor in Portugal, and founding father of the Fuertes Cartel, he had groomed me to run the family business with an iron fist. They knew me as Ghost because I'm good at making problems disappear. The young lady sitting across from me in a chair gave me a forced nod of agreement, which told me I had failed to persuade her to do as I requested. A deep frown crossed my face. This bitch was looking to destroy not only the De Luca Cartel but ours as well, here in Italy. Queen was known as a hardass, and Antonio had made it clear not to cross his family again, or her entire bloodline would be extinct. I stepped out of my chair as she sat with tape wrapped around her mouth, keeping the screams at bay, blood dripping down her body from numerous injuries.

She had a chance to leave when Antonio confronted her back at the meeting. Afterward, she continued with her plan, and Antonio agreed for me to put an end to her plans. Both the De Luca and Fuertes' Cartels had an agreement that as long as we made money together, we wouldn't interfere with each other's territory. I'm not an abuser, unlike other men in the Cartel. I had my ways of getting what I needed out of my enemies. Raising the sleeves of my crisp white shirt, I stepped forward as my enforcer, Gabriella, continued the ritual of cutting off one finger at a time when she didn't comply and answered my questions. I didn't need to have a gun on me like my counterparts. I've lived in Italy for the past two years, and recently an opportunity came up for me to visit America, more specifically the Big Apple, for a business exchange that would extend the Fuertes Cartel territory in the illegal underground dealings.

"Take the tape off, Gabriella."

"Joaquin, you don't want to do this. We can forge a new deal, and I can get you all the territory you need plus guns. Your father isn't the only one with ties in America," Queen said weakly, trying to convince me to betray my father. Not wanting to hear any more of her lies, I winked, and Gabriella smiled, knowing this was the signal to end her life. As she prepared to have fun, I gathered my jacket off the chair and walked out of the back of Antonio's; the restaurant was a front for the De Luca Cartel, even though it was the top celebrity spot for politicians. Everyone knew what happened here. As Queen's screams finally died down, I walked up the stairs and opened the door. I bumped into a soft body, and before we both fell, I gripped her by the waist.

"Ohh...Excuse me."

A light, sweet smell invaded my nostrils. Our eyes connected, and my grasp grew tighter.

"Hello, you can let me go now," she said with a chuckle as we both leaned against the wall away from the restaurant.

"Joaquin, the car is here and Gabriella texted you. What's going on here?" Monica pointed between the mystery goddess and me. I somehow could not make myself let go of my thoughts of her. I was only trying to prevent her from falling, but my eyes never left hers. Something about them kept me hypnotized.

"Mira a donde vas hermosa?"

"Huh?" she asked as I grinned at the perplexed look across her face, dropping my hands from around her waist. Monica followed behind me and passed my phone over as Gabriella texted the package was cleaned up.

Gabriella: The package is secure.

Me: Inform De Luca, and let him know we should make dinner plans while he's here.

Gabriella: Any other guests?

I looked back over my shoulder as the woman I just knocked into headed toward a seat that a man pulled out for her. A strange suspicion came over me, and I couldn't explain it as she peered up and caught my eye. Turning away, I opened the car door and got inside, ignoring whatever odd feeling came over me from being in her presence.

"Joaquin, are you listening to me?" Monica asked, sitting beside me in the limousine, rubbing a hand over my thigh.

"Not right now, Monica," I said, moving her hand off my thigh and focusing on texting Gabriella back.

Me: My father.

PART I

SOFIA

Three Months Later

  I'd finished the tenth performance of my Broadway show, *Regret, My Love*. Sitting in front of my vanity mirror I turned down the radio low as Nina Simone played in the background. I needed a shower and bed from being on my feet for over four days with two shows daily, back to back. I removed my makeup, tightening my robe over my sweatsuit. A knock on my door interrupted me, and my assistant walked inside without waiting for a response to come in.

"Your stalker just left." Cassidy closed the door, walking inside with a bouquet of red roses and placing them down on the vanity mirror. I pulled one stem out and took a sniff. It smelled fresh, sweet, and clean. Nothing like the man that I had come to know as Joaquin Fuertes. A dangerous, angry, menacing, but deadly Cartel boss I met a few months ago. It was in all the journals about the Fuertes family. In New York, they were untouchable, as from the stories I saw, people went missing because of them. They seemed to have multiple businesses here and their connections reached up to the top of the food chain from the cops to governors to politicians in Washington. The rumors said they came together with the De

Luca Cartel, which was run by club owner, Antonio De Luca, who was married to Sabrina Washington.

"Did he do anything to you?" Her head moved to wagging back and forth. Opening up another Revlon makeup remover, and wiping the foundation and lipstick off my lips, I glanced up through the mirror and saw her shake her head no.

"No, he does what he always does when you have a performance. Come up here, sit in the back, watch you, bring you flowers, and then leave. Should I contact the police to have him removed from the property?" Cassidy questioned.

I should probably be afraid of him. As the daughter of a southern father and mother, Latoya and Leroy Chambers, they were a regular hardworking family, and their three children were everything to them. I was born and raised in Mississippi with two brothers, me being the youngest. I was five-seven in height, twenty-seven years old, single, and working on my career as an actress and singer. I had an oval face and long nose, which my manager wanted me to get fixed. My lips were full with a small gap in between, and I had a copper skin tone with dimples in both cheeks. I was told repeatedly that I'd never make it in this business; five years later, I'm the lead actress in a Broadway show. I also had done ten movies and one TV show, with one album release, which still blew my mind coming from the south to live in New York. I was making a living doing what I loved. Things were opening up for me and having a distraction like this would be stupid.

"Has he threatened you, Cassidy?"

She sighed, running a hand down her face, turning toward me, walking closer to read the card. "Beautiful performance by a beautiful woman. I don't know, Sofia, the man never speaks to anyone, but he has a box seat to watch you perform. You've never gone out with him or had sex. But he sends you flowers for every show," Cassidy said.

"I know it seems strange, but we met one day by accident. I ran into him when I was coming out of the restaurant the day I had a meeting with the producer for the show."

I had immediately noticed the man who was tall with broad, muscled shoulders. I noticed men don't like to consider themselves beautiful. There was nothing too special about me and it made me curious as to what he wanted from me. We had never held a single conversation ever since I bumped into that muscular broad chest of his that day. I tried one time to send the flowers back and ended up with more in my room the next day.

"What did you think about my performance tonight?" I asked.

"Don't change the subject, Sofia, I expect you like the chase from the baby boy."

"I don't have time for that right now. I have the play, my family, and a movie coming up; dating is the last thing on my mind," I told her while removing my robe. I grabbed my jacket and flowers to leave Cassidy to follow behind. "I'll call you tomorrow once I hear back from Jordan about the audition," I added.

Opening the door and walking outside through the back alley, I saw a long sleek black limousine sitting and running with the door wide. The driver said to me, "Ma'am, he's waiting for you."

"I'm not getting in your car," I respond.

"The boss doesn't take no for an answer, please get in. He's had a long day; all he wants to do is take you home." The driver took my flowers, and I looked around, there was no one behind me.

"What are you doing here?" I asked.

He said nothing; he just sat near the window, turned his head to stare at me and my mouth. He then licked his lips and turned back, looking out of the window. "You can get into the car, beautiful, I won't bite. I'm safe." He held his hand out for me to take while staring at my face. I fidgeted with my hands as I hesitated to take the next step and he extended a hand out and I grasped it, then looked out the window. The driver went around to get into the driver's side; he pushed the partition up to give us privacy, and I sat near the door crossing my legs, wondering if this was the worst mistake ever.

"Thank you for the flowers," I commented. He nodded in response.

"You're welcome," he answered.

"Are you always this quiet? You're a big-time mobster from what the paper says so I figured you'd have some backup." It was very quiet in the limo as we drove home, so I kept rambling.

"I live near Waterline Square in Manhattan. My assistant feels you're crazy, and I'm crazy for indulging you; sending these flowers, she thinks you're probably a stalker."

"And what do you think?" he asked.

"I guess she's right." He smiled at me as the car pulled up in front of my apartment building. I moved to open the door, and he grasped my hand. I turned to look at him.

"Joaquin Fuertes."

"I recognize your name from the papers."

"Have dinner with me," he commanded.

"My story is simple, and one dinner can't change everything," I spoke.

"Does that scare you, Sofia?" he questioned.

"It depends, are you planning on hurting me?" He held my hand as I stepped out of the car, then I stood on the sidewalk, watching the limo leave with him inside while thinking about The Tonight Show and the audience applause, knowing he was there watching me in the private booths. I turned to walk inside and saw Mr. Simon, who has worked as one of the doormen for the past ten years.

"Wonderful evening, Sofia. How was your performance?" Jerry questioned.

"It was sold-out, Jerry; remind me to get tickets for you and your wife." He held up his hands in a grateful gesture. Living in a condo had its advantages. I was staying at the penthouse level while I was here until I wrapped up the show in six months. I had a private gym and pool. My laundry got picked up once a week, and I had a chef that prepared my breakfast, lunch, and dinner when I'm home. Although on nights like tonight, I knew I'd find some gourmet meal waiting for me. I rode the elevator up to my Twenty-fifth floored penthouse before stepping off. I opened the door, hung up my coat, then checked my mail that my housekeeper left. Passing through the living room to the kitchen, I saw food wrapped on the counter. She made my favorite tonight, a zucchini bowl with red sauce and sweet potatoes. I lifted the tinfoil, opened the cabinet, and picked up a plate and fork. I warmed everything in the microwave, then went to shower to get the day washed away. Fifteen minutes after showering, I was dried off and had put a long sleeper shirt with my hair wrapped in a scarf. I walked back into the kitchen, grabbed my food and planner to look over my schedule for the following week as I sipped from the red wine I previously bought at the store. I had a full schedule coming up the following week and being distracted by a man that appeared to want me, who was dangerous on top of that, was the last thing I needed in my life right now, especially since I suspected he'd be the type to want to control my every move.

"I won't be on his list of women," I muttered to myself and turned on the tv to watch a movie while I planned everything with my music recording. Two hours later, I was under the covers dozing off to sleep.

SOFIA

Joaquin...Ughh...this is- his large, strong hands gripped my neck while his fingers gave me pleasure beyond imagination. His whispers of how good my pussy tasted, the groans and moans mixed between us caused me to shudder while gripping the sheets, and our juices trailed down onto the tousled bedding. He surprised me with a trip to Spain. We had his entire villa to ourselves. He gripped my thigh, squeezing gently as I called out his name.

"Sofia! Sofia! Are you listening?" Edward asked, snapping me out of my daydream.

"I'm sorry, Edward, what did you say?" While I had the day off, with so many things coming up, Edward arranged for a car to pick me up for the back-to-back meetings about a potential movie, as well as discussions concerning a future album with the label now. My first album had launched, and I was lining up a tour potential along with a new film. And now we're sitting at the same restaurant that I crashed into Joaquin a few months back. There's a part of me that wondered if he still came by.

"If you would ever focus, you'd realize I said we have four meetings with producers that want to work with you." Edward's gaze cut to mine.

"Sorry, I haven't been sleeping lately."

He reached over and caressed my cheek, and I moved out of his hold, before looking around and making sure no one saw us. Edward Anderson had been my manager for the last seven years of my career. The first three years, I was struggling with playing small roles, until my big break in the comedy, *Riley Home*.

"Cassidy, did you set up the recording with Deras Jones?" I asked.

"I did and scheduled you to do a few social media interviews with influencers. It could be beneficial to show your face online a little more."

"I don't know, that ends up being more time than it's worth. I have to study my lines. And getting distracted by weirdos on the internet is too draining."

"Cassidy has a point, Sofia, this could be good for us, especially with your music coming out soon."

"Let me think it over for a few days."

"I have a photoshoot set for you, so make sure you don't hang out with your boyfriend all night," Cassidy stated.

"He's a distraction. Get rid of him," Edward demanded.

"Edward, focus on my career only, please." All eyes bore into me.

"Sofia, what do you think of doing a brand endorsement with a new clothing line?" Cassidy asked as she obsessively texted someone.

Cassidy took a bite of her burger and drank from her strawberry lemonade.

"Who's the company?" I inquired. My phone rang and I lifted it to see that my mom was calling.

"A sportswear line for women," Cassidy replied and I held a finger up to give me a second.

"Hello?" I answered the call.

"Hey, superstar," Mom said, laughing through the phone.

I laughed at her. "Hey, lady, what's going on?" I asked.

"Checking in on you," Mom said.

"I'm good, how's the family doing?" I asked.

Edward pointed toward his watch to finish the call soon.

"Everybody is good. I was planning on coming to visit you with your dad," she stated.

"Okay, send me the information for the flight and I'll make sure I'm available to hang out with you guys," I answered.

"Sounds good, baby. I'll call you later," Mom said, ending the call.

"I really need you to focus on the career I'm trying to help you build," Edward stated as his face glowered at me.

I was over him being condescending and I grabbed my purse, stood up, and turned to leave before we got into a shouting match. I knew Edward meant well but he overstepped his bounds constantly. I held my arm up for a cab and my phone started blowing up with Edward telling me to come back inside.

"Where are you headed to?" Cassidy asked, closing the door of the restaurant.

"To the recording studio," I replied.

"I'll go with you. We can continue talking about the clothing brand," Cassidy said, and I nodded in answer as the cab pulled up. I opened the door and Cassidy climbed in behind me.

* * *

...

TWENTY MINUTES LATER, the cab arrived in front of Sunset Studios in lower Manhattan and I tipped him forty dollars while we thanked him for driving us fast.

"Hey, Sofia," Keon, the security guard, said as he passed the sign-in form around to me.

"What's going on, Keon?" I asked. He was an aspiring singer and worked here part time as a security guard to cut the cost of recording down for him. Keon was only around twenty-two, but extremely talented and I wanted to do a song with him one day. He reminded me of the singer, Joe, from back in the day of smooth R&B singers with the bald head. He was tall, around five-eleven, and had a nice well-trimmed beard, and nice full lips.

"Nothing much. You hitting the booth tonight?" he asked.

"Yep, is the last room free?" I asked and he said yes.

Cassidy and I strolled to the back and I pulled my notebook out of my purse. I opened the door and saw Chauncey, one of the in-house engineers and producers sitting at the booth. I bent over and gave him a hug.

"I didn't know you were coming through," Chauncey said as he shook hands with Cassidy. I dropped my purse on the couch and flipped to one of the songs I was working on.

"I just needed to get in the booth for a few minutes and record a few bars." He rubbed his hands together gleefully. Chauncey and I went way back to my first album and I thought of him as not only a producer in the industry, but a friend as well.

"Perfect, get on in there so we can hear what you got," Chauncey said, turning the volume up on the sound. Cassidy continued texting and making notes as I walked inside the booth and placed the headphones on my ears. I picked up the bottle of water on the seat next to me and took a sip. I closed my eyes, took a few breaths as a beat slowly came through. I motioned for Chauncey to turn it up a little more.

I don't need your love
I don't need your love
These feelings seem to change
I don't need your love, baby
Ohhh, ohhh, ooohh

"How does that sound?" I yelled through the door and Chauncey motioned for me to come in to hear the playback.

"I can do that as a single." Cassidy spoke up after we listened to the playback.

"I agree, just from the early lyrics," Chauncey said as he twisted some knobs and pushed buttons to tighten up the instrumental. We continued on throughout the day and night recording two then three songs until about midnight. I went home afterwards and listened back to the tracks and fell asleep with multiple texts and messages from Edward apologizing for his behavior.

JOAQUIN

"Joaquin, are you listening to me?" Monica screamed, while she accompanied me out of my office building. She showed up without calling and wanted to talk. I never returned her calls two months ago after I bumped into who I now recognize was Sofia Chambers. Something about her was mesmerizing and calmed me down. Those brief moments played in my mind repeatedly until I had my people investigate and locate her information when they left Antonio's that day. She didn't acknowledge my question about dinner, but over time, she'll open up to being my friend and then my lover.

"Monica, go home."

Gabriella pulled up in the black SUV that we did business in that called for a fast exit. Tightening my black gloves, I kissed Monica on the forehead and told her I'd be in touch with her later. She stepped in front of me, blocking me from leaving.

"What is this?" I questioned, anger making my tone harsher than normal.

"No, you are not leaving without me. I don't see what I did wrong, but please forgive me," Monica whined, running her hand up to my chest, then standing on her toes to plant a kiss on my lips. I turned my head and it landed on my cheek.

"We're work acquaintances, Monica, nothing more."

"Do you have all your work acquaintances sucking your dick?" she snapped harshly.

"Did you think embarrassing yourself in public would get me to agree to speak with you privately?"

"I-"

"No, I've never thrown you the impression we had anything other than friendship. Go home, and I will call you. Never come up here again without calling me first."

"But you never answer my calls, Joaquin, and you know Gael hates me." She leaned her head into my chest, and I gently leaned her head up, wiping the tears off her cheek.

"Go home. I have a business to handle."

Monica agreed, smiling weakly, and stepping out of my way, and I headed in the car's direction before getting inside, and Gabriella drove off.

"She will be a problem, boss," Gabriella implied, typing in the warehouse's address where the guns were located. Gael got a call late last night that a shipment of our weapons had been stolen, and they suspected it was the Russians. I had my own suspicions; there was a local gang poking around our business. Antonio could negotiate a three-way sale of guns from Germany without going through the Russians, and we'd split everything down the middle. Now to have a shipment come up missing not even twenty-four hours later, I had my concerns. It was only two in the afternoon, so traffic was heavy, and everybody was out. The warehouse was near the loading dock. Antonio shuffled things around after his situation with Queen months back, and destroyed the old warehouse that was closer to the city. This was further out by the Hudson River.

"Monica is needy and weak. Her entire existence is based on my approval, and I've never given her that impression. She doesn't even know my parents' names or where I live," I answered in my native Portuguese.

"If she becomes a problem…"

"Then I'll take care of her making sure she understands that being in my life won't be her end result." I grunted, lifting my gun out of my holster and removing the safety and cocking it back. Gabriella pulled into the entrance of the warehouse. Gael, Hugo, and a few more men were standing by. I walked out of the car and slammed it shut.

"Any visitors?" I interrogated.

Gael rubbed the back of his neck, looking nervous.

"Speak," I urged.

"There are women working inside; we can't go inside. I think it was a false call," Gael responded.

Turning and wandering to the front door, I opened the gate to see a room full of women of all ages and races sewing. The low hum of merengue played in the background. Searching around, it looked like a sweatshop as the racks of jumpsuits were labeled Fashion Den. Grating my teeth, I shot my revolver in the air and everyone screamed and scrambled to run off. I pointed at Hugo to block the front door. Scanning around the room, I looked everyone in the eye to see if they'd give away who was in charge.

"Excuse me for my interruption. Who is in charge here?" I demanded, marching down the aisle.

No one spoke and I pointed at Gael to help. He was more of a negotiator. He came over and got out some money, and one woman stepped up and took it in exchange for giving us information.

"The supervisor stepped out, he said that he would get back in an hour after dropping off a package," the young lady explained; she didn't look over the age of twenty, and was dressed in worn jeans and a dingy blue vest with Fashion Den spiraled across her chest.

"How long have you worked here?" I sought answers and she seemed like she was willing to provide information.

"One year, sir."

"Any other rooms in this place? A basement or office?"

She nodded and pointed to the exit sign. I waved for Gael to follow me, and for Hugo and Gabriella to stay up front.

I jogged over to the door and pushed it open. It was a dark hallway that led to another door. There was rat shit on the ground and empty food containers. It looked more like the trash area than a business office and I wrinkled my nose at the noxious odors that surrounded us. Gael and I drew our guns and opened the door on the count of three. Crates, small and big, sat open. I walked over and checked one and noticed serial numbers on the inside of the container. Gael checked another box, and we continued for the next five minutes, coming up empty-handed. We left the room and ran back to the front entrance. Hugo was standing at the window and cocked his shotgun.

"We have company, about three cars and eight men that I could see," Hugo whispered.

"Take the women to the back and find an exit," I shouted at the young lady who was in charge. She pushed them to follow behind her right as Hugo busted a hole in the window and started shooting. I moved to the other side of the window and peeked out as gunfire was returned.

Pop! Pop! Pop!

"It has to be Vitale's men," Gael yelled.

"Go through the back and come up on the side. I'll hold them off, and you get a clean shot. Gabriella, go with him," I yelled as I motioned to the two of them before running a hand down my face, sweat staining my shirt.

Narrowing my eyes, I aimed the handgun toward his ankle and pulled. He screamed in pain, falling, and the other men tried to help him, which opened a doorway for Gael and Gabriella to get off a few more rounds until Hugo and I walked outside to clear the area. I kicked the gun away from the only one that was left alive. Stooping down, I smacked him in the face, getting him to focus.

"Aye, focus!" I snapped my finger.

"Fuck you, Joaquin!" he shouted in pain. I took the tip of my gun and pushed it into his wound as he cried out.

"Who sent you and where are my guns?" I sneered, cocking my gun in his direction.

"I know nothing."

Gabriella grinned, thirsty to kill.

"Then, you're of no use to me," I responded, shooting him in between the eyes, and walking off toward my car to leave. I wiped the sweat off of my brow as Gabriella started the car and drove me home. Twenty minutes later, I stepped in the shower, and cleaned the blood off my hands and face. I had guards all around my building watching for any blowback. If I heard that my enemies were working together to sabotage me, hell wouldn't be good enough for them once I was finished with them. Throwing on a t-shirt and jeans, I stalked to my office and turned on my monitors then watched outside to see if anything was off. I stood and walked to my wall safe, typed in my password and grabbed a gun, checked the chamber, and sealed it back up. I sat down in my chair and sent a text to Gabriella to make sure the area was completely cleared.

Me: I don't need any surprises.

Gabriella: Job is clear and clean.

Me: Good.

Gabriella: Have you seen her?

Me: I will, soon.

I closed my messages and continued to look over the photos and video of the restaurant where I bumped into Sofia, and watched to see if I missed anyone watching her. I planned to spend the rest of the night putting security in place for her in case this was the beginning of a new war.

JOAQUIN

wo Days Later
    I was born in Spain and raised in Portugal as the son of Mayor Joaquin Fuertes and Italian mother, Alba Fuertes. They're still married to this day, even though he was now retired from politics. When you joined the Cartel, you never retired, and his hands advised me when needed. Mother wasn't happy about her oldest son getting involved in the lifestyle while also being groomed with two grandfathers who were also involved in the underworld. Tiago Fuertes, on my Dad's side, was an underboss to his brother that started the Fuertes Cartel, and my mother's father, Piero Giordano, was his accountant. Growing up, I watched my dad work both sides of the law. He was able to walk into dinners with politicians and governors, then at the drop of a hat cut a man's throat that betrayed him. They set life for me before I was born. My younger sister, Alessandra, who was now twenty-two, wished to follow me to America, but I refused to allow her to do so.

I promised my mother that I'd never put her in a position that she'd have to lose any of her children. I was the one behind Queen's death, and time was ticking because someone out there was waiting and planning to bring an end to my door. At twenty-nine, I should be out dating, living life, traveling around the world, preparing for a future with a wife and children. But here I was, standing in my office thinking about her. The minute our eyes connected, my heart felt inclined to protect her and have her near me. It didn't matter if she was with someone at the restaurant that night. If I hadn't had business to attend to, she would have been with me for the rest of the night. That's the side of me that pushes the other part away in order to have a moment of happiness. Ghost was the one I go around as all day and night. The amount of death and destruction, bloodshed, and ripping families apart has forced my soul to harden, and I refused to push the darkness onto Sofia. Could I have protested? No. My family would have made sure that they immediately changed my decision. Even when I came to America to get an education, it was under strict protection. Not only am I the don of the most prominent underworld Cartel family, but I also have my investment company that I've built from the ground up with my right-hand man, Gael Velez. We've been childhood friends since we were five years old in boarding school. The Velez and Fuertes families ran all over Spain and parts of Italy that we gained through our collaboration with Antonio De Luca and his clan.

"He's right here. I'll tell him," Gael responded, hanging up the phone. I was peering out of the window of my office on the tenth floor while he dealt with a phone call. Instead of having to share the space, we bought the entire building. This way, we don't have anyone around who shouldn't be there.

The Alba Industries was a venture firm with more than two hundred clients with our money tied into everything from sports teams, entertainment, and local mom and pop shops that we helped refinance while taking a small percentage as repayment.

"What is the problem?" I slid my hands in my pockets.

"That was Carlo updating us from his contacts in Italy. They've found out that Queen was involved in something with Antonio, and now that she's dead, they think he was assisted by us because the last sightings had you photographed with him and Bruno."

Scratching my neck, I squinted my nose, looking at the guy

harassing the young woman sitting at the bus stop. Working on Madison Avenue, people think because it's full of business people that things are clean. The shit I've seen from here to Italy would blow your mind. *Filho da puta*, which meant son of a bitch in Portuguese, because the guy yanked the woman by her jacket while getting in her face and no one stopped him.

Grabbing my gun out of my desk, I strode out of my office, avoiding the elevator and my assistant and Gael calling my name.

"Joaquin! Joaquin!" Gael yelled, chasing after me. He knew my temper and how I felt about abuse. My mom taught me about men treating women with respect and love. When I became of age and capable of fighting, she took control of her life and wanted to do things outside of the mafia family. I said I would never love someone that much to the point of controlling their happiness. Alba Giordano was a strong woman that only wanted to be a teacher. Once she fell in love, her dreams slowly faded, and she became a stay-at-home mom and wife. The same was now happening with Alessandra, and she had to fight to have some freedom.

I stormed down the stairs, pushing the entrance of the door open. At ten in the morning, I could see a small crowd of people standing at the corner waiting for the light to change so they could cross. A typical day on Madison Avenue as folks tended to their lives. I narrowed my eyes at the guy and acknowledged he wasn't as big as I originally thought when I saw him out of my window. Placing my pistol behind my back, I walked toward him.

She tried to push him away. "Please, let me go!" she cried.

"Shut up, bitch!" he growled.

Stepping behind him, I tapped his shoulder; he didn't remove his grip on her and turned his head toward me. I punched him with my right fist, and he fell on the ground. The young woman started screaming, and I strolled back to my office.

"Joaquin, you can't do shit like that and bring the heat to us." Gael texted on his phone as I opened the door to return to the office. A black car pulled up and Gabriella stepped out with Hugo. She nodded at Gael and me.

"He's not dead," I stated.

"That's not the point," he argued.

"Brother, you need to calm down; you looked stressed. Tonight, we have bevande," I insisted.

Lately, we'd worked a great deal of overtime with the business. I had him not only as my underboss and right hand, he also served as the VP of Alba Industries. His family had ties to the gun sales, and we'd brokered deals with even the worst enemies of the Velez mafia. Gael was a year older than me at thirty-two, and more rational and patient. I'm called Ghost for a reason. I like to get in and out without being noticed.

"You need to call her." Gael followed me back into my office and shoved his hands in his pockets.

"Call whom?" I questioned, headed into my office taking a seat at my desk.

"The American actress and singer, Sofia Chambers. You know, the one you're consumed with and keep stalking."

I glared at his comment, and he held his hands up in apology.

"I'm not obsessed, she's a talented actress and I've attended a few of her shows."

"Stop following and ask her out. Maybe she can help you release some tension."

"I will forget you're my brother and expect to never hear you mention her name again and release anything in the same breath," I said through gritted teeth.

"We have a meeting tonight to discuss the Queen situation, and then a new shipment is coming in from Italy," he advised, effectively changing the subject.

"Has the shipment been inspected?" I watched as Gael walked to the bar next to the window, picked up the glass of scotch and poured two glasses. He angled the glass toward me, and I grabbed it and took it straight.

"I'll have it inspected, but I'm running thin on men to trust," Gael admitted as he took a seat on the couch. He wrapped his hands around the glass and stared at me.

"I agree, maybe have some people come down from Italy to help. My father would be fine with me bringing in reinforcements."

"The shooting has me worried and now you're all over the place beating on strangers in public." Gael's mouth turned in a twisted smirk.

"He deserved it."

"Joaquin, you're taking over as the head of the family. I keep repeating you need to leave certain things to me," Gael commented, leaned back on the couch.

"I don't tolerate disrespect, Gael."

"I understand that, and as your right-hand man, some things shouldn't have your name involved, especially with this Queen mess brewing around," Gael spoke, causing an icy panic to creep into my chest.

"The families have no clue it was me," I answered.

"Ghost," he said and I held my hand out to stop him.

"I'm done talking about Queen. I want to get security on Sofia." I shoved my hands in my pockets.

"Don't you think it's too early?" Gael grabbed the bottle and poured another shot, then waved it at me but I declined.

"She's important to me. I need her protected at all times." An email popped up on my desktop. I turned in my chair and checked the encrypted file with more details on a Russian trade deal that Antonio wanted me to investigate.

"Have you talked to her yet?" Gael inquired.

"No, but I'm planning to very soon."

"Try not to chase her off this time. What about Monica?"

"Monica's a little different," I responded as I sifted through the order that was planned to be shipped. I heard Gael chuckling as he finished off his drink.

"Brother, we both know Monica is a ticking time bomb," Gael told me.

JOAQUIN

The best way for the family to go unnoticed was by staying a productive member of society and working to keep our money clean. Laundering it through some local business was what my father wanted me to do, and I'd been fighting him on it for the last few months. The situation of killing Queen was resurfacing. We paid off some police officers to keep things out of the paper. A week ago, it popped up all over social media about a high-ranking mafioso being killed in America.

"Where's your assistant? The last girl got attached to you because you slept with her and you had to fire her," Gael asked, looking out into the lobby of my office.

"That's the problem with women, they get too attached. Monica's constantly calling me like we're a couple. She's known for the last year that she's just sex for me." I shrugged, leaning back in my chair, raising my hands behind my neck.

"Have you talked to Alessandra?"

"No, why?"

"She texted and requested if I'd convince you to let her visit."

"No."

"Joaquin."

"She's not coming, and she can stop asking and going behind my back to everyone except her brother. She's too young for this city," I said, standing, picking up my black trench coat off my hanger, and heading out.

"Alessandra is twenty-two. A grown woman that you and your father seem to refuse to let grow up." I stopped walking and turned to him, narrowing my eyes.

"Are you sleeping with my sister?"

"Joaquin, you know me better than that. Alessandra is like a little sister to me, and she wants to be taken seriously and not smothered by her family."

"I'll talk to her, and I propose you stop talking to her," I suggested as we walked to my limo parked out back. Leonardo, my longtime driver and bodyguard when I needed him to cover my back, was waiting with the door opened.

* * *

"Boss, Gabriella said I needed to take the trash out," Leonardo advised, leaving the passenger side door and walking back around to the driver's side. I had hundreds of men that depended on me, and unfortunately, I didn't trust any of them in this business.

"Thank you, Leonardo, take us to Ryde. I need to speak with Carlo and Antonio." He nodded and stuck the key in the ignition and pulled off into traffic. While living here in New York, you became hyper-focused on the next thing you had to do, and the fast pace ended up making you crash and burn if you didn't take every little moment and enjoy the people or things you loved. Gael was more sensible about things than I was, because the second someone crossed me, I killed them. I learned from the best, and my grandfather Tiago was no pushover. He and my father took me to my first kill at twelve. I didn't understand at first when we walked into the basement, and I saw a man was lying on the floor naked. Tiago explained that he stole from the family and needed to be punished. They handed me a gun and I held it up, pointed it at the man as he writhed, crawling and crying to be free.

I smiled and pretended like I would shoot him, and he peed on himself. I was taught to always put the Fuertes family first. My mother knew what was happening; she cried all night about me being taken to be initiated into the lifestyle. My father promised her I wouldn't have to do anything except observe, but that was a lie. I passed the gun back to my father and he asked why I was giving it back. I said it was too loud, and the feel of a knife to someone's throat, while you're staring intently into their eyes as they take their last breath, was what brought me joy. Am I a serial killer? Yes. Do I go around killing random people? No. Am I heartless and cold-blooded? Absolutely, and I wouldn't change a thing about me. That's what gets you through life, not caring, not letting anyone get too close.

"We're here, boss," Leonardo shouted and got out of the car to assist us. I waved him off that we'd be fine as Gael and I got out of the limo.

"We'll be awhile here, make sure Miss Chambers gets my delivery and send my regrets about not being there." He agreed with a thumbs up, and I shut the door weaving through the afternoon lunch crowd outside of Antonio's.

"So, you don't believe in love or dating, and yet you send flowers to a woman you don't want any relationship with?" Gael started patting his side to make sure his gun was ready. We had a working relationship with Antonio and Carlo, but we don't even trust our allies.

"I'm not interested; like I said, I think she's a great actress."

"I heard you asked her out to dinner the other night."

We saw Carlo sitting in his usual booth, eating and laughing with the bartender. She was tall and lean, with big breasts and a small butt. The uniforms they wore had the girls in black dresses and men in black slacks and dress shirts. The smell of fresh garlic sauce and Italian meatballs drenched in marinara caused my stomach to rumble. Last year, I was here and I'd met Sofia.

"Carlo, we've heard the rumors about your wife, Janice. I suggest you try not to enjoy yourself too much with your staff."

"Alana is a friend and Janice knows I would never cheat on her," Carlo replied, gesturing for us to take a seat.

I smirked, taking a seat opposite him in the booth. Alana sauntered over with a glass of wine and menus for Gael and I. Taking it out of her hand, Gael smiled and winked at her as she giggled and walked away.

"No," Carlo replied.

"No, what?" Gael asked innocently.

"Stay away from her," Carlo informed him.

Gael chuckled and winked at Carlo.

"So, tell me what you've heard from your contacts in Italy," I demanded, changing the subject.

He sighed, driving a hand down his face, before he leaned forward, clasping his hands together.

"We can look at this a few different ways. She came after us first and tried to take down our family, we had no choice but to retaliate. Antonio is onboard with whatever you need to do, but Vitale wants blood as a replacement for killing her. Basically, Queen went off on her own with trying to make moves that went above her pay grade."

"Should we prepare for retaliation?"

Alana strolled back over with the second plate of fettuccine pasta for the table this time. I needed to be clear on what Carlo was telling me to be prepared for before I carried out some calls to Italy and Portugal. My parents split their time between Portugal and Italy, and Alessandra was in Italy last time I learned.

"Antonio explained that Vitale was making moves with the Russian mob, and we've already had a strained relationship with them over the past few years after they tried to kill him. Ghost, I know you like to kill in silence, but they're coming with big guns compared to your knives. De Luca's family is finally content and happy; I cannot pull our children and wives back into any drama. Move fast and in silence."

"Cut off the head and the rest will fall," I mumbled to myself.

Gael scooped some pasta onto his plate, taking a bite of the famous dish that Antonio's sold.

"What are you thinking?" Gael questioned.

"Traveling to Italy may need to come sooner than expected. Ensuring the family is protected is my only concern and stopping this before it gets out of hand and they strike us in New York. I'll contact my sister tonight and see if our parents stayed in town or not. Mother likely has. I pushed my father to travel more with her, thinking it would slow him down from sticking his nose in Cartel business. The man is sixty-five years old; he'll never stop pulling strings."

"Uncle Joaquin is dangerous when your mother isn't around to keep him preoccupied and focused on her. As his junior, your personality is the same, brother. You're silent and deadly."

"Leave my father out of this and tell me more about the Vitale and Russian partnership," I demanded. Right as Carlo spoke, I picked up a familiar laugh that caught my attention.

I took in the sight of Sofia and the same guy she was here with last time, laughing together. He held her around the waist, running a hand up and down her back. I felt a twinge of jealousy. This was the second time we had seen her out with him in public. Maybe that's why she turned me down; because they had a relationship together. The hostess walked them through the front section of the restaurant and down to the side and sat them at a table near us with her back to us. Our booth was more toward the corner enclave, but I still had a perfect view of her sweet smile. He caressed her cheek, and I grabbed the fork in my hand, ready to push it into his eye. "Do you know why this is all happening? I mean, the real reason behind the hate between Vitale, Fuertes, and De Luca?" Carlo questioned.

"Didn't it originally start with Joaquin's grandfather, Tiago, killing someone that stole from them a few years ago?" Gael asked.

"Joaquin, you want to explain?" Carlo suggested.

"It wasn't Tiago that killed someone; it was me."

"Wait, you?"

Rehashing my first kill over twenty years ago always stirred up bad memories, not from the killing, but the aftermath. Like Carlo said, this war was long standing because the man that I killed was Queen's uncle, Federico's twin brother. I had Gabriella investigate deeper and if it ever came to light that it was me, this war would be personal. Perio Vitale was working with my grandfather and father, and tried to cut them out of a deal that would have made them millionaires. Over the years, a truce was called if we paid them a set amount, and when I refused to continue the payment of fifty million to be transferred to them, and then Queen died, it must have all come full circle and we'd be back to destroying each other.

Loud laughing brought me out of my daze; looking at the cause of the giggles, I stood ready to put an end to Sofia's lunch. Gael reached out to stop me. "Joaquin, no. We're in public, and she's well-known. Let them be."

He knew my temper and what I was capable of doing.

"Am I missing something?" Carlo asked.

"I'm just going to say hello. I won't hurt him, yet," I informed him.

"Every time you say you won't hurt anyone, it's a code for calling Gabriella to clean up the mess," Gael joked as I was removing his hand from my jacket. I grinned, and observed Sofia remove her hand from her little boyfriend's grasp.

Marching over to the table, I slid my hands in my pockets so I wouldn't get the urge to kill him in two seconds. Clearing my throat, I stated, "Sofia, I see you were able to get out to have lunch. I hope you haven't filled out too much and have left room for me."

"What are you doing here?" Sofia questioned, as her eyes scanned around the restaurant.

"Come talk to me, your boyfriend won't mind. Right?" I requested, furrowing my brows, just waiting for him to say the wrong thing.

"Uhhh, no. That's fine. The food hasn't come out, anyway," he spoke.

"Grazia." I thanked him in Italian. Having two different languages after having an Italian mother and a father from Portugal came with the privilege of me getting to travel the world. Speaking multiple languages was something our mother instilled in us.

Sofia stood up, and I let her walk in front of me toward the back. I nodded to Carlo that I was going toward the office at the end of the restaurant. Either he or Antonio would work out of there when they came here.

Opening the door, it didn't look like anyone had been in here today; it was spotless.

"Have a seat."

"I'd rather stand, and why did you choose to talk with me?"

"I want to have dinner with you."

She sighed, rolling her eyes, and I grinned at her annoyance. Antonio told me the story of how he pursued his Sabrina, and she always pushed him away.

"I can't."

"That's not good enough."

"I know who you and your family are. I don't consider this to be a great idea. Sorry, but I'm not trying to get involved with a mob family."

I chuckled at her statement and stepped closer, filling the gap between us. "I'm a legit businessman, Sofia Chambers."

"I don't think that's true, and besides, you don't seem like the one-woman type of guy. Am I missing something, or did you not arrive with your girlfriend from the last time we bumped into each other?"

"She's not my girlfriend."

"At least you're honest and admit the woman that showed up with you."

"Monica is of no importance. I'm talking to you, wanting to spend a few minutes of your time getting to know you a little better, is that so sinful?" I lifted her palm and caressed the top of her knuckles.

"It is if it ends up with me having a bullet to my head because of your mobster friends," she spat and jerked her hand away.

"You don't think I would protect you? Sofia, I'm a simple man and my family has dealings in that world, I won't lie. But I'm a businessman," I lied, and she seemed to believe me.

"What type of business do you have?" she quizzed.

Explaining myself to anybody was a death wish any other day. Seeing the determination in her eyes to push me away only caused me to want to press forward.

SOFIA

$\mathcal{I}$t felt like a standoff in the room—me on one side and him on the other. Neither one willing to give in. I couldn't help but admire what he was wearing and how sexy he looked in his black trench coat and dark grey suit. Usually, I saw him at nighttime when he came to the show, and the one time I rode with him in the limo. His beard and mustache were nicely trimmed and his black hair was slicked back. Tall, at least over six feet, and well-manicured sideburns made him look distinguished. His eyes were the color of black coal and when you stared into them, it made you feel as though he was looking into your soul.

"I run an investment firm called Alba Industries, named after my mother."

"Still can't go out with you, my life is public, and being seen with you would bring unwanted attention toward my career."

"Is that your boyfriend out there?"

"Who? Edward? I'm single and I plan on keeping it that way for a while. He's my manager. Now, if you'll excuse me, I have to go finish a business meeting," I explained, leaving out of the office. He grasped my wrist and turned me around, pushing me up against the door.

"What are you do-?"

"Mmm... have dinner with me," he moaned, gripping my waist, pressing his entire body against mine.

"I...I...shouldn't," I stuttered, losing all sense as my legs automatically opened wider for him. Feeling his erection against my stomach, it pulled me back to the realization of what I was doing and where I was at. Shoving him again, I announced, "No, this isn't right. I need to leave and forget this ever happened." I opened the office door, heading back up front to Edward and my lunch.

* * *

EDWARD JUMPED up as I approached him and lifted my chin. "What are you doing?" I asked. I'm annoyed with all his touching and reaching for my hand today, making it seem like we're a couple.

"You looked flushed, and I was checking to see if he hurt you. Did he?"

"Did he what?"

"Do anything to you?"

"Uhhh..."

"Sofia, bellissima, I'll call you tomorrow for our date," Joaquin stated behind me, walking back over to join his friends in the booth that I just noticed was close by. At least now, I knew how he saw me enter with Edward. I knew *bellissma* meant beautiful in Italian. I'd learned a few distinct words when I worked in Italy on a movie shoot a few years back.

"Sofia, what happened back there?" Edward pointed to where we came from. I picked up my purse to exit and glanced over my shoulder at Joaquin, and he smugly winked at me as I stared. Edward followed behind and met me at my car, opening the door to my Tesla. He wanted us to drive together, and I said no because I wasn't going back to the studio when I had a studio session tonight.

"Tell me what he wanted to talk to you about. Isn't he the guy from the news who's a gangster or something? Sofia, stay away from him and his friends. Nothing good can come from this little date."

Edward closed my car door and leaned through the window. Turning the key in the ignition, I rubbed my temples hoping my headache wouldn't turn into a migraine.

"My dating life isn't your concern, Edward, you manage my career and that's all, we have no personal relationship, and we've discussed this plenty of times."

"Fine. Get involved with New York's most wanted, at least call me when you finish looking over the contracts for the album." I waved goodbye and was pulling out into traffic when Joaquin walked out of the restaurant with another guy. Talking, they headed to his Mercedes limo that sat in front of my car and got inside. He didn't notice me because the only time he'd ever seen me was inside of the theater. I rarely drove my car unless I had a meeting to attend. Shaking off today's events, I left and drove to the music studio Edward rented for me to do a recording session for my next album. I arrived forty minutes later uptown. I left my key with the valet and stepped inside as the music blasted through the walls. Edward set up a meeting with a writer and producer that was hot right now in New York and LA, he was a little younger than me, but he was talented and worked with all the major artists. Deras Jones was the person to call when you wanted a hit ballad or a hot one-hundred song on the billboard charts. Tapping on the door, I heard him shout to come inside, and I slowly opened the door to see he was sitting at the booth, mixing some beats.

"Deras Jones? Hi, I'm Sofia Chambers, nice to meet you." I extended a hand, and he shook it, gesturing for me to sit. I did so, sitting my purse down on the mixer board.

"*The* Sofia Chambers, wow! I'm honored to be in your presence. You're a stunning woman, sorry if that makes you uncomfortable, I mean. I apologize. Damn."

I chuckled at his nervousness, I was the one that was starstruck when on a movie set with a major actor and to have someone feel the same way about me outside of my usual fan base was flattering. He was an industry person who understood the way the business worked.

"No worries, I'm flattered and a huge fan of yours. I loved that song, "Sinful Touch" that Kimberly Maxine sang. Outdid yourself there, sir."

"Thank you. Did Edward tell you what was happening today?"

I shook my head no.

"Okay, no problem. Well, I wrote a few songs already, since I met with him and he gave me your vision of what you wanted to do with this album. All we'll do today is read through them and cut the list down."

"May I look?"

"Sure."

He passed the folder to me and I noticed it was labeled with my name. Impressed, I opened the envelope and turned over ten pages of musical lyrics written.

"There are over fifty songs in here."

"I know."

"When did you meet with Edward?"

"Two weeks ago," he answered, taking out another folder that had nothing written on it, and he grabbed a pen and passed me one.

"Wow! I didn't think you'd have this much done for me in two weeks."

"I eat, breathe, and sleep music. Sofia, between the two of us, we can come up with a few hits."

"I believe you," I replied and picked up my purse, removing my vibrating phone to see a message from an unknown number.

Unknown: 917-4340575 save this number.

Me: Who is this?

Unknown: Your date for tomorrow night.

I frowned at the comment. Then a light bulb went off, and I remembered my earlier interaction with Joaquin. He must be sitting there with a hard glare on his face waiting for me to answer. He didn't seem like a patient man at all. And from my past relationships, the men I've been with have all been fickle with being consistent. The moment I invested any interest, he'd pull back and ghost out.

Unknown: Still there?
Me: Thank you for the offer, but I have to decline our date.
Unknown: Save this number.
Me: Did you not see my earlier response?
Joaquin: 😉

He sent a winking emoji, ignoring what I said earlier. I didn't have time for stroking a man's ego. My career, family, and friends were more important. Closing out of the chat, I turned my phone on silent and stashed it back in my bag.

"Boyfriend problems?" Deras inquired, offering me a bottle of water. I thanked him and screwed the lid off the top, taking a sip. On my off days, I tried to focus on my singing and recording; most often, I'd have a small tour planned for the summer. Edward was an egomaniac like every other industry manager, but he was loyal and worked hard for my career and believed in me. We needed to get past his little crush so we could continue to work together. The last man I was with was about a year ago. I wasn't practicing celibacy or anything, far from it. I loved sex. The problem was finding a guy that could understand that I was not looking to become what they wanted me to be. I needed someone that supported my goals and saw the real me. The blogs could say I'm a diva or whatever. The biggest reason I've stayed so long in the industry is by being sure of myself and demanding my worth.

"No, why do you say that?"

"The little wrinkle in your nose when that text came through, you looked pissed off about something. I'd hate to be on the receiving end of you being mad," he joked.

"I'm free as a bird. Not interested in dating life. Besides, I'm not into the same things as I was before in my early twenties. I can't hang in the clubs and be asleep by ten if I'm not on set anymore," I answered, laughing at my comment.

"Whoever you spend that time with, he's a lucky man."

The entire room went silent as he stared into my eyes, then stood up and went to the recording booth. He gestured for me to follow him, and I stood, grabbing my pen and notepad heading into the booth to record a few verses. Over the next three hours, we recorded about twenty songs repeatedly until I felt right with each concept. We ordered food and laughed, talked about our childhood and beginnings in the industry. Deras was a cool, laid back type of guy. Not too flashy or in your face about all the money he had or flaunting it like a massive star. We worked well together, but I'd do nothing more than friendship with him. One thing you never do is mix business with pleasure. You just ended up on the first paper of a gossip magazine saying you'd gotten married, had a baby, and divorced within a week. Arriving home, I noticed Jerry still standing at the door, and he tipped his hat to me, then opened the door for me to pass through.

"Late recording, Sofia?"

"Yep. I have to get this album ready for my fans. Been over four years since I've released music, I hope that they'll still remember me." I laughed and walked off to my private elevator then rode up to my penthouse.

Plopping my bag down, I kicked off my shoes and checked the clock on my wall. It had just turned one in the morning and I felt beat up from the long day I had. Removing my clothes, bra, and panties, I walked to my bathroom and dropped my clothes in my hamper for my housekeeper to pick up in the morning. I had one more performance, then I was done with my Broadway show, and I moved on to filming full time. Juggling both and trying to make music was taking a toll on my body. I stretched in front of the mirror, then picked up my toothbrush and paste. I was thinking of remodeling my place and renting it out and moving into a house. Mom always talked about creating roots and having stability and foundation. Glancing around my bathroom, it was the modern-day style with a clean, off-white color, more eggshell. I had my goddess tub installed with the gold trim at the bottom. A walk-in shower with four different heads installed for the front and back. My personal vanity mirror with my name up above. Stepping in the shower, the heat sprayed against my back, and I let my hair get wet this time to cleanse the day away. I began thinking about Joaquin and the kiss. Even considering a date with a man whose family had been in the news for years would be the end of my career. I couldn't risk being seen in public with him. Imagine what he could do to me based on that kiss in private. Twenty minutes later, I stepped out of the shower and dried off with my towel that hung against the wall on the shelf rack. Drying my hair wasn't an enormous deal tonight, and I could open it up and throw my bonnet on top to keep it down and not frizz up. Sliding the covers back, I pulled my phone out of my purse and plugged it into the wall charger and checked it since it had been on silent. I noticed a barrage of text messages and emails pop up. Mostly from friends, family, and a few from Edward about filming starting soon. The next one that piqued my interest was the one from the earlier number that I now knew was Joaquin.

Joaquin: You have a good recording session?

He's following me, I thought to myself.

Me: Are you stalking me?

Joaquin: Have a good night, Sofia, and see you tomorrow after your show.

I bit my bottom lip and grinned at his response. I shook off any weird vibes because if he wanted to do anything to me; he had the chance a few weeks back when he drove me home or while sitting in the VIP booths and watching me perform. He had many opportunities to ask me out. As a well-known actress, if I went missing, people would talk and notice, I had to shake him out of my mind and get focused. Pulling the covers up, I laid down and closed my eyes, drifting off into a deep sleep.

JOAQUIN

Sleeping alone wasn't easy these days when you had the entire world on your shoulders. Running a business that dealt in the public eye and masked my underworld dealings caused many sleepless nights. I was in my car, heading to a meeting with Lin-Sae of the Chinese mafia. The underboss was meeting me at neutral territory at Antonio's restaurant, a place where most deals were struck. Gael was driving, as I had let Leonardo have the day off to be with his family. Gabriella was driving behind us with Hugo and a few more men. She was the only woman on my team who was a better shooter than me. Even though Gael was my right-hand man, I called on Gabriella to handle the cleanup as the enforcer. We met when she tried to steal from my family's store back in Portugal, and my father wanted to make an example out of her and murder her in the middle of the street. I pleaded with my mother, and she convinced him to give her a job at fifteen, and we'd been friends ever since.

"Antonio will be there today," Gael said out loud, stopping at the light. The cars honked at each other; bikers rushed through the streets, cutting off pedestrians. A typical Friday in New York. The smell of street vendors and barterers on every corner yelling to get a sale. I smirked—my kind of town.

"He told me. Gabriella has more weapons stashed inside if we need anything."

"Today shouldn't be anything but getting answers about the Russians and their dealings with Vitale," Gael told me.

"I appreciate how you stay optimistic, my friend. I go nowhere without my knife beside me."

"Have you spoken to your actress?"

Shaking my head no, I replied, "I texted her last night to say goodnight."

"Did she take you up on your offer to go on a date?" He finally parked, and we stepped out, and he handed the keys off to the valet. Gabriella and Hugo followed behind me, and I waved for my other men to stay in the front and back on post. I hadn't killed anyone since Queen, and I was itching for someone to step out of line.

"Her show is tonight. I plan on taking her out afterward," I said, walking through the door, nodding a thank you to the doorman. The hostess pointed to the back room where the men were sitting waiting on us. I observed the place was closed today. Antonio came over and extended his hand.

"Joaquin, really think about what you're doing before she gets hurt," Gael suggested.

"Why would she get hurt? I'm not asking her to marry me, one date, simple and possibly a friendship. We're both adults, and my lifestyle will never cross into her world."

"My wife is angry with you," Antonio stated as he pointed at me.

Gael and I looked at each other then back at him.

"What did I do?"

"I'm not home with her and the kids," he replied.

"Admit you're happy to be out of the house and not around four kids constantly screaming your name. I hear you're thinking of a fifth baby?" I questioned. He smirked, rubbing his chin in thought.

"If it were up to me, I'd have ten kids by now, but Sabrina's the boss at home, and she's put that on hold. Anyway, let us meet with our guests."

We trailed behind him, and he opened the door to the private room in the back. Three men standing and two sitting at a table looked over at us. I nodded in respect, they did the same, and everyone took a seat at the table.

"Mr. Fuertes, how are you?" Lin-Sae asked. He was the under-boss to his brother and brought his enforcer, Jin, and his body-guards with him. In the past, we'd handled business together without any problems, and I expected the same today if they answered my questions truthfully.

"Lin, you know why we requested your presence today?" I asked, unbuttoning my jacket and showing my gun on the side. Knives were my favorite killing tool, but in certain situations, when I needed to be quick and deadly with one person, I brought along my backup — the nine-millimeter Glock that I used for special occasions.

"My counsel brought to my attention you have some Russians upset with you about the killing of Queen Vitale. Joaquin, I've known you and your family a long time; this brings me distur-bance," Lin-Sae answered.

He'd been the underboss for the last fifteen years and had aged rather quickly, with gray streaks in his hair and beard, and wrinkles on his forehead and around his eyes. For someone that was only forty, he looked sixty.

"Your counsel has misinformed you. I had nothing to do with Queen's death. Antonio can vouch for me," I lied, not wanting to play my hand too fast.

"Lin, cut the bullshit. We know the Vitales are working with the Russians to start a war and bring it here on our turf. I recommend you convey how wrong that would be for everyone's safety," Antonio informed him, leaning back in his chair and nodding for his security to bring something to the table.

"What is this?" Lin-Sae questioned.

"I took the liberty of getting insurance in case this meeting didn't go in our favor. These are the documents that show Sae Mafia selling drugs to the undercover FBI agents. Now we don't work with the police, but I can't say it wouldn't unanimously get out to some of our friends in the Cartel if they knew you were giving the product to the very people trying to stop their business," Antonio announced, before he opened the briefcase and pulled out a manila folder then spread pictures of the Sae Cartel talking with the FBI and handing off bags of money and drugs.

Lin-Sae slammed his hand down on the table, cursing us out in Italian.

"Sae Cartel does not work with the police. These are fake," he spat, pulling his gun out, pointing it at Antonio.

Neither of us flinched as our enforcer and bodyguards drew their guns right back at him. Gael stepped up, gesturing for calmness, for everyone to put their guns down. "Gentlemen, we're on the same side. Put your guns away, and let's talk about this."

"Gael, you told me he'd be reasonable," Lin-Sae stated, and I glared at Gael for overstepping and thinking someone could control me.

"Lin, everybody in this room knows I can't be controlled. You want to know if it's true about Queen?"

He nodded his head in answer.

"She's dead, and I enjoyed every minute of torturing her when she came after this family. All the Bosses know that the families are off-limits, and she stepped out of bounds with no authority, and I took care of the matter."

"Then you will pay for killing the daughter of Federico Vitale," Lin said, waving for his men to put their guns away. He stood and walked out, stopped at the door and looked over his shoulder back at us.

"Family for family," he said, walking out of the room.

Antonio jumped up, ready to shoot.

"No, we need to think and regroup," I responded, cracking my knuckles and neck.

"They're working together, any other time he'd be neutral, and you see how quick he was accusing you about the murder," Antonio murmured.

"Carlo told us this would have an aftereffect behind her death. The only way to secure protection was to keep them out of New York."

"The Russians won't be quick to come here unless they have to, but the Vitales will hop on a plane fast. If they get the Sae Cartel to help, then a war is bound to happen," Gael informed us.

"Should we have someone following them?" Gabriella spoke, checking the chamber on her gun. I nodded for her to take the men and leave.

"The warehouse is empty tonight, and we can gather everyone up. Bruno is visiting from Italy with Liz; we can call him to help," Antonio suggested.

"This is my problem; I can't get you involved. It will be fine."

"Joaquin." Gael started to speak, but I held my hand up for him to stop.

"I'm not worried about them. Gael will be in touch once we've spoken with my contacts in Italy. My father is retired, but he knows a few men higher up that can get information on what Vitale is thinking about doing."

"Try not to get blown up or shot, my friend," Antonio stated, patting me on the back, as he walked us out of the private room toward the front entrance.

Gael and I laughed at his response and shook hands with him before leaving out of the restaurant. Heading toward the car, I opened the passenger side door, and he went around to the driver's side. Turning the key in the ignition, we pulled off with two black bulletproof SUVs tailing us for protection.

"Where am I dropping you off?"

"The theater on Forty-fifth Chelsea Street and Broadway."

"I forgot you had a date."

"Two people are having dinner and getting to know each other."

"Is that what you do with Monica?"

"Monica knows her purpose in my life."

"Last I checked, Monica was stomping into your office looking for you, when you did not call her for a week after you got back into town from Italy. Joaquin, she's the only woman you've kept for the last five years for fun. How do you think she'll take it when you date this Sofia actress?" Gael queried.

"I can handle Monica."

* * *

Forty minutes later, Gael arrived at the back of the theater. A crowd of photographers started taking pictures and yelling our names. I checked my watch and noticed she was near time for ending her final show and had Leonardo come with flowers. He was near the entrance, and I walked up to him to grab them with Gael behind me.

"She's inside, boss, and I hear they sold the show out. They reserved your seat as usual."

"Thank you. Gael, leave the keys with me and ride back with Leonardo," I requested.

"Joaquin, you shouldn't be out here in the open alone. At least call Gabriella or have Hugo follow you tonight," Gael said, shielding me from the cameras as we headed through the back entrance.

"I'll be fine. Keep me updated on what you find out and set up a flight to Italy," I reminded him as I walked toward the dressing rooms and found her door. I knocked and waited for an answer.

"Come in!" I heard and opened the door.

The girl I always saw her with was packing up her things.

"It's you!" Cassidy said.

"Excuse me."

"Her stalker boyfriend," she called me.

I chuckled and placed the flowers down on the side table. Peering around the room, I saw all the posted pictures of her performances in various newspapers and magazines, saying the show was superb and continuously sold out.

"Hello, I'm Joaquin," I introduced myself, reaching out to shake her hand. She shook it and crossed her arms over her chest, tapping her index finger to her chin.

"I'm Sofia's assistant. My name's Cassidy, and she told me all about you."

"All good things, I hope."

"Mostly about you being the quiet, brooding type of guy. Except you've been dropping flowers off to her every time she's performed on stage. Why is that?" she questioned.

"I'm a fan."

Before she could delve more in-depth into questioning me, the door swung open, and Sofia came inside with Edward behind her. Gabriella researched him and found out he was some big-time manager and producer. A little shorter than me with a thin build, probably a jogger. He'd been her manager for the past seven years and lived on Long Island. He had a girlfriend he occasionally saw from time to time and his parents were still alive.

"What are you doing here, Joaquin?" she questioned nervously, and I pointed toward the flowers.

"This room is off-limits to fans, and we need you to leave," Edward said, opening the door and waving for me to leave.

SOFIA

The entire time my stomach turned into knots watching the two of them glare at each other. I knew Edward was no match for Joaquin, and I'd hoped he'd keep his mouth shut and not cause a fight. Tonight was a huge success, I sold out my show, and the cast was getting ready to go out to a wrap party and celebrate. When he texted me last night, I didn't think he would really comment on the dinner. I cut the tension before Edward said anything to cause Joaquin to hurt him.

"Uhm… I have plans tonight. I didn't believe you were serious about dinner."

"What are these plans? Maybe, I can come along," he replied in his strong accent, staring at me and licking his lips. Clearing my throat, I walked over and grabbed my bag to change.

"I have to change, and then we have a party to attend for my show. Sorry, maybe another time," I suggested.

"I like parties, maybe I can call my friends to meet us there." He pulled his phone out of his pocket, and my eyes rose in fear.

"Wait!" I shouted, trying to think of a way to get out of this without causing an even bigger issue.

"Sofia, you can't be serious," Edward fussed, gripping my arm, turning me toward him.

"Take your hands off of her," Joaquin demanded with a low growl. Edward probably didn't think Joaquin would do anything in front of me, but his posture was giving off mysterious vibes. Yanking out of his hold, I stepped in front of Joaquin to calm him down. His eyes twitched, and his fists clenched at his sides.

"Where did you park?" I queried to get him to leave; I cupped his chin, forcing him to look me in the eye and away from Edward. It was like he transformed into a killer gearing up for his prey.

"My car is out back. I can take you to this party," he answered, sliding his hands on the lower half of my back. Cassidy smiled, and I rolled my eyes. She'd always been attracted to the bad boy types, and anytime someone put Edward in his place, she loved to see it.

"Okay, we can go. Edward, I'll see you at the party. Cassidy, are you coming?" I questioned, grabbing my purse and shawl. She was dropping off all my gifts and flowers, as well as clothes from my dressing room later tonight, so I only needed my keys and wallet for the evening. I'd already changed into my black bodycon dress, adding light makeup and a few pieces of jewelry.

Everyone followed out behind me, and Joaquin reached for my hand and escorted me over to his car. It differed from the limo I rode in the first time, and he seemed more typical in an SUV compared to being chauffeured around by Leonardo. Opening the door for me, he helped me slide in and winked once the door closed. The second Edward mumbled something under his breath, Joaquin glared, ready to go off. Coming around to the driver's side, he hopped inside before putting his seatbelt on and turning the ignition.

"Here's the address of the party." I pulled out my phone, locating my email with the address. He drove off toward a club called Ryde. I'd never gone there before, and he seemed to know exactly where it was located.

"Why do you hate Edward?" I investigated.

"He's not worthy of my time or yours, and he wants to sleep with you."

"And you don't?" I challenged snarkily, crossing my arms over my chest, leaning back into the seat against the window.

I must have hit a nerve as he glared over at me.

"I want to be your friend." Joaquin pushed the loose hair behind my ear.

"Tell me something about you, Joaquin?" I questioned, changing the subject to lighten the mood.

"What would you like to know, sweetheart?"

"Let me see— your name, age, parents dead or alive. Siblings, the usual."

"Like a date," he responded and grinned.

"Ughh, you're an ass."

"I'll tell you everything about me if you have dinner with me right now."

He turned down near Ryde, a local night club.

"What about the party?"

Shrugging his shoulders, he stated, "Come with me right now for dinner and drinks, and I'll answer your questions."

"That's it? Dinner and drinks only?"

"Yes," he replied, stopping in front of Ryde. Not turning the car off, we peered into each other's eyes, neither one willing to open the door and leave. Internally, I was cursing myself out for falling for this man that I had no business being with right now. The photographers started clamoring and noticing us in the car and began filming. I shielded my eyes and nodded to go.

"Okay, fine, I'll have dinner with you, just hurry and go before it becomes a madhouse."

Signaling to get in the left turn lane, Joaquin pulled off right as a mob of fans and photographers captured us together. Even one picture of us together plastered in the media would have Edward going crazy. Bad enough I was still upset about the other day at the restaurant and he tried sending me flowers to make up for his attitude.

"You're thinking hard over there," Joaquin spoke, slowing down at the yellow light as it turned red.

"Thinking about if I'll end up making a big mistake," I commented.

"Sometimes mistakes are good when it gives you the best pleasure you've ever experienced," he stated then pushed the gas a little harder, when his phone buzzed in the cup holder. He replied to a text message.

Joaquin

Security: All clear Boss.

Me: Make sure you get information on her manager.

Security: Yes Sir.

Sofia

"You drive this fast all the time?" she asked as she held onto the door knob.

I grinned, flashing an innocent smile.

"You want me to slow down, Sofia?" he asked.

Her hands folded in her lap.

"I want you to focus on the road, Joaquin," I spat and he laughed then slowed down right as we pulled up to my home.

JOAQUIN

I didn't want to do a regular restaurant, so I had dinner arranged at my apartment. I've lived in the Flatiron district for the past two years. No other woman had came here and usually when I met Monica, it was either at a hotel, or I'd stop by her place. Ever since I pushed her away at my office, she hadn't called to see me. Parking in my parking space, I turned off the car and leaned over, cupping her chin and capturing her lips in a tender kiss.

"Where are we?" she muttered through the kiss.

"My place," I replied, and her eyes grew wide in shock.

Opening the door, I got out, walking around to her side and helping her step out. Right as we headed toward my door, Hugo and Gabriella pulled up and got out.

I nodded, and they returned the gesture, following behind us into the building.

"Are they having dinner with us?" she asked.

"No, I need to talk to them quickly. You can take my key and head up to the penthouse. I'm right behind you."

"Joaquin."

"I promise, just a minute." I leaned over and kissed her forehead.

Sofia sighed and took the private key and left toward the elevator. I watched until she got on and the doors closed.

"What did you find out?" I questioned Gabriella.

"Sir, Lin-Sae drove off to the meatpacking district and then the loading dock where most of the shipment of cars come into the city. He could have been throwing us off, but I doubt it."

I ran a hand down my face.

"Keep an eye on him and let me know what happens. I don't trust him, and if we need to remove him from power, we only have one chance. The Bosses are meeting in two months to sign off on expanding into a new bureau. Last minute interruptions will not be tolerated. Do I make myself clear?"

Hugo and Gabriella nodded in answer and walked off. I didn't need overnight security, the same way my parents had in Italy and Portugal. They have trained snipers on roofs and posted twenty-four hours a day. A few minutes later, I was unlocking the door to my penthouse and stepped inside to find Sofia standing near the balcony. I shut the front door and removed my jacket, unbuttoning my cufflinks. Stepping out to the balcony, I stared at her, leaning against the door. She turned, facing me, and had a sly smile lifted at the corner of her mouth.

"I'm here at your place, which you didn't tell me we'd be going to for dinner. So, you owe me."

"What would you like to know?" I asked, heading toward her.

"We can start with your background. I mean, I can imagine you've done a background check on me and probably know my blood type," she joked.

"I'm Joaquin Fuertes; nice to meet you, Sofia Chambers."

"Nice to meet you, Joaquin." She held her hand out for a shake.

"You're right, I did do a background check on you, mostly the basic information; your name, age, and your birthplace. More interested in hearing it from your beautiful lips," I said, running a finger across her bottom lip.

"Where are you from?"

"My father is Portuguese and my mother is Italian. They've been

51

married for over forty years. I was born in Portugal and split my time between both places because my father was the mayor."

"Any sisters or brothers?"

"I have a younger sister, Alessandra, who's twenty-two, and I'm thirty-one."

"Are you one of those big brothers that won't let his sister date?" she teased, walking out of my hold and entering back inside. Sofia plopped down on the couch, crossing her legs, exposing her left thigh.

"I am, and I don't want to talk about her. Tell me something about you," I initiated, walking over to pick up the two champagne glasses on the table. I had dinner already set up with candles, and I wanted to move at her own pace. Passing her a drink, she thanked me.

I sat down next to her extending my arm around her shoulders on the couch.

"You know I'm from the south, and I moved here to pursue my career. At twenty-nine, I'm in the prime of my career with multiple films, TV, and Broadway shows on my resume. So, if you're looking for a wife or girlfriend, I can't be that, and I won't put my dreams on hold."

"I'm looking for friendship, nothing more."

"We can be friends."

"Close friends?" I placed my glass down. Running a hand alongside her cheek, she smiled, taking another sip.

"What do you want with me, Joaquin, and be honest?"

"Are you hungry?"

"I am, but not for food," she answered, surprising me.

She initiated the kiss, leaning into my space at the same time putting her glass on the table. Sofia attempted to straddle my legs, and I restrained her by the wrists.

"Sweetheart, what are you doing?" I cupped both sides of her cheeks.

"Putting our cards on the table. We've been at this for months with the cat and mouse games, we're both grown adults that are interested in only friendship with benefits and nothing more. You can tell your little girlfriend she can have you back by tomorrow. The last time I've had sex was a year ago, so this right here will break the streak and satisfy my appetite."

"So, you're using me," I commented, brushed my tongue across her lips.

"We use each other," she muttered out in a low breath.

"What if one of us wants more down the line?"

"It can't happen."

"But, what if it does?"

Sofia sighed, removing her wrists out of my hold. "Joaquin, men are a dime a dozen, even if I wanted more, I wouldn't be able to commit because my career is ever evolving. I travel almost every other month for acting, plus my music career. I can't give any man a long-term answer. I was only fulfilling our sexual desires. I need to get home, I'm filming tomorrow, and need to sleep. Can you call for a cab?"

She stood up, ready to leave, and I reached for her hand before pulling her into my chest.

"Stay, it's late, and you've been drinking with no food. Tomorrow, I'll take you home personally."

"I can't do that."

"Why not? You would be here anyway if we'd slept together."

"Normally, a one-night stand doesn't sleep overnight," she joked.

"I wasn't planning on sleeping at all."

She hiked her eyebrow. "Fine, and the food is probably cold by now. Answer me this. How many women have you brought here before?"

We headed over to the dining room table, and I slid the chair out for her, and she thanked me.

"None. You're the first one," I answered truthfully.

"A part of me thinks you're lying."

"Why would I lie? It doesn't gain me anything in your favor, sweetheart. Do I have women friends? Yes, I take them to a hotel. Never my home."

"What if I never agreed to come to dinner? All of this food would have gone to waste."

Shrugging my shoulders, I placed the napkin on my lap and picked up my fork, removing the top lids off her dishes.

"Eventually, we would have had dinner. I say our paths would have crossed one day."

"As a mob boss, do you kill people personally?" she asked out of the blue.

"Would that cause you to not want to talk to me if I did?"

"I don't know. A part of me is saying run for the hills, and the other part is curious about those deep black pearl eyes looking back at me, making me feel like you have a lot of secrets to tell."

"Do you know what I see when I look into your eyes?"

"What?'

"Loneliness. Someone that has everything they've ever wanted except someone to share it with. You're afraid to get close because you think they'll leave you unless you have them in some capacity at arm's length. Dangling them on a string to want to be in your presence, but not too close that they'll see the little girl that's still dealing with the loss of her father."

"Mob boss, business owner, and therapist. Do I have that right?"

"You're only right if what I said is truthful. Does the reason for your celibacy have anything to do with keeping me on a short leash because you'd instead prefer not to get close and get your heart broken?"

The stare off continued for three minutes straight. The tension was thick as her eyes narrowed in slits. I leaned back in my chair, waiting to see her response. Was she a flight or fight type?

"How did you find me in the first place after our initial run-in at the restaurant?" Sofia inquired, as she ran her hand up my shoulder and through my hair. I closed my eyes feeling her comfort and peace with her presence near me.

"I had my people look you up." I said, glancing at her.

"So you did do a background check."

"Something like that."

I wanted to avoid the mention of me finding out where her parents lived and tracking her Broadway schedule with me buying off the theater owner. If she found out that I knew everything from the car service she used to her favorite restaurant, then this date would be over fast.

"Did you speak with any of my coworkers at the theater?" Sofia asked. I laid a hand on her thigh and rubbed gently as I stared in wonder at her beautiful heart-shaped lips.

"A few people, but nothing too invasive." I smirked and she chuckled.

"Something tells me you're lying, but I won't push."

"In time, you'll know I have reasons for everything I do, Sofia."

"When that time comes, be prepared to not like how I respond." Sofia's left brow lifted.

I inched closer and lifted her chin.

"You have beautiful lips. Makes me wonder how they'd feel on top of mine."

"Do you have any more wine?" she questioned, pointing to the glass on the table.

"Is that your way of changing the subject?"

Our fingers entwined in a loose grip.

"I feel like I might regret this date."

I leaned back and smiled. She looked over and cocked her head as she appraised me.

"Can I give you a reason to regret?" I announced then reached for her hand and placed it on top of my dick. The tension between us rose to a ten, right as her hand tightened around my large girth.

SOFIA

*H*e dragged his lips across my soft skin and nibbled at my hip bone. I paused and chewed my lip in thought.

"Mmmmm...Yes, Joaquin." I gripped his hair in my hands. We never got a chance to eat dinner. He told me I was his meal. It was the reason why my dress was thrown on the floor with my heels, as I was arching my back, and gripping the back of his head. He was still clothed and running his tongue up my inner thigh. Logic faded a long time ago when I agreed to get in the car and let him take me to the party. There was something so explosive about our interactions. A deep gravitational pull where both of us needed to be in each other's presence. Was I a fool? Probably. But neither of us could change the turn of events with me in his bed as he skimmed his fingers over my wet sex. I kept my legs apart, giving him room as he used both index fingers to open my slit and swipe his tongue across.

"Ohhh..."

The scent of my arousal drove me mad. I needed him to be inside me. He grabbed my hips, keeping me from locking his head between my thighs.

"Shit!" I cried out as his tongue explored my backdoor.

No man had ever taken it there with me by licking my asshole. This would be new territory for me.

"I love your taste, sweetheart."

"Ughhh...Please don't stop," I begged, my breath ragged and shallow.

He released my left thigh and claimed my breast, squeezing gently as his tongue speared my canal. I cried out, digging my nails into the covers on the bed.

"Don't worry; I won't."

Joaquin licked and teased me with his tongue in long strokes. In and out, slow, then fast.

My hips pumped up from below, meeting his rhythm. As he held my left breast, I squeezed and tweaked my right one. The sight of him, exploring my body after all these months, was bringing tears to my eyes. No one had ever focused all of their energy on pleasing me fully without wanting anything in return.

"I'm commmming!!" I shouted as he slowly kissed his way up my stomach and breasts.

I gasped right as he pressed against my spot that had me leaking on his sheets. I was exhausted and ready for bed. He teased my soft nipple with his tongue as he lifted my left leg and curved it around his waist. I felt his hard erection pressed against me and the sensation was torturous with every inch. Joaquin ran his palm across my cheek, hovered over my lips letting me taste myself as I dozed off.

"Mmmm..." he mumbled as his right hand pressed against my lower lips.

* * *

Two hours later, I woke up alone in bed, under the covers in a white t-shirt. Admiring his bedroom, I saw it was neat, nothing was out of place. Almost as if he didn't have any clothes. The room was large, with a TV hanging on the wall. His closet was open with all of his pants and shoes tidy. I got out of bed and walked over to the mantle with the fireplace underneath, and it held pictures of a couple with two kids, a girl and a boy. I assumed it was him and his family. They looked happy while posing in front of a house. I saw more photos on the wall of him in Italy and Portugal, posing with other men wearing suits. His father was prominent in the middle with a Portuguese flag. Checking his drawers, I saw all of his shirts, socks, and pants folded neatly.

"Find anything interesting?" he asked, startling me. I turned and looked at him wearing only pajama pants and no shirt. A large tattoo across his chest spelled out Fuertes, along with an arm tattoo of the Italian flag.

"Sorry, I didn't mean to snoop," I told him.

He walked further inside, closing the door.

"I have nothing to hide, sweetheart," he replied, taking a seat on the bed.

"Did I pass out?" I inquired, sitting on the edge of the bed.

Joaquin chuckled, staring at me, running his tongue across his lips. He leaned over and kissed me on the lips.

"You did."

"That's never happened before."

"You're welcome."

"Ugh, you're an asshole."

"And you're beautiful with a fiery tongue that needs to be disciplined properly."

"Let me guess, you'd be the one to dole out the punishment," I commented.

He smirked.

"Are you hungry?" he questioned.

"No, I need to get dressed and go home, though."

"It's late, Sofia, stay here. I promise I'll take you home in the morning. You shouldn't be out this late."

"What time is it?" I looked around the room for a clock. He lifted his wrist and showed me it was midnight.

"Tell me about your tattoos?" His boldly handsome face smiled warmly down at me as I tucked myself under the covers. Joaquin pointed toward the tattoo on his arm.

"I take pride in where I come from. My heritage is important to me, both Italy and Portugal. This tattoo on my chest is my family crest. All the men in our family have them."

"Tell me about the woman that I saw you with, the first time in Antonio's. She seemed overly jealous of anyone being in your presence that was the opposite sex."

"Monica-"

"Monica, nice name. She's cute."

Joaquin chuckled at my response.

"Monica is a friend; I've known her for the past five years."

"Wow! I need to go."

"What does that mean? Sofia, stop, talk to me." I attempted to get out of the bed and leave. He'd been dating her off and on for five years and never proposed.

"She's your girlfriend, Joaquin. I'm not a cheater and refuse to be friends with anyone that would allow that to happen!" I spat.

"Shushh. Calm down, sweetheart. Monica understands that I am not interested in her for a relationship. We had an arrangement that was beneficial to us both. I don't cheat, and I would never put you in a position of being a cheater."

"I don't know. I think we took this too far."

"Get some sleep, I'll be in the guest room, and I set the alarm to wake you at seven. I'll take you home after we have breakfast in the morning, and I don't want to hear any more about Monica. Get her out of your head. Besides, I've had a taste of your pussy, and I refuse to give it up to the next man," he informed me, gripping my chin before he leaned over to peck my lips and forehead. He walked out of the bedroom and left me alone with my thoughts of the past few hours. Had I invited more trouble in my world? I wasn't built for endless nights of worry and pain if something happened, I thought to myself, drifting off to sleep.

* * *

THE NEXT MORNING, I snuck out of his place and covered my face as I walked through the lobby. I wasn't against one-night stands, it was something about the look in his eyes that told me this wouldn't be the last time we would be together. I opened the door, glanced around and saw two of his bodyguards talking.

"Boss know you're out here?"

"What's your name?" I asked.

"Alex, Miss Chambers," Alex said and I looked out of place honestly, because most of the men I'd seen around Joaquin were at least six-two or taller. Alex was just shy of six feet.

"Yes, Alex, he knows, and I have an Uber pulling up right now."

"We can drop you off. Let me confirm with the boss."

"No need to do that. I can get myself home on my own."

"Are you sure?" Alex inquired, and followed me toward the Uber. I opened the back door and the driver called my name to confirm.

"Sofia?" the young girl questioned.

"That's me."

"You're that actress, right?" she questioned and I shook my head no.

"Listen, Alex, don't worry about taking me. I got it from here," I said and closed the door and told her to pull off immediately.

I looked out of the window at them arguing back and forth with the other guard and I blew out a breath of relief.

SOFIA

Two days later, I was home in my apartment with Cassidy going through pieces of the sample collection that Expressive Designs sent over for me to check out.

"This jacket is cute," Cassidy said, handing me the jacket.

"Yeah, I like the side zippers and the hood being able to detach." I tested out the side zippers and slid my hands inside standing from left to right in front of my mirror.

"So, tell me what happened with Mr. Boyfriend?" Cassidy asked as she took a photo of me in the jacket. We had about ten pieces to mix and match. Once that was completed, I had to try and get online and do some blog interviews.

"Nothing happened, nosy pants." I removed the jacket, wearing only the sports bra and black tights.

"You want me to believe that?" Cassidy remarked, labeling the jacket as a possible choice.

"He had arranged dinner for us at his place, then we talked."

The doorbell rang and Cassidy jumped up and ran to the door to grab our lunch that I ordered. She paid the driver twenty dollars for the steamed rice, vegetables, and egg roll bowls we always got from the corner restaurant near my building.

"Dinner only," Cassidy replied as she opened the food on the table and separated out her pork and vegetable bowl.

"Do I hound you about your dates?" I questioned before I picked up the fork from the bag. I headed to the kitchen to grab us a bottle of water and came to sit next to her on the couch.

"You can't hound something that I don't do. This job takes up too much of my time."

"If you're overwhelmed, let me know," I said and nudged her in the shoulder.

Cassidy sprinkled pepper and salt on her food and took a bite, moaning in satisfaction.

"I love this job, so that's not the problem. Finding a good man is," Cassidy mentioned and I couldn't agree more. I wondered if I was self-sabotaging every man that tried to date me because I didn't want to go down that path of hurt and pain that I sang about.

"What time is the interview again?" I checked my watch on my wrist and took a sip of the water.

"In about an hour," Cassidy responded.

"He gave me oral sex," I blurted out and buried my head in my pillow. Cassidy jumped up and screamed in excitement.

"I knew it...he looked like the type that could eat some pussy and have you climbing walls," Cassidy joked and I rolled my eyes at her comment.

"Don't tell anybody I said that." I shoved her away when she tried to hug me.

"Wow! Edward's going to be pissed," Cassidy reminded me, before she scratched her nose and sat back.

"Edward needs to worry about managing my career and nothing else."

"That's true, but you know how protective he gets over you," Cassidy remarked and passed me an egg roll.

"He will be all right."

"Joaquin seems very intense," Cassidy said, then picked up her laptop and typed in her password to set up for the interview.

"That's an understatement."

"Why do you say that?"

"I ran out of his place and haven't called him back."

"Wait, you skipped out on morning sex?"

"Yeah, I sneaked out of his place like a teenager. Which reminds me, did my mom send you her flight information?"

Cassidy checked her phone and nodded.

"In a month, she's coming with your dad for a few days," Cassidy said, putting her phone on the table.

"I really like the short set with the see through on the side," I said as I picked up the black and pink jogging shorts.

"Okay, I'll let them know you want the first five pieces," Cassidy said.

"The deal is for the editorial, correct?" I investigated, going through my contract after I placed my food down on the table.

"Editorial and opening of the shop, walk red carpet, and photo-shoot." I bobbed my head in agreement and looked over the documents. Cassidy continued jotting down her notes when my phone beeped with a notification.

Actress and Singer Sofia Chambers in love with a Mob Boss- Gossip Times Blog

Sofia Chambers and Joaquin a new item- Celebrity Style Magazine

I threw my phone on the table and groaned.

"What's wrong?" She looked over at my phone.

"It's probably in all the news now." Cassidy started to close out of the video chat and pick up her phone when it rang.

"Edward." Cassidy held the phone up for me to see.

"Ignore him, it might blow over."

I sighed as I raked a finger through my hair.

"I need to put on some makeup." I jumped up, ran to my bath-room and applied light foundation and lipstick. The interview would play back on social media most likely. I puffed my hair into a high bun and walked out. Cassidy was talking to the blogger and I sat down next to her on the couch and waved.

"Hey, Kelly," I spoke.

Kelly had her own platform called Katch up with Kelly, a

celebrity-driven video channel. She sometimes got into the gossip, but overall, she focused on the new movie releases, music, and TV's latest news.

"I'm super excited to talk with you, Sofia," Kelly responded.

"As long as we keep it to work, Kelly. I know how you can get," I replied, pivoting my body to the camera so she could see the back white wall of my apartment.

"I understand, but can you make one comment about your new boyfriend?" Kelly queried.

"I'm single."

"What about the pictures that paparazzi have of you in a car with some guy named Joaquin Fuertes; allegedly a mobster," Kelly stated.

"You can't believe everything you see, Kelly."

"That's true, but your fans want you to be happy," Kelly said.

"I am, but not because of a man. My passion is singing and acting." I waved to the wall where my plaques of my platinum album and film awards hung.

"That's the best statement an actress has said on my platform," Kelly said.

"We have twenty minutes for the interview, Kelly," Cassidy jumped in to say.

"Let's start with the first question. How is the Broadway show going?" Kelly held up a playbill of the show I'd been working on.

"Everything is going well. Super proud of my work."

"Do you have plans of doing more Broadway?"

"You just have to wait and see."

"What about music?" Kelly questioned.

"I'm in the studio as we speak. So look for more music soon," I answered, drinking from my water bottle.

"Do you see it more of an R&B or pop inspiration?" Kelly asked.

"Right now, I'm just recording songs. I have to enjoy what I do before planning a full album."

Joaquin: Still ignoring me?

Joaquin: I don't like talking on the phone.

Joaquin: We need to meet in person.

"Sofia! Sofia! Do you hear me?" Kelly wondered, calling out my name. In the middle of answering her call, my phone caught my eye with back-to-back messages from Joaquin.

Joaquin: I can tell you're scared of what we could be.

"Huh…Oh sorry…Can we finish this through email and I'll have Cassidy send you my answers?" I replied as I turned my phone over.

"Sure, is everything okay?" Kelly wondered.

"Yeah, sorry, just a last-minute business request," I said, trying to avoid all conversations about Joaquin. Cassidy moved the computer to herself and finished talking with Kelly to set up another session. My heart thudded in my chest when I walked over to window, scanned around, and saw a dark luxury SUV at the corner.

Everyone went on about their business as though nothing was strange about a car sitting on the corner near any restaurants. *Was it a mistake to take things that far with Joaquin?* I thought to myself.

"What just happened, Sofia?" Cassidy asked.

"I just wanted to cut it short to get over to the studio. Chauncey texted he was there," I lied, closed the curtain of the window, and picked up the trash from the food and threw it away.

"Are you sure? You seem out of it right now." Cassidy folded her arms and stood in the doorway of the kitchen.

I wiped down the table and pointed at her to ask if she wanted to finish it before I tossed it away. She gestured she was finished.

"Cassidy, stop worrying, girl. I'm fine, just call a cab or Uber so we can go," I said.

"I can't make it to the studio, I want to get some of the photos and samples sent over," she replied as she strolled to the table and grabbed her laptop to put it away.

"You want to share an Uber?" I asked.

"That's fine since it's on my way home."

She snapped her fingers.

"Don't forget you have an Atlanta trip coming up," Cassidy announced, and I bobbed my head in answer.

"I won't," I responded and grabbed a jacket off the coat rack, then my purse. We left together as I locked up and hopped on the elevator when the doors opened. Five minutes later, we came out of the elevator and I waved at the receptionist and doorman as Cassidy followed me out to the awaiting car.

"Here we go," Cassidy said to the red Prius with the older gentleman driving.

"For Sofia?" I asked to make sure and he checked the name on his phone and nodded his head. I climbed inside and Cassidy got up front.

He pulled off into traffic, passing by the SUV, and I kept my head at a low angle, but still managed to see out and I noticed Alex, the bodyguard, waving at me. I rolled my eyes and knew I would have to have some words with Joaquin if he thought I would allow anyone to babysit me.

"We're here, Sofia," Cassidy called out.

I slid my Coach bag around my neck and stepped out of the car and told Cassidy I would see her later. She waved goodbye and I walked inside running into Chauncey coming from the recording booth.

"Hey, what are you doing here?" he asked, checking his watch.

"I wanted to get a little time in and hoped you'd be here," I said as I followed behind him and took my backpack off.

"All-nighter?" he queried.

"Yep, I need the break," I responded, pulled out my notebook and pen, ready to get all my frustrations out. Chauncey went in and set it up for me with a bottle of water and lit candles.

JOAQUIN

*S*ofia hadn't called or texted me once since our night together about slipping out when I was asleep and she wouldn't respond to my texts either. I tried to be patient and go at her speed, but I wasn't a patient man in any aspect of my life. Currently, I was in the United Kingdom after taking a red eye to sign a potential deal to have our guns operation shipped from England to Portugal. Even while dealing with the Russian situation, I needed to make sure business would continue without any interruptions.

"This is just the preliminary meeting, Joaquin," Gael said as he glanced around the room at the men gathered together.

"I won't shoot anyone, if that's what you're worried about!" I cocked my head to the side and winked. He was the only one that got my humor.

"Fuck off, Joaquin," Gael grunted, then he pulled out his phone and texted with someone.

"Gentlemen, thank you for coming to meet with me," Maricio Caputo said as he marched in the room and extended a hand for us both to take.

"It sounded like an emergency. I thought we were meeting with Laurent?" Gael questioned.

"Yes. I know and I apologize about the last-minute change," Maricio said.

Gael and I peered at each other to see if this was a setup or not.

"I only talk with people that make the decisions," I said, cutting off Gael from responding.

"I understand, but as his right-hand man, I can assure you that I speak for him on any major decisions," Maricio stated. The man was only about five-seven with a large round belly, bushy eyebrows, and crooked teeth. Something about him made my gut turn.

"What does he want?" Gael asked.

"He wants to cut a deal that leaves you with a thirty-seventy split," Maricio told us and I laughed.

"I'm not wasting my time on this." I stood up and all of his security reached for their guns.

"Ghost," Maricio spoke and I glared at him.

"Maricio was taking all the risk, if we decided to go in on this," Gael stated.

"How do we know you didn't work with the Russians?" I barked out and slammed my hand on the table while I pointed at him.

He menacingly stared.

"We had nothing to do with that setup," Maricio said.

"I don't trust you," I spat and my phone chimed with a text message.

Alex: She just left on a flight.

Me: Where is she going?

Alex: The flight said Atlanta.

Me: Call our tech to get her exact location.

"Joaquin, I can go to a forty-sixty split," Maricio informed me and I shook my head while texting to find out Sofia's destination.

"Our final offer is sixty-five to your thirty-five and that's final. I need to be somewhere," I told him as I motioned for my men to follow behind me. If he had any sense, he would get Laurent on the phone and give in to my request. Fuertes would bear the brunt of

68

the load and reload through different channels. There would be extra security we'd need to hire to watch the drop off as they unloaded. Carrington was a friend of my father's, but I'm no fool and getting anything less than the top percentage then he could handle it on his own. The distribution alone would raise a red flag with our associates.

"What's the rush?" Gael asked, strolling alongside me.

"I need to head out on another flight."

My phone ran with my sister's name scrolled across.

"Where to?" Gael inquired, getting in on the other side of the limo. We were only here for two days to confirm the transaction and then head back to the US.

"Joaquin!" Alessandra said.

"Yes, Alessandra. I already sent you an allowance," I responded while buckling my seatbelt. The security team packed into two more SUVs behind us.

"What makes you think I want money?" she asked.

Gael held up his phone showing a message from Maricio saying it was a go.

"Alessandra, I need to call you back. Something has come up." I hurriedly ended the call and texted Maricio back.

"What did your sister want?" Gael questioned.

"Nothing important," I mumbled and sent the message.

Me: Glad you see things my way.

Maricio: You know this wasn't the way to do things with the Carringtons.

Me: I'll speak to Laurent when the time comes.

Maricio: Will you be there for the first shipment?

Me: My people will handle the details.

"Make sure they watch every last load. I don't put anything past anyone," I stated as we headed to the airstrip to get on the private jet.

Fifteen minutes later, we pulled up and I jumped out, while they grabbed our bags that we already had in the car since we came to London. Today was checkout anyway and we pre-planned to leave right after the meeting. Only now, my destination would not be New York. Sofia was playing games and I wasn't going away after I had the pleasure of her moans and groans as I tasted her sweet nectar.

"Welcome back, sir," the flight attendant said.

"Thank you. Can you let the pilot know there have been a change of plans?"

"Sure, where are you headed to?" she asked, placing a drink in front of me and Gael.

"Atlanta," I said as Gael had a perplexed look on his face.

"What's that look about?"

"You always fight your feelings and now she has you wrapped around her finger," Gael chuckled then took a sip of his bourbon.

I flipped him off and dug through my phone looking at photos of her in the media and red carpets.

"I saw a few social media posts. This won't be good for her career, you know."

"Get them removed," I demanded.

"Everything doesn't happen at the snap of your fingers, brother," Gael argued.

"I pay to get what I want and if anything gets in my way..."

"Just try to hang back and not to do anything irrational," Gael said as he glanced out of the window while the plane was being loaded up and the doors closed. I relaxed in the chair and thought about the first night we were together.

"I can't promise that." The pilot got on the intercom, announced the plane was heading to the runway to take off. It was a bright sunny day and I planned to try and keep my emotions under control when I saw her again. The taking off while I was sleeping, and now flying out of state without a word, was something I wouldn't tolerate.

SOFIA

*C*week later, I still hadn't spoken with Joaquin since that
night. I blocked his number when he texted and I worked
overtime with getting my tracks laid down with Deras and started
filming my latest movie in Atlanta. Being out in Atlanta temporarily
was a nice distraction without having anything or anyone
reminding me that I entertained a cartel kingpin. I could hear my
parents yelling and cursing at me that I was crazy for even giving
the time of my day to someone like that. Right now, I was running
lines with my co-star in my hotel room. Edward was on the phone,
taking phone calls and managing my schedule with Cassidy.

"Dante, what do you think about this line?" I asked, highlighting
in my script, sitting next to him on the couch. We had today off and
decided to run through our lines and rehearse. Meanwhile, Cassidy
was managing my schedule and social media, and returning emails.
We were here for a month and then back to New York to continue
filming. It was something more dramatic with a romantic under-
tone. Atlanta was the place to be for film production and network-
ing, almost rivaling Los Angeles.

"Tomorrow we'll need to have the director rehearse with us a
few times, that's a big scene," he responded. I nodded in agreement.

"Sounds good. Cassidy, how is everything with my schedule? Deras texted me earlier about coming to his showcase when I got back into town," I investigated, replying to his text.

"Right now, you're free; you only have two off days when you get back, and then two photoshoots, a magazine interview, and then you're back to filming and recording," Cassidy informed me.

"Get an appointment for a spa day in the hotel. I need to get these kinks removed in my back," I requested.

"Okay, uhmm, Sofia, have you seen the latest gossip?" Cassidy probed, passing me the laptop computer with my name and photo on the front page of a major newspaper— New York celebrity with a shot of Joaquin holding his hands up to block the cameras. It was taken when we were in the car heading to dinner. Then there was another one of him trying to punch a photographer.

"OMG!" I jumped off the couch, pacing back and forth.

"Let me call you back," Edward said, walking toward me and looking over my shoulder at the article.

"Sofia, WTF! I told you to leave that thug alone," Edward fussed as he planted his hands on his sides.

"I really don't need an 'I told you so' from you. How about you just be my manager and help fix the issue?"

"Fix it. Your name's plastered on every news gossip site with you named as the next Donna of the Fuertes Cartel. Do you understand how this could set your career back, shit... my career?" Edward murmured.

Dante comforted me with a hug when all of a sudden, loud banging came from the front door.

"Did you order room service?" I asked, walking off to answer.

Edward and Cassidy shook their heads. Opening the door, the last person I ever expected to see was standing in the middle of two big burly men and one woman. All were wearing black suits and ties. I suspected the handguns, but the trench coats easily covered them from being detected.

"Who's at the door?" Edward yelled.

I hurriedly slammed the door behind me and leaned against it with closed eyes wishing this was all a dream.

"What are you doing here?" I whispered harshly.

His bodyguards moved aside, and he stepped forward, closing the space between us; the hard glare and bushy eyebrows stared into my eyes, willing me to say the wrong thing.

"Can I come inside?" he asked.

"No."

"Why is that? Are you entertaining someone? Having a party? I like parties, invite my men and me inside," Joaquin queried.

"I'm busy."

"I'll ask you again, invite me inside, or I'll force my way in, and you won't like my way, sweetheart," Joaquin insisted, winking at his bodyguard he called Gabriella. A smile crept on her face, and she pulled a gun from behind her back.

"Put that away, are you insane? We're in a hotel room. You can't go forcing your way into people's private rooms. I'm busy like I said."

He gripped my waist, pulled me in close, bent down and whispered in my ear, "I missed you, sweetheart." He gently moved me behind him and opened my room door. I tried to stop him, and his bodyguards grasped my arm, stopping me. He glared at his men, motioning to let me go.

"I want to meet your guests. I remember you, Cassidy, correct? The assistant," Joaquin stated. He moved into the room, taking my hand, reintroducing himself to Cassidy. As a sick love puppy, she was giddy when he kissed her hand.

"Who is he?" Joaquin pointed at Dante, and I attempted to respond, but Dante cut me off.

"Hi, I'm Dante, her co-star."

"Hello, Dante, her former co-star."

My mouth dropped open in shock.

"You can't do that," I snapped, yanking my hand out of his hold.

"I can and I did. Grab your things, we're leaving." He pointed around at my clothes and shoes.

"Joaquin, I don't know what goes on in your world, but this control and trying to force my client to become your alibi won't stand. Sofia is not your mistress, girlfriend, or any of that bullshit that happens in your country," Edward shouted.

Joaquin peered from Dante to Edward, sliding his hands in his pockets.

"Edward, let me talk to him," I said.

"Sofia, grab your things, please. I am only going to ask you this once. We have a lot to talk about."

"Sofia, I'll see you tomorrow, hopefully on set." Dante tried to hug me, and Joaquin's men moved in closer. I couldn't believe he came all the way here acting an ass.

"Cassidy, can you and Edward go downstairs and reserve a table for dinner? I need to talk with Mr. Fuertes for a moment."

"Sure," Cassidy said meekly.

Edward refused to budge until our eyes connected and I silently asked him to leave. Joaquin wouldn't hurt me. I was more worried about him getting hurt.

"Hell, no! I've put too much money into your career and mine," Edward shouted, as he tried to get in my face and Joaquin grabbed him by the neck.

"I suggest you do as the lady said, Edward," Joaquin said through clenched teeth. I stood at his side and stared in his eyes to plead with him to let Edward go.

"Let...me...goooo...," Edward sputtered out.

Joaquin's eyes narrowed in anger, like he became another person.

"Joaquin, let him go. I'll talk with you," I told him.

"Are you sleeping with him?" Joaquin glared at me.

I sighed and tried to shove his arm away from Edward.

"No, and if you'd let him go, we could talk."

Joaquin stared back at Edward and smirked before letting him go. Edward dropped to the floor coughing and I bent down to try and help him.

"You see this!" Edward yelled, trying to catch his breath. I went to step around Joaquin and get Edward some water, but Joaquin stuck his arm out to stop me.

"He's fine," Joaquin commented.

"You're insane," I argued and pushed him in the chest.

Edward finally stood up and I helped him to the door, then turned to glare at Joaquin. I knew this was a bad idea from the first time I accepted those flowers at the show. I thought it was an innocent gesture and it would end with a dinner and drinks, something casual. Now, my entire life was upended with me being attached to a Cartel boss. I covered my face with my hands to calm my beating heart rate.

JOAQUIN

*H*er people stepped out, and I motioned for my men to leave us alone. She looked beautiful, dressed down like this in a large t-shirt and leggings, displaying her curves. Sofia walked up to me after the door closed and slapped me across the face. I smirked, rubbing the sting away. When I reached out to caress her cheek, she smacked my hand away.

"Sweetheart."

"I'm not your sweetheart, and who do you think you are coming up here demanding I leave with you?"

"Why did you run?" I shouted angrily.

"What?"

"The second I fell asleep, you disappeared. What did I do?"

"I don't have time to babysit your feelings. My career could be over because of you,"

she snapped, picking up the open laptop and shoving it into my face.

"I don't read gossip or entertain it, sweetheart. They'll have something new to talk about by tomorrow. We need to talk." Putting the computer back down on the couch, I followed her to the window, standing behind her as she looked out into the park.

"Talk then," she stated.

I ran a hand down my face, stepping back away from her; I removed my coat, suit jacket, and gun. I eased my hand across her shoulder and toward her neck, applying a little pressure.

"I'm done playing these games, sweetheart." I moved my left hand under her shirt. Gripping her left breast, I brushed a gentle kiss across her lips once, twice, smoothing her lips with demand. No woman had ever caused an ache or need that I had to be in their presence until I met Sofia Chambers.

"Mmmm...Joaquin," she moaned as she wrapped her hand around my neck.

"No talking," I muttered in between kisses, lifting her up by her ass and carrying her to the bedroom.

I turned the knob and plopped her on the bed, removing my shirt and pants, she tossed her shirt on the floor and eased out of the leggings. Capturing her mouth once more, I was shocked at her eagerness. Whirling her around, I nudged her to bend over and spread her legs. Grabbing my wallet out of my pocket, I removed three condoms, tossing them on the bed. I reached around, and her nipples firmed instantly under my touch.

"Ahhh!"

"Bellissima." My favorite word to call her; beautiful in Italian. She writhed, tossing her head back. I grasped her chin, crushing her lips to mine, challenging her to not want what was building between us.

Smacking her left, then right butt-cheek, I bent down to kiss the sting away. Licking my thumb, I spread her ass cheeks and ran a finger from her sweet sex to her asshole.

"Ughhh...shit!"

I tasted her with a slow lick; I inserted a finger and curled over her hard bud.

"Baby!"

"Louder!" I shouted, smacking her ass again. She quivered in anticipation. The moist flesh between her thighs glistened.

"Mine."

Deepening my tongue lashing, I slid a hand down and kissed her pussy again, praying I didn't go too fast. She was so soft and smelled the same as the first time we met.

"Oh, God."

I finally sheathed myself, gliding into her pussy. There's no way in hell I'd ever let her go now.

"Fuck!" I yelled, rocking in and out slowly.

She almost fell over, screaming, "Ahhh!"

Kissing up her back, we soon found a matching rhythm.

"Sofia...Mmmm." I leaned into the mattress, covering her back, grabbing both breasts as I picked up the pace, cursing and grunting in her ear, whispering how beautiful she was the first time I met her and saw her show. Thanking her for giving herself to me. Flipping her over with me still inside, one hand slid down her taut stomach to the swell of her hips. I bent down, showering kisses around her lips before thrusting my tongue inside for her sweet taste. Sofia cupped my face briefly before pulling me into a tight embrace.

Her arousal bloomed throughout the room and I felt myself get hard again. She couldn't tear her gaze away as my finger explored her sex again. I drove my tongue inside one more time, and lifted up to turn her around and positioned her on her knees.

Not stopping at only the front, I probed her tight sweet asshole.

"Joaquin! Please, don't stop," Sofia cried out.

"I'll never stop, baby," I responded, squeezing her ass cheeks. Her slick folds leaked onto the bed and I groaned in anticipation of being back inside of her. Rage and hunger exploded inside of me at the thought of never having her again. I grabbed another condom and pressed my swelled dick up against the tight rim of her ass. I teasingly rubbed once, then twice, letting her feel what she'd done to me. After five minutes of foreplay, I slid into her tight warm sheath and stopped, trying to catch my breath. I had to count to ten and think of anything that would distract me from coming too fast. Her pussy was so warm and weeping with need.

"My God, Sofia...I'll kill anyone that stands in the way." I slowly started to move inside of her and nudged her legs wider. I was lost in sensation as my movements picked up and I gave her deep strokes. The beads of sweat poured down my face onto her back. I bent down and licked the spot that my sweat fell on the lower part of her back, then trailed up to the back of her neck.

"Ohhh...Fuck!" Sofia screamed and tried to pull away. I chuckled at her trying to run from me. I circled my hips and picked up my strokes then stopped suddenly.

"No! What are you doing, Joaquin? Keep going...," Sofia shouted.

I leaned over her and grasped the back of her head to turn her around and kiss her lips.

"Mmmmmm...stop running from me, beautiful," I grunted, as she tangled her fingers in my hair.

"I won't run anymore...Ugh....keep going."

"Shit...baby...you're everything," I groaned out, now filled with a wild neediness when my pumps became sporadic as I went balls deep. I felt a raw act of possession as she pushed back into me finding the rhythm as her orgasm showed and she shivered in my arms. We continued to explore each other for the next two hours using up all the condoms.

JOAQUIN

A MONTH LATER

Sofia was in the car with me as we drove over to the hotel to visit my parents. They were in town with my sister for a few days. Gael was meeting me there with Gabriella and Hugo as extra protection for them. They didn't want to stay with me at my place, so we compromised with the hotel that was only a few minutes away. Sofia was nervous and changed her clothes at least three times because she was worried about what they would think of her outfits. I didn't care what she wore. The only opinion that mattered was mine.

"Are you sure your parents are okay with me coming? I hate to be the surprise girlfriend you've only known for a few months."

I chuckled at her comment. We never really talked about how people would perceive our relationship. A few times, she had to beg me not to put a bullet in a photographer's head for following us.

"You'll be fine, sweetheart."

"Have any women of yours ever met them?" she questioned. I groaned because I knew the second I told her that Monica met them, she was going to explode. Even though, it was by accident. Once, while I was talking to them on FaceTime, she interrupted me in my office, and they asked who she was. It ended quickly before it even began.

"Monica met them once."

"Of course, she did."

"Sofia," I grunted, squeezing her hand.

She tried to move closer to the window and out of my hold.

"I like this jealousy."

"Don't flatter yourself."

"It was by accident, she burst into my office, and they asked who she was. Please, sweetheart, not today."

"The big bad mob boss can't take the heat from his girlfriend."

"Don't flatter yourself," I repeated her statement.

"Tell me why you came for me in Atlanta a month ago. What caused you to take a leap from just wanting to be friends to us being a couple?"

Flashback

One month ago

I pounded my fist into his face over and over. He groaned, trying to cover his face. He set up the guns being stolen and then tried to get us killed. Lin-Sae was a snake, and I was ready to bury him.

"Joaquin, that's enough!" Gael yelled, trying to push me off of him. I kicked him in the stomach.

"Pussy," I said, spitting on him. Antonio and Carlo stood aside with their guns drawn.

"Where are the guns, Lin?" Antonio inquired, bending down to hear him speak. Blood was all over his face and clothes. We picked him up in the early morning on his way to the city. We managed to box him in since he only took two bodyguards with him when traveling.

"Fuck you," Lin-Sae grunted, holding his stomach.

Walking over to the table, I grabbed my jacket to take my knife out.

"Joaquin, hold up, you can't kill him. He's a cartel leader," Gael pleaded.

Grinning, I bent down to the ground, taking the knife and placing it in the middle of his forehead. I watched as his earlier bravado bled out and fear replaced it in his eyes.

81

"See you in hell," I whispered in his ear, stabbing him in the heart.

"Fuck!" Gael shouted. As my best friend, he knew I couldn't be controlled, and with Sofia running off and not taking my calls after the other night in my apartment, I hadn't been able to focus. Everything pissed me off.

"A war will start because of this, and we're still dealing with Vitale and the Russians behind Queen," Antonio stated.

"He's right, Joaquin; I understand your hurt is behind your girlfriend leaving," Carlo said, pulling his phone out of his pocket and calling for the cleanup crew.

"That has nothing to do with me killing him."

"It has everything to do with you not keeping your cool and jumping off and killing people without really thinking it over. I had you kill Queen because you're methodic, clean, and think things through. I've been where you are. Carlo can tell you about when Sabrina and I butted heads early on. Then she was kidnapped, and all I wanted to do was kill anything that ever harmed her," Antonio reminded us of his relationship conflicts.

"Queen Vitale was a gift to you. This one was fun. Call me when you locate the guns," I replied, grabbing my coat and walking out with my men following behind.

Present

"I needed you," I said.

"Like someone to talk to?"

I tried my best to avoid any type of conversations regarding my work since we'd started really dealing with each other. I never told her about my London trip and I wanted to avoid having her name tied to any issues that involve my illegal business.

"Something like that," I stated, kissed the top of her hand.

"My parents are coming to visit," she blurted out.

"Do you want me to meet them?" I queried, peering at her mischievously.

She bent over in laughter.

"I don't know, Joaquin. You have a lot to handle."

I licked my lips and grinned.

"I like the way you handle me." I kissed her cheek and her hand lifted to caress my face.

"I know because you have me bent over every time we see each other."

"Are you complaining, baby?"

"No, but I think since I'm meeting your parents, it's only right you meet mine," Sofia stated.

"Sofia, you know I'm not the typical business," I said.

"Yes, I know."

I cleared my throat, adjusted my suit jacket and worked through my uncustomary nervousness. I didn't fear anyone, I was feared, so this unknown and unwelcome feeling had me unsettled.

"I don't want you afraid of me, sweetheart. Everything they report isn't all true," I explained.

"What *is* true?"

"Just know that I have a big responsibility."

"If I was afraid, I would have left the first time you sent the flowers," Sofia told me.

"The media has camped out at your place?" I questioned, already knowing the answer. My people had to get rid of some photographers that went through the garbage outside of her building and also talked to her neighbors.

"I was already a media hot topic, you've only elevated it more," Sofia told me.

"I have security watching you."

"That's not necessary. I can take care of myself," Sofia fussed.

"As my woman, I need you safe at all times."

Monica had started leaving voice messages and I tried to avoid any confrontation, because she truly did mean something to me as a friend. But she couldn't grasp the fact that I chose Sofia and wanted her in my life. We finally made it to our destination and I turned at the light and headed to the valet area.

"Let's talk about that later," Sofia replied.

SOFIA

*J*oaquin stopped in front of the Hilton Hotel, stepped out and passed the keys to the valet. He came around to open my door and helped me out. I wore wide black pants and a wrap top that looked like a suit jacket. All of his men came and opened the door for us to walk through. I nodded thank you. I thought we were headed to their rooms, but he pulled me into the restaurant and pointed at the older couple and the young woman sitting at a table with six tall men standing around them.

"Father, Mother, good to see you. Alessandra, don't you look beautiful!"

Joaquin's sister and mother jumped up in excitement and hugged him around the neck; he switched between them both for a hug. I glanced over to his father, and he stared at me with a harsh glare. Clearing my throat, I extended my hand to introduce myself.

"Hello, I'm Sofia; nice to meet you, Alessandra, Mr. and Mrs. Fuertes." His mother gave me a hug, and his father sat without acknowledging me.

"Joaquin, get up, and hug your son," Alba said. I smiled, standing behind as he continued talking with his sister and mother.

"Son, nice to see you again; we need to talk," Joaquin Sr. demanded.

"We will, later," Joaquin said.

"You're so cute, Sofia, I'm a huge fan of yours. I can't wait for the second album," Alessandra said excitedly, hugging me.

"Thanks."

Joaquin stepped off with his father, and I hung back talking with his mom and sister.

"How did you meet my son, Sofia?" Alba questioned.

"He stalked me," I joked.

They both laughed and asked if I wanted anything to eat.

"I'm fine, thank you, but we actually bumped into each other a few months back, almost a year now, and then he appeared one day with flowers at my show, and we've been in each other's lives ever since."

"Joaquin is like his father. They're sincere and forward with what they want. I get the hesitation, honey. I was the same way when his father asked me out over forty years ago when he saw me standing in a window in a boutique, trying on perfumes," Alba recalled.

"Yeah, I've learned that about him."

"Sofia, tell my brother I would be okay living here. He thinks I'm too young to move here. I could live with him and go to school," Alessandra begged, grasping my hand. She looked like the girl version of Joaquin, except with long black hair. She had a small dainty nose, plush pink lips with a thin build, like a model.

"How old are you?"

"Twenty-two."

"He can't tell you what to do; you're an adult."

"Not in this family," Alessandra groaned in frustration.

"Alessandra, stop pouting. We will discuss this later," Alba commanded.

Joaquin and his father came back over and sat down. He kissed my cheek and held my hand under the table.

"Sofia, do you love what you do? I mean dressing up and playing characters?" Alba asked, taking a drink from her glass of white wine.

"I love it a lot. Especially the traveling."

"Sofia, I heard you just signed to be a spokesperson for Expressive Designs," Alessandra said as she pulled her phone out and scrolled through pictures of me wearing the designs.

"I did and hopefully if everything goes well, I can design my own line."

"The clothes look fabulous on you," Alessandra complimented me.

"Thank you. If you want, I can get you a set or two," I replied and she gasped in excitement, leaned over and gave me a hug.

"My sister doesn't need any more clothes," Joaquin huffed in annoyance as Alessandra tried to push him away. He stretched his long arm behind my chair.

"Stop being mean to your sister."

"Yeah. Stop being mean to me," Alessandra stated, and I chuckled at their banter.

"Joaquin, when are you coming back to Italy for a visit?" Alba wondered.

"I'm not sure, mother. Work keeps me pretty busy," Joaquin said as he lifted his glass of water, turned his head toward me and winked. He stayed up in my bed or I was in his bed unless either of us had to work. I've never had a relationship that was so passionate and sometimes over the top. We'd gone on dates that ranged from seeing the opera to flying me in a private jet across the country to Miami for dinner at his favorite restaurant.

"You should make time for your mother, son," his mother said.

"Alba, the boy is obviously busy with this young lady," Joaquin Sr. said, having a stare down with his son.

"Don't start," Joaquin stated.

"Did he tell you about his London trip, Sofia?" Sr. said before he pulled out a cigar and started to light it when his wife jerked it out of his hand.

"Stop being an ass," Alba fussed and they got into an argument in Italian. Alessandra and Joaquin tried to get them to calm down.

"Enough!" Joaquin shouted.

The entire restaurant got quiet. I started to speak up when his phone rang and he checked the number and declined the call.

"Who was that?" I questioned.

"No one important," Joaquin replied.

"Sofia, can you walk with me to the restroom?" Alessandra asked.

"Sure," I answered and stood up to grab my purse. His security started to walk with us and

I gestured they didn't need to. Joaquin stood up, lifted my chin, and pressed a kiss on my lips.

"For me, sweetheart, they'll stand outside, away from the door," Joaquin explained and I gave in when his hands rubbed the lower part of my back in comfort. One of my favorite things about him when we were alone together in bed was when we talked about our days. Having his attention and comfort, listening to all of my problems, and even though he wanted to solve everything, he allowed me the space to fight my own battles.

"Okay. But only one of them."

Alessandra smiled and locked her arm with me, and we headed to the bathroom chuckling at the pout that Joaquin had on his face.

"I have never seen my brother be so quiet before," Alessandra said, pushing the door of the bathroom open and walking over to the counter. She checked her makeup in the mirror and pulled her lipstick out of her purse.

"I'll probably have to hear about it later tonight."

"You really are something special. My brother has never brought a woman around us," Alessandra told me as she patted a little more foundation on her cheeks with the sponge from her bag.

"What was it like growing up with Joaquin?" I questioned while I washed my hands and checked my own makeup.

"He was just as crazy when we were younger. Gael can sometimes keep him on the straight and narrow," Alessandra commented and clasped her tube of lipstick closed.

"Did he tell you how we first met?"

"No."

"He came to the Broadway show and sent flowers every time and sat back in the rear corner," I remarked, chuckling in amusement.

"I like you, Sofia. Word of advice, make sure Monica isn't sniffing around him," Alessandra replied.

"He told me they never dated."

"True, but she's been a part of our world and wants more from my brother than he's willing to give," Alessandra said before a knock on the door interrupted us. A group of women came inside and we grabbed our purses and stepped out to head back to the table.

JOAQUIN

I could tell my father was not happy with my choice in Sofia. Dating someone that's extremely high profile brought a lot of unwanted attention the family didn't need. She thought it was because of her race. I knew better. My father hated drawing attention, and if we're involved, the public will want to know more about me and dig into my background and family. Sofia was quiet, partially because I kept her up all night having sex.

"Miss Chambers, my son tells me you're an actress and a singer," my dad questioned.

The waitress came over to pour Sofia and me a glass of water. I wasn't hungry, so I passed her a menu.

"Yes, sir, I'm currently filming a movie and recording my second album," Sofia answered.

"How long do you plan on doing this?" he asked.

"Uhm… Well, I've been in the business for over ten years, so hopefully for another ten or fifteen."

"Do you ever want to get married and have kids?"

"Drop it," I insisted. He was getting too personal and making her uncomfortable.

"She's your girlfriend, correct?"

"She is."

"Then she can answer my questions."

"Joaquin is happy, that's all that matters. Please, honey, let's change the subject," my mother said, kissing his cheek.

He did, but only because my mother requested him to do so, but later on, he'll bring it up to me in private.

"Joaquin, tell papa to let me move here. I want to go to fashion school, and I can stay on campus," Alessandra pleaded.

"You're too young," I said.

"She's twenty-two. I moved out when I was seventeen to pursue my dreams. You can't smother her forever," Sofia stated calmly toward me. My father squinted his eyes, offended that anyone would come into his relationship with his daughter. Our family was very traditional, even to the point of arranged marriages. Mother and I convinced him to not push that on her because Alessandra can be headstrong at times. Her love of fashion and photography was what she wanted to study in America.

"This isn't the time right now, Alessandra. I'm busy and can't watch you while I'm working."

"That's not fair! I'm twenty-two. Sofia can help me find a place to stay, right?" Alessandra whined.

"Silence!" Father shouted. The entire room went quiet, other guests gasped in shock. Gael walked up to the table and kissed my mother, then Alessandra on the cheek. He then gave my father a handshake before taking a seat next to Alessandra. He tucked a piece of her hair behind her ear, and she blushed like a high school girl with her boyfriend. My gaze cut between them; if he was interested in my little sister, it was something he would need to forget about before it ever became an issue. My father wasn't paying attention, but I was.

"Gael, you're looking well, my dear," Alba said.

"Yes, ma'am, eating healthy and following behind your bigheaded son." Gael whipped his head around to face me.

Sofia shifted back in her seat; I lifted her hand to lay a kiss on her palm. Hugo and Gabriella stood around us along with my father's men.

"You seem tired, are you ready to go?"

"I don't want to put you out with your family. I can take a cab and meet you back at your place later. I need to meet with Cassidy and Edward about Deras's upcoming performance. "

"I can take you." I started to stand up, and she tugged at my coat jacket to sit back down.

"Stay here with them; your mother hasn't seen you in two years. I promise I'll call when I get done," Sofia assured me by kissing me on the cheek.

"Take Gabriella or Hugo with you. I'd feel better when I'm not around that you have protection."

Sofia smoothed down her shirt. "What do I need protection for? Is there something I need to know about?"

"Take someone with you for my peace of mind."

"Okay," Sofia commented, pointing to Hugo.

Hugo nodded and walked behind Sofia as she left the restaurant.

"Alba, take Alessandra up to the bar and look at the desserts. I want something sweet and would prefer you personally pick it out for me." Father patted her hand, and she stood up, grabbing her purse. Alessandra did the same. He watched as they looked over the wall case of the cakes and pies.

"Joaquin, I'm getting phone calls that Lin-Sae is no longer with us. Tell me how this happened?" Father asked.

"He stole from us, and I sent a message."

"The type of message that has me getting phone calls all the way in Portugal from the President that talks about how you've created a new dynamic that will have the family in the newspaper for the wrong reasons. They say it's a drug deal with Fuertes Cartel," Father muttered angrily, shoving the empty plate away.

The waiter appeared with their food and we both got quiet.

"The calamari and stir-fried rice," the server announced.

"Thank you," he said.

"We have two strawberry salads with oil and vinegar," the server informed us, placing the dishes on the tables and walking away.

"Antonio spoke with Bruno this morning since he travels back and forth between Italy and New York. He stated a council wants you to come out there and speak with them about the killing," Gael explained. Alessandra walked over and sat down.

"What are we talking about?" Alessandra questioned.

"Nothing of importance," I said. Easing my phone out of my pocket, I sent a text message to Sofia.

Me: Dinner tonight, my place?

Sofia: Not tonight, I'm hanging with some friends.

Me: Where?

Sofia: Deras's performance.

Me: Keep me updated.

Lunch continued without a hitch, and my sister talked about her favorite actors and seeing Sofia's movies. Mother gushed about her garden and getting father to eat healthier. The day was going to be long because I ended up going shopping and talking for the rest of the day.

...

"I like her for you," Alessandra said, sifting through the racks at the Versace store inside of the mall.

"I'm glad," I answered, returning text messages to Monica.

"Joaquin, what do you think would happen if Monica met Sofia?" Alessandra questioned.

That statement caused me to cock my head to the side and stare at my sister trying to gauge what she was attempting to say.

"What are you talking about?" I asked.

"Sofia told me that you said Monica was just a friend," Alessandra said.

"She is," I replied.

"You cared about Monica at one point, correct?"

"Where are you going with this topic, Alessandra? My patience is very thin."

"Monica could become a problem if you don't take care of her soon." Alessandra grabbed two dresses off the rack and held them up toward me and I ran a hand down my head and sighed in annoyance.

"They're too short, Alessandra."

"You're my brother, not my father, Joaquin!" Alessandra spat loudly, slamming the dresses back on the rack.

"A brother that pays all of your damn bills," I fussed, tired of all the women in my life except for my baby, Sofia.

"Fine! But I want a bigger allowance, and I won't tell Sofia that Monica was texting you through lunch today."

"Monica wasn't texting me," I lied, already knowing my little sister would rat me out if money wasn't involved.

She stood there with her arms crossed over and her lip poked out. I was about to respond when again, my phone texted.

Monica: You're throwing me away like some trash for her.

Me: You knew what it was from the beginning.

"Is that Monica?" Alessandra asked as she laughed. I glared up at her until she walked off to go try on another dress.

Monica: Does she know you fucked me every time you went to her show.

Me: She knows about you, Monica.

Monica: Joaquin, I won't allow you to play me.

Me: I suggest you find a place to stay.

We didn't live together or anything, but I did pay for her place, and sometimes if the hotel wasn't convenient, I went to her condo. I know I was wrong for keeping it from Sofia, but she wouldn't understand the dynamics of my friendship with Monica.

"Okay. How about this one?" Alessandra questioned. I nodded my head and passed her my credit card.

"I'm going to drop you off and head to see Sofia."

"Where, at the studio? Can I come, please?" Alessandra inquired.

93

"She doesn't like a lot of people when she's recording," I replied, then patted her leg as my driver closed the door of my car.

"Fine." She pouted and I decided to call Sofia to check if she was still at the studio or home.

"Hello." I heard her raspy voice.

"Are you sleeping?" I questioned.

"Long day and tired from recording, I'm home in bed," Sofia said.

"Get some rest and I'll be there soon," I spoke and listened to her yawn through the phone.

"Drop my sister off and then take me to Sofia's apartment." Our driver nodded in answer and hit the left signal to do a U-turn in the middle of the street to take Alessandra back to the hotel. Twenty minutes later, I kicked off my shoes, dropped my pants, and climbed in bed with Sofia, pulling her to my chest.

SOFIA

Three days later, my parents were here visiting and I brought them to the recording studio and then shopping and lunch. I was supposed to do another photoshoot for Expressive Designs, but it was canceled last minute and I could use the break since lately, I'd done back-to-back recording or rehearsals for filming.

"Here's where I do the recording," I said and introduced them to Chauncey.

"Finally, we met the famous Chauncey," Mom joked and hugged him.

Latoya and Leroy were the most humble and sweet people you'd ever meet. Being born and raised in the south, my upbringing was always focused on making sure my dreams were met and supporting me.

"You have an amazing daughter here, Mr. and Mrs. Chambers," Chauncey said, then motioned for them to sit down.

"Do you want to hear a few tracks?" I asked.

"Yeah, let us hear the magic for the new album," Latoya insisted as she plopped down on the seat of the couch.

"It's not fully done, but here's a little snippet of what we're working on."

Chauncey turned the knobs and adjusted the sound as my melodies came on for a new single called "Tainted Love".

I feel different around him.

Yes.

I feel he's the one.

Yes.

Can this be love?

Yes.

This tainted love.

My mom clapped her hands in excitement and my phone rang. I answered and stepped out of the room for a second.

"How is your day going?" Joaquin asked.

"Everything is going well, I'm here with my parents."

"Are they having fun?" he wondered.

"Yeah, I have them listening to my music now."

"Do you want to do dinner tonight?"

"Can I take a rain check? I wanted to have dinner with them tonight," I explained.

"Of course, baby. Let me know if you need anything," Joaquin said.

"Great, thanks, babe," I said and ended the call, then headed back into the room.

"These are great, Sofia. I'm so proud of you, sweetie," Mom said.

I dropped my phone back in my purse and sat next to Chauncey at the booth.

"Thank you. I know you guys got in early this morning. Do you want to go out to eat?" I inquired.

"That's fine, what do you have an interest for?" Mom asked.

"I can eat anything, honestly."

"What about your boyfriend? We see you in the pictures with him," Dad stated and stood up.

"Joaquin is probably working."

"We want to meet him. I heard he's a dangerous man, Sofia,"

96

Mom commented. I glanced at Chauncey and he kept his head down in his phone ignoring my glare.

"Did you say something to them?" I asked.

"You know I don't get into your business, Sofia. The tabloids have you plastered on every weekly magazine with him," Chauncey remarked.

"Joaquin isn't perfect."

"So, it's true that he's in the Cartel and kills people?" Mom asked.

"I can't answer that question, because he doesn't put me in those situations," I answered, grabbed my bag, strolling out of the room then past security to outside. They unlocked the rental car and we got inside to head out of the parking structure and back into the food district. Fifteen minutes later, my phone rang so I hit speaker phone.

"Hello?"

"Sofia," Joaquin said.

"Who's that?" Dad asked, hearing the thick accent.

"Joaquin, I'm with my parents in the car, keep it clean," I said and he chuckled.

"Anything for you, sweetheart. Hello Mr. and Mrs. Chambers," Joaquin said.

"Hello, Joaquin," Mom said.

"What's up? I'm taking my parents to dinner."

I stopped at the red light.

"If you want to bring them to Antonio's, they could have a meal on me. I've already arranged for you to have the entire place to yourself," Joaquin advised.

"You don't have to do that."

"I want to," Joaquin answered.

"What do you do for a living, Joaquin?" Mom asked.

"I'm in investments, Mrs. Chambers," Joaquin responded.

"Are your men following me?" I asked as I noticed two black SUVs turning at the same time. They had followed me from the time I had left the studio. He promised to give me a little space to enjoy my parents and now this.

"For your safety, sweetheart," Joaquin said.

I went down the street where Antonio's was located and parked in front. This was one of my favorite places and I hoped it wasn't swarming with a lot of people.

"We're here now, call off your people and give me some distance," I told him and hung up the phone. I turned the car off and took the key out and picked up my purse as my parents followed and the doorman tipped his hat at me and the valet took my keys to go park the car.

"Sofia, it's nice to see you again," the hostess said.

"Hi, I was told the place was set up for dinner," I stated.

"Yes. Mr. Fuertes arranged everything, and you have the place to yourself."

"Perfect."

"This is a nice place, Sofia," Mom spoke as she looked around. Antonio's was an old school Italian feel of a restaurant and one of my favorites. Not just because I met Joaquin for the first time here, but during my early years of trying to make it in the industry, this was the place we'd have most meetings.

"Antonio's is one of the places I used to go to for meetings early in my career," I explained, and the waitress came over with a bottle of wine and water. She placed everything down on the table.

"I remember you telling me about this place," Dad said.

"How is retirement going for you, Dad?" I wanted to change the subject and get their minds off Joaquin's background.

"Retirement is fine, but boring. Your mother wants to travel," Dad replied, and asked for a beer.

"Sure, a beer for you and would you like bread and butter? Your meals are being prepared," Stella informed us.

"We didn't order yet," Mom said.

"Joaquin told us to prepare the special for you three. Lasagna, baked ziti, penne, steamed vegetables, and Tiramisu for dessert," Stella said.

"That's fine. Thanks Stella."

"Tell us the truth, Sofia. Are you happy?" Dad queried, as he reached over and touched my hand on top of the table.

"I am, Dad. Please, don't worry. You're not here for long so I want to talk about you guys."

"Everything is good with us, the house is beautiful and we recently upgraded and added a swimming pool," Mom said.

"Let me know if you ever want to move up here, and have a condo like mine." I noticed a text message come through on my phone, I lifted it up and went back to Joaquin.

Joaquin: Enjoy your dinner.

Me: Thanks, but this is too much.

Joaquin: Nothing is too much for you.

"New York is too fast paced for us, baby. We like the quiet Memphis traffic," Dad told me and I chuckled at his grimace looking outside; all we could hear were the loud honks from cab drivers. Stella came out five minutes later and brought our food to the table. We talked about my high school days and how I wanted to be an actress and we laughed about my first auditions and red carpet looks. Also, they explained that some photographers had come to their house to get a story about me and I told them I would get Edward to look into getting a restraining order if they kept it up. Photographers will go into your trash and talk with your friends to make up a story about you.

SOFIA

Two months later

Edward and I were inside my dressing room as I prepared for my scenes with Dante. I was starting to regret signing on to this project, knowing once Joaquin found out we had a love scene, he was going to go ballistic. Dante, on occasion, flirted after we hung out in Atlanta, but I prayed he kept his thoughts to himself, unlike Edward professing his undying love. He was always telling me to leave Joaquin because I was too good for him, and he was a better man for me. I tried establishing a professional relationship. Now he was looking to destroy that.

"Sofia, this guy is dangerous. You know how I feel about you," Edward stated.

Tonya's eyes rose up in surprise. I was wearing a robe, with a lingerie set for the next scene; today was only this scene that was the big compilation of our characters coming together. The sound-stage on the studio lot was booming with film and TV shoots all around. My nerves were still a little off-balanced after meeting his father in the restaurant. Over the past month, the arguments between us came back to my insecurity of him trying to make it seem as though I was crazy for feeling the way I did. Seeing up close and personal the Cartel lifestyle was giving me doubts our relationship would last.

"Edward, now is not the time. I have a scene in a few minutes," I remarked, pushing him off.

"Funny, you've brushed me off all these years, and yet the second this mafia motherfucker threw himself at the door, you dropped to your knees!" Edward snapped, and before I could react, the door swung open, and Joaquin walked inside with his men behind him.

"What the fuck did you say to her?" Joaquin questioned, popping his knuckles.

I started to speak, and he held his hand up, cutting me off.

"No, let him speak," Joaquin said, standing in front of Edward as he cleared his throat before speaking.

"You aren't allowed on the studio lot without permission," Edward told him, trying to throw his weight around.

Joaquin smirked, winking at me before punching Edward in the face with a right hook.

"Joaquin!" I yelled, bending down to help Edward up.

"Leave him," Joaquin demanded.

"He's hurt, and I could have handled him."

Joaquin scowled at me, adjusting his tie.

"As your boyfriend, I take it upon myself to handle things for you. It's my job, sweetheart. What are you filming today?" Joaquin tugged on my robe.

I was shifting on my left foot, placing my hand on my hips.

"I'm working, and you need to apologize to Edward and leave. I'll contact you later."

"Baby, I'll do a lot of things for you; apologizing to him is not one of them." His bodyguards laughed, and I broke eye contact with him to glare at them.

"Get out and take them with you now," I demanded, pointing toward the door.

"The director stated we could watch you perform. I haven't seen you on stage since your Broadway show. I'm your biggest fan, sweetheart." He threaded a hand through my hair. I smacked it away.

"Joaquin, you can't see the filming today. It's a closed set, and I don't care what the director said. Mhmmm...wait." He gripped my hips, pulling me in close, covering my mouth and shoving his tongue inside.

Someone cleared their throat.

"Joaquin, she's right. We should go and meet with your contractor for your house," Gabriella said, winking at me to distract him. I mouthed thank you, and he pulled away.

"You're buying a house?"

"I am, will you decorate it for me?"

"Depends."

"What does it depend on, Sofia?" he slyly questioned as he ran his palm down my arm.

"Alessandra and I have kept in touch, and she wants to move here. I was thinking if you talk with your father, then he would agree with letting her come here. Maybe, I could decorate and do other things." I fluttered my eyes, trying to seduce him.

Joaquin grinned and gestured for his team to leave and take Edward with them.

The trailer door closed, and he pushed me up against the wall, both his hands on the wall closing me in, loosening my robe running a hand down my chest. His chest rose and fell.

"Would this make you happy, having my sister here?"

"It would make her happy."

"What would make you happy?"

"You leaving and letting me work."

He chuckled at my statement. I drew in a shallow breath as he lightly bit my shoulder, easing his hand down my thigh, lifting my leg up, wrapping it around his thigh.

"Joaquin we can't, I have to be on set, baby."

"Give me five minutes."

I chortled; he damn well knew he wouldn't be only five minutes.

"Five minutes will turn into an hour with you."

"Then give me what I want, and I'll grant my sister her wish," he said, unbuckling his pants, pulling his dick out and rubbing it against my slit, sliding inside.

"Yesss...fuck."

Grabbing my other leg, he picked me up, holding me against the wall. I wrapped my arms around his neck as he pounded inside of me.

"Ugh...shit."

"Right there, Joaquin!"

"You like this, sweetheart? Let me hear from you."

Someone started banging on the door, calling me to set. Sweat clung to my brow, and I tossed my head back as he walked us over to the couch. He laid on his back, and I lifted up, riding the tip of his dick.

"Ughhh...You feel so good, Sofia," he groaned, squeezing my ass.

"Is this all yours, baby?" I teased, reaching behind my back inside his pants, massaging his balls. I needed him to come fast so I could clean up and get back to work.

"Aghhhh!!!" He gripped my knees, pumping from below, as we both came at the same time. I fell on his chest out of breath, and he dozed off to sleep. I smirked slowly, crawling off of him and rushing to the bathroom to clean up. A few minutes later, he was still sleeping on the couch, and I left him there to go start filming. Stepping out of the trailer, his men stood at attention.

"He's taking a nap. You may want to wake him up in an hour or two," I said, then swung my hair and walked off to the set. I overheard them snickering behind me as I walked away and entered Stage Five for filming. The entire crew was setting up the shot for today with me and Dante.

"Sofia, you ready?" Thomas, the PA, asked with an earpiece and walkie talkie.

"Yes, where do they want me?" I replied as he helped me to step through the cords and wires on the floor. I saw the director's chair with the video monitors on the side and Dante talking to the director. The background set for this scene was the living room of my character's home and I was home reading when Dante's character came over to confess his love. They even took some concepts of my idea to replicate the color scheme of my apartment with black and cream for the couch and rug set.

"Can I have quiet on set?" Thomas yelled and the bell for filming rang. The sound guy held the boom mic up high over my head. Lights clicked on and Tonya came over to do one more look on my face.

"Is he still here?" Tonya asked and I shrugged.

"Hopefully not."

"Okay, Sofia, this is about you and Dante realizing your feelings for each other. Let's see that chemistry," Jeremiah said.

I grabbed the bracelet and rings from the wardrobe lady and thanked her for putting last minute touches together. I sat down and picked up the book that my character was supposed to read. Out of the corner of my eye, I could see Dante on the outside of the fake stage door.

"Action!" Jeremiah called out. A few minutes went by then Dante knocked on the door.

"Who is it?" I asked.

"Jessica, it's me," Dante responded, calling me by my character's name. I stood up and walked to the door and opened it.

"What are you doing here, Terrance?" I questioned as he stepped aside so he could come in while I closed the door.

"I needed to talk to you, Jessica," he said, sitting on the edge of the couch and pulling me into his embrace by my waist.

"We don't have anything to talk about."

"I wish that was true. I care about you," he said, staring into my eyes. I lifted his chin as his hands moved up my back.

"Cut!" Jeremiah shouted; Tonya stepped in the shot to reapply our makeup.

"How does it look?" I asked.

"So far so good, we should try it with Dante opening your robe. Same dialogue," Jeremiah stated.

"Quiet on set," Thomas announced and we got back in positions.

"Action!" Jeremiah yelled. Dante knocked on the fake door.

"Who is it?" I asked.

"Jessica, it's me," he replied and I sighed, standing up to answer the door.

"What are you doing here, Terrance?"

He stepped into the apartment and moved around me and headed to sit on the edge of the couch. Dante extended his head for me to come toward him. I closed the space between us as he stared into my eyes.

"I care about you," he answered as he untied my robe slowly, licking his lips and eased his hands around my waist.

"Hey! You can't walk into the scene," I heard Thomas shout as my eyes grew wide when Joaquin stormed on set and yanked me out of Dante's hold and punched him in the face.

"Oh, my God!" Tonya screamed.

"Keep your fucking hands off her!" Joaquin shouted as he gripped Dante around his neck. I was so embarrassed and wanted to crawl into a hole and shut the world out.

"Somebody call security," Jeremiah said.

"Joaquin, stop it! I'm working," I spat and tried to shove him away.

Gabriella and the rest of his men came on stage to push back the crew.

"Joaquin! Gabriella, please, stop him," I pleaded and she nodded getting in between Joaquin and Dante.

"Dante, are you all right?" I questioned and tried to check his neck and he slapped my hand away.

"Motherfucker! Did you put your hands on her?" Joaquin snapped and tried to reach around Gabriella and me to get to Dante again.

"God damn it, stop this shit!" I screamed, then shoved him back.

Joaquin's chest heaved up and down in anger.

"Jeremiah, I need to call it a day. I'm sorry," I spoke tying up my robe.

"Who is he?" Jeremiah asked.

"Who the fuck are you?" Joaquin shot back while he cursed in Portuguese.

I rubbed my temples trying to figure out how to salvage the day, but I doubted Joaquin could control himself.

"Joaquin, get out now," I demanded, pointing toward the exit.

"Sweetheart," he started to speak.

"I will speak to you later when I have something to say to you," I fussed, and stomped off stage toward my trailer to get dressed. He followed behind me, gripped my arm to turn me around and I was getting more aggravated with this over the top macho bullshit.

"He wants to fuck you!" Joaquin shouted and I pushed his hand away.

"Guess what, every man probably wants to, Joaquin. I'm an actress and singer."

"I'm not stupid, Sofia," Joaquin argued back and opened my trailer door, held my hand so I could walk in first.

"No, but you're acting like an ass. You promised you wouldn't interfere in my career."

"How many love scenes do you have with him?" Joaquin inquired. I walked to the corner of the trailer and grabbed my pants out of my bag as well as a t-shirt.

"For this movie, about two or three. That's not the point."

"It's the main point, why can't you just hold hands and not wear that?" Joaquin asked as he sat down in the makeup chair while I changed back into my clothes.

"I don't let my daddy tell me what to do, so what makes you believe you can run my life?"

He clenched his jaw and rolled his eyes.

"I am your man, correct?" he asked and I nodded.

"Yes, Joaquin."

"Then respect my wishes. Find someone else or cut out love scenes."

I chuckled then bent down to tie my shoelaces up.

"Respect me as your girlfriend and trust me," I stated, grabbing my bag, keys, and phone.

"Where are you going?" he asked, stepping out of the trailer with me.

"Home, I need to call my parents. Besides, I need space away from you."

"Sofia."

I held my hand up to cut him off from speaking.

"No, I need you to give me a minute if you want this to continue."

"Let my people follow you home," he replied, and I scoffed as I walked off.

"Whatever."

Thirty minutes later it was going on eight at night. I ended up home locked in my apartment in the bubble bath watching video of today's incident on FMZ's gossip blog. Somehow, they got a video clip of Joaquin acting an ass. I closed my eyes and tried to prepare for the onslaught of attention this would bring us. Maybe Edward was correct about me and Joaquin being too opposite and not working.

JOAQUIN

The next day, we finally found out that the Russians had help from Lin-Sae to steal our guns. I got word from the council about having a sit-down meeting to go over the details of how we could rectify the situation for all parties. I was in a war with myself to end things or continue down a destructive path. Antonio talked about slowing down when he got married and finding a woman that understood him. Sofia was that person for me, and if we got to that level and decided to get married, I knew she'd want me to leave this lifestyle. Tightening my bulletproof vest, I was in the car with Gael, Hugo, and Gabriella as three more cars followed behind. A source said the Nigerian gang in the Bronx was meeting with some Russians for some crates of guns.

"Are you sure about this, Joaquin? The money can be replaced," Gael exclaimed.

"It's not about the money anymore, it's about principle and the disrespect of stealing from this family."

"I know better than anyone about disrespect toward the family, but you've killed two high profile leaders of rival families without any consequences. Now, going into a possible shootout would put a bigger target on our back," Gael explained, his face twitching in irritation.

I ran a hand down my face as a sigh escaped my lips.

"I did what needed to be done. Am I not Ghost? People call me because they are not willing to make hard decisions, and I am."

"Si, I understand, brother, but you're putting a bigger target on the wrong people's back."

"What are you talking about?" I demanded to know as the car pulled up to an abandoned building. Our contact said the men would be inside and to go through the back.

"I received photos of Sofia, and this came from Italy, and your father doesn't like you together."

"My father doesn't tell me who I can date."

"Is she going to be your Donna?"

"Focus on today," I answered, getting out of the car, checking to make sure my guns were locked and loaded. We had on fake FBI vests and hats to get in and out without any questions.

I motioned for Gabriella to follow me as Gael took Hugo to the left side, and we went on the right. The other men stayed in front in case someone tried to get out or come in and see what was going on.

The sun was shining in the afternoon with the streets empty, less witnesses before kids were let out of school and decided to play outside. I met Gael's eyes and pointed to the count of three, we would go in quietly. He nodded in agreement with a dark shadow marred over his face.

Tilting my head over to look through the back screen door, it was open with no one in the kitchen. I placed my hand to my lips for everyone to be quiet as we walked inside so as not to be detected. Holding the gun and knife in my hands, I edged in further, not seeing any people around. Staring at the stairs, I heard talking, and we followed the voices; stopping at the door, I noticed it was slightly ajar.

The Russians had three men, and the Nigerians had two; the crates were open as they inspected them. I tapped Gael on the

shoulder without talking, showing five fingers, and he acknowledged, pulling out a second gun. Taking the lead, I closed my eyes,
thinking of Sofia, and smiled. Opening them back up, I wore a
devious smirk because I was out for blood.

Pop! Pop! Pop!

Right as I held my gun up to shoot, we heard shots outside, and
it alerted the men, so I started blasting in the room, and one got a
chance of hitting me in the arm. Running inside, I punched the guy
that held the automatic rifle, and he stumbled. Slicing his throat and
shooting as many people as I could, I never noticed the adjoining
door that connected to the bathroom. I miscalculated, and someone
peeking out pointed a gun in my direction. One bullet hit me in the
leg, and I shot back, hitting him between the eyes.

"Aghhh!!"

"Joaquin, hold on!" Gael shouted.

Gabriella would cover us so Gael could pick me up and take me
outside. As the firing stopped, all of the Nigerians and Russians
were dead. Gael picked me up, helping me walk as Hugo started
packing up the guns. Gabriella was still in front of us, keeping an
eye as we ran to our cars. The bodies laid out on the ground were
more Nigerians.

"Russian, Vitale, Chinese, and now Nigerian mafia are going to
be looking for your head," Gael informed me.

"I'll be ready."

"How are you feeling?" Gael asked.

"Like I've been shot."

"What happened with you at the studio, it's all over the media."

"I heard. Alex told me Sofia had a swarm of photographers
outside her place the night I busted Dante up for touching her."

I felt the wound and tried to keep pressure on it as they drove
away.

"Ughh… shit," I groaned, feeling lightheaded.

"Hang on, we'll be there soon," Gael advised as he handed me a
ripped piece of cloth from his shirt while he weaved in and out of
traffic honking the horn.

"Shit, I need to talk to Sofia," I mumbled as I tried to sit up in the back seat.

I felt my eyes rolling.

"Give her some space and worry about not dying," Gael huffed, then took a sharp turn at the corner of Antonio's. He made it to the back of the restaurant and cut the car off and jumped off, then yanked the passenger door open to help me out.

"We're almost there," Gael said as he banged on the back door. The security camera adjusted to us and scanned our faces then clicked to allow us entry. Antonio's men watched as Gael helped me through the back entry of the kitchen over to the back stairs and toward the elevator.

JOAQUIN

*A*ntonio walked inside of the basement of his restaurant. He didn't look happy to see me. I removed the vest, as the in-house doctor tore my shirt open to look at the bullet wound.

"Joaquin, you need to be in a hospital, I can only patch you up," the doctor said.

"What happened?" Antonio asked, sitting on the edge of the conference table.

Carlo sat his gun on top of the table, keeping the safety on. I furrowed my brow.

"I had a disagreement with some people." I shrugged as I tried to play it off.

"How many people?" Carlo questioned.

"Russians, Nigerians," I answered.

"You realize that you will end up having a bigger issue now. Did you get things cleaned up before anyone saw you out there?" Antonio pressed.

Waving them off, I tried to push through the pain. It wasn't life-threatening, but it hurt, and I'd probably be sore for a while.

"You have anything for the pain?" I questioned.

"Yes, and you need to take a few days off," the doctor suggested.

I shook my head in denial.

"I have too much work to get done, and I'm flying to Italy soon, and my sister is moving here," I said.

Gael's jaw dropped at my comment. "When did your father agree to this?"

"A few weeks ago. She's going to be staying with me, and that was the biggest condition by him agreeing to let her come out here."

"Can we get back to the problem that could potentially destroy all of our lives? If the Russians team up with Chinese, Vitales, and Nigerians, we won't be able to fight them," Carlo fussed.

"Pay the Nigerians off, and the Chinese won't do anything if we have something bigger that they want. At the end of the day, killing Joaquin off is more of a threat for the Russians and Vitale's people," Antonio stated.

"What do they want more than my head on a platter for killing their leader?"

"Territory, which you will happily give up to end this feud with them," Antonio commanded, staring into my eyes.

"They can have New Jersey."

"Jersey is your lowest profitable location; they'll want more than that," Carlo insisted.

"What if we give them Jersey, Brooklyn, and Atlanta?" I questioned.

"What! You can't give them all of Atlanta. That's your second-biggest market, Joaquin," Gael shouted.

"You're right I can't keep bringing on more problems, and I need to smooth a few relationships over before we get to Italy. Let them have Atlanta and we'll regroup," I told them.

His emotions flitted across his face. As my best friend, he was the only one that could tell me when I was wrong and cause me to question my motives. Ever since I came to America and killed Queen, things had gone downward except for Sofia.

"Sofia," I mumbled to myself. "Where is Sofia?" I asked Hugo. As her bodyguard, unless he was with me on a mission, I assigned a man on her to keep her safe.

"At a photoshoot," Hugo answered.

"Call her."

He took his phone out of his pocket and dialed her number. Her voicemail picked up. He then tried her assistant, and no one answered. Snatching my phone out of my pocket, I dialed her number and still no answer. The doctor finished cleaning up the wound, and I leaned up off the table, standing upright. I slid another shirt on then my jacket, preparing to go find her. Gael and my bodyguards started out of the basement and up the stairs and went to leave when Monica called my name.

"Joaquin!" Monica shouted and marched toward me.

I scanned her over and she wasn't as unkempt as she normally was.

"Monica, what are you doing here?" I grasped her elbow and moved her toward the back corner out of the exit.

"I've been calling you," Monica snapped and jerked her arm out of my hand.

"We have nothing to talk about."

"You kicked me out of my home." Monica shoved me in the chest and I grunted from the pain of her hitting my wound.

"Keep your hands off me." I leaned both hands above her head and bent down and stared into her eyes.

"What do you think your little actress girlfriend will think about you paying for my place?" Monica inquired, her neck craning to look up at me.

"Tell her and find out why they call me Ghost."

"You're pathetic." Monica sucked her lip inside her mouth.

"What's pathetic is a woman standing in front of me trying to get back into my bed if I agreed."

"I'm pregnant," Monica blurted out and tried to grab my hand, stopping me from leaving.

"That's a lie and I suggest you find out who's the father." I slowly started to stalk off.

"Sofia will believe me," Monica yelled, and I stopped at the exit door, turned my face, twisted in disgust at her stooping so low. My expression wiped the smirk off her face, giving me a brief moment of satisfaction.

"Do you want me to hurt you, Monica?" I questioned.

"Why can't you see how much I love you?" Monica whined, her eyes filling with tears.

"I've never wanted you for more than what we shared, Monica. Understand that I won't let anything or anyone hurt Sofia or cause her pain." I gave her a look that let her know I wouldn't hesitate to show her why I was called Ghost if she messed with my woman.

Hugo held the door open and I walked away as she continued screaming and crying for me to come back and not end things. Monica was becoming a problem that I never thought I would have to admit to myself. I slid inside the back of the car, avoiding eye contact with Gael and Hugo.

"What do you want to happen?" Hugo asked.

"Keep someone on her for now. I need to talk with Sofia first before I make any decisions," I explained as I looked out of the window thinking about the last time I was in Sofia's presence and the anger in her eyes.

SOFIA & JOAQUIN

 wo days later

Sofia

I was on a photoshoot with Edward when Cassidy came inside, followed by a huge gift box.

The shoot was supposed to be about four hours, and it looked as if we'd already hit over eight hours and it was not looking like it was going to end any time soon. Cassidy placed the gift box down on the table. She picked up the card and passed it to me as I stood getting my makeup retouched, along with my hair. This was a shoot for a Destiny magazine spread as the hottest star this year. I had deals across my desk for multiple movies, TV guest appearances, and even starting my own makeup line if I wanted to venture in that direction. My first love was acting and singing; having a big responsibility on my plate I knew would be a challenge, starting a new business and partnership with a company would send me into traveling a lot more, testing the products and not just adding my name onto something just to have a product out that would have my fans ending up disappointed.

"Seems your boyfriend sent you a little surprise, read the card, Sofia," Cassidy said. My brow arched because he figured I was out of town the last time I talked with him earlier today.

"We aren't ever far apart.

Love,

Joaquin."

I said, reading the card out loud.

"Sounds romantic," Cassidy swooned, removing the ribbon and the wrap around the box. It was the size of a square flat box that looked like it held a book. Something Joaquin knew I loved doing was reading on my down time.

Right as Cassidy was about to lift the top, Joaquin and some of his men busted inside with guns drawn out.

"Don't open that!" Joaquin screamed, running toward me, pulling me behind him.

"What are you doing? Joaquin, I'm working, and you are embarrassing me," I hissed, pushing his hands off me.

"I let a lot of things go, but this bullshit is ridiculous. Sofia, tell your gangster boyfriend to leave, or I'm calling the cops," Edward stated, pulling his phone out of his pocket.

Joaquin glared at Edward and gestured for Gael with his right hand to grab Edward's phone. They scuffled for a second, and Gael gripped Edward by the neck.

"Joaquin, stop him now. Gael, stop it!" I yelled, trying to move around Joaquin to help Edward.

"Hugo, take him outside and wait for me. Cassidy, step back from the table," Joaquin commanded.

"Why, what's wrong?" I questioned.

"Where did this package come from?" Joaquin asked.

"I don't know. I thought you sent it over to me. Cassidy brought it in from the delivery guy." He balled his fists up at his side. I swallowed a lump in my throat. Did we do something wrong?

Cassidy was scared shitless; she hadn't been around Joaquin for long periods of time when he was dealing with any mafia business. If he got her caught up in any type of violence, I would never forgive myself.

"Boss, look at this," Hugo insisted, holding the top of the lid. I leaned over Joaquin's shoulder, and the box contained a clock running down on top of dead flowers, possibly a bomb inside with another note that said, "We can get her at any time."

"OMG, I have to go, where are my keys? Cassidy, call the police!" I cried out, trying to pull away from Joaquin's tight hold.

"Sofia, baby. I promise nothing is going to happen to you. They were sending a message and wanted my attention and knew how to go about doing so."

"I can't do this with you; I need to leave now."

"I'll take you," Joaquin suggested, entwining our hands, and I jerked back in fear for the first time of what this could have been. My friends could have lost their lives because of me.

...

"No! Edward can take me. We need to call the police. OMG! Somebody tried to kill me." I fell to the floor and Joaquin tried to pick me up and I shoved him away, holding my hand up for him to give me space.

"Sofia, please, it's me, baby. I'm not going to hurt you." He slowly approached me, and I slapped him across the face, hitting his chest and cursing him out as he tried to calm me down.

"Stay away from me. This has gone too far; I don't care what you're involved in but to bring this to my door is unforgivable."

"Silencio! You knew who I was, Sofia, you're mine and nothing is going to happen to you. Understand?" The line of his mouth tightened a fraction more, the dark eyebrows slanted in a frown.

Shaking my head, I couldn't pretend this was going to be a fairy-tale whirlwind romance anymore. I was blind to think he was untouchable when at the top, but that's the spot everyone is gunning for, so his entire life is about watching his back and making moves to protect his family. Removing myself from this situation was my only chance at getting things back on track. Already the newspapers and gossip blogs had my name mixed in with drug dealers and killers. I was foolish, and my pride wouldn't let me see the love I had for him was overshadowing my life. Grabbing my purse and keys, Cassidy followed behind me toward the door carrying her jacket and purse. Right as we got to the door, Joaquin's men blocked the front entrance, cutting us off from leaving.

"Let me through," I demanded; even though he towered over me and could probably snap my neck in a split second, I would make sure to go out with a fight.

"He moves at my orders."

"Then tell him to step aside so I can leave, or I'll call the police."

"Like that? You won't let me fix this, mi amor?" I knew that translated to my love. I learned a few words while dating him for the past few months.

"I need to think and make sure my people get home safely. Release Edward and let him go. I will talk with you once I'm able to clear my head."

"That's not enough; I need to make sure you're safe; let Leonardo take you home and put some security outside your building. I promise not to contact you for a few days."

"Fine, but I'll call you when I'm ready." He did not like my response, but nodded in agreement and kissed my forehead. I flinched at his touch and backed up, waving to his security to allow me to walk away.

...

Joaquin

I WAS STILL DEALING with a gunshot wound from earlier today, and having Sofia stand in fear was breaking me down. Sticking my hands in my pockets, I eyed the room, wondering how they found out about this place, and that she'd be here at this time. Gael came strolling inside once Leonardo and Hugo pulled off with Sofia and Cassidy.

"Edward was sent home with a warning. Hugo will stay and monitor her place. That Cassidy woman is staying with her tonight."

"Fuck," I shouted, tossing everything off the table. Rubbing my temple, I needed to regroup, and figure out if this was a warning from the Russian deal or coming from one of Antonio's crew. Too much shit happening all at once to deal with and I refused to lose the woman I loved.

"She needs time, Joaquin. I usually stay out of your affairs, but this fucked up her image of you. The most important thing a woman wants is security, and brother, you failed to protect her. In time, she will come around." Gael slapped me on the back and headed to the photographer to pay him off. My phone vibrated in my pocket. I pulled it out and saw it was a message from an unknown number.

Unknown: *That was a warning.*

Me: *I'm the wrong person to fuck with; who is this?*

Unknown: *We'll meet in due time.*

Walking out of the studio, Gabriella was waiting on the driver's side, and I hopped inside as she pulled into traffic. It wasn't too late, and so it wouldn't take us too long to get to the loft. I let the window down to get fresh air. "What's the plan?" Gabriella asked as she stopped at the light.

"I need you to look into Edward and follow Sofia. I don't want anyone thinking they can touch a single strand of hair on her head and think I would not skin them to the bone. Their entire family will be shot in front of them and tossed in the trash like I believe they are," I snapped.

"Who do you think is behind this?" Gabriella asked.

"It could be anyone, hell, even Monica as far as I know."

"Maricio seems more likely. I doubt Monica would have the brain power or support to pull this off," Gael said.

"I can't take that chance. If Sofia disappears, I can't say what I would do."

"We can put in some calls. Have Antonio contact his people," Gael stated.

"Take me by her place."

"I don't think that's a good idea, Joaquin. We should investigate where the threats are coming from," Gabriella said and I clenched my fists until it hurt.

The car went silent as they drove me to my home and I got out, went inside with Gabriella and Gael to look into evidence and talk over a strategy.

"I need a shower," I said.

I went to the back and lifted my shirt off, stood in the mirror and looked at my wound. I shoved the bandages off and tossed them in the trash and headed to the shower. I turned the water to luke-warm, stepped in and held my head against the wall as the warmth helped sooth the pain. Twenty minutes later, I came out and joined the team in the living room and scanned over the photos they had placed on the table as well as printouts of various documents and text messages.

"Anything new?" I asked as I hovered over them.

"So far, nothing," Gael said, passing me photos of Sofia walking into her place.

I scanned my finger across her face and smiled. I knew she was upset with me right now, but we would be together soon.

SOFIA

our months later

Security walked me to my car after the media had a field day with the bomb scare. The movie was put on hold until things smoothed out in the media. I hadn't really shown my face in public after the photographer sold his story to a tabloid about the situation at his shoot. Talking about Joaquin busting into his building, yelling, and screaming to leave. Saying that he was almost killed by my boyfriend, and he'd never work with me again. Giving photos and interviews of bruises he had on his body saying Joaquin's men tried to torture him so he would keep his mouth shut. My entire life was under a microscope, but the music was still helping to keep my mind at ease. Joaquin and I hadn't spoken in over four months, my heart and mind are conflicted. He tried calling and texting as soon as things went down, but Edward finally convinced me to take a break from him when the movie was shut down, and all of the news outlets wanted to only talk about my love life. Social media didn't help because some fans started accounts with our photos of us together and saying I should take him back.

Tonight, I was headed to The Blue Bell, a local nightclub for singers, and Deras was performing, and he wanted me to sit and relax. I was going to try and take my mind off things. Cassidy was in the car with me. Edward flew to Los Angeles to try and find some work for me. The cab stopped in front of The Blue Bell, and we stepped out. I had on a baby blue jumpsuit that zipped up and left a little bit in the cleavage area. My hair needed a change, so I cut it into a shoulder-length bob. Turning my phone off, we walked in together. The bouncer knew that we were coming and showed us to a reserved VIP section.

Cassidy pressed a hand to her mouth to stifle her giggles. "What's so funny?" I questioned.

"Nothing, Sofia."

"No, tell me, Cassidy."

"I had a serious moment of thinking that your life is more like a movie than the actual movie you were filming." Cassidy laughed.

The whole world was moving in slow motion. I felt like I was walking in a dream world, a nightmare. Some people saw him as a corrupt businessman, a mobster. He showed me the softer side of him, and maybe in the future, we could be friends again. But right now, I needed to focus on me.

"Hey, you came," Deras said, approaching us.

"We did, and I can't wait to hear your set. Deras, this is Cassidy, my assistant."

"Hi, nice to meet you, Deras. I'm a huge fan," Cassidy stated.

"Nice to meet you, Cassidy. Do you guys need anything? Please let the waitress know if you need anything. Everything is on me."

"We're fine. Go, so we can get to twerking in our seats," I joked.

"You got it," Deras said, heading to the stage.

Cassidy took a sip of the wine and swayed her hips. The section had champagne, wine, fruit, and cheese trays. I placed my purse on the couch and clapped my hands as Deras started talking.

"Ladies and gentlemen, I want to thank you all for coming tonight and hanging with my people and me. I'm going to start it off and sing a few songs, and then the rest of the evening, you'll be joined by a few friends of mine. Is that all right with you?" Deras asked.

"Yesss!!" the crowd cheered.

Cassidy jumped up and down, clapping.

"Slow down with the drinks, ma'am. I'm not babysitting you," I told her.

"I'm fine, you need to take a few shots and get some dick," Cassidy commented, the corners of her mouth curled upwards into a smile.

"I can't stand you."

"You know you love me, friend." Cassidy wiggled her hips from front to back joking of missionary sex.

"Let me get drunk, so I can ignore you," I announced.

"That's my girl!" Cassidy cheered.

"Mhmm...huh."

The music started and Deras smiled at me, and started to sing a sweet melody.

When I see your smile, it lights up my day
When I hear your laugh, it brings calm to my heart
When I talk to you, baby, you are all I need
Everything comes back to you
Back to you
Back to you
Back to you

He never took his eyes off me as he sang. He thanked the crowd and plopped down in my seat, and Cassidy stared at me. I didn't know how to feel about this new revelation.

If he was interested in me, I had no clue. Whenever I was around him at the studio, he never made it known that he was concerned.

"Wow, you have all the luck!" Cassidy said, joining me on the couch.

"Cassidy," I groaned, sitting back on the couch, closing my eyes and covering my face.

"Sofia, if Joaquin finds out-" I cut her off before she even finished putting that thought in the air.

"Sofia," Deras called out for me. Opening my eyes, I sat up and looked at him.

"I'm going to go to the bar and get another bottle of Moscato," Cassidy explained, holding the bottle up.

"I know this comes as a surprise," Deras stated.

"A big surprise."

He reached out and grabbed my hand, entwining our fingers.

"Am I interrupting something?" Joaquin questioned.

"What are you doing here?" I moved away from Deras to put space between us.

"I haven't seen you in almost four months and this is the first thing you say." Joaquin pressed his palm against my cheek.

"Do you not remember what happened?" I swallowed the lump in my throat.

His nostrils flared and I tried to step in front of Deras.

JOAQUIN

Sofia didn't know that she was being watched even over the past four months. She should have known from the last time that I would never allow anything to happen to her. The break was needed because I had business to take care of making sure that my enemies didn't see she was important enough in my life to cause her harm. The family wasn't in the clear, but I bought some time before going out to Italy in the next few weeks.

I stalked over glaring at her little boyfriend that professed his love up on stage. I had Gael check him out when I saw them going in and out of the studio a few nights. The owner of the studio didn't mind a few extra dollars in his pocket when I asked to get information on Deras Jones. A famous writer and producer, but he still performed in local clubs. Sofia didn't know the spell she put on men because her personality not only matched her beauty, but she was genuine and caring with her friends and family.

"Joaquin, how did you know I was here?" Sofia queried.

"Do you want him here?" Deras asked.

"The question is who are you? And why are you holding her hand?"

"Joaquin, that's enough. I'll call you tomorrow."

"I don't think so."

"Listen, man, she doesn't want to talk to you. You're the mobster ex-boyfriend, right?" Deras pointed his finger in my face.

"Put your finger down," I commanded, balling my fists up.

Sofia jumped up, standing in between us and pushing me back.

"I'm out with my friends; we can talk tomorrow when you've cooled down."

"Come home with me now."

"Sofia, you can stay with me; you don't need to listen to him," Deras advised.

"What!" I reached over Sofia and grasped his neck. Sofia screamed as Gael and Hugo attempted to pull me away.

"Joaquin, please, let him go. I'll leave with you, I promise."

"Let...me...go..." Deras stuttered out.

Cassidy came back over during all the commotion and tried to pull Sofia away. I cursed him out in Italian and then Portuguese for his interference, trying to act tough in front of Sofia.

"I mean it, Joaquin, let him go, or I'll never speak to you again." Sofia shoved me back. I stumbled, and Gael caught me before I fell.

"Are you all right, Deras?" Sofia asked, checking his neck.

"Grab her," I demanded and walked out as Gael gestured for Hugo to pick Sofia up and grab her purse.

"NO!! Put me down! Joaquin! You can't do this," Sofia screamed. Cassidy followed behind as we walked out to my limo, and Hugo put her down on her feet. Leonardo was standing at the driver's side door.

"Get inside," I gritted through clenched teeth, peering into her eyes.

"Joaquin," Gael called my name, and I threw a hand up for him to hush.

"I'm not leaving with you."

"Yes, you are, willingly or forcibly. But you're coming home with me tonight and we're going to talk," I explained.

"Gael, please tell him to leave me alone and lose my number." Sofia tried to walk off, and I blocked her exit. She smacked me across the face, and I didn't move; she raised her hand again to slap me and I grabbed it, kissing her palm, then her lips.

"I'm sorry, sweetheart; please come home with me so we can discuss some things. We've drawn a crowd, and I don't want to stay out here arguing and cause more photographers to show," I said, caressing her cheek.

She looked over at Cassidy for assurance.

"We can drop you off, Cassidy," I reassured.

"I'm fine; my Uber will be here soon," Cassidy informed us.

Shaking my head no, I snapped my finger for Hugo to take her home in the other car.

"Hugo will drive you home, you've been drinking, and I wouldn't feel right leaving you alone with a stranger. Hugo has protected Sofia with his life, and he'll do the same for you," I said.

"Are you sure?" Cassidy replied.

"Positive, and Sofia will call you tomorrow," I stated. Hugo took the keys from Gabriella and walked off with Cassidy. Sofia sighed and finally got in the car, and I slid inside next to her. She sat closer to the door, far away from me. I was left staring out into the night sky.

Leonardo pulled off as Gael followed, trailing us to my new home in New Jersey. With Alessandra moving here, I thought it was best to live out of the city with more privacy with security twenty-four hours.

"Where do you live now?" Sofia queried.

"New Jersey. Alessandra is moving here, and I wanted her away from the city."

"So you can keep her under lock and key," Sofia mumbled under her breath.

The drive was long, but we finally arrived. She looked in awe as the spiral gate opened, and Leonardo drove up the winding road. I lived on eight acres of rolling lawn. It was a brick and slate colonial manor with a main reception room, each with the finest woods and marble floors. There were eleven spacious bedroom suites throughout the house on two levels with a separate guest house that had its own entrance off the side. I hoped to make this our home as a union one day. She had no clue how much she controlled me. The past few months without her left me broken. The engagement ring still sat in my pocket.

"Thank you for coming."

"Did I have a choice?" she muttered, rolling her eyes as she closed the door, and stepped aside. Her hips had spread, and she'd gained a few extra pounds on her ass. I couldn't wait to be inside her again; she was teasing me. I hadn't even thought of another woman since meeting Sofia a year ago.

I opened the door and stood off to the side, and gestured for her to come into the kitchen.

"You want anything to drink?"

"No, so get to talking."

Groaning in frustration, I calmed down, not letting her attitude get me out of character and give her an excuse to leave. Grabbing a bottle of water out of the fridge, I took a sip and leaned against the counter, peering into her eyes. She looked away, and I stepped around the island that kept us separated and turned her around in the chair and stepped in between her legs.

I bent down and kissed her lips. She allowed me that moment of passion.

"Did I ever tell you that I'm grateful to you for coming into my life?"

She drew in a sharp breath. "You have a funny way of showing that side of yourself, Joaquin, when I constantly have to defend you to my friends, family, and the public."

"Never apologize, I'll never act like someone I'm not. This, around you is me, my life. Can you understand it? As the son, brother, and friend, born into this lifestyle, I had no choice."

"What I understand is that you've been on a destructive path during these past four months with killing people and closing down businesses. I'm surprised your little girlfriends aren't complaining about you pulling me out of the club tonight."

"What girlfriends? You're the only one for me."

"I want a simple boyfriend, not a crazy kingpin called Ghost!" she screamed, shoving me away and jumping up, storming toward the front door.

"Who told you about that?"

"It's all over the blogs about you being a killer for the mafia. I knew you probably sold drugs, and I could try to distance myself, but killing people, Joaquin. I don't know if I can be with you."

"Do you love me, Sofia?" I asked.

"What kind of question is that, Joaquin?"

"Answer me."

"No!"

I chuckled, not believing her at all.

"What's so funny?"

"If you didn't love me, Sofia, you would have never gotten in the car with me from the beginning."

"I didn't have a choice, if you remember. Hugo would have hounded me until I came with you."

"Not tonight."

"Then, when?"

"Since the first time you walked out of the building and I drove you home, sweetheart, you've been in my heart and mind. Every second of every day, I think of you. All of my thoughts are about making sure you're okay, and no harm comes to you before I even think of myself."

"That's not love, Joaquin."

"It's my love."

I pulled the ring out and got on my knee. She was speechless.

"Can you see yourself loving a crazy, mafia, obsessed, and extremely in love with you, man?" I questioned.

"Yes," she whispered.

I slid the ring on her finger and pulled her into a kiss.

"No more killing, crazy kingpin. I need the sweet Joaquin more than the other one. Promise me you'll work on being mindful of not overreacting at certain situations when I'm with someone else," Sofia suggested.

"I promise." I gazed down at our hands clasped together.

"Is there anything else that I should know about?" she questioned.

"Nothing important, sweetheart." Now that she had said yes, the exhaustion I had ignored came crashing down. I walked us to my room and stripped us both down before lowering her onto the bed and crawling in beside her.

"I don't want to be blind out here again, Joaquin." She shifted the covers and moved them across her shoulders.

"Sofia, you know I'll do anything to keep you safe."

My eyes slowly lowered, and I yawned ready to fall into a deep sleep.

"I believe you." She kissed my chest.

"Good, now let me catch a little sleep before we make up," I said and she chortled at my statement.

SOFIA

*J*oaquin was sleeping on his stomach in my bed. The sheet showcased his thick broad shoulders. The night we had reconnected played again in my mind, and I was fully ready to commit as his Donna and take his engagement ring. I slid the sheet off completely, and he didn't stir in his sleep. I removed my robe, climbing to the edge of the bed, tightening my hair in a bun on top of my head. I ran my hands up his legs slowly. Positioning my legs on both sides of his body, I kissed behind his left and right ear; he finally mumbled under his breath and turned around facing me with his eyes still closed. I smiled, knowing he was about to get a big wakeup morning. Getting the chance to visit Spain with him after the movie shoot was done later this year, I couldn't wait to explore Spain with him.

I moved down, gripping his dick; it hardened at my touch. I sucked the tip into my mouth, placing kisses on the sensitive head. Joaquin shifted his left leg wider giving me more room, grasping my hair. I moaned, sliding him further down my throat. His smell was still fresh from the shower we took together before bed last night after our fourth round of sex. Our short nap helped us and my body was deliciously sore from his avid attention. Every time we made love felt like the very first time. My soul was shifted, mind ignited, spirit rejuvenated with his touch. He was a bad guy; my parents taught me to stay away from that type of man, yet I agreed to be his wife. Was I making a mistake? Possibly. But the limits that he was willing to go to make me happy did bring a smile to my face. As I massaged his balls, I slid my tongue across, taking them individually into my mouth, breathing through my nose and fondling his pubic hair. Removing his balls, I spit on each one, pushed my breasts up against them, rubbing against the base of his dick.

"Fuckkkk! Stop before I come."

"Not yet."

I kept stroking him up and down between my breasts, taking the tip of his penis down my throat, squeezing between my pillows as he moaned out. Joaquin jerked in my hands, spilling his seed, a small drizzle spilling down my cheek.

"Shit! Get up here," he groaned, reaching for my shoulders to pull me up to ride him.

"This is my show, Mr. Fuertes," I replied as I licked across his balls.

Once I got to spend more time with Sabrina and the girls, I learned how she coped with being in this lifestyle. Anticipation for more launched through my body, I paced our time together because neither one of us had to be anywhere today.

"Sofia, don't play with me, get up here now," Joaquin demanded, gripping his dick and stroking himself. I crawled up his body, slapping his hand away and straddling his lap, planting my hands around his neck, pressing gently.

"This is mine, and you can't touch it until I allow you to." He slipped his arm around my waist, grabbed the back of my head, leaned up, and captured my lips. The cruel ravishment of his mouth was punishing and angry.

"Never deny me." His slow drugging kisses had teased me so much, I was ready to take him into my mouth again.

"Take me."

I was burying my hands into his thick hair, pushing his head back. His black brows winged down. I lifted up, placing his dick at my opening; the searing contact of our bodies moved through us and a low groan left his lips. I grabbed a handful of the sheets as I rode him slow and steady. I felt his heart pound underneath my fingertips. His gaze turned soft as we made love for the rest of the morning.

* * *

JOAQUIN HAD a few errands to run, and I decided to invite Sabrina and Janice over to hang out while he was out before I started running my lines for the movie I just signed on to film.

Hearing a knock at the door, I headed to place the plate of snacks and wine down on the table. Changing into a pair of leggings and Joaquin's shirt, I felt more comfortable around the house without all the makeup. Hopefully, they wouldn't think I was superficial like other actors that have to stay on point at all times.

"Sabrina, Janice, welcome, please come inside."

They hugged me and walked into the living room.

"Your home is beautiful, Sofia," Sabrina said, picking up a bottle of water.

"Thank you."

"For real, how many bedrooms are in here? I can see Carlo and me fucking in every room," Janice joked.

"Janice, don't you start," Sabrina insisted.

"It has eleven bedrooms and eight bathrooms, plus a guesthouse."

"Where's your boo?" Janice questioned.

"He's probably out with your husband cooking up some problems that we'll hear about on the news."

"Yeah I heard about your man. Honey, you need to make sure you have insurance on him when you get married because the way he's running around, you'll need something to cover the expenses in this place," Janice said, gesturing around the room.

"Janice, please don't start, and that's rude," Sabrina spat out.

"It's fine; I get it now. You two have been in this world for years, and I'm still fairly new to being in love with someone like him."

"You can say it out loud, Sofia; your boyfriend is a mafia boss. A leader, the boss of all Bosses, sweetie, and you need to understand that's never going to change. The only advice we can give you is to own and embrace your status as his woman and be his peace, never question or doubt him in front of his men. Let the women know you own that dick and let him know that you run the family in the household, and he runs the people in the streets. The moment you lay down those rules, your life will be much easier," Janice exclaimed.

Joaquin filled me in on his friends' wives and the stories of how they met at Ryde nightclub almost ten years ago. They were way more forthcoming than I thought they would be, and I needed someone to keep things real with me.

"I agree with Janice, maybe I would have said it a little nicer. I've been through everything with Antonio and tried to end things many times. I still remember him sending his bodyguard over to me with a gift, and I turned him down. You can't win my heart with gifts, and Antonio thought his charm would do the trick. Let's not get me started on when he thought I was sleeping with Spencer. That man is so jealous and possessive," Sabrina said, shaking her head.

"Joaquin's the same way."

"So why did you take his ring?" Janice questioned.

"I love him above all of his flaws," I responded.

"Has he met your parents?" Sabrina asked.

"Not officially, but I plan on having them meet. Are you guys hungry?" I responded.

"Can we order from Sybil's? I want a huge lasagna, sweet potatoes, and pork chops," Janice rounded off her favorites. I grabbed the phone and ordered through DoorDash and sat back on the couch.

"The first time I met Antonio's parents, his mother was more open to us dating than his father," Sabrina told me.

"What about you, Janice?"

"Carlo's family lives out of the country. I'm lucky not to deal with any crazy in-laws," Janice stated.

"I asked him to promise not to lie to me again. I have not only my career, but my family to think about," I said.

"If I can give you any type of advice, Sofia. Don't take offense," Sabrina said.

"I can handle it, go ahead."

"If you're going to be with a man like Joaquin and in his world, you can never really get out," Sabrina told me.

"What do you mean?"

"This Cartel world doesn't allow you to step away easily. Sabrina tried, and you see, she's still here ten years later," Janice explained.

"What Janice so eloquently stated is that if you love him, understand that some things will need to be kept from you to keep you safe," Sabrina informed me.

The doorbell buzzed and I knew it was the food delivery that the doorman let up. I jumped up and ran to the door, thanked him for being fast and shut it carrying the over to the kitchen table to arrange everything to dig in buffet style.

"Time to eat," I announced, holding the bag up to them.

"Great because I'm starving," Janice spoke as she danced her way to the kitchen and grabbed a plate and fork off the table. For the rest of the afternoon, we drank and talked, they showed me photos of their kids, and we made plans to do this often.

SOFIA

A *week later*
    I stepped off the elevator walking toward the front door as Jerry stood at the door laughing with other residents as they left. "Miss Chambers, how are you doing? I know that the bomb scare was rough."

"I'm fine, Jerry, thanks for asking. The police are still investigating; they even added around-the-clock security when I leave this place or go to the studio, but I declined."

"That decline wouldn't have anything to do with Mr. Fuertes?" he quipped.

"Something like that. I'm moving in with him soon; I'll see you tomorrow, I'm heading out for the evening."

"Be safe." He waved goodbye and I waved and smiled back at him as Leonardo held the door of the stretch limo open. It was a beautiful Saturday night and couples were out walking. I checked my watch. It just turned eight o'clock. Joaquin called earlier. He had a surprise for me and said to get dressed up.

I was wearing a black dress rouched on one shoulder with a split on the side. "How are you?" I asked Leonardo. With me starting a new movie tomorrow, I decided to keep my hair pinned back and accessorized with stud diamond earrings/diamond studded earrings and a bracelet as my only adornment.

"Doing good, Sofia. Mr. Fuertes is calling on the car phone." I slid inside picking up the phone hearing his deep, dark raspy voice.

"What is the surprise, Joaquin?" I questioned biting my bottom lip, crossing my legs.

"I have Leonardo driving you to my yacht. I am taking you on a trip," Joaquin said. I sighed, not sure about taking this trip. With my commitments with a new movie and album, this wasn't the best time to leave.

"Don't disappoint me, Sofia. We need this, just the two of us alone. I've already told Antonio I was taking some time off, so we have two weeks together to travel by sea." These past few months, Joaquin and I had grown closer even though the work he does puts him at risk, but our bond has never wavered. Even when his ex-plaything, Monica, didn't understand the connection we had. The door closed a few minutes later and Leonardo got in on the driver's side and headed into the traffic.

"Appreciate the thought, baby, but what about my movie and album? My manager wants me to do a tour."

"You've been through a lot, Sofia, and it's partially my fault. Can't you push the movie back for when you get back in town, and I'll talk with your manager about postponing the tour?" he asked. The car arrived at the dock fifteen minutes later. I smiled, tilting my head against the window. Looking out at the stars, I noticed another limo pull up and park. A tall man wearing a business suit, trench coat, and gloves got out and I noticed he had a harsh scowl on his face. He had a medium build, short black hair, bushy eyebrows, and thin lips. It made me wonder who he was married to.

"I told you already, Joaquin, you don't run my life."

"I'm not trying to run your life, I'm trying to love you," he responded, groaning in frustration. I turned toward the shouting outside and saw multiple cars arrive.

"I love you too; what's the name of your boat?" I watched Leonardo get out of the car and shake hands with a man I'd never seen before. They exchanged words, and he passed Leonardo a black bag.

"It's called Sofia. I had all your favorite foods ordered and clothes picked up, so you don't have to worry about anything."

Leonardo turned, headed toward the car, and opened the passenger seat. I grabbed my purse as he opened the door, then yanked the phone out of my hand. "Leonardo, what are you doing?!" I shouted.

"Bitch, let's go!" he shouted at me angrily and shoved me to a man. "She's all yours!" he spat. I screamed at Leonardo, trying to get out of his hold on my arm. I tried yelling for Joaquin to help me. Leonardo placed his hand over my mouth as I kicked and screamed to get out of his arms. I could hear Joaquin yelling through the phone. "Sofia! Sofia! Leonardo, I swear to God, if you hurt her, your entire bloodline will be extinguished." I heard Joaquin yell.

"Bitch, you bit me," Leonardo yelled, before he slapped me across the face. I fell on the ground in shock and pain as he ripped the back of my dress trying to pull me back.

"No, let me go! Please... Please, I won't tell," I begged, as he handed me off to the other guy.

I should've known something was wrong when the smell of rotten eggs was in the air, and my tears spilled down my face as the guy holding me shook his head in disgust.

"Please, let me go," I begged and tried to push away from him.

He grinned, licking his lips, not caring. Leonardo walked off, heading back to the limo, while we went in the opposite direction toward the loading dock. He dragged me up the steps pushing me through the door, and I fell to the floor. I looked around until the smell of a cigar caused me to look up.

Into the eyes of the last person I expected to see. He sat there in a white suit with his legs crossed, puffing on his cigar. I'd seen him before in the newspapers. I'd never forgotten that scar over his right eye.

"Hello, Mrs. Chambers," he said in his Portuguese accent. He was grinning down at me.

"You can't do this."

"I can and I will. Now remove your clothes, including the jewel-ry," he demanded as the ship started to move, and I jumped up trying to run out. I banged on the door, tears pouring down my cheeks as I saw men with guns standing at every corner of the ship.

"You can play nice, or I can get ugly, it's your choice, Sofia," he suggested, puffing on his cigar, before standing up and walking toward me as I continued calling for help.

PART II

JOAQUIN FUERTES

THE FUERTES CARTEL BOOK 2

SYNOPSIS

Joaquin

I never expected things would get this out of control. My sins have come back to haunt me and affect everyone I love. I forced my way into her life and turned things upside down. Not only am I dealing with snakes in business, but her family, and friends think we shouldn't be together. The only problem is that I'll never let her go.

Sofia

It wasn't meant to be like this. I think back to the first time I laid my eyes on Joaquin Fuertes, and thought I could control my feelings and not get caught up with falling in love. Now I'm in a position to never see my family and friends again. I ask myself should I leave my life behind or try to make things work with him? The only problem is that I doubt he'll ever let me go, but do I really want to be away from him anyway?

JOAQUIN

I tried calling Sofia's number again to try and get some type of location of where she could be. I had no clue of who could have done this since my line of work puts me in the line of fire from not only rival cartels, but also, the police in both America and my home country have me on their radar. I try to keep a low profile as Ghost, but if anything happened to Sofia I couldn't promise not to kill off every head of all the cartel families.

"Speed up and get me to the dock now!" I shouted to my driver. Dialing my car phone again it was finally answered.

"Sofia! Sofia!" I yelled and heard an evil laugh.

"Boss, good to hear from you," Leonardo said.

"Where is she?" I questioned.

"She went on a little trip and said for me to tell you not to bother calling again," Leonardo spoke in a menacing yet annoyed tone.

"Do you really want to play with your life, Leonardo? You know what I'm capable of doing," I stated. Chilled silence lengthened over the phone before I spoke once more. "I suggest you contact your mother and say goodbye now."

"What are you talking about?" Leonardo fearfully asked.

"You'll find out soon," I replied then ended the call as he

screamed my name. Loving another person while being in this business was one of the reasons I didn't get involved with women. It only brought out the other side of me that I tried to keep hidden and now Sofia would see the real Joaquin "Ghost" Fuertes because I planned on hunting down everyone that had a hand in hurting her. From the captain of the ship to Leonardo's mother for giving birth to a spineless piece of shit son.

The car finally pulled up at the dock, and I could see the boat was already halfway in the middle of the ocean. I could only hope and pray Sofia was able to stay calm and not get hurt by fighting back. I knew the way these men thought and worked. When I killed Queen it was quick and smooth, no witnesses or anything tying it to the organization. I looked down as my phone started ringing from an unknown number. Normally I wouldn't answer, but something in my gut told me this wasn't an ordinary call. I hit answer while still watching as the boat got farther away.

"Mr. Fuertes." I heard a voice I couldn't recognize come through the phone.

"Who is this?" I asked.

"I have something you want," he stated.

"Joaquin! Help me!" I heard Sofia cry out.

I closed my eyes trying to control my emotions.

"Shush...sweetheart," he told her over the phone, and I heard Sofia whimpering don't touch me.

I felt my heart pumping fast and clenched my fists.

"I know Leonardo helped you," I ground out through clenched teeth. My whole being boiled with fury. My jaw ached from my actions, but my focus, my priority was Sofia.

"I figured it wouldn't take you nothing but a second," he remarked.

"What...do...you...want?" I spoke, my voice low and deadly.

"You took something from me Ghost. It's only fair that I do the same thing to you."

"*Ahhh! Stop please,*" Sofia screamed.

"Since you know my name, it's only right I know yours."

I paced in front of the dock back and forth as Gabriella, Gael, and Hugo pulled in next to my car.

"I think that will be arranged really soon. But in the meantime, I'm going to have a little fun with my guest," he said and hung up abruptly.

"Fuckkkk!!" I shouted, removing my tie to stop the suffocation I was feeling. I knew I wasn't really suffocating, but my rage and anguish were such I felt like I would combust if my tie was on one minute longer. I watched as the boat faded out to sea and my stomach dropped knowing that I'd probably never see her again.

"Joaquin you need to see this," Gael said and stepped next to me holding his phone. I froze, my eyes wide as I struggled to comprehend what I was reading.

Actress, Singer Sofia Chambers Kidnapped-The Daily Blast

Sofia Chambers Worldwide Superstar is Missing-Celebrity Gossip Magazine

"Fuck!"

"Exactly, we need to regroup at your place and call her people," Gael mentioned.

My jaw tightened further at having to call her manager and parents. They would only use this as a means to keep her away from me. Gael tapped me on the shoulder and we walked back to my car and I got inside while Gael slid next to me as Gabriella and Hugo rode in the next car.

"Your father wants to meet tomorrow," Gael stated, and I waved him off.

"I don't have time for him."

"He might be able to help, Joaquin," Gael told me, and I sharply turned my head toward him.

"You think he had something to do with this?" I questioned as the driver drove back to the city.

"I doubt he would stoop to that level," Gael replied, once again scrolling through his phone.

"I wouldn't put anything past anyone," I said as our eyes locked.

"I agree, but you know I've always been loyal."

"Let's hope so," I mumbled to myself.

Thirty minutes later we made it back to my place, jumped out of the car, and walked inside to head toward the elevator. I checked my watch and it was going on ten o'clock. Since the blogs already had the story I could only imagine the major news stations would blast the story soon. Gabriella and Hugo followed us onto the elevator. I stood in the corner with my head angled up and my eyes closed trying to will myself not to go crazy. The elevator dinged and we stepped off. Hugo stopped to pick up a yellow envelope.

"Take Gabriella and check out back to see if you can find anything. This is preposterous that someone was bold enough to leave an envelope in front of my door."

"Stay calm, Joaquin," Gael said.

"Fuck being calm!" I shouted as I stepped in Gael's face.

He held his hands up and took a step back. I could feel myself slowly slipping into that dark place again. Without Sofia, there was no reason for me to spare a soul on this planet. I opened the envelope and pulled the photos out of Sofia showing her in various scenarios—alone at the studio, entering the recording booth, and out to eat. Some of the photos even had me with her or with my people. I slapped the photos in Gael's hands.

"How was someone able to get these without me knowing?" I forced my key in the door and tossed my jacket on the couch before I headed to the bar and poured a drink.

"I'm starting to think it could be an inside job," Gael said as Gabriella and Hugo walked inside shaking their heads.

"We didn't see anything." Gabriella bit her lip.

"Check the cameras," I said before I gulped down the scotch and poured another glass.

"What do you want me to do about her people? We need to get ahead of this," Gael informed me.

"Call them over first and then we'll see what they think about calling her parents."

Gael stood up and walked out of the living room as he talked on the phone. My gaze lingered on each person in the room as I wondered if they had betrayed me.

"Boss," Gabriella muttered and walked over to the couch and looked at the screen.

My face reddened. "Who is that?" I questioned as I glared at the person wearing all black with their face covered up.

"I think it's Leonardo, just from the body build. No one has access besides him and us," Gabriella stated and rewound the footage of the guy as he stepped into the frame and placed the envelope down without ever showing his face.

"He knew the cameras were there," I spoke.

"Exactly, which means we have a snake in the camp," Gabriella sneered before she cracked her knuckles.

"Cassidy is on her way here now. Edward didn't answer the phone," Gael remarked.

"He didn't answer his phone? The same night Sofia is kidnapped?" My brows drew together.

"Edward's a sleazeball, but I doubt he could pull something like this off on his own," Gael told me.

"Should we call Antonio?" Hugo asked.

"No."

"He's gone through the same thing, Joaquin. Maybe he could help." Gael's eyes burned with frustration.

"The less people involved the better."

"I disagree, we need everyone that can put in calls," Gael replied.

"I said no. I'm Ghost, this can be fixed without more people getting involved."

"Do you hear yourself?" Gael questioned.

"Gael, drop it."

"You're not invisible, Joaquin."

"I fucking know that! I'm Ghost for a reason," I yelled in Portuguese.

"Brother, I just want to help you." Gael jammed his hands in his pockets. The doorbell rang and Hugo opened it slowly and I saw Cassidy standing on the other side.

"Thanks for coming," I spoke as I waved for her to take a seat.

"I had no choice when you said something happened to Sofia," Cassidy remarked, and my chest tightened. I sat down on the chair opposite of Cassidy; my hands clasped together in my lap.

"Sofia's been kidnapped," I muttered.

"What! OMG...I need to call the police." Cassidy jumped up out of her seat and I motioned for Gabriella to take her phone.

"What are you doing!" Cassidy screamed.

I watched as Gabriella tossed Cassidy's phone in her pocket.

"Cassidy, we can't get the police involved."

"Are you crazy? The police should have been called the second you found out," Cassidy grumbled, holding her hand out for her phone.

"Cassidy, my work is not the most conventional," I said.

"I know you're a gangster or something," Cassidy mumbled.

"Something like that, but Sofia has always been protected."

"Until today," Cassidy spat.

"Yes and the reason being is because someone wants my attention and they decided to get me back by taking Sofia," I informed her, and stood up, grabbed my glass and refilled it.

"You need a clear mind, Joaquin," Gael said, pointing toward the glass.

"This is the only thing keeping me sane," I stated, and went back to the couch.

"Hugo, go back to the dock with some men and see if anything was left behind, maybe Sofia fought with them." Gael crossed his arms over his chest.

I stood up and walked to the bedroom to change my clothes. I turned and saw one of my shirts on the bed and lifted it up and smelled it remembering this was Sofia's favorite shirt whenever she came over and spent the night.

"I knew you thugs would hurt Sofia in some way!" I heard a gasp and yelling back and forth. I ran back into the living room and saw Gabriella choking Edward as Hugo and Gael tried to separate them.

"Let him go," I said as I dropped the shirt on the back of the couch. He bent over trying to catch his breath as Gabriella glared at him.

"She's an animal," Edward spat.

"I see you got our message."

"Where is Sofia? I don't think this is a kidnapping plot." He straightened his jacket and tie.

"She's been taken and before you start, I'll cut your fucking tongue out if you say anything else besides *How can I help?*" I demanded.

Edward glanced over at Cassidy then back to me with a grave expression.

"I don't understand why we can't call the police," Cassidy spoke.

"Because the police will only make things worse," Gael responded as he focused his eyes on Edward.

"What can we help with?" Edward mumbled.

"Two gossip magazines or whatever you call them have posted about Sofia's kidnapping. I want them shut down and for you to find out who did it."

"We can try, but most times they'll say an anonymous source," Cassidy explained, raising her arms wide.

"Take Gabriella with you," I stated and both their eyes darted over to Gabriella checking the bullets in her gun.

"You have any idea who did this?" Edward questioned.

"An enemy. I can promise that once I find out who, they'll wish they were never born," I said.

"I'll help, but just know the second we find Sofia, I'll do everything I can in my power to convince her to stop dating you. If you truly love her, I suggest you leave her alone," Edward responded, before he turned to yank the door open and walked out. Cassidy and Gabriella strolled behind him. I lifted the bottle of scotch to refill my glass and Gael grabbed it out of my hand.

"Get your head out of the bottle. We need you clear and focused," Gael said, placing the top back on and I nodded in agreement. We both stayed silent for a few minutes until Hugo spoke.

"What about her apartment?" Hugo asked.

"Take Alex with you and report back to me," I said and grabbed my jacket off the floor not even thinking to change clothes.

"Where are you going, Joaquin?" Gael asked.

"I need to talk with Antonio." I swiped my keys off of the table.

"I'm going with you," Gael insisted.

Hugo, Gael, and I left my apartment and went our separate ways, leaving through the back alley. I jumped into the driver's side of my Ferrari and Gael went to the passenger side. I stuck the key in the ignition and headed out, not waiting for him to slide the seat belt on.

SOFIA

That same night.

I was sitting inside of the room on the bed, looking out the window as he talked to one of his men. I tried my best to fight and jump off the boat, but he locked me inside of the bedroom. I was beyond terrified of what he was planning on doing and where he was taking me, and I still had no clue who he was or what he wanted with me. I saw them stop talking and he came back down to the lower deck and I heard the lock turn before he stepped inside.

"Please let me go," I said as I wiped the tears from my cheek.

"You're really a fabulous actress, Miss Chambers. Bravo," he replied and grinned.

I scooted back further as he stepped further into the room. One of his men stood behind him with a gun.

"I have some food for you."

"I'm not hungry," I responded.

"Do you want to go home? See your family and Joaquin?" he asked.

I nodded yes before verbally responding, "I do."

"Then follow my instructions," he replied then turned to walk out.

"Then I can go home?" I asked as I followed behind.

"Maybe," he answered and sat down at the table and picked up the napkin, placing it on his lap. He had a candlelight dinner with two plates that held steamed vegetables, baked salmon, oysters, and pasta with cut up lobster.

"Why are you doing this?" I questioned, lowered down in the chair.

"He took something from me."

"Who?" I inquired.

"Ghost," he spat, with a hard grimace.

"Who's Ghost?" I inquired.

"You have no clue, do you?"

"No dammit and I want to get out of here!" I shouted, and tried to stand up. The man with the gun pushed me back in the seat.

He flicked his hand and the guy with the gun nodded and walked out of the room.

"Joaquin *Ghost* Fuertes is a dangerous man, Sofia."

A chill went down my spine.

"Who are you?" I asked.

He smirked.

"Ciro Vitale," he responded as he reached his hand out for me to shake.

"Why are you doing this to me?"

"Joaquin killed my niece, Queen Vitale," he replied.

"That has nothing to do with me," I said.

"It has everything to do with you, because Ghost decided to kill the daughter of a Cartel Boss," Ciro spoke.

"I don't know anything about that."

"Eat, we can finish our talk tomorrow," Ciro stated.

"Are you going to kill me?" I queried, gripping the knife beside me. His eyes darted to my hand and smirked.

"I wouldn't do anything stupid if I were you. A lot of sharks in these waters," he responded as he cut into his meal.

"I can pay you. Please, I have money, if I go missing a lot of people will worry."

"That's what I plan on," he said, sneering.

"If Joaquin or Ghost is the person you say is so crazy to kill the daughter of a mobster what do you think he will do if something happens to me?"

"While he's distracted by you missing? A few friends of mine will take what's owed to them," Ciro explained. I jumped up, raised the knife under his chin and he grinned as I glared at him.

"Have your men turn around and take me back."

"Don't worry, Sofia, we're not leaving the country," Ciro said as he grasped my wrist, twisted it around and almost broke it making me drop the knife as I screamed.

"You little bitch!" Ciro yelled.

"Please, let me go," I cried out.

"I should punish you for that move, but I won't this time. I have plans for Joaquin and they include you."

"Ciro turn on the news." His henchman marched inside, picked up the remote and turned on the tv.

"We have some reports that Sofia Chambers is missing," the Channel 5 news anchor announced.

"That's right, Elizabeth, so far we have Celebrity Gossip magazine reporting. We still have not confirmed," Jonathan, the second news anchor reporter, replied.

"Good," Ciro said.

"Good! I'm all over the news and probably social media. I demand to be sent home," I shouted, and he backhanded me.

"Take her to the bedroom," Ciro said.

"No, let me go. Get your fucking hands-" He pointed the gun in my face.

"My men will treat you with respect on my orders or they can treat you like the whore that you are, Miss Chambers," Ciro seethed as he sparked up the cigar he'd taken out of his pocket.

"Move," his man said and pushed me forward to the bedroom.

"Can I get the food?" I asked, hearing my stomach growling.

"No," the guy blurted out with a raspy voice.

I crawled on top of the bed and curled my legs up to my chest, and cried to myself as I felt the boat stop. All of a sudden I heard gunfire and yelling from up top.

"Go grab her now!" Ciro shouted.

Pop! Pop!

"OMG!" I screamed as the bullets went back and forth, hitting the window of the room I was in. The door burst open and two of his men came in and dragged me out.

"Let me go."

"Hurry up," yelled the shorter guy wearing a military vest, dark boots, and a patch over his eye.

"She's acting like a bitch," the taller one stated as he gripped my arm tighter and pulled me out of bed.

"I can walk," I said, stumbling to get up right.

Finally, he let me go and shoved me to keep me walking forward.

The shorter man with the hard glare, souless eyes from out on the lower deck, stood talking with another gunman. I could hear Ciro on top barking orders. Gunfire was still going off as I looked out further and saw a smaller boat. I squinted my eyes, but it was hard to tell who was on the other boat and if they were here to save me.

"Take her to the boat," Ciro commanded as he continued firing shots. I was still wearing my dress and heels without a jacket, but I'd rather die trying to get away than stay with these men. We continued down the right side of the boat and I saw another one with a gun holding a guy and wearing a life vest.

"Get in," the guy with the eye patch told me.

I looked down then up into his eyes and behind me. Thinking this was my only chance, I decided to shove him away and run further to the edge of the back of the boat near the engine and I jumped off as I felt the sting from a bullet then the cold freezing temperatures of the sea as I plunged beneath the water.

"Ahhh!!" I felt a sense of relief as my eyes slowly narrowed. I thought I saw a light shining, and a part of me was trying to will myself to start swimming. The wound in my side was something I'd never felt before and all of a sudden, I drifted off as the currents pulled me below.

* * *

ONE DAY LATER.

I felt whispering around me and heard crying. It sounded like my mom and dad, but they were back home. I wanted to wake up, but my body was weighing heavy, like something was sitting on my chest. I prayed that wherever I was, it was away from those men and they'd never find me again. The way Ciro spat Joaquin's name and how he killed his niece, and having that burden of wanting to save myself and warn him was too much to bear. Hearing gunshots over and over again and the cold icy water where I almost drowned caused my body to heat up again.

"Doctor, is she all right?" I heard a voice say.

All of a sudden the beeping noises became elevated.

"Sofia, we need you to calm down."

My eyes felt like they were moving at a rapid pace.

"Let me go!" I screamed.

"Sofia, you're safe, sweetie."

"No, he's going to kill me," I yelled.

A soft gentle voice said, "Doctor do something."

"Nurse, give her a sedative to calm her down. Let her get some rest," the doctor spoke and I drifted back into that dark place. Eased into a deep sleep, like a movie replaying, I watched myself in slow motion jumping into the water and felt the sting of the bullet hit me.

Two days later I slowly opened my eyes and glanced around the room. I lifted my hand to check my side still feeling the pain from the gunshot. The room was white, more than likely I'm in the hospital and still in America since the tv was running an entertainment show about me.

"Where am I?" I questioned. My mom jumped up and came to my bedside, caressed my cheek.

"You're awake, thank God."

"Where am I?" I asked again.

"You're in the hospital, baby. Your father and I have been here every day," Mom said.

"How long have I been sleeping?"

"Three days," Mom replied.

She picked up the jug of water and poured some in a cup.

"Here drink this," she said.

"Mmmm...thanks," I said and gave her the cup back to place on the food tray.

"We thought we lost you for a moment," Mom said as she kissed my cheek.

"What did the doctor say and where is Dad?"

"The doctor is checking your test results and Dad went to the cafeteria for food."

"How did you find me?"

The second I spoke those words the door opened, and I smelled that same cologne that had taken over my mind and body since the first time we met at Antonio's.

"I was hoping you'd be awake," Joaquin stated as he stalked to the edge of the bed. He ran a hand across my foot. He didn't look like the clean cut Joaquin I was used to being around in suits and all clean shaven. Instead, he stood before me, slightly disheveled with a beard and mustache.

"What happened to me?" I questioned him and he darted his eyes toward my mother.

"We can talk about that later," Joaquin stated.

"No, I want to talk about it now!" I demanded, and the heart monitor started beeping.

"Sofia, relax, baby. Your blood pressure will go up and they'll put you back to sleep," Mom explained.

"I need to talk to Joaquin, can you give us a minute?" I looked up, and she nodded in answer.

She went over to pick up her purse and walked out of the room as Gael held the door open. Joaquin's entire demeanor was off and I felt somewhere in my gut that he was lying and probably hiding more secrets. I was very aware of who he was when I agreed to go out with him, but he promised to keep me protected and now I was sitting in a hospital bed with a gunshot wound and three days missing from my life.

"I need to know everything that happened," I said.

"Sofia, you're safe. That's what matters," he replied in his thick accent.

"Gael, can you leave us alone please?" I continued glaring at Joaquin as Gael stared between us.

"I'll be right outside," Gael said and turned to walk out. Joaquin came around from the end of the bed to the top and bent down to kiss me on the lips and I moved my head out of the way.

"Don't do this," Joaquin said.

"You need to explain to me how I ended up getting kidnapped by some maniac and then woke up here in a hospital bed."

"Did he touch you?" Joaquin questioned, trying to change the subject.

I felt myself starting to get frustrated and heated. I drew the covers close to my neck and laid my head back on the pillow and closed my eyes for a moment to recall the events on the boat.

"Tell me what's going on, Joaquin. If you want this to work." I pointed between us and his brows narrowed in slits.

"If!" he arrogantly chuckled.

"I just want the truth," I spat, pushed his hands off my leg. He sighed and bobbed his head up and down, grasped my hand and sat on the corner of the bed and stared into my eyes.

"Are you going to sit there and stare at me or tell me the truth?"

The way his eyes bore into me I felt something was missing. He knew more than he was willing to tell me and in a weird way it was probably best that I didn't know anything for my own protection. But if I decided to continue dating him, then all of our cards needed to be on the table.

JOAQUIN

Three days prior.

I ran the red light not caring if the police saw me driving down the road at a high rate of speed. I needed to find Sofia and that all depended on what Antonio could tell me. I gripped the steering wheel even tighter as I blew through the yellow light causing a car to honk at me.

"Joaquin, slow down, you won't be any help to Sofia if we're dead," Gael grumbled and I pushed the gas even harder, swerving away from a truck that almost hit the right passenger side at the next light. Ten minutes later we pulled up in front of Antonio's restaurant, and jumped out, headed inside pushing the valet and security out of the way and went to the back of the lounge and got on the elevator toward the basement. I walked up to the guard and he nodded before he opened the door for us. Walking in, I saw Antonio, Bruno, and Carlo sitting together talking.

"I expected you half an hour ago," Antonio stated as he leaned over the conference table.

"Who the fuck took her?" I spat, throwing a chair into the wall.

"Has he been like this all night?" Carlo asked, and Gael motioned with his hands out that he wasn't answering that question.

"I know how you feel," Antonio said, and marched around the table to extend his hand out to me.

"I want everything you have on who took her."

"Right now the word is that Ciro Vitale planned this," Bruno told me.

My eyes bugged out in shock.

"He's alive?" I questioned.

"Looks like it and we can't touch him. After killing Queen our hands are tied," Carlo explained.

"You can't kill him, but I will."

"No, Ghost, you've been in the media too much lately," Antonio informed me.

"That's bullshit!" I snapped before I started to punch the wall, only Gael stopped me.

I jerked out of his hold.

"Queen was my call and I take responsibility for that. We need to think about our next steps," Antonio said.

"The bitch deserved to die. Ciro should be next to her."

"Which is why you can't touch him. We have a team preparing to go get Sofia," Carlo said.

"So you have eyes on them?" I asked, getting pissed the longer we stayed there.

"The minute we got word Ciro came into town we had eyes on him," Bruno said.

"No one thought to tell me?"

"Joaquin, you're a hot head like me. The chance of Ciro surviving one day with you around was not something we could take a chance on," Antonio stated.

"He's not only looking to get revenge on Queen's murder, but we haven't figured out what else he's here for," Carlo said as he pushed a folder down the table toward me. I leaned over and picked it up, then flipped through documents and photos of Ciro talking with Leonardo and Edward.

"I'm going to kill him!" I shouted as I started to leave the room only to be stopped.

"Joaquin calm down," Carlo said.

"I swear to God if you don't let me go, Gael, I'll kill you right now."

"What's in the folder?" Gael asked, and I shoved it in his hands. I ran both palms down my face. All this time I underestimated Edward and thought he wasn't a threat and all along he was playing me.

"That's her manager," Gael spoke up.

"Which makes things even more complicated," Antonio said.

"People go missing all the time."

"Joaquin, we know you're ready to suit up, but you need to listen," Antonio said.

"Explain to me why I shouldn't walk out of here and kill them both?"

"Because Edward and Sofia are both high profile; it's already bad enough that she's been kidnapped," Carlo stated.

"Ciro is looking to take you down and he's started with Alba Industries and working his way with taking Sofia on top of that," Bruno said.

"Does my father know about this?"

"Not yet," Antonio said.

"Where are they now?" Gael asked.

"He's still on the water moving toward Long Island. Ciro's not getting out of the country," Antonio explained.

"How many men are on standby?"

"We have two boats with guys locked and loaded, you can come, but you need to stay on land," Carlo said.

"I need to be there when she gets off the boat."

Antonio shook his head.

"That would only cause Ciro to retreat and kill her. If we go in the dark and take them by surprise, we have a better chance of getting Sofia home safe," Antonio stated.

"What if this was Sabrina?" I snarled. My control was nearly gone and despite knowing what they all were saying was the right thing, I needed to be there, do something. Do damage and seek vengeance upon the man who thought it'd be wise to touch my woman.

"I wasn't there when she was kidnapped in Italy. Sonny found her and sent word," Antonio explained.

"Be smart about this, Ghost, we know she's important to you," Bruno remarked.

"She's the reason my heart even beats."

The door opened and one of his men motioned with a wave of his hand to speak with him."Go ahead, Sonny, you can speak freely," Antonio stated as he went to the cage in the corner of the basement, typed in a code and grabbed two guns.

"The men are set up and ready to go on your word. We have the front of the dock covered," Sonny explained.

"Sonny, ride with me, Gael, and Joaquin. Carlo you go with Hugo and Bruno in the other car," Antonio said as he offered me a gun.

"I have that covered."

"Joaquin if things don't-" Antonio started to say and I held my hand up to stop him.

"She's coming home," I responded before I marched out of the room with my team behind me and headed back up the stairs to the top and out to the back entry and loaded up in the black SUV. Mere seconds later, Antonio and Gael climbed in and gave directions to Sonny of where to go. He drove down the street and onto the freeway. My phone vibrated with a picture of Sofia in a bedroom banging on the door.

Unknown: Keep this photo as a reminder.

Me: Ciro I suggest you remember who you're dealing with.

Ciro: Do You remember?Did you give my niece the same respect?

Me: Test me and see what happens.

The car stopped in the parking lot of the loading dock and we filed out and stalked over to the grassy knoll. Antonio had more men wearing life jackets and two speed boats ready to go. I checked my watch; it was going on midnight and I still hadn't heard form Cassidy or Edward.

"You ready?" Antonio asked as he passed me a bulletproof vest.

"I thought you wanted only two people in the boat," I replied.

"If this was Sabrina, I would do the same, just be careful," Antonio said, then waved for his men to start up the engines. I ran to the edge and hopped inside sliding on the vest, grabbing my gun from behind my back. Gael jumped in the other boat as Hugo and Gabriella got back in the car and rode to the other side of the dark woods. It was getting chillier as the night went on. I could see my breath in the air. Antonio stayed at the dock and directed his men as Sonny drove us out to the spot where he had located Ciro's boat. I thought about hearing Sofia's voice again and worried that if he touched her in any way that would cause her to close herself off. I'd never prayed for anything in the world or cared to even think God listened to me after the things I'd done. Right now looking up to the sky at the full moon and stars I closed my eyes and wished to get her back safe in my arms. A tap on my shoulder brought me out of my thoughts. The bright lights flickered in our direction.

"Get more lights!" the guy that shot at us yelled.

I looked back at Gael as he pointed to the left at the boat that was about a few minutes away from us. We heard some commotion and yelling.

"What's the plan?" Gael asked and I lifted my gun, lined it up and took the safety off right as a gunshot was sent at our boat.

"Focus the light!" the guy that shot at us shouted again.

All three of us ducked as more shots went over our heads. I lifted my gun and sent shots off from my Glock nine. I heard someone scream out in pain.

Pop! Pop! Pop!

"Joaquin, look at the left side," Gael yelled out.

My eyes narrowed as I saw Sofia being pushed from behind and I didn't know what they were planning to do.

"Sonny, head to the other side," I commanded, removing my vest and jacket, preparing to swim over if needed.

The boat picked up speed and took off in her direction while we continued shooting back at the boat. What I wasn't expecting was for Sofia to jump in the water to try and get free.

"Fuck!" I shouted before I jumped in the water and swam to catch her. Not knowing if she survived the gunshot, I was prepared to wipe the entire Vitale family line out.

"Sofia...baby, listen to me," I said as I grabbed her around the waist right when Ciro saw us and started shooting at us in the water.

"Mmmm...help me." Sofia choked on the water.

"Baby, hold on," I said and shoved her back under the water and tried to glide her away from the bullets. Her body went limp in my arms until we got a little more distance away, and finally came up for air two minutes later. I saw Sonny and Gael approach and I lifted Sofia into the boat first.

"Ughhh....don't hurt me," Sofia muttered, trying to fight Gael.

I climbed out of the water and got on the boat and took Sofia out of Gael's arms then placed my jacket over her body to warm her up.

"It's me, baby, Joaquin. You're safe," I repeatedly said, while I rubbed her arms up and down to continue giving her warmth.

"We need to get out of here," Gael responded, and gave me his jacket to put on Sofia.

"Joaquin...Joaquin..." Sofia's eyes rolled to the back of her head as her mouth fell open. She had apparently gone into shock, either due to the gunshot wound or the chill of the water. Regardless, time was of the essence; I refused to lose the woman who owned me, mind, body and soul.

"Faster, God damn it!" I demanded as I tried to give Sofia mouth to mouth. It felt like a lifetime, but only a few seconds before she spit up more water. The boat made it back to land and I picked her up and walked off to the truck that Hugo and Gabriella were in.

"Keep me updated. We have a lot to discuss," Antonio said before he slid the window of the SUV up and drove off. I had Hugo drive to the nearest hospital as I cradled her in my arms. Thirty minutes later we made it to the emergency area, and I got out yelling in order to get some help.

"I need a doctor!"

"Sir, what's the emergency?" a nurse asked as she motioned for a gurney.

"She was in the water a long time and she was shot."

"You stay here and let us take it from here," the short blonde, gray-eyed nurse stated, and I refused, trying to walk behind them, wanting to be with her when she woke up.

"Sir, we need you to fill out some information. Is she your wife?" I looked down at her badge.

"Naomi, she's more than my wife. If anything happens to her," I started to say, and she somberly smiled.

"I understand, sir. Please let us do our jobs and we'll update you soon," Naomi insisted. I nodded and sat down in the waiting area. Gael, Gabriella, and Hugo came in and stood around guarding the front and back entrance.

"Ciro got away," Gael said as he slid his hands in his pockets.

"I want him dead, Gael."

"I understand, brother, but we have to think about our next steps. Your picture and Sofia's are all over the news."

"Fuck the news," I screeched then stood up and kicked the chair away from me, trying to control my temper.

"Your father called and so did your sister," Gael informed me.

"My phone fell in the water."

"Okay, I'll get Alex to get you a new one," Gael said. As he picked the chair up and put it back, the security guard came over with a grimace on his face. If he thought he could intimidate or kick me out, he had another thing coming. People came in and out of the emergency room all night while we waited. Finally, I saw Cassidy run in as the doctor came out to talk to me.

"You brought in the young lady from the water?" the doctor asked as he extended his hand for a shake.

"Sofia Chambers," I said, and his eyes got big.

"We should probably put her in a secluded area away from any prying eyes."

"Does that mean she's alive?" I questioned, holding my breath.

"She is, but we had to perform emergency surgery to get the bullet out, plus being in the water for so long exacerbated the situation."

"What does that mean?" I wondered.

"She's sleeping right now, we didn't want to wake her too early," Doctor Johnson told me.

"How long will she be asleep?" Cassidy asked.

"It's up to her, but if she doesn't wake on her own once the anesthesia wears off, it might end up being a few days. Her body suffered a trauma so right now, rest is important in the healing process."

"Where is she?" Cassidy questioned, hugging herself.

"She's in recovery right now, but we'll move her in a little while to a VIP area," Doctor Johnson informed us as Cassidy and I sat back down in the chairs to wait.

SOFIA & JOAQUIN

*S*ofia

    "So, you've been at the hospital since they first brought me here?" I asked as the nurse came in, smiled at me and started to check my vitals.

"I went home to change clothes after your parents got here on the second day. I left my men here for your protection."

"How are you feeling, Sofia?" Naomi asked as she started the blood pressure machine.

"Exhausted, but hungry," I replied.

"Food will be delivered soon, I just want to make sure you're not having any residual issues," Naomi explained, writing on the chart.

"When can she go home?" Joaquin asked.

"That's up to the doctor, but if everything is looking good, either later today or tomorrow," Naomi stated as she pushed back the cover to check my bandages.

"Does it still hurt? Do you need any extra pain medicine?" Naomi lifted the white bandages and tossed them in the trash.

"A little, but not as much as a few days ago. Will it leave a scar?" I questioned.

Naomi walked over to the door and grabbed what she needed to clean the surgical site.

"A little scar, but nothing to worry about," Naomi said.

I heard a knock on the door as Cassidy stepped in with balloons and a teddy bear.

"I saw your parents outside, and they said I could come up. Am I interrupting?" Cassidy inquired.

"No, you can come in and tell me what's been going on. I'm still trying to process everything," I said.

"Did you tell her?" Cassidy asked.

"Yeah," Joaquin replied.

"Have they caught the guy?" I questioned.

"No, but we have people working on finding him."

"Joaquin, you promised me," I said as I leaned back against the pillow.

"Try not to get upset, dear. I'll bring your food in a few minutes," Naomi told me before she strolled back out. Cassidy sat the balloons on the couch with the teddy bear and handed me the card.

"Edward isn't taking my calls. I'm doing my best to get the blogs under control," Cassidy said.

"Are they camped outside?" I questioned.

"They are and of course they knew me, so they tried to follow me," Cassidy fussed as she rolled her eyes then sat down on the chair next to my bed.

"Put out a statement saying I'm thankful for all of their prayers and well wishes. Keep it simple, but don't feed into anything," I stated. I watched as Cassidy pulled out her phone and started typing up a note.

"You sure that's needed right now? The added stress is probably not good for your recovery," Joaquin advised.

"The stress started with you and look where I ended up!" I fussed, causing the monitor to spike.

"I understand, sweetheart, but I'm working on fixing it so you'll never experience this again."

"How are you going to fix it, huh? Go out and kill everyone that had a hand in this?" I sneered as I motioned around the room I was currently ensconced in.

Before Joaquin could answer, my mother and father peeked through the door. I smiled and waved them inside.

"She's awake, Leroy," my mom, Latonya said, bending down to hug me and kiss my cheek.

"Baby, you scared us to death," my dad, Leroy, stated as he pressed a kiss on my forehead. They were both in the middle age range, around their late fifties or sixties. But they looked far younger, which I was thankful for as I had inherited their genes.

"I'm sorry you guys had to deal with this." Naomi pushed a food tray in and my mother took the top off and helped to get things organized for me to eat.

"We can talk about that later. The most important thing is you're safe," Mom said.

"When can she come home?" Dad asked Naomi.

"The doctor is checking her chart, most likely later today or tomorrow if everything is clear," Naomi informed him.

"Once the doctor clears you, Sofia, we should talk about you coming back home," Mom blurted out.

"That's not happening," Joaquin said and the room went quiet.

"Excuse me?" Latonya responded.

"Joaquin don't start," I said as I cut into my salad.

"My daughter needs rest and to be away from you," Latonya demanded.

"No offense, but Sofia needs to be with me for her own protection."

"We know what you're into, it only takes one phone call to the police," Latonya spat.

"Okay, enough, Ma, I'm not leaving New York. I refuse to be chased away," I explained.

"Sofia, I sent out the press release. I know they'll be calling for you to do an interview soon," Cassidy stated.

"I know and once I talk with the lawyer about the case we can plan out the details," I replied.

"You can't talk with your lawyer, sweetheart."

"What do you mean?" I queried, biting into my burger then taking a sip of water.

"It's complicated and we need to keep it out of police hands."

"Joaquin, you are not making sense."

"We'll discuss this when I get you home," he advised. He stood up to leave and leaned down to kiss me, but I turned my head, unwilling to allow that contact with the current state of affairs so up in the air. I didn't understand why he wouldn't allow the police to get involved; I'd been kidnapped then shot!

"I'll be back."

"Yeah," I mumbled as he walked out leaving my parents and Cassidy in the room.

* * *

Joaquin

Gael was on the phone arguing and I headed in his direction as Gabriella and Hugo pulled away from the door of Sofia's room where they had been standing guard.

"Hugo, I want you to stay here. I have some business to handle."

"Sure boss," Hugo replied.

"Where to now?" Gabriella asked as we stepped out of the hospital and headed to the car.

"Did you get that package for me?" I turned to her as we stopped at the car door.

"Nicely packaged for you," Gabriella commented, and I nodded and opened the door of the passenger side.

"That was your father, it's all the news in Italy about Ciro and Maricio said the next shipment they want to double up," Gael told me. I wasn't too excited to add more product and strain on my men so early.

"Manage it for now and keep an eye out. He's operating under Laurent's orders."

"If something goes wrong," Gael stated as he looked up making eye contact in the rearview mirror.

"His death will be on Laurent's hands."

Gael passed me a phone and I scrolled to see all of my numbers set up and a message from Antonio.

Antonio: We have Ciro coming out of the Westin Hotel.

Me: Keep your men on him.

Antonio: He's trying to do business with Russia.

Me: Fuck doing business, put the word out.

Antonio: How is she doing?

Me: She woke up today and we talked.

Antonio: She knows everything?

Me: I explained how we found her and Edward.

Antonio: He's still MIA?

Me: Yeah, that motherfucker hasn't returned one call.

Antonio: You need me to locate him?

Me: I got my tech people looking into him.

* * *

FORTY MINUTES later we pulled in front of the warehouse that was out in the middle of nowhere. No interruption would stop me from doing what needed to be done. I looked down at my phone and checked the time. I knew the doctor would probably discharge her by tomorrow, and I wanted to be the one to bring her home so we could talk about everything. I shut the car door and as I got out, Gabriella passed me a gun.

"I won't need that just yet." I handed the gun back to her and removed my jacket and rolled up the sleeves of my white shirt. Usually we handled the torturing together or I let her have free reign, but today I would take pleasure in killing the bastard that thought he could get away with hurting my Sofia.

I looked around the area, the sun was shining, birds chirping. It was more peaceful now than being out in the murky water trying to save my baby's life.

"Arghh ..." she screamed as they saw me walk inside with not one ounce of remorse. I never wanted to stoop to this level, but he left me no choice and today he'd have to watch as I killed his mother in front of him.

"Joaquin, please man. I fucked up," Leonardo said, his face whitening in the chair next to his mother.

"Shut up!" Gabriella shouted as she punched him in the face.

He was picked up by Gabriella two days ago trying to board a plane with his mother. I guess he thought I would spare her, but once you stepped over that line and deliberately tried to hurt the one thing that mattered to me most, then Ghost would come out.

"Shush... save the tears. I mean Sofia had tears when you were sending her off to Ciro right?" I asked, bent down to stare into his eyes. Snot and blood were mixed in with his tears.

"I promise, it wasn't like that. He forced me to do that," Leonardo pleaded.

"Really? Because from what I heard on the phone you took joy in smacking my woman around."

I snapped my finger and Gabriella lifted the knife off the table. I would make his mother suffer a death by torture like I planned on doing with her son. I grabbed it out of her hands and smiled at her.

"I hate that things have to be like this," I said as tears poured out of Leonardo's mother's eyes.

"Ughhh... ahhh..." She tried to move, but we had her arms and legs tied up and a towel inside her mouth.

"Please, Joaquin, I can help you, man...Don't do this," Leonardo begged as I placed the knife under her chin.

"The world we live in states that mothers and children are off-limits, but the minute my woman was taken I didn't exist in this world anymore," I spoke and gripped her hair tight, pulling it back as they both continued to cry and beg.

"Ciro is working with someone close to Sofia," Leonardo yelled out.

I slowly slit her throat as her eyes widened in shock. Leonardo screamed and cried for his mother.

"Tell me something I don't know...Huh...you piece of shit." I stabbed him in the knee and punched him in the stomach.

"Ahhhh!!! Fuckkkk...please don't kill me," Leonardo cried out as I whistled, and my pit bull came running out of the back corner he was chained up against.

"Sit," I commanded.

"Too late, Leonardo. If I were you I would close my eyes and pray God forgives you, because I don't give second chances," I told him and stabbed him in the left eye.

"Eat." Alessandra went for Leonardo's neck and continued feeding off of him as I stood to clean the knife off with the towel on the table.

"When did you name your dog after your sister?" Gael asked.

I chuckled.

"She's just like my sister, spoiled and angry unless she gets her way."

"That's true," Gael answered as he looked off in thought. I shook off his comment and removed my bloody shirt and tossed it to Gabriella to dispose of as we left the warehouse to head back to the city.

"Who were you arguing on the phone with at the hospital earlier?"

"Nobody," Gael said as he reversed out of the parking lot then headed toward the city.

Gael had never made me not trust him, but lately he'd taken calls more and more that weren't about business, well at least he said they weren't. Every time I tried to talk to him about any problems he blew me off. I'd really hate to have to kill my best friend for working with my enemies.

"If you say so."

He glanced back at me as he drove, and I never lost eye contact. Everybody around me must have felt I went soft with Sofia around me. She'd only made me stronger and I'd prove to everybody not to underestimate why they called me Ghost.

"Burn the building down tonight," I said, and he nodded in answer.

"I need a house out of the city for me and Sofia."

"What about her parents?"

"They'll jump on board in time." I relaxed in the seat.

"Do you think she's ready for that?"

"It's for her safety. Contact the realtor and find something gated." I closed my eyes as we drove back to the hospital to check on Sofia.

SOFIA

"*You* *should mind your manners, Sofia," he said as he reached out and gripped my arm.*

"Let me go," I shouted. I attempted to bite his hand when he covered my mouth.

"Bitch!" he shouted and smacked me across the face. I fell to the floor and raised my hand to my sore cheek as tears pooled into my eyes.

"I see what Joaquin likes about you." He bent down and grabbed my chin then squeezed.

"He's going to kill you," I muttered as he pushed me down on the floor, pulled out a switchblade and traced it across my cheek down to the top of my dress.

I vainly tried to push his hands away.

"Then, I should make my time worthwhile."

"Get the fuck off me, you bastard," I screamed as I kicked my legs to force him up off me.

"My men wanted to take you for themselves; I said you shouldn't be touched. Are you going to make me change my mind?"

He stood up and placed the blade back in his pocket.

"Joaquin will kill you if anyone touches me."

He smiled and walked toward the door. I pulled myself up from the floor and watched as his henchman came to the door, and they whispered back and forth.

"Would you like something to eat, Sofia?" he asked.

"I want out of here now."

"That's not going to happen. I suggest we become acquainted with each other since you'll be here for a while." He smirked as the door closed behind him.

I ran to the desk drawer to look for anything that could help me get out of here. The entire room only held a bed, tv, and boarded-up windows with bars. Why was this happening to me? I cried and cupped my face, sat down on the bed and was thinking of my family when the door opened again, and two of his men walked in with their guns.

"Get away from me!" I screamed.

Ring! Ring!

"Shit!" Sweat beads ran down my face, and my heart was racing fast from a nightmare of being held captive on a boat. I glanced around my room as I calmed my breathing.

Ring! Ring!

I picked up my cell phone.

"Hello," I said groggily.

"Are you all right?" Joaquin asked.

I checked the time, and it said two am. I'd never had nightmares growing up, but this felt so real.

"It's two am, Joaquin," I responded, wondering why he was calling so late.

"I couldn't sleep," he said.

"That makes two of us."

"You want me to come over?"

"No."

"Baby."

"I promise I'm fine, just a little nightmare."

"I'm coming over," Joaquin spoke. It sounded like he was getting out of bed.

"Joaquin, stop worrying. I have work in the morning."

"Then, I'll drive you, sweetheart," Joaquin insisted, and I smiled.

"You'll probably drive me and stay with me all day."

"I don't see a problem with that," Joaquin stated.

"The problem is that you can't fix everything."

"I won't bother you; I'll even sleep on the couch," he joked, and I knew that would never happen.

"No, you'll stay home, and I will talk to you later. Goodbye," I said then hung up the call.

...

The next day I was looking at my calendar and emails with Cassidy before I headed home. Cassidy typed on her computer as I read over my schedule and poured myself some water.

"Sofia! Sofia!" Cassidy yelled out, and I realized I was making a mess as water spilled over the glass.

"Sorry."

"Are you okay?" Cassidy questioned.

"Huh."

"You seem distracted," Cassidy mentioned, and I stood up, walked to the bathroom and grabbed a paper towel to clean up my mess.

"I had a nightmare last night."

"You want to talk about it?" Cassidy asked, and I shook my head no.

"No, Joaquin wanted to come over and talk, but I'll be fine."

"If you change your mind, let me know."

"Thanks, but work is all I need," I replied and tossed the towels in the trash and continued to read over what I needed to get a handle on before my career got overshadowed by my personal life.

* * *

TWO DAYS LATER.

I woke up refreshed today knowing I would be leaving the hospital. Joaquin came in last night to spend the night on the couch after my parents left. Neither of them spoke to him and the tension could've been cut with a knife. Doctor Johnson came back yesterday afternoon and explained that all the tests came back fine, and I was clear to head home, but I still needed to rest and take things slow. I was too far along with filming and recording my album to stop the momentum. I asked Chauncey if he could come to my apartment to run through some songs together and Cassidy would be coming over to figure out a plan for my schedule. Social media was nonstop about my shooting and the reason I was in the hospital; some people said I was pregnant or having cosmetic surgery. I wanted to curse Joaquin out for bringing all this drama into my life. Nurse Naomi helped me out of the wheelchair and Joaquin assisted me into the car. I looked up front and saw Hugo was driving. My eyes peered at Joaquin and he assured me Hugo could be trusted, but we thought the same thing about Leonardo and look at how that turned out. The car door closed after Joaquin slid inside and helped me with my seatbelt. He grasped my hand as the car turned into traffic.

"Did they find Leonardo?"

"He's nothing to worry about," Joaquin said, then lifted my hand to press a kiss to my palm.

While he was with me last night, we mainly watched tv and avoided talking about the events that occurred on the boat. I knew it was coming, though, and my stomach clenched in dread.

"He never touched me," I blurted out and waited for his response.

"I know."

"I prayed that you would save me, and things would go back to normal."

"Things would never be normal, Sofia, once I stepped into your life."

"I see that now."

"Do you have regrets?" Joaquin asked as he cupped my chin to stare into my eyes.

I shook my head no.

"I love you, but we need to talk about where things go from

here," I responded, sitting back against the seat as he picked my legs up to massage my feet.

"We move forward together, starting with you moving in with me," Joaquin spoke and my eyes widened in shock.

"What are you talking about?"

"I want you to move in with me."

"Do I have a choice?"

"Sweetheart, you always have a choice, but it's for your protection and my peace of mind."

"You prefer we live together," I stated.

"Yes. Gael found a few places we can go check out this weekend," Joaquin replied as the car stopped in front of my apartment building. I saw Cassidy and Chauncey standing outside.

"What are they doing here?" Joaquin asked as he helped me out of the car.

"I wanted to record some songs. I still need to work, Joaquin," I fussed, pushing him out of the way to walk ahead of him.

"Sweetheart...Sofia, stop walking," he demanded and I stopped.

"Are we interrupting?" Cassidy asked.

"Yes," Joaquin said.

"No, come on up and we can get started." I ignored him and walked them through the lobby and to the elevator.

"How are you feeling, Sofia? I heard about what happened," Chauncey asked.

"Still tired but recovering slowly."

"Glad to hear it, and what about your boyfriend? Is he cool with us being here?" Chauncey inquired.

"This is my home," I said as the elevator doors opened and we stepped off. I walked to my door and unlocked it, sighing in relief at the instantaneous comfort I felt just stepping inside. Feelings of being back home in my own space did something to me. I took a seat on the couch, picked up the pillow and held it against my chest.

"Should we order food? I know you're not up to cooking," Cassidy questioned.

"That's fine, but tell me about Edward. Any news on him?"

Cassidy started to answer when Joaquin stalked inside and glared at me.

"Come talk to me," Joaquin said.

"I'm busy," I responded.

"Sofia, if you expect to have a peaceful evening you need to come and speak with me right now," Joaquin said. I rolled my eyes and jumped up and marched to the back of the apartment away from Cassidy and Chauncey.

"What do you want?"

Joaquin pulled me into his chest, and I hugged him back automatically. He brushed his lips against my shoulder blade, up my neck and down my cheek toward my lips.

"Stop fighting me, sweetheart, I only want the best for you."

"Do you love me?" I questioned.

"Yes. What kind of question is that?"

"Then tell me about Edward."

He sighed and removed his hands from around my waist and sat on the edge of the bed.

"I plan on killing him if I see him," he said and shrugged his shoulders like it was the simplest thing in the world.

"Baby you can't kill him."

"Are you defending him?" Joaquin shouted.

"No, are you crazy? Listen, I want more than anything to see the bastard dead, but he's a very important person. Let the police handle him."

"Sofia, putting the police on him would be a piece of cake. I want him dead now."

"Joaquin."

"No more talking, you need to rest, and I have to leave and handle some business," Joaquin said.

"Are you coming back tonight?" I inquired while I tugged at my earlobe nervously knowing that Edward would be dead soon and it was all my fault.

"I am so don't be long. I want you in bed resting."

"I promise."

"Perfect, I'll leave Alex and Hugo here with you." Joaquin's eyes implored me not to fight him on getting revenge.

"Okay."

He stood and kissed me again and left the bedroom. I followed behind and saw Hugo and Alex already at the door.

"Cassidy, can you order enough food for Alex and Hugo as well please?" I asked and she nodded in answer.

"Joaquin, don't forget what we talked about." He smiled as he strolled out of the apartment as Alex and Hugo stood at the door watching us.

"You guys don't need to stand. Take a seat or something."

"Boss wants us by your side at all times," Hugo mentioned.

"Hugo, please it makes me nervous."

"We'll be outside, call us if you need anything," Hugo stated.

"Thanks."

"Okay, so that was the director. He put a hold on the movie until you're fully recovered," Cassidy commented, and I kicked off my shoes and laid back on the couch.

"First thing I need Cassidy to do is to get my schedule updated. I want to get back to work."

"What about Edward?"

"Fuck Edward, that motherfucker was in on trying to kidnap me."

Cassidy and Chauncey both gasped in surprise.

"Sofia, you can't be serious," Cassidy said.

"Serious as a heart attack."

"I can't believe he would do something so vile," Cassidy stated, wiping away a tear before it fell down her cheek.

"You're not the only one, but Joaquin told me the guy that kidnapped me had help."

"So, Edward wanted you dead. For what reason though?" Cassidy questioned.

"That's some crazy shit, man," Chauncey responded.

"Chauncey, you haven't been around my personal life the way Cassidy is, but Edward wanted me and I rejected him."

"So he decides to plan a kidnapping." Chauncey wrung his hands in front of his body.

"I don't know what he thought he was doing, but he's fired now."

Hugo peeked through the door holding a bag of food. Cassidy took it from him and put everything on the table and I stood up to get plates and utensils from the kitchen. I picked up some bottles of water since I was still recovering and needed to be alert without alcohol in my system. I passed Cassidy and Chauncey the water, she gave me a plate of ribs, baked beans, mac and cheese, and greens. I had my cheat days and it started today until filming started back up.

"I never knew how much I needed this until now," I muttered as I stuffed my face with more baked beans.

"I know you may not think I'm good enough, but what about me managing you?" Cassidy asked.

"That's a lot of responsibility, Cassidy."

"I mean I already help with so much now. I think I can handle more," Cassidy said.

"She helps with the concerts, way more than Edward ever did," Chauncey responded.

"Am I still set for Expressive Designs? I know I missed the launch because of the mess with Joaquin."

"Yeah, I just told the owner you had a family emergency pop up a few days before the launch," Cassidy said.

"Great, put in a call and set a meeting for later this week."

"What about your album?" Chauncey asked.

"Push it back, everything that Edward is behind I want removed," I demanded then took a bite of the short rib.

"What do you think of a photoshoot and interview letting the world know you're back?" Cassidy asked.

"That's fine, do the shoot with a magazine that's friendly to us."

"I have some songs I wrote that I haven't given to anyone else," Chauncey stated, gulping the rest of his water.

"Let me hear them."

"The demo starts a little slow, but it picks up." Chauncey hit the button on his computer and a smooth melody came through. It sounded more jazz and blues rather than old school R&B. I bobbed my head to the lyrics of a woman singing about not needing love anymore and coming into her own.

"I like that, I would want the second verse a little harder."

"That's fine," Chauncey stated.

I grabbed my phone, and checked social media as we continued talking about new changes.

SOFIA

"Hey, Ma," I answered, pointing to a cute dress Cassidy was showing me on her iPad.

"We're back at the hotel, baby. Your father and I wanted to check in on you."

"I'm fine, just sitting here with Cassidy and Chauncey."

"Is that boyfriend of yours around?" she questioned, and I blew out a breath of frustration.

"No, but I want you to have lunch with us this weekend," I stated.

"I'll talk to your father and see how he feels about it," Mom said.

"Thanks, but we know how stubborn your husband can get," I joked before I reached over and grabbed another piece of rib out of the box.

"Keep me updated, sweetie and we'll check in later," Mom said.

"When is your flight back?"

"This weekend, so try not to get caught up with work so we can spend some time together," Mom suggested.

"Okay. Let me call you when I figure out my plans," I said and hung up the phone.

I chuckled thinking about my father fussing about his little girl. That man had been my protector forever and now that someone new was in the picture he'd had to step back. I finished eating and checked the time on my phone then strolled to the kitchen to clean up. I started singing the lyrics to the song that Chauncey played when we heard yelling and gunshots.

Pop! Pop!

"OMG!" Cassidy screamed and dropped to the floor. Chauncey followed suit and I ran back to my couch and grabbed my phone to call Joaquin. As soon as I started to dial his number the door burst open and the man that I now knew as Ciro was standing there.

"We meet again, Miss Chambers," Ciro stated.

"Let them go, it's me you want," I pleaded, speed dialing Joaquin's number. I had him saved as my number one emergency contact.

"Kind of sad your boyfriend left you alone again," Ciro said.

"What's sad is a man taking out his revenge on a woman that had nothing to do with your niece," I spat.

He grinned as he marched into my house with two more men behind him.

"Where's Edward?" I questioned.

"Your little manager friend is hiding from me," Ciro said.

"Look, Joaquin is not here."

"We have some unfinished business, Sofia," Ciro said as he ran his hand across my cheek.

"What happened to Hugo and Alex?"

"They're fine, unless you come with me now."

"No," I said before I head butted him and ran to the kitchen where I grabbed a knife. He was a little dazed, but I was able to put some distance between us. One of his men grabbed Cassidy by the arm and stood her up.

"If you don't want anything to happen to your little friend," Ciro threatened through gritted teeth.

"Let them go first," I responded as I waved the knife back and forth.

"I'm running this show, Miss Chambers," Ciro said.

I glanced over at Chauncey and one of the guys kicked him in the stomach.

"Stop!" I yelled.

"That's for disobeying me," Ciro said.

"You son of a bitch." I lunged at him and he caught my wrist and twisted my hand making me drop the knife. I clenched my left hand and punched him in the nose and kneed him in the balls.

"You bitch!" Ciro shouted and tried to grab for me again and I picked up his gun.

"I'm only going to say this once. Let my friends go or I'll kill you."

"Sofia! Sofia!" I heard Joaquin call out.

"In here!" I replied. He rushed through the door with Gabriella and Gael. It was a full-on standoff in the room. Cassidy and Chauncey were bystanders in the bullshit of my life that came with dating Joaquin.

"Baby put the gun down," Joaquin said and I shook my head no.

"I want him to leave and take his men with him," I said as tears fell down my cheeks.

"You have no idea who you're messing with, little girl," Ciro stated. I shot a little above his head and everyone ducked.

"Get out," I snapped then pointed the gun right in between his eyes. I grew up in the South; I wasn't afraid of guns. My father taught me how to protect myself, I just chose not to carry a gun in New York.

"I can handle it from here, sweetheart," Joaquin stated, before he motioned for them all to leave. They released Chauncey and Cassidy while Gael checked on Hugo outside of the door. Joaquin started to come toward me and I held my hand up to stop him.

"Leave."

"What?"

"I said leave, Joaquin. This is too much for me."

"You don't get to decide that," Joaquin spat.

"Like hell I don't, they just burst into my home and tried to kill me and my friends."

"Sofia, baby, you're scared, I get that. Leaving me is not an option," Joaquin said. He tried to come close and I held the gun up. His eyes widened in surprise.

"Sofia," Gael said.

"No, I want you gone. My life was simple before this bullshit came around."

"I'm not leaving you."

"Then I'll leave." I started to walk off and he grabbed my arm stopping me.

"Wait! Wait... Shushhhh."

"Just go, Joaquin."

"I'll give you some space, but we're not through."

"Take care of Hugo," I stated and placed Ciro's gun in his hand. I ran over to Chauncey and Cassidy to make sure they were okay. Gael talked Joaquin into leaving before he blew up even further. I could see in his eyes when everything went blank that he was ready to become this Ghost person. Maybe my parents were right, and I needed to get the police involved, because Ciro didn't care where I lived and who I was with. All he wanted was to get revenge by any means for his dead niece. Everyone left and an hour later I was soaking in the tub with my eyes closed thinking about how I went from preparing to go out to dinner with my boyfriend on a boat to being kidnapped, shot at, jumped in freezing cold temperatures. Rescued then almost kidnapped again. I could probably write a book about my life at this point. I pulled the plug and stepped out, dried off and removed the wrap from around my hair. I already brushed my teeth before getting in the tub, so I just lotioned up and jumped into bed then checked a few messages.

Joaquin: I'll give you space for now.

Me: It doesn't work like that.

Joaquin: Try me.

I let out a harsh breath and turned my light off in my bedroom and sunk deeper under the covers. I wouldn't let Joaquin's possessive ways get to me any longer. My mind was made up and I might even start to see other people.

Joaquin: Goodnight beautiful.

...

The next morning I blinked my eyes open slowly, feeling like someone was watching me. I adjusted in the bed, wiped the crust out of my eyes, and looked over to the couch under the window. I got it several months ago so I'd have something for me to sit on and read. I jumped when I saw Joaquin staring back at me, wearing the same clothes from yesterday.

"What are you doing here?" I muttered groggily, sitting up against the headboard.

"I needed to make sure you were safe."

"No, you're doing the control bullshit again. I'm fine, you can leave now."

He leaned over, clasping his hands together.

"You know why I pursued you?" Joaquin asked as he stared into my eyes.

I turned my head, not wanting to deal with more stress. I was planning on meeting with Cassidy today at a photo studio to get my life started back up and running.

"Joaquin."

"I wanted you the moment I saw your smile," he spoke.

"What do you mean? We only bumped into each other at the restaurant."

"I stood outside of the door and watched you have lunch with Edward for a few minutes and something made you smile. Your presence stilled me, calmed the noise in my head," Joaquin stated and stood up slowly.

"I think it's best we both focus on other things and get space. I need to get my career on track," I said, pushed the covers back, stood up and made the bed.

"You can have your space, but I want you to have security at all times."

"That's not necessary," I replied as I walked to the bathroom and turned the light on.

"Edward is still involved somehow and Ciro is still missing," Joaquin responded, standing at the door of the bathroom.

I started to brush my hair up into a bun then tied a scarf around it to keep it from getting wet.

We stared at each other through the mirror.

"I trust you'll find him, but I'm not stopping my life or career."

"Sofia," he groaned and started to come closer. I held my hand up to stop him from getting closer to talk me out of wanting space.

"Cassidy is meeting me at the studio, I can't do this with you right now," I told him, and removed my nightshirt, standing naked in front of him as I closed the door in his face.

An hour later I jumped out of the cab and headed inside of the photo studio texting Cassidy to make sure she was here.

"Sofia!" Cassidy called out.

I waved and she came over with the designer of the clothing brand we signed a contract with to become their brand ambassador. With me going back into the studios, and finally getting back into acting, hopefully I could put this nightmare of the past few days behind me.

"Hey Maggie, thanks again for pushing back the shoot," I said, removing my jacket. She was around my age, maybe a few years older. Shorter in height and with an athletic build, she reminded me of a younger Serena Williams mixed with Jill Scott. Someone that loved working out, but was still laid-back and doesn't get overly stressed about things.

"When we heard everything that was happening, we wanted to make sure your safety and recovery was first," Maggie, the owner and designer of Expressive Designs, said.

"Maggie and the team were really supportive and sent flowers to the hospital," Cassidy remarked. I held my hand up to my heart thanking her for the support.

"What's the plan for today? Cassidy said you looked at the notes we sent over."

"Yes we did and I know you recently came out of the hospital so we'll need to do alterations in the moment," she replied and we headed to through the lobby of the photography studio that Expressive Designs built for their company. The colors matched the brand with maroon, orange, and black. The front held a wall display with mannequins wearing the latest fashions. There was a huge tv on the wall with the fashion show that debuted the collection. She escorted us back to the makeup area. It brought back memories of the situation with the bomb scare and I felt a little jittery, but I didn't want to alarm anyone and end the shoot before it started.

"Today is mostly shots of you wearing each outfit as a test look," Maggie said, showing off the pieces that were hanging on the rack next to us. The photographer was setting up shots with his crew as the makeup artist strolled in from the back employee section with more lights.

"Bridget, you remember Sofia and Cassidy right?" Maggie asked and Bridget held her hand out and we shook.

"I'm a huge fan of yours, Sofia. Are you working on another album?" Bridget asked.

"Most definitely am, my fans have hounded me enough," I joked as we all laughed in conjunction.

Cassidy stood on the right side of me with her phone and iPad out.

"I forwarded all of your emails to me now. So far, I've spoken with your lawyer and accountants," Cassidy rattled off.

"Can I get some water?" I asked Cassidy and she grabbed a bottle of water from the craft table.

For today's shoot the setup was a white and gold backdrop with me standing in the front of the Expressive Designs logo.

"I have the first two outfits. A legging one-piece jumper set that we can interchange," Maggie commented, holding up the two outfits.

"I didn't need to do too much on you, Sofia. You can get dressed now," Bridget said.

"Perfect, thanks, Bridget." I took another sip of water and stood up, grabbed the pantsuit and walked into the dressing room to change.

I slipped on the maroon and black suit with the side belts hanging and large pockets. The wardrobe stylist dropped down to the floor to help me slip on the shoes, then touched up my hair.

"We're ready for you, Sofia," Tobias, the photographer, said and I strolled toward the front of the backdrop. Cassidy took shots on her phone for social media.

Tobias motioned for me to put my hands on my waist and turn to the left side, while looking directly into the camera. The flash of the camera went off as the music turned on with Jazzmen Sullivan playing in the background.

"Nice, Sofia, like that, keep going," Tobias said as he turned the camera sideways then moved in closer toward me.

I squatted down on my knees with my hands on top, looking directly into the camera.

"Stay like that, show you're a badass," Tobias announced.

"Let me get a photo we can use for your social media header," Cassidy insisted. She walked next to the photographer to grab the shot.

"Check out what we have so far," Maggie remarked, standing behind the video monitor.

Bridget strolled over and checked my makeup and passed me a bottle of water. I felt renewed and vibrant with getting things moving in the right direction for my career.

"Cassidy, can you pass my phone please?" I said.

"Sure, here you go," Cassidy replied. She marched to my purse, lifted my phone out of my purse and brought it to me. I checked for messages and nothing was there from Joaquin so I guessed he got the message that I wanted to be alone and focus on my work.

"Anything major?" Cassidy wondered, taking the phone back.

"Nope, quiet thank goodness. Maggie should I change?" I questioned.

"Yep, do the sports bra and pants," Maggie responded as she grabbed the pants and shirt for me to change.

I slipped into the dressing room and changed into the next outfit while Tobias set up the next shot. It had more lighting and a short box for me to step up on.

"Sofia, can I get you to put one foot up on the box and turn your body facing the wall?" Tobias asked.

Once I was in the position he requested, I checked to make sure my breasts looked good then smoothed my hand down to make sure all the lint was gone.

"Ready," I said.

Tobias picked up the camera again and started taking shots. I put my right arm on top of my left, then smiled into the camera.

"Looking good, Sofia," Tobias said. Bridget stepped into the frame to add gold bronzer to my back. The next four hours went well and everyone decided to go out and have a few drinks together to celebrate. It was me, Maggie, Cassidy, Tobias, and Bridget that jumped into his car and headed to Bar One. I put the hood over my head to keep the photographers from noticing me as the crowd grew bigger.

"Welcome to Bar One. Are you looking for a booth or did you want to sit at the bar?" the hostess stated.

Bar One was the spot that all of Hollywood and the music industry came to hang out. They had it decorated with clear glass throughout the room. Gold lights hung throughout the club. The bar sat in the middle of the entire room with four televisions mounted around and the DJ had his own stage set up in the corner pumping music.

"Booth please," Maggie said, and the hostess motioned for us to follow her to the back booth in the corner.

"OMG! It's Sofia Chambers." A girl wearing next to nothing in a skimpy dress tried to come over for a hug and Tobias blocked her from moving in close.

SOFIA

I scooted into the corner and Tobias squeezed in next to me. The hostess placed drink menus down for us as the bass of the music started to pick up. Different strobe lights flashed around the room with women getting up out of their seats. I could see people in the VIP area in the top level throwing drinks in the air.

"Today was great, Sofia, we need to set up another one with you," Tobias muttered in my ear over the loud music.

"Set it up with Cassidy, I like the way you guys work and don't hang around wasting time," I said, as the hostess brought over a bottle of Ace of Spades and a martini.

"We didn't order this," Cassidy said to the hostess.

"This was a gift from the owner," the hostess said.

"Who's the owner?" Tobias queried, happily opening the bottle.

"Mr. Fuertes," she said, and I almost spit the drink out. Everybody peered at me while I scanned the room trying to see if Joaquin was nearby.

"Is he here?" I asked her.

"No, he saw you on the monitor remotely," she replied.

"That's your boyfriend, right?" Tobias questioned.

"No. It's a complicated situation," I replied.

"We saw on the news about your kidnapping," Bridget brought up and Maggie glared at her.

"What?" Bridget asked. Her expression was perplexed as if she couldn't understand why Maggie would be upset.

She didn't seem like the type of person that was aloof or just gossiped about things back at the studio; now that we were not on set she must have felt more comfortable.

"That's not your business, Bridget," Maggie told her.

"Sorry, I mean it's all over the news about you dating some big time cartel boss," Bridget commented.

"The media is always twisting stories," I said.

"We should make a toast, to a successful launch and new album, Sofia," Cassidy said, raising her glass in the air. The rest of us joined in and clinked glasses. I chuckled at Cassidy dancing in her seat.

"Come on, Sofia, you should let loose a little," Cassidy suggested and pointed to the dance floor.

"I'm not really dressed to be seen. You go ahead... I'll stay relaxing with a drink." I sipped the rest of the dry martini down and waved for the bar girl to bring me another one.

"I'll go with you," Bridget responded and Maggie let Cassidy out of the booth and the three of them switched to the dance floor.

"You have to excuse Bridget," Tobias commented.

"She's curious like everyone else. No worries," I responded. Maggie and I continued glancing around, observing the other patrons.

Tobias stretched his arm out on the back of the booth and smiled. He was tall with a nicely trimmed beard, full lips, and dark brown skin. He reminded me of the actor Morris Chestnut with the low cut waves.

"Tell me about yourself, Sofia," Tobias said.

"Not much to tell, I'm an actress and singer. Trying to make it in New York," I responded.

"What do you find harder, singing, or acting?" Tobias investigated, nudging me in the arm.

"Probably singing, since it's more intimate."

"You do have a beautiful voice," Tobias replied and smiled.

"Are you flirting with me?"

"Is it working?" he replied as we both broke out in laughter.

My eyes raised in shock when Hugo and Gael stepped in front of the booth. I looked around for Joaquin wondering if he saw us and thought this was a date. Gael cleared his throat and glared at Tobias.

"How are you, Sofia?" Gael asked.

"Gael, no."

"He's not here. We just wanted to make sure you're okay, with your new friend," Gael spoke.

"Who are you?" Tobias asked while trying to stand up out of the booth. Hugo pushed him back down.

"Hey!" Tobias shouted.

"I wouldn't raise my voice in someone's business establishment, sir," Gael suggested with a harsh glare on his face.

"Gael, I'm hanging with friends. Tell him to back off."

"You know we can't do that," Gael answered.

"Ohh... look what we have here," Monica said as she walked up with a group of women behind her.

"I don't have time for this." I rubbed the temples of my forehead.

"Monica, you know you're not allowed here," Gael said.

"I can do what I want, Gael, Joaquin doesn't run me like his little bitch over there," Monica spat, and I tried to jump up and punch her in the face. Tobias held me around the waist and pulled me back down.

"Is this the new boyfriend? I guess you couldn't take Joaquin's lifestyle," Monica responded.

"Get out of here," Gael said.

"No, I'll leave. I had no idea he owned this place," I said.

"Sofia, we can go somewhere else," Tobias mentioned, getting out of the booth to help me up. I didn't have the heart to tell him that I was very much still in love with Joaquin. Dating anyone new right now wouldn't help me at all with the press still hounding me and me trying to get back to work.

"She's not leaving with you," Gael announced and stepped in front of Tobias.

"Tobias, he's right. I can't leave with you. I'll be fine."

"Are you sure?" Tobias queried; Hugo tried to shove him away when he grasped my elbow.

"Hugo, stop it!" I shouted and pointed at Gael.

"Tobias we'll talk. Send Cassidy the edits for approval."

"Hey, are you leaving?" Cassidy came over, fanning herself.

"Yeah, I'm tired, and it's getting crowded," I fussed as I rolled my eyes at Monica who was whispering in her friend's ear and laughing.

"I'll leave with you," Cassidy said, and grabbed her things off the table.

"I have a car out front," Gael stated as he motioned to follow him and I stormed out to the car he had out front. He chuckled and I wanted to smack that smirk off his face.

"Have you talked to Alessandra?" I asked and the smirk washed off his face.

"You play, Sofia," Gael spoke as he opened the door for me to get inside. I looked around to make sure Joaquin wasn't there.

"I haven't talked to her since before the kidnapping."

He closed the door and walked around to the passenger of the SUV and Hugo slid the key into the ignition and drove off into traffic.

"She moved here to the city. She's taking fashion classes," Gael said.

"Oh."

"What's your name?" Cassidy remarked as she tapped Hugo on the shoulder.

"He doesn't like to talk," Gael responded, and Hugo looked through the rearview mirror at Cassidy. I wanted to laugh at the grimace that had crossed Hugo's face at Gael's answer. Cassidy seemed to not care at all because she checked her makeup in the mirror.

"Finally."

"Let Hugo walk you up," Gael said, and I shook my head no.

"We'll be fine and make sure to tell your friend he doesn't have to send drinks over anymore," I said. Cassidy opened the rear passenger side door and I climbed out.

"Sofia, you're being unreasonable," Gael said as he leaned over the car door.

"I might be, but your boy should keep his little fling under control."

"You know she doesn't mean anything to him," Gael told me.

"Goodnight, Gael." I waved him off and stalked in the apartment building with Cassidy behind me.

Cassidy came in behind me and dropped down on the couch and I locked the door, kicked my shoes off and dropped my jacket on the couch. I headed to the kitchen and grabbed a bottle of water to work through the alcohol.

"You can crash in the guest bedroom," I said and shut the fridge.

"Uhhh...huh," Cassidy replied, snorting a little as I laughed. I strolled to my bedroom with my purse to check for any messages. I took my phone out and saw Joaquin had sent a text message.

Joaquin: Dinner tomorrow.

Me: No.

Joaquin: You have fun tonight?

Me: Goodnight Joaquin.

JOAQUIN

A month later.

The last time I spoke to her was the night I texted to go out to dinner. I wanted to work on what was broken between us and figure out a compromise. In her mind we were broken up, but I let her think this for now until she was fully healed from everything. After today there would be no more being apart now that I'd found a home for us to live together. There was so much going on in my life from my sister living here now to my parents constantly wanting to know what my plans were with Sofia. Surprisingly my father was coming around to liking Sofia now and I'd been told my sister had hung out with Sofia and Cassidy a few times since she moved back here. Today I woke up with an agenda and a plan to end the drama in Sofia's and my life for good. It would only happen after I took out the trash that kept popping up so I called to have dinner with Monica and she jumped at the chance to see me again. When I got word she was at Bar One and got in Sofia's face I wanted to strangle her right then and there if I didn't already have a plan to get rid of any obstacles that stood in our way as a couple. I had Gael and Hugo already at the bar doing a drop off, and I had cameras set up on my phone to monitor all my businesses. To see

Sofia walk in with another man was a hit to my ego, but I needed to stay calm and not overreact like I usually did. The plan for today should be enough to show Sofia I was serious about what I wanted and nothing would get in the middle of us ever again. The car stopped in front of Antonio's with Hugo and Gael following me inside.

"Make sure you call your sister. Something about dinner as a family," Gael spoke, as the door opened and I buttoned my suit jacket. I had Bruno close the restaurant down for me to have this conversation privately. I noticed Monica in the back at the private section with a closed off door, but the window was glass. People could only see in the back, but not hear.

"Is she all right?"

"She's having lunch with Sofia," Gael said and I nodded in excitement. Alessandra knew how much Sofia meant to me and if she could convince her to put the past behind us, then I wouldn't have to have more bloodshed in the city.

"Text and tell her to check my calendar," I responded as I slid the door of the private room to the side and Monica grinned before she stood up to give me a kiss as I motioned to stay seated.

"I missed you, Joaquin," Monica whined as she licked her lips.

"Give us a few minutes, Gael, before we order lunch."

Gael turned and left the room to stand at the door.

"I knew you would be back," Monica stated, shifting her glass of wine back and forth.

"You're right."

Monica extended her hand and stroked the top of my palm.

"So that means you're finished with that tramp Sofia," Monica said.

"Do you enjoy the wine?" I questioned as I pushed the glass closer toward her.

"I did, it's one of my favorites. You remembered, baby," Monica spoke while a nervous smile played along the edges of her full lips.

"Always remember a predictable bitch."

"Whattt…" Monica stuttered in shock.

"In about a minute your body should lock up on you. Because of the drug I had put in your wine."

Her eyes popped wide.

"What did you do?" She tried to lift her hand to her throat but was frozen in place.

"It's an odorless, tasteless drug that should keep you from moving so my men can take you away without restraint."

A tear started to fall down her check.

"Please…" Monica whispered slowly, her lips not moving.

"All you had to do was leave things alone. What we had was only sex."

A small screech started to come through her voice.

"Save your voice. They can't hear you and even if they did, no one is coming."

The door opened with Hugo and Gael coming inside and I lifted her up out of the seat by her arms as her eyes darted back and forth in fear.

"How much did you give her?" Gael questioned.

"Enough to stabilize her until you get her to the warehouse."

"I paid off a photographer and got word that Edward was out in New Jersey," Gael spoke, carrying Monica out the back of the restaurant.

Carlo came from the back of the office with some papers in his hand.

"What's all this?" Carlo inquired as Hugo loaded Monica in the back of the white van.

"Taking out the trash."

"You get word on Ciro and her ex manager?" Carlo asked.

"Headed to the third stop now," I said and started to walk out through the exit.

"Try to keep your emotions under control, Joaquin!" Carlo yelled out and I waved him off.

I jumped in the second car with Gael as we followed Hugo and Gabriella in the white van.

"She misses you," Gael announced through the silence.

"Did you send a message to her little photographer friend?" I asked.

They turned down the street heading onto the freeway.

"A quiet message, but deadly warning," Gael responded, and I pulled my phone out of my pocket to see a message from Sofia.

My wife: You're a complete asshole.

I smirked at her text message.

Me: How can that be if we haven't spoken in a month?

My wife: Gael threatened Tobias.

Me: I had nothing to do with that.

My wife: I don't believe you.

Me: Go out to dinner with me.

My wife: I have dinner plans already.

Seeing her reply about having dinner plans caused a lump in my throat. Maybe it was with my sister and I was overreacting.

Me: With who?

My wife: None of your business asshole.

Me: Sofia, I don't like secrets, beautiful.

My wife: Good, because I don't like arrogant, jealous, assholes that try to boss me around.

"Ughhh..." I groaned and closed out of my text messages to check her location from the tracker. It showed she was on set filming. She might have made that statement to throw me off and get under my skin.

Me: Soon we'll be together again.

My wife: No. I'm done with you and you can tell all of your henchmen to stay away.

I chuckled at her last text and closed out of my phone as the car stopped at a house out in the suburbs of New Jersey. It was mid-day so the neighbors weren't going to be around to hear anything or see anything they shouldn't.

"He should be coming out to take the trash to the curb. You want us to grab him then?" Gael asked.

"Is that his car in the driveway?" I questioned, seeing a black Lexus jeep parked.

"Yeah, based on the license plate he got it two months ago," Gael responded.

"Have Hugo slash the tires and cut all the lights out," I said, opening the glove compartment to grab my black gloves and silencer.

"We're taking him alive right?" Gael asked.

"Depends on how I feel when I see his face." I shrugged, opened the car door, stepped out and looked around.

I walked around to the back of the house with Gael while Hugo went to slash the tires and Gabriella stood at the front door monitoring things. I peered through the side window, noticed it was the kitchen and his back was to me. I motioned for Gael to follow and we headed to the back door and slowly slid it open since the music was loud and he was obviously in his own thoughts. I eased into the hallway, looked to my right, then left to see if another person was around. Feeling more confident that the place was secure, I tapped Gael to check the rest of the house while I confronted Edward. I strolled into the kitchen calmly and he still wasn't noticing anything while the music was blasting loud. I turned the button down low and he jumped in fright.

"Shit!" Edward shouted.

"Edward."

"Uh… I can explain," Edward said.

"Can you?" I questioned and sat down at the kitchen table.

"Listen, I was looking out for Sofia's safety. Ciro said he worked for you," Edward told me.

I grinned, letting him fall into more rabbit holes of lies. Gael made an appearance on the other side of Edward as he tried to back up out of the kitchen.

"Edward have a seat."

"I...I...please, man," Edward stated, fidgeting with his hands.

"Edward, I wasn't asking."

Gael pushed him forward and Edward took a seat in front of me.

"I think we got off on the wrong foot. Do you agree?"

Edward looked behind himself, then back at me.

"Yes."

"The one thing I asked you to do was not to get involved in my business."

"I didn't know he would kidnap Sofia," Edward explained.

"Silence!" I slammed my hand on the top of the table.

"Please don't kill me, I'm a high-profile person. The cops will come looking for you," Edward said before he tried to rush to grab the butter knife. I grabbed his wrist and twisted it back.

"Aghhh!!! Please…" Edward screamed, falling to the floor.

"Gael," I said and he stalked over and stabbed Edward with the same poison in his neck.

"We need to hurry up before Monica comes out of it," Gael mentioned and I agreed.

"The faster we get this done, the sooner we can get Ciro finished."

Gael and I lifted Edward off the floor, carried his body through the front door and put him inside the van. The house was locked up by Gabriella as we loaded up to leave.

...

Two hours later I was sitting with both Monica and Edward hung up on chains naked in my warehouse. I stared at them both as they started to come out of the poison. They still couldn't move, but they could talk.

"Arghhh…Joaquin, I love you," Monica screamed and cried trying to get me to let her go. I picked up the machete and walked up to Monica as she tried to get out of the chains, but there was no leaving this building besides in a body bag.

"You had your chance, now you must die."

"Please…I beg you, let me go and you won't hear from me again," Monica pleaded as I ran my hand across her thigh. I used to enjoy what was between them, but the sight only brought misery and regret now.

"That I doubt, but I will give you a choice."

"Anything, I'll take it," Monica said, not knowing what I was about to bring up.

"Then you'll die second." I waved the machete in the air.

"Ahhh…" she gasped as I plunged the machete across Edward's chest. As blood spilled out, Monica started crying and throwing up as Edward screamed and passed out.

"No one can hear you, Monica." I took Edward's legs off, then dropped the machete to the floor, wiped the sweat off with the handkerchief from my pocket.

"Joaquin, you know me," Monica cried out as I started to walk toward her.

"You know I don't tolerate disrespect." I grasped the bottom of her chin and stared into her eyes.

"I don't want to die," Monica whimpered.

"Should have thought about that before confronting my wife."

"You…You…Aghhhh," she screamed as the snake I picked up out of the box that Gael brought out and placed next to her feet slid around.

"Don't fight it, let it happen naturally," I said as I placed the snake in a bag. Gael lowered her down from the chain and the bag went over her head as she screamed and cried.

"Aghhhh…" Monica twitched, then her limp body fell over.

"Finish her off," I said and left the warehouse to hop in my car to go home and shower. Forty minutes after making it home at the new house I received a message from my tech guy that Ciro was spotted coming out of the hotel. Antonio said his people were watching him and this was my chance to grab him without interruption.

I dialed Gael's number while I hopped in the shower.

"Yeah," Gael said, with loud music coming through the phone.

"Our guest arrived today," I said in code through the phone.

"Perfect, I'll have dinner reservations texted to you," Gael responded and hung up before I could ask about the music in the background. I had a weird feeling so I called my sister.

"Joaquin! I miss you," Alessandra said excitedly. Loud background music made it difficult to hear her.

"Where are you, Alessandra?" I questioned, giving her a chance to be honest.

"Out with friends," she replied.

"What friends?" I turned the knob up hotter, to let the steam fill the room.

"Some friends from school," Alessandra spoke.

"We'll do lunch and I want to meet these friends," I said.

"Joaquin."

"Yes, princess?"

"I have to tell you something," Alessandra muttered lowly.

"Over lunch, we'll talk and tell your friend or friends that if you're hurt in any way…"

"I'm fine and my friend is sweet."

"I'll talk to you later," I said and hung up.

JOAQUIN

*M*idnight.

I was parked outside of Sofia's apartment fresh from getting changed and showered. My thoughts were on hearing my sister over the phone wanting to meet for lunch and tell me something that I already suspected. The thought of her being with a man that was like me, and I thought of as a brother had caused a knot in my stomach. Gael was just as ruthless and only leveled me out when I went too far, but we had many years of drinking, women, and killings between us. Now to see him possibly want to start something with my little sister was unnerving.

I removed the key out of the car, got out and headed into her building. I nodded at the receptionist and security guard. I'd paid them to keep an eye on when she comes and goes. The people that enter the building had all been checked out with a background report. After the shit with Edward I wasn't taking another chance on something else happening to her until I could convince her to move with me to our new house. I stepped on the elevator, hit the button for her floor as the doors closed and I saw my reflection in the door. I was a man that was relentless and heartless for the past few years until she stepped into my life.

Beep!

The elevator dinged and I got off chuckling at her probably being in bed snoring. I pulled the key I had made out, opened the door, then locked it behind me.

I removed my jacket and kicked my shoes off in the hallway.

Her door was partially open, but her light was off. I slowly eased inside and watched as her chest moved up and down slowly as she lightly snored. I dropped my jeans and t-shirt on the floor only wearing my boxers and pulled the covers back gently admiring her naked frame.

I exhaled a long sigh of contentment. The prolonged anticipation of wanting to be back in her arms, and her sweet, warm sex caused my dick to twitch. I crawled in on the side of her body, and slowly glided my hand down her chest, to her stomach, and thigh. Her eyes blinked slowly, but she didn't move.

I leaned over and kissed her shoulder.

"Sweetheart," I whispered, then pressed a kiss behind her ear as she moaned.

"Mmmm... Joaquin," she faintly said with her eyes closed.

"Baby, I want you to come home." I trailed my tongue across her shoulder, down her chest to her nipple.

"Ssss...mmmm," she moaned.

"I miss tasting you."

"Ughhh..." she cried out with her eyes still closed.

"Can I taste you baby?" I asked as I dipped my index finger in her fat, wet sex.

"Arhghh...fuck...Yes, Joaquin." She opened her legs wider.

Her eyes popped open. The sound of her voice affected me deeply, each time I saw her the pull was stronger. My fingers softly caressed her body as I sealed my mouth over hers.

"Mmmmmm..." I groaned and pushed my boxers down lower as her arms wrapped around my neck.

"Yes...Yes..." Sofia cried out as I eased in at a slow pace. I hadn't been with her since before the incident or any woman because no one else could cause this deep longing and feeling of happiness. She folded one leg over my back, and I bent at the knees, with my head back as I thrusted my hips forward.

"Ughhh...fuck," I murmured, grabbing the top of the comforter with my right hand. Beads of sweat popped out on my forehead. Her soft curves molded to the contours of my lean body.

I watched her carefully from the corner of my eyes.

"Joaquin," she called out.

"Shushhh."

I captured her mouth in a slow, affectionate kiss. She clutched at my arms, pulled me in closer as I pushed in deeper.

"Ohhh...God."

"I love you, Sofia. Sweetheart, you're my wife," I said as I dipped my head down to taste her nipples again. I felt a primal ownership now; a deep powerful surge started to explode. My strokes became erratic, as she ground her pelvis against my groin.

"Yeah...Tell me again," she demanded as she ran her long nails up my chest. My knee nudged her legs wider as wetness seeped out and I let out a raw groan as our thrusts became rhythmic. Her pussy squeezed my dick and I had to pull out fast before I came too early and taste her. I was rock hard as I sucked on her clit and the dam of her release broke in a frenzy of need and desire.

"Baby...Joaquin...Ahhh," Sofia cried out.

"Move in with me." I smacked her gently on the ass. She grabbed the tip of my head and ground herself against my tongue.

"Joaquin."

"Move in with me, sweetheart, you'll have this every night." I grazed against her sensitive center as she shivered in my hold. I pushed back inside picked up my pace, drove faster, hearing our groans and cries of pleasure until she came and cried out my name. A second later my dick swelled and I released inside of her feeling worn out and exhausted. I fell on top of her, kissed all over her face and lips.

"Move in with me please, baby."

"Okay," she responded and fell back to sleep. I smirked hearing her snores and fell to the side of the bed and pulled the covers up, wrapping her under my arms. We both had a lot to talk about in the morning and hopefully this wasn't just sex for her. I planned on making her my wife officially with the Fuertes last name.

* * *

I GOT UP EXTRA EARLY to have breakfast delivered and coffee ready to keep her from running out and avoiding the conversation. I had pancakes, waffles, eggs, fruit, and toast, with juice and oatmeal if she didn't want a big meal. I showered in the guest room as not to wake her up. I cut the toast in half and grabbed the butter to put on the table.

"Morning," I said as I stared at the most beautiful angel that had a harsh grimace on her face.

"What happened to space, Joaquin?" Sofia mentioned, wearing only my t-shirt that I had left here a few months back.

"You look good in my shirt. I was wondered where I left it."

"Don't change the subject. I want my key back."

"That's fine, let the landlord know you'll give your notice today," I replied as I poured orange juice in a glass, and held it out for her.

"I'm not moving."

"Yes you are," I said.

"Did you find Ciro and Edward?" she questioned.

"I did, but I wanted you to move in even before this happened."

I dropped the spatula, strolled over, and wrapped my arms around her waist.

"Last night you agreed, sweetheart." I kissed the nape of her neck.

"I was in the heat of the moment."

I sighed, pressed my forehead against hers.

"I love you and being apart has only caused problems."

"For me or you?" she asked as she peered up into my eyes.

"Me, I need you and not being able to see you, talk to you is not good for my heart."

211

"I thought you didn't do love, this was just a fling," she spoke before she stepped out of my hold.

"What are you saying?"

"Are you really in love with me or is this just about in-house pussy?" she probed, took a bite of the toast and sat down.

"If it was just about sex, do you think I would buy a house?"

She choked on the orange juice and I patted her back.

"Hold up, you bought a house? When?"

"It was going to be a surprise during the boat trip, but things went off plan."

"What about kids? We didn't use protection last night," she asked.

"I want children with you."

"Did you kill Edward and Ciro?" she questioned.

"That's something you don't have to worry about."

"For us to move forward I need you to be honest with me."

"I took care of our problems, that's all you need to know."

"Monica?"

"A faded memory." I pushed my chair next to hers and started to fill my plate with food.

"What do your parents think about this?"

"Sweetheart, you ask too many questions," I said, and kissed the top of her nose.

"Where is the house located?" she asked.

"New Jersey in a gated community and you'll have a car driving you around."

"I have to go back on set in a few days with Dante."

"I understand, my men won't cause a problem."

"I haven't agreed to anything yet. This doesn't mean I'm going to fall back into your charms," she spat as she rolled her eyes.

"Would you like some more convincing?" I teased, as I pinched her nipple through the shirt.

"No, you're on probation."

"What!" I shouted and she bent over laughing.

I grabbed her up and carried her to the couch and tickled her stomach and side.

"Okay, okay. I'll move in, but you have to meet with my parents for dinner soon," Sofia explained and I agreed with a kiss.

"My sister wants to hang out. Can you meet with her for lunch or something?" I said while I pushed a piece of hair out of her face.

"I knew she was back and in school, we made plans to have lunch."

"When were you going to tell me?"

"I didn't think I needed to tell you. Everywhere I go your men follow."

"For your protection, baby."

"Is Antonio like this with Sabrina?" she asked.

"Like what?"

"Crazy, possessive, arrogant, bossy," she rattled off.

"Is that your description of me?"

"What would you call it?" she replied as she eased her hands up my chest.

"I would say a man that was so struck by your intelligence, beauty, and confidence that he needed to know everything about her."

"What conclusion did you come up with?"

"Love."

"Love doesn't hurt, Joaquin."

"My love is pure, Sofia, but it can be dangerous when someone hurts what I love."

"Has the Cartel ruined you?"

"How is your music coming along?" I questioned to change the subject.

"I need to set up studio time with Chauncey, mostly been working on modeling for now."

"You're a natural."

"Thank you."

"Let's finish breakfast and then you can tell me all about the music and acting."

"I'm not hungry anymore," Sofia spoke.

"You want to go see the house?" I asked.

She shook her head no and slid her palm further down in my boxers.

SOFIA

The intensity in his eyes bore into mine. I reached up to grab his face with my free hand and kiss his lips. Last night, I couldn't fight the pent-up anger inside of me. I can admit I missed him and loved when we just sat around and talked about life. I knew some people would look at him as some thug, but he was everything I wanted and needed. Putting the walls back up and pushing him away would only cause us heartache and living life without the one you loved because of ego and pride was a crutch of a burden. His breath tickled my neck as I felt his first stroke. Dark curly hair smelled like my strawberry shampoo that I kept in the guest shower. His hands slid over my waist, as I clutched at his back.

"Fuck! Sofia."

I teased his mouth as his hands gripped my breasts under my shirt.

"Yess...Ohhh."

"Baby."

My concentration was scattered as his pace picked up and my belly quivered. Hot tingles were shooting up and down my spine.

"Joaquin, don't stop!" I cried out.

The rush of his kiss, the intensity of his hands all over my body;

it was coming too fast and hard. Molding our flesh together was the ultimate spark that gave me a rush of excitement since the first time we made love.

A low groan left his lips.

"Ughhh…"

"I love you, Joaquin," I whimpered as he drove deeper. My climax surged through me as I screamed in ecstasy.

"Ahhhh…I'm coming."

"Fuck! Me too, sweetheart."

"Shittt…" I could feel the tremors of his release as he fell forward and clutched me tighter. He kissed me on the lips and looked down between us. He licked his lips and eased a finger across the head of his base with remnants of our orgasm and brought it to my lips. I stuck my tongue out, he eased his finger in slowly, never taking my eyes off of him as I tasted us together.

"I'm never letting you go again," he spoke.

I knew he was serious this time and by the way he avoided telling me how he killed Edward and Monica, meant Joaquin went off the rails when I wasn't around.

"Kiss me?" I asked, and he bent down like he was about to kiss me and then bit my upper lip.

"Don't ever think this is over, beautiful. Space doesn't exist in my world," Joaquin commented as he gently brushed his tongue around my bottom lip. I glided my hand up around his neck, he smirked as I gently squeezed.

"I know you're crazy, but I can get even crazier, Mr. Fuertes."

* * *

TWO HOURS later after eating breakfast and going for a second round on the couch and floor, I left Joaquin sleeping in bed and I met up with Alessandra, Sabrina, and Janice at the house Joaquin purchased. I texted Cassidy to meet me there since she'd need to help me with finding an interior designer. Hugo drove across town getting on the highway after picking up Alessandra.

"How are you liking fashion school?" I asked.

"I wish I had done it sooner. Sofia, it's amazing and the people I get to meet," Alessandra rushed out.

"How many classes are you taking?"

"Right now, I'm taking three. Joaquin and my parents want me to be available for family events," Alessandra responded, rolled her eyes.

"What's that look?" I chuckled at her pretending to vomit.

"He doesn't know about me and Gael," Alessandra confessed.

"Oh."

"Exactly."

Hugo stopped at the light, looked through the rearview mirror then sped off into traffic.

"Gael's his best friend, right?"

"Yes, right-hand man. He's like a brother to him."

"That can be tough when you're dealing with two alpha males."

"Can you talk to him for me?" Alessandra begged.

I held my hand up.

"No, I have enough problems with your brother now."

"Please, Sofia, he listens to you," Alessandra pleaded, grasped my hand.

"I'm sorry, Alessandra, you're an adult. Stop acting like a little girl," I said.

"Gael said the same thing."

"He's not happy with being a secret."

She shook her head no.

"No, we've been talking for the past year. I've loved him for the past three years."

"Let me guess, he only saw you as a little sister."

"Yeah." She sighed as she looked out of the window as the car approached a gated area.

"Just be honest, all he can do is say no. You're grown," I said then watched as Hugo typed in the code for the security gate and drove on for another five minutes through a winding road.

"Wow," Alessandra said.

"This place is huge."

"I knew Joaquin had money, but this is insane," Alessandra stated and I nodded in agreement. It had to be more than twenty thousand square feet. It looked to be on its own island.

"Hugo, how much did he pay for this?" I investigated. My mouth dropped open when I opened the door. It was like something out of a fairy tale, the grand sixty-foot marble entrance with double staircase, and a high, probably over thirty feet ceiling. It had a unique hexagon shaped atrium with a two-story colonnade reminiscent of an Italian Palladian Villa. I walked toward what I thought was the kitchen but instead found an impressive thirty-five foot dining room, and a two-story library around the corner. The bar room, media room, and walk-in coat room were ideal for entertaining on a large scale as well as everyday five-star living. I saw a private patio, and the outdoor terraces off the breakfast room which led to the Olympic sized pool.

"I can't believe he did this," I muttered, held my hand to my mouth in shock.

"He loves you." Alessandra approached behind me.

"I...I...don't know what to say."

"Say you'll make me an auntie very soon," Alessandra teased, and I nudged her in the shoulder as we laughed.

"That's not happening anytime soon. I have too much I want to do with my career."

"I understand, it's one of the reasons I want to get out from under my father's thumb."

"I'm moving too, Carlo. You can have the kids because this house is crazy." I heard a loud boisterous mouth. Janice and Sabrina were walking toward us in the backyard.

"Ignore her," Sabrina said.

I chuckled at Janice flipping Sabrina off.

"Pack my bags and ship them here," Janice told me.

"Is she always like this?" I questioned.

"What, new Mommy? Carlo don't get fucked up," Janice spat then hung up the phone in his face.

"You two are hilarious," I said as I gave her a hug.

Her phone started ringing again and she turned it on silent.

"He's going to kick your ass when you get back," Sabrina stated to Janice.

"Carlo don't run me," Janice said.

"Are you sure because last time we talked you wanted to give him another baby?" Sabrina taunted and Janice smirked.

"Don't worry about my man, little girl," Janice said.

"Sabrina and Janice, this is Alessandra, Joaquin's sister," I introduced her and they shook hands.

"What do you do, Alessandra?" Sabrina questioned.

"Shop," Alessandra responded.

"See I like her," Janice said, and pointed at Alessandra.

"She goes to fashion school," I said.

"That's great, I love seeing women taking charge of their careers," Sabrina said.

"Hopefully one day I'll be a famous fashion designer," Alessandra mentioned.

"So what's the plan, Sofia, we've heard some things and know how the media can get them?" Janice asked, standing next to me.

"Honestly, I'm still trying to fit into this world of Joaquin's and not leave mine behind."

"We can most definitely understand that," Janice responded.

I turned and walked back inside of the house as I saw the door open with Hugo letting Cassidy inside.

"After the kidnapping, I just want to forget everything and him."

"Let me guess, he wouldn't let you," Janice answered.

"Not only did he show up at my apartment the next morning where I kicked him out, he also has had his people following me."

"In a weird sense, that means he was giving you space," Janice said.

"How do you guys deal with these men? I can't keep up."

"It took a few years and some kids that distracted them," Sabrina commented.

"I'm a long way from having kids."

"Hey everybody," Cassidy said and waved.

"Thanks for coming on such short notice."

"No worries, I needed to talk to you anyway," Cassidy responded.

"Well, Joaquin bought a house and I agreed to move in with him."

"Wow...Okay are you getting married?" Cassidy questioned.

"No, we talked and are no longer doing the space thing."

"Big Daddy Dick, put that in her life," Janice joked and Alessandra covered her ears and we all laughed as her face closed up in a scowl.

"Ignore Janice, we talked and decided to give our relationship another chance."

"You need a decorator asap," Cassidy said.

"Yes and set up a dinner for my parents and Joaquin," I explained as she took notes.

"Can we go to the mall?" Alessandra asked.

"Mall and then grab some lunch. I have to run through my lines for the show."

"What do you all have a taste for?" Sabrina queried as we walked out of the house and I locked up. I saw Sabrina's blacked out limo with her driver talking to Hugo, and Cassidy's car out front.

"I could go for some lobster," Janice stated.

"We'll do the mall first and then lunch at *High Step,* a new restaurant that opened up and they have everything from fish and barbecue to burgers and Mediterranean.

"Sounds good to me," Alessandra said and followed me to the car.

"Cassidy, do you want to ride with me?" I asked.

"What about my car?" she responded.

"Hugo can get someone to bring it back to the city," I said and Hugo nodded.

"Okay," Cassidy answered.

"Are you all right? You seem a little off."

SOFIA

"Nothing a drink won't cure," Cassidy mumbled.

I could tell something was going on with her and having everybody around wasn't the right time to talk. Hugo followed behind Sabrina's driver and pulled back on the road that led back to the main street. I took my phone out and texted Joaquin about the house.

Me: The house is beautiful.

Joaquin: Beautiful house, for a beautiful woman.

Me: Do you realize this house is huge for just the two of us?

Joaquin: Once we have babies, it won't be.

Me: You're talking crazy now.

Joaquin: We have plenty of time to practice.

Me: I bet you had it all planned out.

Joaquin: Do everything with a purpose.

I giggled at his statement and shook my head.

"Is that my brother?" Alessandra asked.

"Yes."

"I could tell by the wide smile on your face," Alessandra said.

"He's crazy, but I love him."

"You calmed the beast. That's a good thing," Alessandra said.

"He's said that in not so many words, that I bring him peace."

"My brother is crazy, but I love him. My father trained him to be a machine," Alessandra advised.

"What do you mean?"

"No emotions, especially love or affection. His only job in life was to take over the Cartel until you came along," Alessandra mentioned. I felt a weird flutter in my chest at her statement.

"Are you saying all he does is go out killing people?" Cassidy queried.

"He's a contracted killer, well mob boss. I thought you knew all of this," Alessandra said.

"I knew some of his work, not the extent of what his father wanted him to become."

"He's leveled out now," Alessandra randomly blurted out like having a contract killer for a brother was a normal thing you tell people.

The car finally stopped in front of the Cherry Hill mall. Hugo helped all three of us step out and I put my shades on to try and cover myself so I could shop without being bothered.

"Where do you want to start first?" Alessandra asked.

"We can try Michael Kors first," I replied as I followed behind her as Janice locked arms with me.

"I know that look, you're feeling overwhelmed. Trust your man," Janice said.

"I do, he told me in not so many terms that he killed two people. One being my manager."

"Send flowers to his mother and keep it moving. If he killed him, it means he hurt you in some way."

"Carlo talks to you about what he does?"

"Some things, but we're not meant to be involved like that, Sofia. Your job is to be that place for him to shed the day away," Janice stated as we stepped on the escalator.

"Am I being too naive to all this?" I responded.

"Sabrina was in your place at one point," Janice told me.

"And now."

"She's a gun toting Donna that will cut your tongue out and financial advisor during the day," Janice nonchalantly said.

"What about you?"

"Oh, I'm crazy in general, this doesn't faze me." Janice laughed and I shook my head.

All of us got off then headed to the Michael Kors store that was up front. I went to the dress section and picked over a few cocktail dresses when a flash bulb went off in my face.

"Sofia, is it true your manager is missing?" a photographer asked.

"Step back," Sabrina said.

"We have every right to be here," the photographer called out as a second one started taking my picture.

"Let's just go," I said, covering my face.

"Edward's family put out a missing person's report," the photographer called out.

"Edward's a grown man. Get out of her face," Janice snapped and pushed them back as we walked out of the store.

"Don't touch me, lady!" he told me.

"Get out of the way," Janice shouted and pushed through the crowd that started to surround us.

"What if I don't, you're going to make me disappear too?" he chuckled, and continued filming us.

"I can make that happen if you want," Janice remarked and Sabrina covered Janice's mouth.

"I guess the day is officially ruined," Alessandra said.

"We'll come back another day." I wrapped my arm around her shoulder and we walked back out to the car.

"I need to head home and start dinner. We can set up another day to have lunch," Sabrina said through the window of our car.

"No worries, sorry about this," I said, and leaned up against the back of the seat.

"One of the things I wanted to talk to you about was the news," Cassidy remarked.

"Edward's disappearance has nothing to do with me or Joaquin."

223

"I'm not so sure about that," Cassidy said and passed her phone to me with a picture of an SUV in front of a house.

"Whose house is that?"

"Edward's."

"I don't understand."

"This was posted on social media Celebrity Underdark, they say it's Joaquin's car in front of Edward's house."

"Set up an interview, it's time I talked."

"Are you sure?"

"Positive. I can't let this overshadow my career."

* * *

ONE WEEK LATER.

I was sitting in front of Jean Shaw of *Morning American* news preparing to answer some questions. Cassidy was here officially as my manager now, until I could hire another publicist. The director wanted to meet with me and the executive producer as soon as possible to talk about everything that was going on. The afternoon we walked out of the mall, photographers followed us back to the city and continued trying to force me into conversation about Edward. I even had a call from the police about coming in to answer some questions. I hadn't said anything about the police to Joaquin yet, my goal was to try to handle what I could without him being thrown in the mix more than he was.

"Miss Chambers thank you so much for joining us today," Jean said as the lights shone down and the mic in her ear was fixed.

"Thank you for giving me the chance to talk about everything."

"America loves you and wants to know how you're doing through these terrible times," Jean said.

"I'm doing better, Jean. As you know I went through something awful and wouldn't wish it on anyone."

"Take us back to that day," Jean said.

"It was another beautiful night in the city. I was meeting with my friend for dinner."

"Your boyfriend, a Mr. Fuertes correct?"

"Yes."

"What happened exactly?"

"I trusted someone that didn't have my best interests."

"The police have mentioned Leonardo was one of the men that took you."

"Leonardo and unfortunately, my ex-manager, Edward."

"This Leonardo person has mob ties to your boyfriend?" Jean questioned.

"My boyfriend has been nothing but supportive through all of this and the way stories are being written about him have nothing to do with who kidnapped me."

"Are you saying your boyfriend is not a Cartel leader?" Jean asked.

"I'm saying I was taken and almost killed and if it wasn't for my boyfriend and his friends, the outcome might have been far different. Wherever Edward is, I hope the police find him soon and he gets the help that he needs."

"Thank you, Sofia. We understand this is a difficult time for you." Jean leaned over and passed me a tissue. I wiped the tears that pooled in my eyes.

"Extremely, I just want to focus on my career."

"What do you have coming up for the future?"

"More acting and music hopefully soon," I explained.

"Thank you again, Sofia, and America, you've heard it here first from Sofia Chambers on the kidnapping and rescue," Jean said into the camera. The producer called cut and I checked my makeup one more time and shook hands with Jean then strolled to Cassidy.

"What do you think?"

"I think you're a good actress," Cassidy joked.

"I think so too." I laughed and followed behind her out of the building.

"What do we have to do next?" I asked, checking my messages.

"We need to meet with the director and executive producer," Cassidy said.

"That's fine, give Hugo the address," I told her and pulled my mirror out to fix my makeup.

Cassidy leaned over and showed Hugo the address to the studio. Dante told me they were thinking of recasting my part and I was beyond pissed. That role was made for me and we were halfway with filming before the kidnapping happened. Hugo took a right turned on 23rd and Avenue, stopping at Lincoln Studios. I stopped him from getting out. This wasn't that type of visit and having Hugo walking inside with me would have paparazzi roaming around. Cassidy came around to the passenger side and got out. The security guard let us walk through without any issue as I smiled.

I saw Jeremiah talking with Bob Stinger, the executive producer and vice president of the studios.

"Sofia, thanks for coming." Jeremiah extended his hand and I put on a fake smile and reached over to cup his palm.

"Thanks for calling me, Jeremiah."

"We can meet in Bob's office," Jeremiah said.

"How are you doing, Sofia?" Bob asked.

"I'm good, Bob, we just left *Morning America* news."

"That's why we texted Cassidy since you had an interview already and we wanted to catch you early."

"Of course."

"Have a seat," Jeremiah said, and I took the seat on the couch next to Cassidy.

"I know Cassidy probably told you our concerns," Jeremiah started to say.

"She did and I can assure you my personal life won't affect the filming."

"Sofia, you just dealt with a kidnapping and now your manager is missing," Bob said.

"I'm aware, but Cassidy's taking on more responsibility and Edward as you know was involved."

"We've heard rumors your boyfriend is in the mob," Jeremiah stated.

"Rumors."

"Yeah and I know from the one time when he barged in on set trying to fight Dante," Jeremiah reminded me.

"That won't happen again. He can be a little jealous at times, but we've talked about what my career means to me."

"Can you guarantee he won't interfere if we bring you back on set?" Bob asked.

"Yes."

"How is the investigation going?" Jeremiah questioned.

"I'm not sure, my lawyer handles all of that. Listen, I'm here to work, that's it."

"We understand, but financially we can't take a loss," Bob said.

"Are you saying you'll remove me? The biggest star on this project."

"Try to understand, Sofia. We have to think about the safety of the entire crew and staff," Bob responded.

"I'm telling you everything will be fine; my personal life won't interrupt my business."

"Give us a little time to think it over," Jeremiah told me.

"I'm still in the process of recording my album and I just finished signing a contract to model."

"If the investigation closes we can see about starting back," Jeremiah explained.

"Okay, keep me updated. I don't want to take on another project, but I will," I stated and stood up shaking hands with them both before leaving the room.

"You think they'll call you?" Cassidy asked.

"In three, two, one." Cassidy's phone rang and she answered as I climbed inside of the car.

"Hugo can we drop Cassidy off, then head home?" He motioned in agreement and reversed in the street and headed into traffic.

"Yes, sounds good, Jeremiah. We look forward to working with you as well." Cassidy grinned and hung up, screaming in excitement.

SOFIA

he next day.

Joaquin had an intense stare as he watched me hit the stop button on the elevator. I wasn't a prude or anything, but I knew they probably had cameras in the elevator watching us. I switched in front of him slowly and unbuttoned my coat.

"Cover your ears," Joaquin said.

"Why?"

As soon as the words left my mouth, Joaquin lifted his gun and shot at the camera up top as the bell rang.

"OMG!"

"Sweetheart, I warned you to cover your ears," he spoke and reached out and pulled me in close. He locked his eyes with mine and captured my lips as he kneaded my breasts through the shirt. I turned us with his back against the wall and I slid down in front of him and unbuckled his pants. I lingered over the tip in admiration and licked up the bead of precum that oozed out. Based on his hissing noises I was driving him crazy. I swirled my tongue over the head and down to the base of his balls as he pushed in my mouth to the hilt. I heard him curse and groan in pleasure.

"Fuck!"

I pulled back and spit on the tip.

"You like that?" I questioned.

"Sofia…" His eyes tensed as I took him back in my mouth.

"Tell me. Do you like this?" I asked and kissed the underside of his balls, while squeezing his dick.

"God damn it!"

"Are you going to fuck me?" I taunted, then watched his head fall back and eyes roll back. I gripped the sides of his thighs and took him back in my mouth as he pumped feverishly. After two more thrusts, his release flowed down my throat. He gently pulled out of my mouth and picked me up and pushed in and I felt a shiver crawl up my spine. Hungrily, he took my mouth at the same time and I snaked my arm around his neck.

"Mmmmm." Desire encompassed me and I felt alive once again. He knew what buttons to push and how to take me to the next level without even trying.

Banging on the door came.

"We'll get you out in one minute," a voice yelled.

"Fuck! Sofia, your pussy drives me insane," Joaquin muttered as he bit the nape of my shoulder.

"Baby, we have to stop…Ahhh…" I screamed in pleasure. My hips rose meeting his thrusts as the ache between my thighs called for more.

"No."

"I'm coming!" I cried out as I convulsed in his arms before he pulled out and sucked on my clit. Five minutes later the doors were open, we both looked disheveled, and I couldn't walk so Joaquin carried me to my apartment.

"You shot the elevator camera," I spoke, leaning my head against his shoulder.

He slid his key inside of my apartment.

"I did."

"Joaquin, we talked about this."

"It's better than shooting a person," he replied. I kissed his lips to shut him up.

"What do you have planned for today?" I asked, as he put me down on the couch.

"I have some unfinished business, and then we can have dinner," Joaquin said.

I bent over and laid my head in his lap.

"Okay, my parents are coming back to town."

He ran his hand across my hair.

"If it'll make you happy, dinner with your parents," Joaquin commented.

"Also, I'm going back to filming."

"I understand," Joaquin stated.

"Do you? The crazy, mob boyfriend can't burst on set anymore."

"I promise, I won't go on set anymore."

"I feel like a shift is happening right."

"I talked to Alessandra and she told me about the photographer at the mall." He bent down and kissed me on the lips.

"The media will always hound me because of my job, but I'm not afraid to be with you."

He grinned, ran a finger over my bottom lip then down my chest and thigh.

"Maybe I can skip my meeting."

"Nope, I need to practice my lines and work on my music."

"When are we moving in the house?"

"I can get Cassidy over here to start packing up this weekend," I replied, lifted my hand to his cheek.

"Good, take my card and buy whatever you need," Joaquin insisted as he pulled his wallet out of his pocket.

"You're giving me your credit card," I said and leaned up to face him.

"You can have that and more if you want." Joaquin pressed a kiss to my forehead.

"Well let me call Cassidy now, and get started. Is there anything you want specifically in the house?"

"There's a basement that I don't want touched," Joaquin answered.

"What's in the basement?"

"I'll use it for my office."

"Joaquin, don't do anything that's going to cause the police to come to our house," I demanded.

"Don't worry, have you spoken with the police?"

"Not yet. I know I didn't tell you sooner, but I thought I could handle things."

"Never keep anything from me, Sofia," Joaquin said, standing up.

"Are you going to kill Ciro?"

"Yes," Joaquin answered.

"I want to be there."

"I can't involve you in that, Sofia."

"If we're going to do this, I want to see what you do."

"The second you see me in that environment, you may not stay with me."

"I know what you do. I'm not stupid and I can handle it so let me get changed."

"No, you're not coming." Joaquin followed behind me to the bedroom.

"Sabrina and Janice have seen what Antonio and Carlo do," I argued as I removed my jacket and skirt. I kicked off my heels then opened the closet to grab a pair of jeans and a t-shirt.

He tried to grab the jeans out of my hands.

"Sofia, you're not Sabrina and Janice."

"You think I'm some weak, naive, and fragile girl."

"No, but the less you know about that side of me the better."

I turned and reached my arms around his neck.

"Joaquin, stop treating me like some fragile doll that can't handle herself." I kissed the side of his mouth.

"Are you trying to seduce me?" he asked.

"Only if it's working."

"You still can't come," he said.

"Okay," I replied.

"Good, so order our favorite for dinner and I'll be back soon."

"Sure."

I watched him walk out of the bedroom and leave. I went to my house phone and called the one person I knew that could help me.

"Hello," Janice said.

"Janice, I need your help." I sat on the edge of the bed, unsnapped my bra with the phone between my shoulder and neck.

"What's wrong?" Janice queried.

"Joaquin has Ciro and he's going to kill him."

"That's good right?"

"Yes, but he won't let me be there to watch."

"Just like Antonio and Carlo," Janice remarked.

"So, they treated you guys the same."

"Yep. Antonio tried to run the same thing on Sabrina."

"So can you help me? Find out where they are?" I questioned.

"Yeah, give me about fifteen minutes to get the kids situated."

"Thanks, Janice, I appreciate this," I said and ended the call.

I jumped up and ran to the bathroom to shower and change. I needed to hurry up and get back before Joaquin noticed I was gone for too long. Fifteen minutes later I walked out of the back and picked up my purse and cell phone to call Cassidy. The door buzzed and I checked the monitor to see Janice and Sabrina downstairs.

"Hey, Sofia, I was getting ready to send you an email with the script."

"Thanks, Cassidy."

"Sure, anything else you need?"

"Get tickets for my parents to fly out for me," I said as I walked out of the apartment and took the stairs toward the back exit.

"The police said they wanted to meet with you asap." I pushed the door open of the exit and ran to the side of the wall and waved for Janice to reverse so I could jump in without Hugo noticing me.

"I'll take care of them tomorrow," I responded then ended the call.

"Janice, you didn't say anything about doing something behind Antonio's back," Sabrina fussed, her arms folded across her chest.

"Hurry up, Sofia," she whispered as I slid in and shut the door.

"Sabrina, blame me, I wanted to find out where Ciro was being held," I told her.

"Sabrina, shut up, you act like you've never killed someone," Janice spat, and waved her off.

"Wait what?"

"We both have done some things...She's the last person to be shocked," Janice joked as she drove off into traffic.

"How long ago did he leave?" Janice asked.

"About fifteen minutes."

"I have an idea," Janice said.

"You know where they are?' I asked.

"Antonio still has a warehouse on London off Sixth Street," Sabrina said.

"That's true, because the other one was burnt down after killing the DEA agent boyfriend," Janice remarked.

"He killed a DEA agent?" I asked, in shock.

"Among other things," Sabrina replied.

"Pass me my bag back there," Janice said and I picked it up off the floor.

"Here you go."

"You'll need this," Janice said and passed me a gun.

"I don't need a gun."

"Listen if we do this, you have to be all in or we turn back around," Janice said.

"She's right, Sofia. When you agreed to be with him, this is what happens," Sabrina stated.

I grabbed the gun from Janice and checked the safety.

"You only need protection," Janice said.

"Joaquin's going to kill me."

"He'll be upset for a few days, but put the pussy on him and he'll forget being mad," Janice advised, and winked through the rearview mirror.

"Is she always like this?" I asked and Sabrina nodded in answer.

"We're here, ladies," Janice stated before she turned the lights off as we approached the side street of what looked like an empty building.

"This street looks abandoned," I said, looking out of the window at all the lights out. It was around nine at night. A ghost town with nothing but empty buildings around.

Janice pulled a black ski mask down on her face.

"Janice is that necessary?" Sabrina questioned.

"My husband thinks I'm out grocery shopping," Janice replied as I giggled at the two of them arguing back and forth.

"Ignore her, Sofia."

"Where should we start?" I questioned.

"Take the back and see if we can get in," Janice stated, and turned to lead us to the back. The building didn't have any security out front. Janice looked around the corner and pushed us to go back further.

"One guy standing outside," Janice spoke, her voice quiet.

"What do you want to do?" I questioned.

She pulled her gun out, removed the safety.

"Ready?" Janice asked us.

"Are we seriously doing this?" I inquired.

"This is what happens when you date a Cartel boss," Janice explained and put the gun to her side.

"If you want to go home tonight I suggest you give me that gun, big fella," Janice announced, and he chuckled.

"Bitch, you better kill me or else," the guy said.

"Is that any way to talk to Antonio's De Luca's wife?" Sabrina asked.

"Wait," he said and Sabrina hit him over the head with the back of her gun.

"Let's go," Janice whispered and eased the door open, before she glanced around the room. The back room was old and musty with wires hanging off from the ceilings. Janice walked over to the door and peeked inside.

"Fuck! Carlo's here," Janice whispered.

"Which means Antonio is here," Sabrina said as she wiped a hand down her face.

"Did you see Ciro?"

"He's tied up," Janice responded.

"What angle?" Sabrina asked.

"Literally tied up hanging up from the wall." Janice chuckled.

"Move back, Janice, you're gun happy," Sabrina stated and pushed her to the side.

"Okay, it's your show, Sofia, how do you want to do this?" Janice questioned.

"I want to see him."

"Then lead the way," Janice said and I swallowed the lump in my throat.

I opened the door and all heads turned toward me. Joaquin was wearing all black with blood running down his face and clothes.

"I knew this would happen," Carlo said, and threw his hands up in the air.

"Hey husband," Janice responded, putting the gun behind her back.

"You can take the mask off now," Carlo said.

"Sabrina, I thought you were getting the kids in bed," Antonio stated before he walked up to her and pressed a kiss to her lips.

"Blame Janice."

Janice removed her mask.

"Sofia wanted to be here and she deserves to see this scum get what's coming to him," Janice explained and Joaquin's eyes narrowed in anger.

"I'm not leaving," I said to him.

"She needs to see this," Sabrina said.

Ciro laughed as blood spilled from his lips.

"That little bitch would have made a good pet for me," Ciro muttered, in slow breaths.

Joaquin punched him in the face.

"What was the plan, Ciro?" Antonio asked.

"Kill the bitch like he killed my niece," Ciro shouted.

"Edward," I said.

"He wasn't nothing but a patsy. Motherfucker thought he was going to get rich," Ciro stated.

"You need to leave, Sofia," Joaquin said and picked up an automatic screwdriver.

"No, we do this together," I said and pulled out my gun and aimed at Ciro.

"Once you do this, it can't be undone," Joaquin remarked and I knew what he was saying about taking someone's life. I needed to see this piece of shit die, because he might try and come back if he gets away.

I raised the gun up.

"Ready," Joaquin said.

"Fucking bitch!" Ciro screamed as Joaquin drilled into his left knee.

Pop! Pop!

"Ahhhhh!!" Ciro cried out as the bullets went into his chest.

I aimed and focused on his head with one eye closed and let go.

Pop! Pop!

"That's my friend," Janice called out as the bullets went straight to his head and neck.

Joaquin took the gun from me as I started shaking. He lifted my chin, peered in my eyes as tears started to spill down my face.

"You did good," Joaquin said.

"I just killed him."

"Better him than you," Joaquin replied and pulled me in close then kissed my cheek.

He rubbed my back and led me out of the warehouse as his men started to get rid of his body.

JOAQUIN

A week earlier.

We'd held Ciro in captivity for the past week with only water keeping him alive. My men caught him as he left the hotel to try and check out and fly back to Italy.

They followed him on the highway toward the airport and rammed his car. I took the gun out of the back of my waistband and got out of the car and eased the door open.

"You think this is over," Ciro said as my men dragged him out of the car.

"Only the beginning."

"Fuck you!" Ciro said and I punched him in the face.

"Take him to the car."

"Your little girlfriend still isn't safe," Ciro taunted.

"What did you say?"

"Joaquin, we can't stay out here. He's fucking with you," Gael advised. Hugo and Gael dragged Ciro to the car.

"Motherfucker needs to die," I shouted, and hit the top of the car.

"We have to go, Joaquin, before his people get word," Gael yelled and I hopped in the van as Gael drove off running a red light.

"Call Antonio," Gael said as my phone vibrated.

"We got him," I spoke into the phone.

"Bring him to the warehouse," Antonio commanded, ending the call. I balled my fist up ready to kill him with my bare hands.

"He had his slimy hands on her."

"I hear you, but we need to do it in a place that won't attract police."

"Sofia's going back to work and I want this finished before it happens."

"We'll handle it," Gael said.

Present Day.

"Ughh...Joaquin," Sofia moaned, as I punished her with a smack to her ass, her cries were muffled in the sheets. As soon as we left out of killing Ciro I drove us home and ripped her clothes off and massaged her clit with my finger and tongue. The kiss to the back of her neck was slow and soothing as my warm body hovered over hers, as my hands landed on her full breasts and gently tweaked her nipples. The soft moan out of her echoed through the room. My hips slowly rotated as I focused on her breathless whimpers. Sofia fell down on top of the bed, and I closed her legs with my dick still inside as her pleasure intensified and I growled as my body trembled as her essence poured out. I leaned further on down, whispered in her ear about how much I loved her and needed her in my life.

"Sweetheart..." I grunted, reached underneath us and massaged her clit with my thumb.

"Keep going...Mmmmm."

"Shit...baby." I plunged deeper, succumbed to her trembles as I jerked in the explosion. I fell on my side and lifted her left leg and pushed back inside.

"Don't stop!" she screamed as she reached around to grab the back of my head.

"I'm coming, baby," I said, as her opening clenched and milked me of every drop. My hips pushed in rapid succession.

"Yessss...Oh God!" Sofia cried out, as her mouth crashed onto my lips as we drunkenly fell deeper in love.

My eyes started to close, and I pulled her in my arms. An hour later I ordered dinner as she slept and I put everything on a plate with a glass of wine. I showered and threw on my boxers and came back into the bedroom and she was awake, surprisingly watching tv.

"Hey," Sofia said.

"Hungry?"

"Starving." She took the glasses of wine off the tray and put them on the nightstand. I put the tray down in front of us on the edge of the bed. I moved the covers over and laid down next to her as she grabbed the rice and orange chicken bowl.

"Was that Ghost I saw tonight?" she asked.

"A small piece of him."

"Janice said something interesting to me about how we need to be your escape," she spoke.

"I didn't want you to lose yourself in what I do."

"I'm okay, Joaquin."

"The second you feel you're not."

"I don't look at you differently, I appreciate how you take care of me," she replied.

"Even when I get controlling?" I fed her a piece of my egg roll.

"Hopefully now you'll step back a little."

"That won't happen," I joked and bit her arm gently.

"What happened to Ciro's body?"

"You really want to know?"

"Yes."

"I put his body in acid."

"What about Edward?"

"I chopped him up," I confessed.

"Wow."

"Does that scare you?"

"I need to go to talk to the police tomorrow," Sofia said.

"I'll send my lawyer with you."

She took a sip of the wine.

"They'll probably ask me about Edward's disappearance."

"You don't know anything about his life and what he did outside of managing your career."

"Let's go to bed, I'm exhausted." She yawned and drank the last of her wine. I took the bowls and put them on top of the tray and put it all on top of the dresser. I pulled the covers up, sighed and wrapped her in my arms.

...

The morning came and Sofia was out of the door with Cassidy and I called my lawyer to meet her at the police station. I had a few calls to make and business at Alba Industries until we had dinner tonight. I checked my wallet and tie, grabbed my keys and walked out of her apartment and headed down to the awaiting car. I hopped in the back of the car with Gael.

"Where to?" Gael asked.

"I want to check on Alba Industries and get Mauricio on the phone."

"We need to talk about something," Gael stated.

"What?" I asked.

"I didn't want it to be like this, but I'm dating Alessandra," Gael said.

"How long has this gone on?" I asked as Gael stopped at the stop sign.

He sighed and ran his hand down his face.

"About a year."

"I already knew."

"What do you think your father will say?" Gael questioned.

"He'll probably want you killed," I joked.

"Fuck you," Gael said.

I ran a hand through my beard.

"You dating my sister isn't my favorite thing."

"But." Gael glanced at me in the passenger seat.

I shrugged my shoulders.

"We've known each other all of our lives. You hurt her."

"You kill me," Gael responded.

"We understand each other."

"We do," Gael said.

Gael parked in his reserved space at Alba Industries. We stepped out, and I buttoned my jacket before I made sure my gun was still safe and secure. I nodded at the security guard and valet as I walked into the building and smiled at the receptionist. Gael went over to check with security as I continued onto the elevator and headed to my office. A few minutes later I grabbed messages from my assistant and opened the door to my office then checked leftover voice messages.

"Sir, are you going to be here for lunch today?" my assistant asked.

I checked my watch. It was going on nine am, and normally lunch was at a restaurant if I was meeting with a new client.

"For now order from Bar One and have it delivered," I replied.

"Yes, sir."

I turned my computer on, checked emails and saw two prospective clients wanting to meet about investing in their companies. I responded to both, requesting that they send over a portfolio of their latest numbers and board members.

"Mauricio just messaged to call him."

"What does he want?" I questioned and dialed his number on my cell phone and put it on speaker.

"Joaquin," Mauricio said.

"What can I do for you, Mauricio?"

"Laurent was informed about Ciro," Mauricio stated.

"I don't know what you're talking about."

He chuckled.

"Is this how you do business over a woman?" he spat.

"This is how I do business, Mauricio, does Laurent have concerns?"

Gael took his phone out and dialed a number.

"I'm speaking on behalf of Carrington Cartel. Ciro was a big buyer for us," Mauricio remarked.

"Sorry to tell you, but he will no longer be a buyer."

"Do you think this woman is worth you losing money?" Mauricio stated.

"Mauricio, we do business, don't worry about my personal life."

"The pussy must be really good," he said.

I slammed my hand down on the desk and cursed in Portuguese.

"If you want to continue doing business with me, then you'll never speak those words again."

"You don't scare me, Joaquin. I'm the next underboss," Mauricio said.

"Would you like to meet Ghost?"

"I just want you to remember money is not worth a woman," Mauricio mentioned.

"I'll take that into consideration for next time," I said and hung up.

Gael ended his call.

"That was Laurent."

"What did he say?" I asked.

"He didn't know Mauricio was calling you," Gael commented, sitting down in front of my desk.

"What do you think the angle is?" I twisted my phone in my hand and stared at the ceiling.

"He could be trying to take over Laurent's seat."

"That motherfucker," I said.

"He's moving funny," Gael responded.

"Hugo's with Sofia right now, make sure the house has extra security," I said. Gael left to go meet up with Alessandra and I told him about reminding her about dinner with Sofia's family tonight.

Me: How is it going?

Sofia: We just pulled up.

Me: My lawyer should be inside waiting for you.

Sofia: I know, he messaged he would meet us.

Me: Tell him to call me right after.

Sofia: I will.

Me: If they get disrespectful, let me know.

Sofia: I don't need you doing anything to the police.

I smirked at her text.

Me: Baby, don't worry. The police can't touch me.

Sofia: They just came out to get me.

Me: Okay, keep me updated as soon as you're done.

Sofia: Love you.

Me: Love you more.

I closed out of the messages and continued working for the rest of the day on my legit businesses.

"Mr. Fuertes, your sister's on the phone," the assistant said.

"Thanks," I replied, and picked up my office phone.

"Gael told you," Alessandra said.

"He did."

"Are you mad?" Alessandra asked.

"I'm disappointed you didn't tell me, but if you're happy, that's what's important."

"I wasn't trying to keep it secret, we just happened," Alessandra spoke.

"Alessandra, I don't believe you for one second, but it's your life."

"Fine, but can you be there when I tell father?" Alessandra asked.

"I have dinner with Sofia's parents tonight, I'll call you when my schedule clears," I replied and hung up. The only thing on my mind was how Sofia was doing at the police station.

SOFIA

I slid my phone in my purse, squared my shoulders and looked forward not showing any type of emotion that would cause the police to think I was intimidated by them. I already felt they were trying to set me up or put my name in a bad light because when we pulled up the paparazzi were outside and I know I didn't call them down here. The only people that knew we'd be here were the officers working on Edward's case, Cassidy, and myself.

"Miss Chambers thank you for joining us today," Detective Jones said.

"Of course," I replied.

Joaquin's lawyer, Emilio, motioned for me to take a seat next to him.

"You didn't need a lawyer with you, we're just asking routine questions," Detective Adams spoke with a silly grin on his face. I didn't like him at all because he seemed like he was on another agenda separate from finding what happened to Edward. I was surprised he had a wedding ring on his hand with the way he came across and smelled. He had a large belly that looped over his pants, a bald head, and was sweating profusely with a tooth missing at the bottom right corner; he just gave off a creepy vibe.

"Let's get on with this, Detective," Emilio said.

"When was the last time you saw Edward?" Detective Jones asked while he pulled out a notepad and pen.

"The last time I saw him was before my kidnapping."

"You haven't spoken to him for over two months," Detective Adams said.

"Yes."

"You don't think that's strange?" Detective Adams responded.

"No, Edward and I weren't close friends."

"Where do you think he'd go?" Detective Jones said.

"I don't know," I responded as I crossed my arms over my chest and leaned back in the chair.

"She's lying," Detective Adams spat.

"Watch it, Detective," Emilio said.

"We know Edward was in love with you, Sofia...Are you telling us that he just up and left?" Detective Jones stated.

"I'm not telling you anything...the last time we spoke it was about business."

"I think your boyfriend killed him," Detective Adams said.

"That's crossing the line, Adams," Emilio spoke.

"I'm wondering why his lawyer is down here," Adams remarked.

"My client doesn't have to explain to you who she hired," Emilio insisted.

"He has you wrapped around his finger. The pussy must be good," Detective Adams said.

"Detective! I want him removed," Emilio shouted.

"It's okay, Emilio," I said.

He grinned.

"Edward, like all men, has tried and failed to get me to sleep with them."

"You don't need to explain this," Emilio muttered.

"No, he needs to understand."

"Understand what? That some rich bitch thinks she can waltz in here?" Detective Adams sneered.

"Adams," Jones commented.

"No, let him keep going and see what happens."

"Are you threatening me?" Adams asked, hovering over the table.

I laughed, seeing him turn red.

"I don't need to threaten anyone, Detective, I didn't do anything wrong."

"Then give us a DNA sample and tell us what happened to Edward," Detective Jones stated.

"This questioning is going to be over before it really starts," Emilio said.

"I had nothing to do with Edward missing."

"Then your boyfriend knows something," Detective Jones implied as he pushed a photo of Edward and Ciro talking together in front of a hotel.

"Who is that?" I questioned, pointing at Ciro.

"This is the man that took you. Do you know him?" Detective Jones asked.

"This was the first time seeing him. Well besides the kidnapping," I spoke.

"Ciro Vitale is a powerful man in the Cartel world, the entire family is almost wiped out," Jones said.

"Sorry to hear that."

"Because of your boyfriend," Adams shouted.

"That's it, get him out of here," Emilio said.

"Fine, I'll let you handle it." Jones took a sip of his coffee.

"Ciro came here looking for Joaquin about his niece's death," Jones said.

"I don't know anything about that, I was almost killed on that boat."

"And somehow you're here without a scratch on you," Adams said.

"Detective Adams is this personal to you?" I asked.

"Nothing is personal to me," Adams said.

"It has to be, I mean, you're so hard up about Joaquin."

"The guy you're in love with is evil, he's killed people," Jones stated.

"Joaquin Fuertes is a business owner."

"Is that what you're going with?" Jones asked.

"That's what I know."

"This is over," Emilio said as he grabbed his briefcase and stood up.

I clasped my purse and jumped up and started to follow him.

"He's not a good man, Miss Chambers. Think of your family," Jones said.

I stopped at the door with my hand on the wall.

"Are you threatening me?" I questioned over my shoulder.

"It's a suggestion," Adams commented.

I smirked, pinned a piece of my hair behind my ear and turned to look at them both.

"I'll let Joaquin know about your suggestions. Good day, detectives," I spoke and walked out of the room.

"Don't worry about them, they don't have anything on you," Emilio said as he held the door open letting me out first. I saw Hugo and Cassidy standing in front of the car waiting on us.

"I know."

"Tell Joaquin I'll be in contact."

"Thank you, Emilio."

"Anytime and I'm a big fan of your work, Miss Chambers."

I reached out and shook hands with him.

"Thank you and don't take this personally, but I hope to not use your services again."

"Joaquin will have an update by the time you get home and things will be rectified," Emilio stated, waved through the window.

I climbed in the backseat of the car as Hugo shut the door.

"How did it go?" Cassidy asked.

"It's not something that I enjoyed, but I told the truth," I said.

"Well at least it's behind you now," Cassidy muttered.

I sighed, looked out of the window in thought.

"You have to be on set tomorrow don't forget," Cassidy reminded me.

"I won't and I need to stop at the grocery store for food. My parents fly in tonight."

"Dinner with the parents," Cassidy advised.

"Yep."

"Good luck, I can't see Joaquin being nervous to convince your parents to like him," Cassidy joked.

"Me neither, so more than likely it'll turn into an argument."

"What about his parents?" Cassidy remarked.

"I met them a while back and his mom loves me."

"His father?" she questioned.

"It was touch and go at first, but now we seem to be fine."

"Joaquin doesn't look like the type to allow anyone to tell him what to do," Cassidy stated.

"He's not. Well besides me." I giggled.

I slid my vibrating phone out and saw a message from Joaquin.

Joaquin: I talked to Emilio.

Me: That didn't take long.

Joaquin: I pay him well.

Me: Detectives didn't have real evidence.

Joaquin: Did they threaten you?

Me: In a non-sort of threatening tone.

Joaquin: Ciro had them on payroll.

Me: So you think they're trying to set me up?

Joaquin: They're not stupid enough to do that.

Me: I'm almost home, will talk later.

Hugo turned in front of Cassidy's apartment building and waved goodbye as she got out to leave.

"Hugo, can you run me by the store and then home?" I asked. He nodded in answer and we headed up the street to the store.

* * *

AN HOUR later I was sauteing vegetables, while the steaks cooked on the stove. I opened a bottle of red wine and put another one in the fridge to chill. Joaquin was on his way with his sister and my parents were getting picked up by Hugo from the airport. I made sure to have something for everybody tonight. My parents were still hesitant about us and I wanted them to see that I was fine and protected not only with my heart, but my safety thanks to Joaquin.

Beep!

The buzzer sounded and I dropped the utensils and wiped my hands on the towel and walked to the door.

"Yes."

"Hey, sweetie, it's your mom and dad."

"Finally, come on up." I let them upstairs and opened the door to go back to the stove and check on my food before it burned.

"What smells good in here?" Mom called out as she removed her jacket.

"Steak, lasagna, garlic bread," I said.

Mom kissed me on the cheek.

"Hi, Dad."

"Hi, pumpkin, how are you feeling?" he asked, hanging my mom's jacket up.

Before I answered, the door opened further and Joaquin and Alessandra strolled in together.

"You're right on time," I said as he wrapped an arm around my waist and kissed my cheek.

"I brought some more wine," Joaquin explained.

"Perfect."

"Mr. and Mrs. Chambers." Joaquin extended his hand to my father and I held my breath waiting to see if an argument would start.

"Joaquin," Father responded and reached out to shake his.

"Hello, I'm Alessandra, Joaquin's sister," she said.

"Hi Alessandra, you're gorgeous. Are you a supermodel?" Mom questioned.

SOFIA

I sprinkled salt and pepper on top of the rice and vegetables, tossed them in the pan and drained the excess grease and poured the concoction over the rice and plated it all into my best dish. I passed Alessandra the garlic bread and vegetables to put on the table.

"Joaquin, I'm not going to sugarcoat this. Why are you with my daughter?" my father blurted out.

"Your daughter is amazing, and I love everything about her."

I stayed quiet as my father grilled him.

"She's our baby. For her to get kidnapped on your watch doesn't sit well with us," Mom spoke.

"I understand. But let me make this clear, Sofia will never be in that situation again," Joaquin said.

"My brother can be an ass, Mr. and Mrs. Chambers," Alessandra said and I giggled.

"Sofia," Mom chastised.

"Sorry."

"He's old school about the way men should be protective over their women."

"Alessandra, our daughter was kidnapped and the police said it was because of your brother," Mom explained.

"The police were trying to scare you," Joaquin said.

"Ma, they will say anything to get me to turn against Joaquin," I said, putting the plate of lasagna on the table. Joaquin pulled me into his arms.

"Do you love our daughter?" Father questioned.

Joaquin stared into my eyes.

"She's my soul," Joaquin replied.

"We can't say who she could be with, our baby is grown. But your job is to protect her," Father stated.

"He's done that. He bought a house for us."

"You're moving in together?" Mom asked.

"Yeah."

"I hope a ring is coming?" Father narrowed his eyes in Joaquin's direction and I felt embarrassed.

"Can we focus on one thing for right now?" I asked.

"I consider her my wife now, but marriage is the next step."

"Joaquin why didn't you tell me?" Alessandra asked, offended.

"Because I knew you'd tell her if I did bring it up," he joked.

"What do you do for work?" Father inquired.

"Business," we both answered at the same time.

"If you're happy then we'll leave it alone," Mom told me.

"Thank you and I am."

"That's all that matters," Mom spoke.

"Can we talk about my boyfriend problems?" Alessandra questioned.

"No," Joaquin responded so I slapped his shoulder.

"Stop acting like that."

"I'm fine with her dating my best friend, but don't want to hear about it," Joaquin informed me.

"He's such an asshole," Alessanda mumbled, as Joaquin buried his face in my neck.

"Let's eat," I said, before he could go further.

251

He groaned and let me up out of his lap to take a seat next to him.

We laughed and talked with my parents and his sister all night, then Hugo drove them back to the hotel and Alessandra to her condo.

* * *

"Fuck!" Joaquin shouted, as I sat with my back to him and bounced with both feet flat on top of the bed.

"Mmmm…"

"Ughhhh…fuck you're so beautiful," Joaquin spoke as he smacked my ass.

"Tell me you love me."

"I love you!" Joaquin bellowed as I jumped off and sucked him into my mouth and massaged his balls. I wanted to show him my gratitude for all he'd done for keeping me safe, trusting me with the other side of his world and not letting the darkness keep him away from loving me purely.

SOFIA

The next day.

Early morning call time was not my idea of getting back to work after a long night talking with my parents. Then Joaquin keeping me up all night long as he tried rearranging my insides. I had a crick in my neck now after doing new tricks to keep up with him. All I heard was him cursing at me which I could only understand a little with his accent. I learned since we'd been together that when he really gets upset, his accent comes out more. In his mind I shouldn't have known these different moves and he kept asking who taught me. I wouldn't dare tell him; I liked to keep a few secrets to myself.

"So today, what are we doing?" Tonya asked.

"Not too heavy on the foundation today. It's a small scene we're doing."

"Okay are you glad to be back on set?"

"I am, even though it was touch and go with Jeremiah and Bob."

"Yeah, I heard there were rumors of replacing you," Tonya mentioned.

"Cassidy and I had to meet with them."

"I'm glad you're back, how does your boyfriend feel about things?" Tonya questioned, placing a primer on first.

"He won't be showing back up here anytime soon. We have an agreement." I laughed, thinking about me giving Joaquin an ultimatum.

"That man is crazy about you," Tonya said.

"I know."

"What did the police say? It was in the blogs about you talking with them."

"Basic questions about Edward's and my relationship."

"I heard his family filed a missing person's report," Tonya remarked.

"Good, and I hope they find him," I spoke, taking a sip of the water and reading my lines.

"Did he really work with that guy to kidnap you?"

"Unfortunately, that's what they said."

"Wow."

A knock at my trailer interrupted us.

"Come in!" I yelled.

"It's me," Cassidy said, sipping on a smoothie.

"You look cute."

"Thanks, here's your usual, celery juice."

"Thanks," I said and took a sip.

"I thought you weren't showing up until later."

"I wasn't, but I wanted you to see the numbers from clothing sales," Cassidy stated.

"I forgot you launched that sportswear line," Tonya said.

"Expressive Designs. Let me know your size and I'll get Maggie to send some pieces over," I replied.

"The social media awareness is growing and since launch we've hit fifty million in US sales alone, and twenty-five million global," Cassidy stated, scrolling through her phone.

"I liked the black pants and sports bra, maybe a custom set," I said.

"I'll talk to Maggie, but she's happy with the sales and wants to extend the contract," Cassidy told me.

"Good, did you hear from Chauncey about the songs?" I questioned.

"Yep, all set for whenever you're ready to go back in the studio."

"Girl you're crazy busy." Tonya pinned my hair up into a bun.

"If I want to continue on my career path, I have to work ten times harder," I remarked.

"Jeremiah's ready for you," a PA for the show called through the walkie that sat on my vanity mirror.

"Show time," I said and removed the cape and stood up. I wore the detective uniform of my character and checked myself out one more time in the mirror before heading out to the set.

"Let them know Sofia Chamber never left," Cassidy gassed me up.

"Thanks, girl."

I stepped out of the trailer and hopped on the golf cart and went to the soundstage to start my day with Dante and hopefully complete filming before I had to start the moving process and finish my album.

* * *

"JOAQUIN!" I squeezed my eyes tight as sweat flowed down my stomach. I felt him all the way in my throat, and I was ready to pass out from his powerful thrusts. I knew he missed me since I was out working late. With us both having busy lives, I needed to figure out a balance of everything I had going on with making sure we were still a priority. I planned on finally getting help with packing to move. Now that my parents were on board and respected our relationship, we could move forward with the next steps. Once recording was halfway started and since filming would be done soon the next obstacle was moving. We reconnected all night into the morning. I wanted to get up early and cook his breakfast, but from the moans and grunts, eating food was the last thing on his mind.

JOAQUIN

I was picking Sofia up from her place tonight, I tried to get her to spend the night, but she wanted to still feel independent. Even though I offered to move her into my building for security reasons, she still argued about needing her own space. Once her parents came around to our relationship things started to calm down and now that my sister was here to live, she became close friends with Sofia. I still wasn't too fond of her dating Gael, but I couldn't do anything besides threaten to kill him if he hurt her. I looked through the rearview mirror and saw Hugo and Gabriella following behind me as a precaution. Ciro was no longer a factor in our lives, but I wasn't naive enough to think it wouldn't cause a ripple effect down the road. Collaborating with Edward to hurt the most important person in my life was the biggest mistake they could have done. I made myself clear when I first saw Sofia and told him that she belonged to me, he should have bowed out gracefully and now his grandmother had to mourn his death. I turned right at the light, near Avalon Clinton apartments and stopped in front of her apartment prepared to head inside and I saw she was already outside waiting with the doorman. She pointed toward the car and the doorman strolled behind her to the door. I wanted to say something about her coming down with her body-guard, but I let it go for now. Tonight she was all mine and I planned on keeping her all tied up. She got inside the car, placed her hand on my thigh and I smiled.

"How was your day?" I questioned as I turned the signal on to head into traffic.

"It was busy because I had a photoshoot for my album cover."

"When does it come out again?" I stopped behind a red pickup truck that had a baby on board sticker.

I pointed at the sticker.

"Can you see yourself like that one day?"

"Like what?"

"Giving me a child."

"Once my career slows down, I can see us with kids one day."

The light changed and I pulled into traffic. I sighed thinking about her answer.

"Sofia and what about marriage?" I peered at her out of the corner of my eye.

"You think your parents will be okay with marriage?" She fidgeted with her hands.

"No one has a say in what we do, but the two people in the rela-tionship."

"Glad to hear that," she responded, looking out of the window.

"Are you excited for tonight?"

"I'm a little nervous, but excited at the same time. A listening party is huge." She reached over and grabbed my hand, entwining our fingers. We arrived at Ryde nightclub and I got out of the car and walked around to help her step out. I reserved the place with her family, friends, and a few industry people that she worked with to help celebrate her music. Normally I stay out of the public picture, but I wanted to show her my support and arranging this with Cassidy let her know that I'm hundred percent behind her career. The outside door had a huge sign about tonight and a few fans wanted a picture with her, so I let them take them as I turned my back so as not to be seen. She kissed my cheek and signed a few autographs and we strolled in together where we saw a few of her castmates from the Broadway show dancing.

"We have the section in VIP reserved," Cassidy shouted in my ear. I held my hand on Sofia's lower back. Hugo was behind us and Gael in front.

"You want anything to drink?" I asked her.

She shook her head no.

"Just you is all I need." She cupped my face and stood on her tip toes to kiss me.

"Anything for you."

"Is your sister here?" she asked.

"Gael is here, so probably," I responded, and we walked through the crowd and took a seat in the corner. A bottle girl came over and dropped more glasses off.

"I invited Tonya and your parents," Cassidy said.

"I see her now. My parents are probably asleep in bed by now," I heard Sofia reply.

"We're having dinner with my parents tomorrow," I mentioned to Gael and watched as he gulped on his shot of whiskey.

"Your sister told me," Gael stated as he put his arm around my sister's waist and pulled her back down to the couch.

"I was just dancing," Alessandra said, annoyed.

"In a little ass dress," Gael growled out. I didn't blame him; I wouldn't want Sofia in something so damn tiny.

Alessandra rolled her eyes.

"Joaquin, talk to your friend," Alessandra said.

"I told you, I wasn't getting involved in your relationship."

"Stop going to your brother when I say something you don't like," Gael complained.

I chuckled at the pout on her face.

"Baby, come dance with me," Sofia said.

"Sweetheart, I don't dance, I'll watch you though." I pinched her cheek.

"You're no fun," she said, so I pulled her into a searing kiss.

"Ewwweee, get a room," Alessandra fussed.

"You're trying to start something, Mr. Fuertes," Sofia said before she wiped the lipstick off my lips.

"Is it working?" I replied.

She grinned.

"Maybe, but we have at least another hour. So you'll have to wait," she commented and I groaned before I adjusted myself and tried to think of anything other than sex to get my dick to go down. She was looking too sexy and I couldn't go a day without being inside of her and hearing her soft moans. We ended up partying until the club shut down and I took her back to the house and we made love in each room christening it listening to her music play over the radio.

SOFIA

Three months later.

Today I planned a dinner with my parents and Joaquin's, along with his sister and Gael. The cat was out of the bag with them dating and her father stopped trying to keep them apart after Alessandra threatened to run away. Their mother was adamant about him letting it go and allowing the couple to be happy. I was just glad to have the heat off me and Joaquin.

After the listening party I felt so inspired that I called Chauncey the next day to add a few more songs and today was the big release. We'd been on a media blitz and I was ready to fall asleep, but needed to get this done so I could take a vacation and finish getting the house together. Joaquin left for work at his office and said he would be here later for dinner. I already had a chef coming over tonight two hours early to prep, as well as a cleaning crew to make sure everything was just right. Cassidy followed along with me to New York for an interview with a local entertainment talk show about my music and new movie. Cassidy typed away on her phone as the makeup artist continued putting mascara on the fake eyelashes.

"Everything's all over social media about today's interview," Cassidy mentioned.

"I didn't expect anything less."

"Some are wondering if this album is about Joaquin," Cassidy spoke.

I shrugged, not giving an answer to the question. I had some songs about Joaquin, but not everything.

"Sofia we're ready for you," the talk show assistant said.

"Coming."

I passed my phone to Cassidy and headed to do my second interview for the day.

"You're looking lovely, Sofia," Brandy from *Entertainment Live* said.

I sat down across from her with my hands clasped together.

"Thank you."

"You have a glow about you," Brandy said.

"Probably my new album being out," I teased as I held it up for the camera.

"So, tell us what this album is about?" Brandy questioned.

"It's about my journey over the past few months and years."

"Would you say highs and lows?" Brandy inquired.

"Yes, the music video I did for "His Peace" is probably the rawest I've ever been."

"Your fans are wanting to know, are you in love?" Brandy asked.

"You know I like to keep my personal life private, but I will say I'm happy."

"The new movie looks great, are you planning more acting in the future?" Brandy asked.

"Hopefully, but I'm taking some time off after this press tour to spend time with my family."

"Thank you again for hanging with us, Sofia, I speak for all of your fans when I say we're glad you're back," Brandy spoke.

* * *

"Dad, I wanted to tell you something," Alessandra started to say.

"What is it?" I asked.

"Ummm…" Alessandra hesitated.

"Just spit it out," I said.

"Gael and I are dating!" Alessandra shouted.

He started to turn red and then glared at Gael.

"You knew about this?" he asked Joaquin.

"I learned about it recently and I'm happy she chose someone that I know could protect her the way she deserves to be protected," Joaquin mentioned.

"Mr. Fuertes, I love your daughter," Gael said.

"Alba, do you hear this?" Mr. Fuertes asked.

"I do and I'm happy to have both my children be in loving relationships," his mother stated.

"Father, I promise I'll finish school," Alessandra said.

"What about this Edward situation?" he asked and changed the subject.

"It's no longer an issue," Joaquin told her.

The detectives' bodies were found in a lake in the back of a trunk chopped up. It was all over the news that it was a mob hit; the timeline was poured over of when Jones and Adams were seen last. I remembered Joaquin saying he had to take care of some business one night, but I learned to stop asking questions. If Jones and Adams were smart they wouldn't have continued pressing me about Edward's disappearance. Alba asked for more wine and I smiled then poured more into her glass.

EPILOGUE

SOFIA

Three years later.

I was riding in the back of a limo with Joaquin sitting beside me, holding my hand in a tight grip. Since the moment I was taken from him on the boat, he'd made it a priority to have me protected at all times even when I was working on set or recording my music. I tried to fight him, but he wouldn't listen and only told me for his own peace of mind that he needed me to be surrounded by people he could trust. Ever since then he has had a camera installed inside each vehicle that I used, plus a tracking device on the car and my ring. One night after dinner he slipped a ring out of his pocket and got down on one knee to propose. At first, I was shocked and it took me a few seconds to answer, but I knew I was in love and that I wanted to be with him no matter what. Here we were driving to an event that held the most dangerous people in the world. From what I gathered they held these events to talk business and introduce new players in the Cartel.

I knew Sabrina and Janice were supposed to be there tonight and that made me feel better to know someone and not be hanging on every word that Joaquin said, as he introduced me as his fiancée. The gossip magazines had reported every other day that I was pregnant. One thing I could assure them of was that babies were not my biggest priority at the moment. Continuing my career and planning our wedding was the only thing I wanted, and I knew that Joaquin supports me. He can be reclusive, withdrawn, angry, and possessive at times. He was the man I loved, and I understood how his emotions got the better of him and trying to express them in a normal relationship with communication would be the ideal thing, but dating a mob boss came with bigger issues than a regular relationship.

"You ready, sweetheart?" Joaquin asked as he squeezed my hand as the car stopped in front of the Atlantis Hall in Queens. His driver came around to the right passenger side and opened the door for Joaquin and he stepped out, adjusted his coat, then held his hand out for me.

"Are you ready?"

"Long as you're by my side, I'll always be good," Joaquin replied before he leaned over to kiss my cheek.

The doors opened and we walked inside to a display of white linen draped around the room with high chandeliers in the middle. A small crowd gathered at the front as they went through security. I noticed they allowed us to pass through without being checked, and Joaquin nodded at the security guard. The tables were white and silver with lit candle centerpieces, and silver napkins looked to be engraved. A small band and stage with the De Luca name etched in gold was on the back wall.

"Why didn't they check us?" I questioned as I tugged on his arm.

"Antonio's people are behind the security for tonight," Joaquin responded as Carlo and Janice waved us over. I smiled and held my arms out for a hug and she extended her arms and we complimented each other on our dresses. I was wearing a gown by Carolina Herrera, a one-shoulder, draped, black mini dress.

"Let me see the ring," Janice asked, I held my hand out for her to see. "This is beautiful, Sofia," she responded and tapped Carlo on the shoulder as he talked to Joaquin.

"Carlo, do you see this ring?" Janice asked and Carlo nodded in answer.

"I do, babe," Carlo answered.

"Good, I expect to see something similar by tomorrow after-noon," Janice stated, and Carlo grinned before he pressed a kiss on her forehead.

"I can just imagine the conversations in your household," I said.

"Carlo thinks he's in control, but we both know who's the boss," Janice said as she looped her arm in mine and started to walk off. Joaquin gave me a look to stay close.

"She's fine, Joaquin. Everybody in here knows you'll blow the place up if something happens to her," Janice commented, and I chuckled knowing she was right.

"Where's Sabrina and Antonio?" I questioned as I looked around the room.

"At the front, right there. We can steal her away before it gets too boring," Janice mentioned.

"What should I expect from these gatherings?"

"Nothing but a bunch of men talking and the women gossiping," Janice stated.

Right as we approached Sabrina, she smiled, and Antonio glanced at who she was grinning at.

"Sofia, you look amazing. I need to borrow that dress," Sabrina told me, and hugged me with one arm.

"Same to you. I can't believe you have four kids and look this beautiful."

"I have no choice since I run after them all day, well the younger ones anyway," Sabrina said, grabbing a glass of champagne off the tray that passed through.

"How long do these meetings last?"

"About two or three hours, but we never stayed more than an hour," Sabrina answered, taking another sip of her drink.

I scanned the room, watched all the men laugh or whisper in conversation. It was interesting to see how Joaquin navigated in this world and he wanted me to be a part of it, at the same time to stay myself and not get jaded or scared.

"Who is that?" I heard Janice ask and point. I followed her stretched out arm and saw a young woman next to an older gentleman. She looked bored and ready to go like the rest of the women here.

"That's Gigi Carrington and her father, Laurent," Sabrina spoke.

"I thought he never brought his daughter anywhere because he was afraid she'd get harmed," Janice stated and Sabrina glared at Janice.

"It's fine, Sabrina, I'm past everything now," I said as I plastered on a smile.

"Did you seek therapy like I told you?" Sabrina inquired, and I responded with a curt nod.

"I'm glad to hear that, because I've been where you are, Sofia. Don't feel like you're alone," Sabrina said.

"Joaquin's been amazing and supportive. Plus, he asked me to be his wife so I doubt I could get away from him now." I laughed and waved my hand around.

"He's just like Antonio and Carlo. Once they get you, there's no way to escape their love," Sabrina mentioned, and we all agreed.

"What are you going to do about your career?" Janice asked.

"I have a new manager now, plus Cassidy is still working with me. I plan on keeping my career."

"What about kids?" Sabrina queried, as the men started to walk over to us.

"We're enjoying each other so hopefully one day we'll be blessed," I said.

"Ladies, I want to introduce you to someone," Antonio said as Joaquin came up behind me and wrapped his arm around my waist.

"This is Laurent Carrington and his daughter, Gigi," Antonio said, and Laurent reached out to shake our hands. For a moment, Gigi's eyes hung on the tall guy wearing all black who looked like he was security.

"Joaquin, you didn't mention how beautiful your fiancée is," Laurent said as he lifted my hand to plant a kiss.

"Laurent, you've been a married man for over forty years, don't cause that to end abruptly," Joaquin stated. I tilted my head and rolled my eyes at his comment. Anytime a guy flirted he had to threaten them in some way.

Laurent chuckled and cuffed Carlo's shoulder.

"It's nice to meet you, Laurent, and your daughter, Gigi."

"You too," Gigi responded in a soft, innocent voice.

The security guard's dark eyes shifted to Gigi and something about the longing in his eyes reminded me of Joaquin and I in the early beginning.

"Antonio, I heard your name was being brought up with the DEA and Interpol," Laurent blurted out and Sabrina twisted her wedding ring.

"Nothing I can't handle," Antonio remarked and shot him a venomous look. I bet he didn't want Sabrina knowing what was going on.

"Ladies and gentlemen, it's time to take your seats for dinner," the announcer said.

Joaquin grasped my hand and we went to the first table that held seating cards that said De Luca and Fuertes. Joaquin pulled my chair out and I sat down with him beside me, the conversation turned to legit businesses starting up for Alba Industries. The waiters came out to each table with a lasagna, salmon, or chicken choice, plus a light salad to start. It felt like a coming out party for our relationship and no animosity or crazy enemies trying to break us apart anymore.

An hour later I was withering underneath Joaquin as he kissed up my stomach after we finished our second round of sex once we got home tonight. He laid back against the headboard and pulled me into his arms.

"Thank you," Joaquin muttered and I'd never heard him sound so relaxed and unsure in the same breath.

I looked up into his eyes and ran a hand across his chest.

"Why are you thanking me?"

"For not running when things got bad," Joaquin spoke and I grinned.

"You can't get rid of me that easily," I answered, pressed a kiss on his chest.

"I'd never want to, Sofia," Joaquin replied.

"Mr. Fuertes, do you love me?" I teased as I slid my hand underneath the covers.

He gasped as I slowly stroked his large girth back to life.

"Bellissima Sofia...You are my heart," Joaquin mumbled slowly.

"No matter good or bad...I won't run from you," I told him, as we stared into each other's eyes. He smirked as I eased under the covers to give him the same special treatment that he descended on me tonight. I made a promise when I took his ring for better or worse, and we'd gone through the biggest hurdle and came above water together.

PART III

JOAQUIN FUERTES

THE FUERTES CARTEL BOOK 3

SYNOPSIS

Joaquin

I'd prepared myself to slow down and be a husband and father to my children now that our lives had blown up in public. Sofia was still working and traveling nonstop as an actress and singer. I'd tried not to let my frustrations show and spill over into my family or business, but deep down, I could feel her pulling away more and more. Being the boss of a cartel didn't mean anything to my wife because she fell in love with Joaquin and not the don of the Fuertes family.

SOFIA

"Three, two, one, action," the director blurted out. The camera started rolling, and lights shined down on the set. My eyes were fixed on the mirror as I composed myself before I turned and walked away. Shamar came into view as I tightened my robe.

"Kendrick, I've been your wife for the past five years. I refuse to let them win."

"Cut!" the director shouted.

While the makeup artist touched up my makeup, the cinematographer rolled the lens back to reveal the playback footage. Since Joaquin and I got married almost two years ago, my life had just expanded even more. My last album received multiple awards, and I had been offered a lot of work, which made me a household name now.

"Sofia, let's try it with you really pissed off. Your character was sacrificed."

"Okay, Angela."

"You need me to change up anything, Angela." Liam asked.

"No, you're doing fine, Shamar. The chemistry is there; we need to see the emotions." Angela held the script up for us to look at the lines one more time. Potentially, the film could be turned into a series. An escort falls in love with a former president, based off a book titled *Mutual Agreement of a Former President*. It simply made sense to me to put myself in another light upon reading the book and pitching it to the production studios.

"Try it one more time from where you're standing," Angela explained, stepping over to the monitor and pointing at me.

"Action," she shouted.

I took a few minutes to breathe in deeply, closing my eyes and counting to three. Shaking my head, I turned away then back toward him as my eyes welled up.

I reached up and gripped his chin. "I refuse to let them win, Kendrick. You do what's necessary."

"Cut!" Angela stated, and the crew cheered and clapped their hands. I smiled and bowed, mouthing *thank you*. Shamar held his arms out for a hug, and I embraced him.

"Oscar worthy," Shamar said, and I giggled, pushing him away.

"Stop playing. You know it'll never happen." He chuckled, nodded at Hugo, and followed me as we walked off the set and headed to my dressing room. Hugo was more than a bodyguard since we met and dealt with my kidnapping. I thought of him as a friend right along with Gael. Swinging the trailer door open, I stepped up to find Cassidy on the phone, and my babysitter Madelyn was taking care of my babies. As soon as I reached over, I grabbed my little girl Jianna from the bed and sat opposite JJ. The cartoons on his computer screen captivated him more than anything else. I was always impressed with his big brotherly skills and his protective nature toward his sister.

"How's the filming going?" Cassidy stood across from the door, texting on her cell. Since becoming my new manager, she carried a more significant load in my life. Every day was something new, and I appreciated that she hadn't run off or sold us out, knowing what my husband did for a living.

"Going fine. Did you get the information for the photoshoot?" *Pregnancy Magazine* wanted to do a shoot with the kids and me, but so far, I hadn't built up the courage to tell Joaquin. We fought about keeping the kids hidden, but as an actress and singer, my fans expected to know more about my life. Lately, I'd post a photo with them blocked out, but they knew Joaquin was my husband even though I kept him off my page.

"I emailed everything over. How are you going to convince him?" Cassidy leaned over and tickled JJ's foot. He giggled and reached his arms out for her to pick him up, as Madelyn pulled his shirt down, covering his belly. My baby boy had his father's dark, piercing eyes, auburn hair, chestnut skin tone, and strong temper if he didn't get his way. Joaquin spoiled him, and I knew as the firstborn, he probably wanted him to follow in his footsteps. Something I meant to talk with him about once our schedules cleared up.

"I don't know, but I need to hurry up if they want me to do the shoot soon."

Jianna closed her eyes, and I lifted her across my shoulder to burp her as she slowly dozed off to sleep.

"They would like an answer by the end of the week, Sofia." Madelyn came back into the room with a plate of food. I placed Jianna down to sleep, rose, and kissed the top of JJ's head.

"I'll talk with him tonight. Let me go shower, so we can go."

"Ewww..." JJ clapped his hands together in excitement.

* * *

FOUR HOURS LATER, we arrived at our home outside the city that Joaquin had purchased years ago after the kidnapping. We were fully moved in, and the kids loved to be outside in the backyard to play. My parents could visit and not have to stay at a hotel since the place was big. Once Hugo parked the car, he headed around to the back passenger side to help Madelyn take Jianna out first, then JJ. I unbuckled my seat and opened the door, not waiting for his assistance, and he growled at me. I waved him off, not caring for the attitude.

"Hugo, you need to take a night off," I spoke, reaching for Jianna in her car seat. Rubbing my nose against her, I kissed her cheek. We all piled into the house, Madelyn set JJ down on the ground, and he took off running.

"He needs to be nice first," Cassidy mumbled under her breath. He held a harsh grimace on his face at her comment but decided to leave it alone. Neither one would speak up and say they liked the other, so I stayed out of the relationship. Joaquin never wanted to talk about his men dating, let alone his sister dating. Cassidy was family to us, and we were just as protective over her.

"Mrs. Fuertes, do you need anything before I start dinner for the kids?" The family chef walked out of the kitchen. I had a huge team of help, from Martha managing the housekeepers and the kids' schedule to Madelyn, my babysitter and assistant and Hugo, my bodyguard.

"No, it's just the family tonight. Is my husband home?" I removed my jacket and kicked off my shoes, rolling my sleeves up on my wrist.

"He's in his office," Martha replied, turning back toward the kitchen.

"I have some calls to make, and I'll get the notes from today sent over," Cassidy said, heading back out.

"You're not staying for dinner?" I asked.

She glanced at Hugo playing with JJ on the floor with Madelyn, and I smirked at him, ignoring her harsh glare.

"I had a huge lunch, still full."

"Yeah, right." She flipped me off, and I chortled, heading off to the back of the house toward Joaquin's office.

As I angled to listen in to the whispering on the other side of the door, a voice from behind me finally broke the silence.

"Ohh. I was just—"

"I forgot to tell you a seven a.m. call time tomorrow," Cassidy said. The door to Joaquin's office opened with Gael rushing out.

"What's wrong with him?" Cassidy inquired, and I shrugged.

"I'll see you in the morning." I didn't wait to be called into his office. I closed the door behind me, locking it from the inside and glancing briefly at Joaquin as he leaned back in his chair with his eyes closed.

"You get a good listen?" Joaquin asked.

"What are you talking about?" When he glanced at me, I pressed off the door and sauntered over to him, turning his chair around and plowing into his lap. Suddenly, he frowned at me, and I was taken aback by the change in his mood.

"You have to stop listening in on my meetings."

"I didn't listen in on your meeting." I pressed my palm against his cheek.

"How was work?" He changed the subject, placing his hands on each of my thighs.

"It is fine, work as normal."

"Hugo told me you had a scene with Shamar today, and you wore a robe." Joaquin's left brow rose.

"That's my job. It doesn't mean anything."

"A job you should be ready to retire from."

I tried to get off his lap, and he tightened his grip around my waist.

"Let me go."

"No."

"We've had this discussion before, and I'm not quitting."

"I have a job I need to go out and do. I need my wife to be home."

"What's the job?"

"Something you don't need to know about."

"Joaquin, that's not fair. We promised to not keep secrets."

"Sofia, enough. Where are my children?" He squeezed my thigh, and I smacked his hand away.

"What's wrong with Gael?"

"My sister is coming to dinner."

"You know they're dating, right?"

"Alessandra dates everyone."

"I want to do a photoshoot with the kids," I blurted out, and he stopped rubbing my thigh. I tried to reach for his hand, and he snatched it away.

278

"No."

"They're my kids too."

"I said no."

"This is ridiculous. You haven't given me a good reason. It's a closed set, and we're protected at all times."

"When is this shoot?"

"In two days."

"Move."

"No, I like sitting in your lap. Give me a kiss." I leaned over to peck his lips, but he turned his head, and I ended up kissing his cheek.

I sighed and moved out of his lap to give him space.

"Stop pushing me."

"What are you afraid of, honey? You said we have triple the security now."

"That doesn't mean my enemies aren't looking for you."

"What if Gael came along with us?" I asked, praying he would let this one thing go.

He blew out a breath of frustration, rubbing his temples.

"No photoshoot, Sofia, and that's final." Joaquin turned toward me and pressed a kiss against my lips. Someone knocked on the door, and he answered, seeing JJ trying to come inside.

"My son, you look happy. Did you have fun with Mommy?" Joaquin was a natural with the kids, surprisingly. I never had to beg him to do anything or get up to feed or change a diaper. He loved being hands-on, and I was grateful to have that in a husband for times when I needed a break.

"Where's Jianna?" Joaquin questioned Madelyn.

"With Hugo in the living room," Madelyn replied.

Joaquin took the toy ball out of JJ's hand, watching him giggle in excitement as his father shook it in front of his face.

"I need to study my lines. I have an early call time tomorrow," I told him, strolling toward the door.

"Sofia."

"Yes." I stood with my back toward him.

"I love you."

"I know."

I drew in a deep breath, headed upstairs to our bedroom, and wiped the oncoming tears trying to fall. Picking up my laptop, I checked my emails and social media. Clicking on the forwarded email by Cassidy, I read over the information for the photoshoot and replied to her that I wanted to go ahead with doing the shoot. Joaquin would just have to deal.

"Your phone is beeping."

I jumped in surprise and closed out the email, seeing Joaquin holding my phone.

"What's wrong with you?" he probed.

"Uhhh… nothing."

"I need to head out, but I'll be back for dinner."

"Where are you going?"

"Alessandra," he replied, and I knew something was wrong.

His sister was always in some type of drama, and since moving here permanently, his parents had put him in charge of keeping an eye on her.

"Be safe." When he bent down and pressed a kiss on my lips, he slid his tongue inside, and I dropped my computer on my side, wrapping my arms around his neck.

"Mmmm…" I sucked on his tongue, released him, then strolled out of the room as I watched the long strides of his broad shoulders as he texted on his phone.

I closed out of the group text, tossing the phone on the bed. No matter what, Joaquin would keep us under his wing at all times. I wasn't ashamed of who I'd married, and I refused to hide my children. Lifting the computer screen, I checked over my schedule and informed Cassidy to keep me updated on any changes. I then closed it out and put it on the desk. I twisted my wedding ring, walked out of the bedroom, and went to check on my babies in the playroom. I laughed when JJ focused so hard on Paw Patrol, and Jianna was in her baby chair, giggling at him. My life had expanded from having to handle what state I was singing in for the night to now chasing babies around a playroom.

"Who's hungry!" I clapped my hands together and tickled Jianna on her stomach.

"Hungry!" JJ excitedly jumped up and down.

"Me too. Come on, big boy." I grabbed his hand, picked Jianna up, and went to the kitchen. I helped them sit in their highchairs, and Martha passed me JJ's plate of veggies, cut-up chicken, and water. I picked up a bottle out of the fridge for Jianna and sat at the island to feed her while I listened to JJ talk our ears off. I chuckled at his animated expressions of what he loved and leaned over to wipe his hands clean of the food. I glanced up at the clock and noticed it was getting late. Dinner was almost done, and Joaquin once again wouldn't make it on time.

"I'm going to take her upstairs and get her ready for bed." I took the bottle out of Jianna's mouth and held her over my shoulder to pat her back.

"I'll keep a plate waiting for you."

"Thanks, Martha. He should be finished in another ten minutes." I rubbed JJ's head.

"No worries."

I kissed the top of his head and strolled upstairs to Jianna's bedroom, grabbed a fresh onesie, and took her to the bathroom. I watched her stare up at me with her father's features. Thirty minutes later, she was knocked out in her crib, and I went to check on JJ, asleep in his bed. I closed the door and checked the time on my watch. Still no Joaquin. I released a breath and sauntered to our bedroom to pin my hair up before setting a bath up to soak and fall asleep. He would be more than surprised when he noticed my schedule wouldn't be as available as he wanted. Mob boss or not, Joaquin needed a reminder of who he'd married.

JOAQUIN

The town car stopped in front of the club that was owned by people I didn't care to know, and I glanced out the window as Alessandra was escorted over to my car by my men. It was going on nine at night, and I'd promised Sofia I would be back for dinner, but that was to be determined if Alessandra continued to do stupid things. Gael was out handling another call. I thought it would be best not to get him involved, especially the way Alessandra was dressed. Lenny opened the passenger door, and she slid across the seat, wearing a dress that showed too much skin.

"I'm an adult, Joaquin!" Alessandra fussed.

"Shut up," I barked back.

"I'm telling Poppa!" she yelled, sniffing.

"You're going back to Italy."

"No!"

"The last thing I need to do is focus on my little sister getting drunk in clubs."

"Weren't you going at my age?"

"With protection. I knew not to drink around people I didn't know."

"All you care about is your work and nothing else," she

complained. The car pulled out into traffic. That was the same argument Sofia was throwing at me, but I heard the opposite from my men because they felt I was losing focus on the cartel business. In addition, since I'd gotten married, Gael was responsible for many of the tasks.

"I'm dating Gael," she blurted out.

"He's my second in command; understand that if you get involved with him."

"He didn't want to date me because of you, but I convinced him you would be fine."

"Gael is much older than you."

"He doesn't treat me like a little girl."

"Stop acting like one by doing stupid things!" As I shouted angrily, my face became red.

"School takes up a lot of my time; it was just a night of drinks."

"If you can't handle yourself, I will have you shipped back to Italy."

"I can handle myself." With a roll of the eyes, she looked away.

"Tomorrow, I'm putting more guards on you."

"What! That's too much," Alessandra spat.

"Either you take the guards, or you come live with me."

"I'll take the guards."

She wiped the tears that welled up, and I hated to see my little sister cry, but she left me no choice as the oldest and her caregiver. I gave her money and paid for her apartment, thinking she would be on top of her classes, so I was shocked when I heard she was failing and partying more and more. If this was what I had to look forward to with Jianna, I'd keep her locked in her bedroom until she was thirty. We arrived at the front of her condo, and I unlocked the door to step out. I checked the time on my cell and wiped a hand down my face. Alessandra leaned her head on my shoulder.

"You don't deserve her," Alessandra mumbled.

"No more alcohol; it makes you look foolish," I fussed, snatching her clutch and taking the keys out. I helped her through the doors and up to the elevator. Leaning her against the wall, I tapped on

Sofia's name. The phone rang with no answer, and I cursed under my breath. I needed to make this right before we became even more fractured.

Ding!

"Come on," I told Alessandra and helped her inside the elevator. I hit the fifth floor and rode up, running all the thoughts of how Sofia would punish me for missing another dinner with our kids.

"I can make it from here, Joaquin." Alessandra held out her hand for her purse, and I walked around her, took the key out, and slid it in. I watched her stroll in and pass out on the couch.

"No more drinking. If I hear about this again, you won't like me." I bent down, helped to remove her shoes, and picked up the blanket off the couch to cover her up.

"I promise," Alessandra whispered.

Buzz! Buzz!

I glanced down at my vibrating phone and saw a text from Gael.

Gael: We have a problem.

Me: I'm handling something with Alessandra.

Gael: Is she all right?

Me: Drunk at a club.

Gael: She's trying to act like she isn't a part of the family.

Me: I'll remind her.

Gael: This can't wait.

Me: I'm leaving now.

Gael: It's not good.

* * *

APPROXIMATELY THIRTY MINUTES LATER, the car arrived at the address Gael texted to me, a small mom and pop shop, but there was something a little weird about it. As I walked to the door, Gael's men held the door open, and I stepped inside to look at the perfectly arranged food and drink display machines. A somber look came over Gabriel's face as he stood near the back door of the employee entrance. My attention was drawn to him as I waited for him to speak.

"You're not going to like this."

"What?"

"We have a new player."

My brow lifted in surprise. Everyone knew I ran the biggest gun ring in New York, on top of being the highest paid killer to get rid of any problem.

"Who?"

He motioned to the left of him, and I peered around him and saw a crate on the floor. I bent down to lift the top and saw a logo of a skull and foreign words that I recognized as French.

"Lusting," I mumbled.

"We need to see if more of those are around here."

"How did you know this was here? Who owns this place?"

I lifted the automatic weapon, checked the grip, and found the serial numbers were scraped off.

"One of our customers was approached with a proposal."

As I dropped the gun back in the crate, I stood and looked around the room. It was a normal back office with a desk, TV, chair, and an exit door.

"Did they purchase it?"

"No, but he's interested in negotiations."

My left brow perked at that request.

"We don't give discounts."

"I told him that, and he'd like to speak with you directly."

"Everyone knows you handle all the negotiations."

"True, but if we want to keep this new problem from getting out of hand, we need to handle it now."

"Set up a meeting."

"You're giving him a discount." Gael trailed behind me from the backroom to the front door.

"Set up the meeting."

"Joaquin." He gave me a worried look.

Gael knew me better than anyone. I didn't let anyone steal from me or make my business look foolish.

"Call Alessandra tomorrow," I called out.

"No arguing?"

"She's an adult, but you know who I am and what I would do if something happened to her."

"I would give my life for her."

"Then we won't have any problems, but she needs to understand the people she's hanging with do her no good."

"I'm trying to not force anything."

"If she becomes a distraction for you or my life, I will send her back."

"I'll talk with her," Gael explained.

"Call me when that meeting is ready."

"What about our new friendly visitor?"

"Find out about Lusting."

"If they want in our area..."

I shut the door of the backseat.

"They dictate their futures."

"I thought you were stepping back on killing since the family has grown."

"Never underestimate a Fuertes."

Gael nodded and headed to his car. My driver pulled off down the road to head back home. I sighed and thought about the smile on my kid's face when I wake them up in the morning, and have our alone time together and able to give them my attention. Those two made everything else disappear, and I needed to remember to take in those moments before they grew older, and I missed out on precious time.

Past midnight, I walked through a quiet house, heading upstairs to peek in on JJ. I noticed him sleeping on his stomach like I used to do when I was younger. I closed the door quietly and checked on Jianna in her crib. Her little hands were balled up at her sides. I kissed her forehead and stepped away so as not to wake her, making sure the door was closed. As I strolled a few doors down the hallway, I approached our bedroom and released a long-held breath. I pushed the door open gently and stared up at my beautiful wife lying in bed asleep. I dropped my jacket on the chair, removed my clothes, and headed to the bathroom. I turned the shower on the hottest temperature, stepped in, and let the night wash away from me with my head down in thought. Fifteen minutes later, I grabbed a towel off the door and dried off. Sliding on my boxers, I turned the light off, climbed in bed, and pulled her naked body close to me.

"Mmmmm... you missed dinner," she muttered. I kissed her forehead. She slid her hand in my boxers and automatically, I got hard.

"It couldn't be helped..." I groaned when she squeezed my dick.

"What happened with Alessandra?" she asked, pulled my thick girth out of the boxers, and sat up to ease down on him.

"Shit!" I gripped her hips as she slowly rocked back and forth. Her low eyes exposed she was ready to take control.

Sofia stretched her arms out, lifted her hips, leaned down to take my lips, and guided her tongue to my mouth.

"Ughhh!" My hand firmly grasped her waist as I tightened my grip and pumped into her. She moaned as her head dropped back, her body quivering. We both fought for dominance in the relationship, and I hated when Sofia tried to question me. I smacked her on the ass, rotated us with me on top, and picked up the pace. She scratched my arms and chest as she cried out. She was close to climax.

"Joaquin! Right there!"

"Do as I ask, mi amore." Her hips bucked as her orgasm overwhelmed her. I released and fell on top of her, out of breath. She wrapped her arms around my back, and we fell asleep with me still inside of her.

JOAQUIN

I came downstairs fully dressed the next morning and noticed Martha only having my plate available for breakfast and coffee. She smiled and placed it in the usual spot of the island.

"Where's Sofia?"

"She's at the photoshoot, sir."

"I told her that was out of the question."

"I'm sorry, sir. She told me to pack the kids some food, and she'll have them eat at the location."

"Was Hugo with her?"

Martha nodded.

"I'm not hungry." I left the kitchen, stalked to my office in the back of the house, and slammed the door. I dialed Sofia's number.

"You've reached Sofia. I can't come to the phone right now. Leave a message."

"Sofia, call me back." I hung up and dialed again.

"You've reached Sofia, I can't come to the phone right now. Leave a message."

She knew I didn't want my children paraded around the world and shown off. A man of my position needed to keep his family hidden, or at least my children. The sex we'd had last night I'd hoped would be a wakeup call to her, but something more was brewing between us that I didn't like.

Ring! Ring!

I answered the call.

"Sofia!"

"Joaquin, it's your father."

I sighed, not in the right frame of mind to talk with him about anything. I was slammed with thoughts of why Sofia had defied my orders and went on with the photoshoot.

"I'm here."

"How is your sister doing? We haven't heard from her lately."

"She's fine." I sat in my chair and clicked on the computer.

"I'm hearing differently."

"Then why are you calling me?"

"You seem distracted."

"I'm focused."

"Really? Because from what I see, you're losing a grip on everything."

"Define losing my grip." I clenched my teeth.

"I still have contacts in New York. I hear things."

"Are you trying to call to talk about your daughter or my business?"

"Unlike you, I have control over everything that belongs to me."

"I have control!" I shouted.

"For now. If your sister is getting drunk and showing up in these photos or on the internet, that's a problem for the family," he chastised.

I rubbed a hand down my forehead.

"I had a talk with her."

"Either you get a handle on things, or she comes back to Italy."

"She knows."

"And you'll lose my connection to guns if this continues."

"I can handle my own business."

"You're being watched."

"What do you know about Lusting?" I probed.

"Nothing."

"Gael found their guns being dropped in our area."

"A new dealer."

"Probably."

"You need to handle it."

"I will."

"Let me look into them first."

"A French design and wording."

"I'll send over what I find out."

"Thank you."

"And Joaquin."

"Yes."

"Understand your position."

I listened to the dial tone and held the phone out, then glanced at the family photo of Sofia and the kids. I'd been patient with her ever since the night of the kidnapping and wanted to keep her less caught up in my world, but she was taking her career to higher places and not thinking of the backfire it could have on our family or my business. I checked my business email and saw a few clients wanting me to take some jobs next week on short notice. I needed to think it over before agreeing even though the payment was one million. Anytime I spent away from my children out of the state was precious, minutes I couldn't get back or put a monetary value on. After I closed the email, I turned the computer off and walked to the wall photo of Sofia and pulled it open to reveal my safe. I grabbed a stack of money and a gun and locked it back up.

"Mr. Fuertes, do you need anything specific for dinner tonight?" Martha questioned.

"No, Martha. As a matter of fact, take the night off."

"Are you sure?"

"Positive."

"What should I say when Mrs. Fuertes calls?"

I stood at the open front door.

"Tell her you've confirmed things with me." I winked, shut the door behind me, placed my shades on, and walked to the awaiting limo.

"Anywhere specific, sir?" my driver asked.

"I need to go to Antonio's."

"Yes, sir, Mr. Fuertes."

He shut the door, and I buckled my seatbelt and dialed Sofia's number again.

"*You've reached Sofia. I can't come to the phone right now. Leave a message.*"

Amherst pulled out of the driveway, and I held the cell up to stare at the third missed call from Sofia. This was only fueling the fire, making me want to send my men to bring her back home and lock her away with my children.

Buzz! Buzz!

Gael: Alessandra showed up for class.

Me: Good. I should be at Antonio's soon.

Gael: No updates on the Lusting situation.

Me: Meet me anyway.

Gael: Let me wrap up here.

After I sent a text back to him and said okay, Sofia finally replied back to my missed calls.

Sofia: I'm filming. What's going on?

Me: Where are my kids?

Sofia: They're fine, Joaquin. I wouldn't put my children in harm's way.

Me: We talked about this photoshoot not being a good idea.

Sofia: No, you demanded I don't do it.

The car stopped at a light. I watched the traffic ease through to the sounds of pissed-off people.

Me: We'll discuss this later tonight.

Sofia: Sex won't solve this issue.

Me: Alessandra held me up last night.

Sofia: That's not the only problem we're dealing with.

Me: I have a meeting I need to attend. I will talk to you later.

Sofia: Fine.

Me: Don't ignore my calls again.

Sofia: I was filming, and my phone was in my purse.
Me: I've stated what my concerns are.
Sofia: I'm being called to set.

The car arrived at Antonio's, and I closed out of the message thread, pushed the door open, and stepped out, looking at the surrounding areas. I went around the limo and shook hands with the guard on duty, and he opened the door for me. Looking around the closed restaurant, I noticed Carlo and Antonio sitting together at the back table near the window.

"Joaquin, how are you?" Carlo questioned.

I shook hands with Antonio, then Carlo, and grabbed the chair from the next table.

"I woke up with a lot on my mind."

Antonio picked up his glass of water and glanced at Carlo.

"Tell us," Carlo suggested.

"Do you know anything about Lusting?" I asked.

"Only thing I've heard about them was a few years ago. A gang out of France," Antonio recalled and slid his cup of water away.

"Why are you bringing this up?" Carlo asked.

"I might have a friend uninvited," I spoke in code.

"This Lusting," he quipped.

"Yes."

"We don't like visitors invited to the table." Antonio leaned forward clasped his hands together.

"Do we need to assist?"

"No, I've made a good reputation since I've been in America and New York City specifically. People know where I am."

"Are you still taking jobs?"

"Occasionally."

"How is married life?"

"Work." I smirked, and they chuckled at my statement.

"Give Sofia and the kids our best."

"Janice is constantly talking about a new trailer she saw Sofia in."

"Yeah, she's becoming a bigger star than before."

"I understand about having high profile women," Antonio said.

"Between her and my sister, my life is busy."

"So the ghost isn't ready for retirement?" Carlo pointed at the gun behind my jacket.

"He's always ready for action."

"Keep us updated, and we'll do our own checking on Lusting." Antonio looked at Carlo, and he nodded.

"What else do you need from us?" Carlo asked. Gael arrived, extended his hand to them, and sat next to me.

"Antonio, Carlo," Gael said, picking up the glass of water.

"I'm thinking of exploring new territory in Texas."

Gael took out his phone.

"I went out there a few months ago, after Joaquin talked about how the borders are easily available to get guns in and out," Gael mentioned.

"You able to handle that type of increase?" On a napkin, Antonio scribbled.

"Depending on what the distribution is like, it could be lucrative," Gael replied.

"Keep me updated and contact this person to do research on the prospect." Antonio handed the napkin to me.

"Ezequiel Mota."

"Carlo and I have done business with him before. He's fair."

"I'll keep that in mind."

"Don't be a stranger. Even if your services aren't utilized by us, the girls want to get together," Carlo said, reaching out for a shake. I stood to leave.

"I'm always available for the De Luca Family."

"Again, keep us updated." Anthony tipped his glass into the air.

"Salute."

Upon leaving Antonio's, Gael and I walked to the car, and Amherst held the door open.

"Where to now?"

"Look into Ezequiel and Lusting. I want our reach to cover more shipment areas in case we need to expand beyond the loading docks for incoming deals."

"Expand that far? What if your father doesn't like your choice of business dealings?"

"He's not in charge."

"As long as you know," Gael replied.

"I need another favor."

"What is it?"

"I want to know everything about Sofia's filming."

"Joaquin, we've been through this before. She has her career."

"I know what she has. Her schedule is getting busier, and that's leaving very little time."

"I like Sofia for you, but you'll cause more problems with this request."

"Make the arrangements and see about a flight to Texas."

I climbed in and shut the door, waiting as the car pulled into traffic. The plan was to get back home early after a few more stops and spend time with my family for the rest of the day. Sofia would come home and expect me to be upset and angry, but my plan was to make sure the kids and her were welcomed with a nice dinner. Then we could spend alone time together once the kids went to bed.

SOFIA

The slow jams of the '80s played on the radio as the photographer came forward and took more shots of me holding Jianna's hand. JJ stood in front of me. All three of us matched in the same colors of cream, and red, to fit the background of me as a working actress and mother. We'd been here for over six hours, and I was enjoying myself, laughing, playing, and wanting to do even more. JJ became the star of the photoshoot, and they even mentioned him doing modeling for babies. That would never happen. Joaquin's calls were blowing up my phone, and I eventually had to text him back because Cassidy thought something could be wrong. I'd rather not deal with him being upset about me not returning any calls since the tension was already high with us. The filming project was going into extended shooting, and I needed to add more days on my schedule to do promo work and interviews, plus traveling would happen soon.

"We can break for lunch," the photographer said. We'd filmed together before in the past, and she knew how I liked to not fool around. Having a shoot at her studio in the Bronx was a little farther away from home, but we'd managed to stay on time and not run over.

"Thanks, Rosalie."

Madelyn came over and grabbed JJ's hand, and I sauntered with Jianna on my hip to the play area in the corner. JJ went to grab the toy truck, and I placed Jianna down on the patio and picked up a toy ball for her to take.

"How many more setups?" I asked Cassidy, took a seat in the chair next to the kids, and watched them play.

"Two more and only one of those with the kids."

"Do they need to change?"

"No, I think it'll be fine."

Cassidy passed me my phone.

"Any more texts from Joaquin?" I scrolled through my phone.

"No, and I think Hugo has sent photos or video back to him; it's been quiet since earlier."

"I doubt Hugo would do that, Cassidy."

"I don't put anything past him," Cassidy fussed.

Her upper lip pursed as she rolled her eyes at him.

"You two still haven't talked?"

"No reason to talk."

"You like him, and I think kissed him if I'm not mistaken."

"I was drunk." Cassidy grabbed the truck and bent down next to JJ.

"JJ, are you hungry?" I questioned, and he nodded.

"Yes, Mommy."

"Madelyn, can you grab some food from the bag in the corner please?"

I'd triple-packed for today and brought snacks they'd enjoy so I wouldn't have them on a sugar rush from the junk that was normally at photoshoots. Madelyn pulled out packets of apples, yogurt, crackers, and grapes for them to share.

"What are we doing after this?"

"We have a few video meetings, and then you're free for the rest of the day."

"Good, I'm exhausted."

"Just remember if we get the call to do the filming in Texas, you'll be away for a few weeks."

I blew out a breath.

"I know."

"Plus, you need to plan your next album."

"I can't think about that right now." I groaned, leaning back in the chair.

"Your career is at the top right now. I don't want to pressure you."

I wasn't upset about Cassidy going the extra mile to get me to the point in my career where I could decline certain roles. She'd taken the role of being a manager to a level that my previous management team never even imagined. I received so many offers and requests there was a possibility I'd be booked for the next two years, if I said yes to everything.

"I understand. Grab the opportunity while you can."

Cassidy stood, wiped her hands on her pants, and pulled the chair over to sit beside me.

"What do you think about doing a few appearances in Texas?"

"We're ready, Sofia!" Rosalie called out, changing the lights.

"Coming," I responded, rising out of the chair.

"Send me the details. I need to figure out what Joaquin is doing first."

"Great, give me a few minutes, and I'll send it over to your email."

Madelyn stood up with Jianna, and I grabbed JJ's hand to clean him up and help him stand to get set up for the next scene. Rosalie spoke on what she wanted for the final shoots with her team, and I listened in and helped to keep the kids hyped up and ready.

* * *

TWO HOURS LATER, we were piled in the limo together, and the kids were asleep in their car seats as the limo sped down the highway. It wasn't too late, and I had time to get the kids washed before bed and spend a little time together before I went over my scenes for tomorrow.

"It's so weird how much they look like Joaquin."

"My parents say the same thing."

"You just pooped out another version of him." Cassidy chuckled.

"When are you going to settle down?" I pointed out.

She waved away my question.

"Too busy."

"Life doesn't have to stop for you to have a love life and career."

"Honestly, I like focusing on your career rather than my love life."

I gazed over at Hugo in the passenger seat. I knew they had something going on and were secretly trying to keep it under wraps, but if he wanted something serious, and Cassidy didn't, this would drive a wedge between them even further.

"I appreciate the support, but remember you have a life outside of me and the kids."

"One day, I'll find someone," Cassidy muttered, looking out the window.

The car made it home and drove up to the front door. Hugo got out to help the kids on the left side of the car, and I opened my door on the right and climbed out to pick up my bags. Madelyn carried Jianna's things. I removed my key and slid it in the front door, and there was complete silence as we walked through the corridor to the dining room. My eyes scanned around the room; it smelled like Pine Sol from a deep cleaning.

"I'll take them upstairs to get bathed," Madelyn said.

"Thanks, Madelyn. I'll get dinner started."

Hugo carried JJ in his arms behind Madelyn, and Cassidy followed to the kitchen. I strolled to my bedroom to change.

"Joaquin," I called out, nudging the door of our bedroom open, and it was empty.

I kicked off my shoes, removed the sweatpants and T-shirt, and grabbed my robe from the back of the door, along with a fresh shirt and pants. I pushed the bathroom door open and found candles were lit, with the lights low. I had no clue why. I stepped in farther and saw a note on the edge of the tub.

Relax, dinner will be ready in fifteen minutes .

I smiled, folded the note up, and put it inside my robe. I dropped it on the counter, slid in the tub of warm water, and placed my head on the back of the pillow so as not to get it wet. I let my body soak up the soothing aromas.

"Sofia! I'm leaving," I heard Cassidy yell from the other side of the door.

"Okay, call me later."

"Don't forget call time."

"I promise."

Thirty minutes later, I came downstairs, went to the kitchen, and saw Joaquin sitting with the kids, laughing together.

"Where is everybody?" I walked up to him and kissed him on the lips. He gripped the back of my head and sucked on my tongue.

"I wanted to make dinner for you and the kids alone."

He sat between Jianna and JJ, and I pulled the chair out across from him.

"You want to tell me what that was earlier?"

I picked up the spoon to eat the risotto and veggies.

"We need to make sure we're not losing this time with the kids." He kissed the top of JJ's head.

"I don't disagree."

"How was the shoot?"

"It was good."

"I don't want my children in any more media photos."

"They're my kids too."

"Sofia, you can't expect to have the same life as before."

"I expect my husband to support my goals."

Jianna started to cry for me. I dropped the spoon, stood, and walked around the island to pick her up and bounce her to sleep in my arms.

"You went against my orders."

"I'm not Hugo or any other one of your men."

He whispered something in JJ's ear and helped him to finish eating.

"So you're ignoring me?"

"I'm going to get my son to bed. Then I plan on sleeping with my wife."

"Your wife."

Joaquin pressed a kiss to my cheek.

"Get the kids to bed."

"I have an early shoot tomorrow."

"Hugo will take you."

"I don't like your demeanor."

We walked the kids to their bedrooms.

"I have a lot of work to handle; fighting with my wife is not my goal."

"There is something else."

"Not tonight, Sofia." He pecked my lips.

I went into Jianna's room and took her to the bathroom to wipe her face and hands clean. I placed her in the crib and kissed her on the forehead. Turning the lights off, I headed to our bedroom, slipped out of my shoes, and pulled the covers back to lie down with the lights off. I fell asleep until his strong arms pulled me close to his chest, kissing the back of my neck.

* * *

TWO DAYS LATER.

I was on set, filming another scene with Shamar and waiting for them to call cut as we stood together in a tight embrace.

"Cut!" the director yelled.

"You brought it today, Sofia," Shamar said.

"Thanks, Shamar." The wardrobe department head brought over a robe to cover my dress. My character was going to dinner with his character. I picked up the water bottle, took a sip, and sat in my chair, watching the replay of the scene. We were becoming more and more comfortable bringing the story to life with each other.

Cassidy pointed to the screen and noticed I picked up the fork in the wrong hand.

"We can do another take on that shot," the director said.

I sipped the water and listened to myself, checking to make sure that was the only mistake.

"That looks great," I muttered, pointing to us holding hands.

"We can do one more take of your side profile," the director explained. I nodded, removed the robe, and stood as makeup and hair looked me over one more time. Escorting me back on stage, I released my hand and sat in the chair with the fake food and candlelight.

Shamar sat and joked to keep the fun flowing after a long day of filming.

"One more time, and it will be good for today." The director held the script in front of him on the table and pointed at the setup.

"Ready."

"Picking up from the beginning?" Shamar questioned.

I nodded and scooted closer to the table, picked up the fork.

"Action!" the director called out.

"Baby, I did this all for you." Shamar covered my hand on the table.

"I love how much you care." I smiled back and squeezed his hand.

Shamar leaned over the table and pecked me on the lips.

"Cut!"

Everybody clapped their hands for doing a great job on filming. Shamar helped me out from the table, and we gathered with the rest of the crew.

"Today was great, everyone. Remember we have filming coming up in Texas soon," the director commented.

"You guys have this in the bag for award season," Cassidy cheered.

"I'm just happy to be a part of the film," I responded.

"Are you ready to head out?" Cassidy asked.

I removed the jewelry and strolled off to my trailer with a team of guards as Cassidy talked about the details of our trip to Texas. I pushed open the door of my trailer and smiled at the kids playing with Madelyn. I kissed them both on the forehead and went to change my clothes.

Twenty minutes later, we arrived home exhausted from being gone the entire day once again. I allowed JJ to go to the playroom, and I saw Martha in the kitchen but no sign of Joaquin again.

"Madelyn, can you get the kids fed and ready for bed?"

"Of course."

"Thanks. I need to finalize some things with Cassidy."

Cassidy sauntered into the kitchen with her laptop and phone pressed to her ear.

"We can go to the living room."

She nodded, and I passed her a bottle of water and lifted an apple from the fruit bowl in the middle of the island.

"Where's Joaquin?" Cassidy questioned.

I sat next to her on the couch and shrugged.

"Who knows."

"If you need to reschedule our meeting, we can."

"It's fine."

"Okay, then we can start with a photo." Cassidy was cut off from a loud noise at the front door.

Bang! Bang!

"Move out of my way!" I heard loud familiar voices.

Startled, I put the cap back on the bottle of water, wondering who was yelling at the front door.

"Who is that?" Cassidy asked, and Hugo walked in with a tight grip on Alessandra.

"It's me... Alessandra," she whispered.

"What's wrong?"

"I need to talk to you."

"Can it wait?"

"Please, Sofia!"

"Give me a second," I replied and jumped up to escort her to Joaquin's office, away from the kids being disturbed.

"What?"

I shut the door behind us.

"I need your help."

"No." I tried to open the door and leave, but she pushed it back closed.

"Please, Sofia. I want to go to this party, and Joaquin's men won't let me out of their sight."

"Alessandra, you 're kidding, right?"

"No."

"I was relaxing after a long day of dealing with children and work. Your brother is missing in action."

"But I need you." She poked her lip out.

"No, you need to grow up and focus on why you came to New York."

"Haven't you wanted to be free of this mess and live life, Sofia?"

"That was before I got with your brother, and you know what I went through." I recalled the kidnapping and attempted rape.

Those early days of being with Joaquin should have come with a manual on dating a mobster. I thought I knew everything, but it was becoming clear that his world was more complicated by the day.

"It won't take long; you just slip in with me and leave after five minutes."

"What do you think Joaquin will say when he finds out I went to a club?" I opened the door and left with her behind me. I made it back to the living room with Cassidy and Hugo glaring at each other.

"He doesn't have to know. Besides, you need a girls' night out."

"No."

"I didn't take you for the submissive type."

I placed my hand on my hip, my lips pursed.

"That won't work on me."

"What are you talking about?"

"Trying to manipulate me into agreeing."

"You're right. I knew my brother was in charge, but I just figured you still had your way of handling him."

"Alessandra, I'm a grown woman; nobody is in charge of me."

"Then you'll go to the club with me." She held her hands up in prayer.

"Five minutes, and then we leave." I pointed at her.

"Yay! Yay!" Alessandra kissed me on the cheek and turned to leave the room.

"Don't make me regret this."

She crossed her middle and index finger and smirked.

SOFIA

$\mathcal{I}$ could already tell the night would be terrible soon as we came in and saw how the crowd was acting in the club. Alessandra had us in a section with some guys I'd never met before, but Hugo was close by and made sure we were watched. He didn't like that we'd come, but I promised we wouldn't stay long, and Cassidy was with me as well. The smoke filled the room, and I fanned it away and scooted closer to Cassidy as Alessandra smiled and picked up one of the champagne bottles to pour herself a drink.

"Do you think she knows those guys are expecting something for these drinks?"

"I told Joaquin something was up with Alessandra."

Walls thumped, and the DJ called over the mic for single women to come to the main floor.

"That's my song!" Alessandra jumped up, pulled her dress down, and reached for my hand.

"I'll be fine up here."

"Come on, Sofia. Have some fun." Alessandra extended her hand.

"No. I came with you, but I'm not dancing."

I was glad I'd listened to Cassidy and put my shades on so no one could recognize me.

"Ugh! Don't be boring at a nightclub." Alessandra stomped off down the stairs to the crowd. A hand was placed on my thigh, and I froze.

"Sexy, who are you with?" a drunken voice whispered in my ear.

"Please move your hand."

"You know you like it, sexy," he said.

"If you want to live, I suggest you move it before he does." I pointed at Hugo, whose eyes narrowed on the guy next to me.

He raised his hands in surrender.

"Cassidy, let's leave."

"Thought you'd never ask." Cassidy jumped up and extended her hand to me. I followed her out of the section, down the stairs, and through the crowds of people.

"*Ladies and gentlemen, we have Sofia Fuertes in the house!*" the DJ yelled.

I froze and turned to look over at the booth, and I saw Alessandra waving at us.

"Did she just do that?" I mumbled to myself.

"Where's Hugo?" Cassidy probed as camera phones were pushed in my face.

"Shit, we need to get out of here." I looked around the room.

"Can I have your autograph please?" a girl asked.

"Sorry, I'm not doing that."

"You're a stuck-up bitch!" she blurted out, and I felt a hand push me hard.

"What the fuck, bitch!" another woman shouted and shoved me in the shoulder.

"Sorry, this was an accident—"

Pop! Pop!

The entire club erupted in chaos. People shoved each other, fighting. I reached out to grab Cassidy's hand, and she was yanked down to the ground.

"Cassidy!"

Hugo fought a guy to get through to her, and before I could help her, my hand was yanked back, and my shades fell off.

"Let me go!" I shouted.

A tall figure of a man pushed me into the room, and I tried to get out, but he held his hands up in surrender.

"I'm not here to hurt you."

His accent was different, so I took a step back.

"Who are you?"

He smiled and reached his palm out. I looked down and back up to his narrowed dark, intense eyes. Even though it was nighttime, I could see he was a beautiful man at six-four, wearing a tailor-made suit.

"Emile."

Bang! Bang!

"Sofia! Sofia!" Cassidy yelled.

I strolled around him and opened the door. Hugo and Cassidy glared at the man behind me.

"Are you all right?"

"Yes. What about you?"

"Fine, but we need to leave."

"Where's Alessandra?"

"Who's this?" Hugo held his gun at the side of his body.

"He's okay, Hugo."

"What are you doing here with her?"

"Hugo, it's fine. He saved me."

"We don't have time, Hugo. We need to go."

Hugo tucked the gun back in his side, and I released a breath and started toward the front entrance, but Hugo blocked me.

"The car is in the back," Hugo said.

"Joaquin is pissed," Cassidy whispered in my ear.

I looked over my shoulder and saw Emile staring back at me, and he winked. I climbed in the car, sitting next to Alessandra arguing on the phone with someone I could only assume was Gael. Hugo started the car and drove down the alleyway of the back entrance. I searched around for my purse and realized I didn't have it with me in the car.

"I lost my purse."

"Maybe tomorrow we can call to get it back." Cassidy pulled her phone out, scrolled, and showed her text thread of people mentioning a shootout at the club.

"This is a disaster." I groaned, leaning my head back on the seat.

"I'm not in the mood," Alessandra blurted out.

"What's going on with Alessandra?"

The car went silent as we rode on the freeway to our house.

"Sofia, you can't blame this on me." Alessandra placed her hand on her chest in shock.

"Actually, I can."

Alessandra rolled her eyes.

"You're just like my brother and Gael."

"Are you still going to school?"

I hadn't stayed on top of her lately with my schedule and the kids, but now, after the way she behaved in the club, she was doing more than just hanging with the wrong crowd.

"Yes, school is fine."

Hugo pulled up to the driveaway and parked, and the door was yanked open before he could turn it off.

"Hugo, make sure Alessandra gets home," Joaquin said in a low, even tone.

"Joaquin."

"Sofia, get in the house."

He turned and walked up the steps. I blew out a breath and followed him inside, nervous at how the night was only getting worse if we got into a shouting match.

"I'll call you tomorrow," I called out to Cassidy.

I shut the door behind me, and he set the alarm, slid his hands in pockets and leaned against the door.

"Let me explain."

"Who is the guy you're with?"

"I wasn't with anyone."

Joaquin cocked his head to the side and hiked his brow.

"Do you understand what you've done?"

After removing my heels, I went upstairs to our room, ignoring his questions.

"I'd appreciate you not condemning me for something I couldn't control." I turned the knob and dropped my shoes at the side of the door, removed my jewelry, and picked up the makeup wipes.

Joaquin stalked toward me and closed the distance between us. He gripped the bottom of my chin and put me in his line of sight.

"I won't ask again."

"All I know is that the shots went off, and we ran."

"Where was Hugo?"

"He was trying to get us out of the club, but somebody pushed him, and it turned into a fight."

"The man."

"Emile."

"Emile."

I sighed, dropped the wipes in the trash, and took my dress off, throwing it in the hamper near the bathroom.

"That's what he told me."

"You're not going out anymore."

"I'm a grown woman."

"My wife was almost killed. Do you know what message this will send to my enemies?"

"Is that the only thing you're worried about?"

I covered myself with his white shirt, stomped over to the bed, and climbed in, turning my back to him.

"Never question what I love more, Sofia."

"Could have fooled me." I wiped a tear that fell down my cheek.

"I think Alessandra needs to go back to Italy."

"She's obviously going through something."

"Get some sleep. We'll talk more tomorrow." He pressed a kiss to my cheek and started to leave.

"Where are you going?"

"I need to take care of some work. I'll be back."

"Don't take too long."

* * *

Two days later, I was preparing to do some pre-promo for the film with Shamar. Plus, the photoshoot with JJ and Jianna was trending, with people wanting us to do a reality show, which I'd never agree to do. I sipped on water through a straw Cassidy had brought over and waited for the camera crew to prepare for the interview.

"I think we have lifted off," Pamela, the reporter from Big News Media, said.

"Which one is this? Number fifteen?" Shamar joked, and I chuckled, feeling exhausted from sitting and moving from room to room, answering the same questions.

"That's the life of acting. We have to do promo," I replied.

"Ladies and gentlemen, I'm super excited to be sitting with you two," Pamela remarked.

"We're just as excited," Shamar said.

"Let's get started with the obvious question. How do you two feel about the story?" Pamela questioned.

Shamar motioned for me to answer first.

"I think we're both excited and relaxed, which makes the story come together on screen easier," I explained.

"From everyone I've talked to, this role was meant for you," Pamela said.

"That makes me feel good."

"So do you think you two will work together again?" Pamela asked.

I pointed at Shamar, and he laughed.

"I hope we get the chance; she's been the best screen partner."

"You're just as amazing," I teased him back.

"I can see you two work well together, Sofia. I think my audience and viewers would like to know how life is married to Joaquin Fuertes," Pamela probed.

The smile I had fell. I blinked fast, turning to find Cassidy, and she was around.

"Excuse me."

"Your husband. Joaquin Fuertes is a mob boss, correct?"

"I think we shouldn't be talking about my personal life."

"Your personal life is on social media; I mean, you've recently done a photoshoot with your kids." Pamela clasped her hands together and stared at me.

"I know from being on set, they're lovely kids," Shamar brought up.

"But your husband is involved in illegal activities, correct?" Pamela asked again, and I didn't want to be unprofessional and show that she'd gotten the best of me. They were known to do gossipy stories on me constantly.

"Pamela is here to talk about Sofia as an actress," Cassidy approached, and I felt relief.

"If you're asking the audience to believe you're a clean-cut family, I think you're doing a disservice to our readers," Pamela commented.

"We're done," I said.

"I mean, you were trending from being at a shootout at a club. Was that because of your husband?" Pamela blurted out, and I almost lunged at her and choked her on camera. That would have just put me in a worse position with the studio and industry peers. I walked out of the room and back into the hotel room the studio rented for us to get dressed. I grabbed my purse and keys to get ready to leave.

"That was a setup."

"I know." Cassidy typed on her cell phone.

"Who are you calling?"

"Getting the studio to pull Big News from the press."

"She said the shootout was trending on social media."

"We should put a statement out."

"Was anybody hurt?" I asked.

"Not that I know of." She glanced at Hugo.

"Why do I feel like this is going to get worse?"

"What do you need me to do?" Shamar knocked on the door and peeked his head inside.

"Sorry about this, Shamar. I can't believe she tried to do this right now."

"Don't worry about it. I'm used to the gossip blogs." Shamar placed his hand on my shoulder.

"Thanks."

"I'll see you back on set." Shamar reached over and gave me a hug.

"Well, we might have a bigger problem than I thought."

"What?"

Cassidy passed her phone to me, and I saw a black and white photo of me and Joaquin in bed together.

"What the fuck!" I scrolled through two more photos of me naked with Joaquin having sex.

"You need to call Joaquin." Cassidy paced back and forth.

"Who is doing this?"

JOAQUIN

Standing in the room surrounded by some of my men, I listened to them run down all the information they could come up with on Lusting's character and the shootout at the club Sofia had gone to the other night. My sister was in class because I made sure guards were standing outside the room if she tried to leave. Sofia could feel sorry for her and want to be caring and supportive, but I was done with allowing Alessandra a pass.

"Gael, what do you have?" I questioned, scanning the office and watching the nervous looks on each man who came up short and expected to walk out of here alive.

"From talking with Alessandra, it was two guys arguing."

"Just random men arguing."

"She wasn't close to them, but I suspect it was a setup."

"They knew Sofia was inside."

"Probably followed her and Alessandra for a while."

"Anything on the video footage?" I looked at Steven, our tech guy.

"I ran video stills of everyone who entered the club and left; facial recognition came up."

"What is it?"

Steven turned the computer around, displaying the semi-blurry photo of a tall man with a low-cut buzz, thin nose, and broad shoulders.

"Emile Lusting," I muttered.

"The leader of the French mafia. They've been around for over thirty years," Steven read off the screen.

"Why is he here?"

"He's looking to take over."

"So he tries to go after my wife?"

"I think we need to make contact," Gael suggested.

"Now isn't the time to go to war," one of my soldiers commented.

"That's only the tip of my thoughts."

"He wants to push us out, correct?"

"Joaquin, if we do this and are still trying to expand to Texas, we need to make sure our bases are covered." I listened to Gael explain the details of our deals. My phone vibrated, and I glanced down to see a message with Sofia's name across the top. I typed in my password and pulled the message up. My eyes widened in surprise. I heard the cells go off my other men, and I looked around at their shocked eyes.

"It's him."

"Joaquin, we need to figure out what he wants."

"I know what he wants, and he's going to get exactly what he's asking for."

I gripped the phone tighter and went to dial Sofia and find out where she was, when her soft whimpers came through the phone.

"Why are they doing this to me?" Sofia murmured.

"I'm going to get to the bottom of this."

"Steven, get these photos taken down," Gael demanded.

"On it already."

"Where are you?" I started to walk out of the room.

"Locked in the bedroom."

"My babies."

"With Madelyn."

"I won't let this come back on you."

"This about you?" she probed.

"I won't like it; I think it's a message."

"Are you serious, Joaquin?"

"Mi amore."

"No, don't even think about trying to manipulate me."

"Sofia."

The phone went dead, and I growled and punched the wall.

"Take me to the club."

"We need to be smart about running into the club until we know for sure where Emile is located."

"I don't give a fuck who he is; he came after my family."

We climbed in the car, and I slammed the door and tried to dial Sofia back, but she didn't answer. I called Hugo to make sure he was with her at the house.

"Boss."

"Where is Sofia?"

"In her room, sir."

"My children?"

"Right in front of me."

"Put the house on lockdown; no one in or out."

"What's going on?"

"Lusting, a new enemy, has given the first shot."

"The photos."

"And the shootout at the club."

"What does he want?"

"What they all want. My attention."

"Sofia's supposed to go back to work and fly out of town."

"Out of town where?"

"Texas."

My body heated up, and I became enraged at her not telling me about some work trip that she knew I wouldn't approve of. I promised myself I would never be caught looking weak by giving someone the opportunity to get into my home and near my children.

"She's not going anywhere."

The car arrived at the club, and I had two SUVs deep with more guards. I finished telling Hugo I would be home soon.

"Mr. Fuertes, can I help you?" the security guard asked.

"Where's Emile?"

"Who?"

I passed my phone to Gael and turned my head. Smirking, I punched him in the stomach, and he fell to the ground.

"Arghhh!"

Another guard came out shouting, and I lunged, gripping him around the collar of his shirt and pushing him up against the wall. I pulled out my knife and held it against his throat.

"Tell Emile Lusting his guest has arrived."

The guard held his hands up in surrender and nodded. I released my tight grip and let him lead me into the club. The bartender paused what he was doing, stared at the group of men holding guns, and blocked the door, motioning for the waitress to move toward the bar.

"Where is he?"

"In the back."

I shoved him to move forward and lead us to the back room. As they walked down the hallway, he came upon more guards standing stoically at the door.

"Don't be a hero." Joaquin pushed the knife closer to his throat.

"Emile wants to see him."

The guard nodded, twisted the knob, and pushed the door open. I shoved his man forward and strolled in to see Emile sitting in his chair, smoking a cigar.

"Mr. Fuertes," he said in a deep French accent.

"What do you want?"

"Would you like a drink?"

"Gael."

Gael raised his gun and shot the guard in the leg.

"No need for the anger."

"How did you get in my house?"

"I wouldn't know what you're talking about."

"Do you know who you're making an enemy out of?"

He put the cigar out, stood from the seat, and came around the desk.

"Mr. Fuertes, I'm no harm to you or your family."

"How did you get in my home?"

Emile smirked, rubbing his chin.

"I apologize for being overboard."

I gripped the knife tight at my side.

"You don't want to do that, Mr. Fuertes."

"Why not?"

"My men have your home surrounded."

I glanced at Gael, and he lifted his phone to dial Hugo.

"Gael, I'm a little busy." Hugo sounded annoyed, rustling through the phone.

"Check outside," Gael demanded.

My eyes never left Emile.

"Why?"

"Just do it!" Gael shouted.

"Hold on, JJ," Hugo said.

"You see anything?" Gael asked.

"No, our men are patrolling," Hugo answered.

"Keep an eye out." Gael ended the call.

"We like to be undetected. The same way we got in, we can do it again." Emile grinned.

"What do you want?" Gael asked.

"I'd like to do business with you."

"Threatening my family doesn't prove to me I should work with you."

"I only ask, but we can do things the hard way," Lusting said. I raised the knife up and slid it back in my space place.

"Working together will never happen. I'm warning you now, don't threaten my family again."

"Sorry we couldn't do business together, Mr. Fuertes." Lusting extended his hand to shake.

I turned my back, stalked out of his office, and left the club. A few seconds later, Gael pulled me back before we got in the car.

"Your quietness is going to be called into question."

"He thinks he has the upper hand, but we're going to give him what he wants."

"Are you giving up territory?"

"We're giving him an early death."

Ring! Ring!

I picked up my ringing phone and saw Cassidy's name scrolled across.

"Why is she calling me? I just talked to Sofia."

"Maybe Emile did something," Gael answered, and we climbed in the car.

"Cassidy?"

"Mr. Fuertes, I'm with Sofia."

"What happened? We just spoke to her a second ago."

"It's your sister."

"Alessandra." I looked over at Gael, and he pulled out his phone and tried to dial Alessandra.

"I guess you haven't heard about her hanging out with the wrong crowd."

"I know, and Gael is going to speak with her."

"The club shooting is all over the Internet and now the photos of you and Sofia."

"Where is Sofia?"

"She's upset, but I wanted to see if you'd agree to a statement."

"Statement."

"A joint statement about the photos."

"No."

"But—"

"Cassidy, one thing you should understand is that I don't let things or people dictate my life."

"Yes, sir."

"Put Sofia on the phone."

"Here she is."

"Sofia."

I heard sniffing.

"I'm on my way home."

"Who is trying to ruin my career to get to you?"

"I have something in the works."

"Do you know they have me plastered all over the world, apparently in a sex tape of us."

I closed my eyes for a moment.

"He's being taken care of as we speak."

"I want this finished, Joaquin."

"I promise. Ti amore."

ALESSANDRA

Many people would say I was spoiled because I wanted to be free and away from my parents. I grew up in Italy and Spain under strict rules, having my life dictated from the time I was born. Yes, I liked to party and drink with friends, but I worked hard and went to school to get my degree in fashion. *Have I done a few things that I shouldn't have done?* What twenty-two-year-old hasn't? My brother made a bigger deal out of things than it needed to be. On top of that, my boyfriend and his right-hand man Gael were acting more like him, being over-protective since we'd decided to become a couple.

I stepped out of the bathroom from a long shower with a towel wrapped around my waist and stopped at the sight of Gael sitting on the edge of my bed. I smiled and extended my arms out and approached him, but he nudged me away.

"What's wrong?"

"I should ask you that question."

I rolled my eyes.

"If you're here to yell at me, then you can leave." I placed my hands on my hips.

"Who are you?"

"I'm having fun. Is that a crime?"

"You got mixed up in a shootout with your brother's wife!"

"That wasn't my fault."

"What about you being out with some guy, and he's groping you?"

I forgot about the party I went to with some friends from school. A few guys approached us, and we got to talking and drinking. I told them I had a boyfriend, but there wasn't any harm in dancing with a few friends.

"It was harmless flirting."

Gael jumped up in my face, squinting his eyes.

"We're done."

"Wait… What?"

"You disrespect me, Alessandra. I knew this was a mistake from the beginning."

"Gael, you're making a bigger deal than it really is. Besides, I've never cheated on you."

"You need to live life and explore. I'm obviously not a priority, and I wouldn't want to hold you back."

"That's not true."

"Si, it is, mi amore."

"Did Joaquin tell you to do this?"

"Joaquin doesn't even know I'm here."

I grabbed a pair of high-waisted jean shorts and a crop top from the closet and got dressed.

"I'll listen."

"That's not the only problem."

"What else? I'm doing fine in school."

He tilted his head to the side, and I rolled my eyes.

"All right, I was late a few times and missed an exam."

"Do you love me?"

My hands were on his chest.

"More than anything."

"Then we should take a little break, and you should explore on your own."

"No!" I shoved him back.

"Alessandra!"

I cursed him out in Italian, and he ran a hand down his face and walked off, leaving me behind his back to push and shove to get his attention.

"Please don't do this." I grasped his arm.

"Let me go."

"Who is she? Did you cheat on me? You've hated the age difference."

"The only issue in this relationship is you." Gael opened the front door, and I stood in shock, released his arm, and watched him walk out of my condo.

"Arghhh!" I dropped to my knees in tears at not seeing Gael anymore. All my life, I'd loved him and wanted us to be together. Now, by my own doing, we'd broken up.

Ring! Ring!

"Hello."

"Alessandra? Are you all right?"

I looked around my home in disbelief that Gael wouldn't come back to me.

"No."

"Well, come out with us to the bar." My classmate Odessa was in her last year of design school and popular on campus. She was tall and blond with brown eyes, thin with a model body that had all the guys in love.

"I don't think it's a good idea."

"Why? This will be fun. I already have Rich and Eliot eating out of my hands," Odessa said.

"I just broke up with my boyfriend." I sniffed over the phone.

"All the more reason to let your hair down."

"I can't."

She groaned through the phone.

"Listen, you sound depressed, and I think you should come out. Get some fresh air."

Thinking over her words, I decided I could use a moment away from any memories of Gael and me together.

"One drink, and then I'm leaving."

"One drink," Odessa repeated.

* * *

THE ROOM WAS loud with blaring music, and I was on my third drink, sulking in pain from calling Gael for the third time in a row. My calls went straight to voicemail. I was tempted to go to his house, force him to speak to me, and then cook his favorite meals.

"To the single life!" Odessa held a glass in the air.

I froze when an arm wrapped around my waist, and a husky voice whispered in my ear, "Aren't you Alessandra Fuertes?"

"My friend just broke up with her boyfriend, can you show her a good time?" Odessa winked her left brow and giggled, falling in the arms of the guy's friend.

"He's a fool for hurting you," he said. I ignored him and waved for the bartender to give me another shot of tequila.

"Rich, take her on the dance floor."

"Not in the mood to dance."

"Come on, Alessandra. I won't bite... unless you need a little pain," he growled in my ear.

"Alessandra, if you're going to be bored, you could have stayed home," Odessa blurted out. I nodded and figured it was time to get out of my funk.

"One dance."

"One dance, and then we can have a little party alone." He dug in his pocket and pulled out a bag of pills.

"I don't do drugs."

"Not drugs, just something to make you feel good." Rich opened the bag, pulled a pill out, and popped it in his mouth. Then he gripped my chin, pressed a kiss to my lips, and sucked on my tongue. I felt the pill ease into my mouth.

"Sexy," Rich said, pecking me on the lips. The music changed, and the crowd grew louder. I felt lighter on my feet and smiled.

"What was that?" I asked, swaying my hips. Odessa came up beside us and bumped into me. We laughed.

"Relax, Alessandra, it's fun and harmless."

An hour later, we were inside a diner with a group of six of us, drinking and laughing after hanging out at the bar. My mouth was dry, and I was hot and sweaty from dancing too much. It was going on one in the morning.

"What are you getting, Alessandra?" Odessa asked.

My eyes were low. I could barely keep my head up, and I thought I was seeing two Odessas.

"Huh?"

"Are you all right?"

"I don't feel good."

I fanned myself.

"You need some food in your stomach."

I shook my head.

"Can you call Sofia?"

"Who is Sofia?" Rich questioned, rubbing on my thigh. I pushed his hand away, crossed my legs, and slid my hand in my purse to grab my phone.

"I need to call my brother." I tried to dial Sofia's number when my head got drowsy. Someone yanked the phone out of my hand, and everything went dark. My eyes rolled in the back of my head.

My head was heavy, and I groaned and rubbed my forehead from the massive headache. When I opened my eyes, I saw I wasn't at home.

"She's woken up," I heard a voice say.

"Mhmmmmm…" I moaned.

"Alessandra."

"Sofia."

"Call the nurse," she said.

I looked around the room and saw Gael standing at the window with a hard glare on his face and Joaquin sitting in the chair near my bed. Sofia talked with a nurse, and I realized I was in a hospital bed, wearing a white gown.

"What happened?"

"You were drugged."

"Huh?"

"You're going back home," Joaquin said.

"Joaquin, not now," Sofia snapped.

"No."

"Either you go back home, or you're moving in with us," Joaquin demanded.

"I'm not a child!" I spat, and my head pounded.

"Then act like an adult. You could have been attacked or worse!" Joaquin shouted.

"Joaquin, can I talk to her alone please?"

"Odessa's my friend," I replied.

Gael shoved off the wall, shook his head, and sauntered to the door.

"Gael... wait," I called his name, trying to sit up.

"Don't. I'll check in on you later." Gael opened the door and walked out.

"Alessandra, that girl is not your friend," Sofia remarked, walked over, and grasped my hand.

"I'll be outside," Joaquin said.

"They hate me," I muttered.

"No, they're disappointed, and we have a lot going on."

"Don't let them send me back."

"You should think about what you're doing; it's interrupting our lives," Sofia argued.

"You're just like him, trying to run my life," I fussed, yanking my hand away.

"Anytime we get a phone call in the middle of the night with the words drug overdose, what do you expect us to do?" Sofia questioned.

"Can you leave me alone please?"

"Tonight, you sleep, but you need to make a decision. Tomorrow, you're not going back to your condo." Sofia kissed me on the forehead, and I closed my eyes and let the thoughts of Gael consume me as I drifted off to sleep.

CASSIDY

The next day.

The door of my bedroom squeaked open, and I wanted to yell at him for not answering my call again. I liked when he got pissed off. I bit my bottom lip, scooted up in the bed, and let the sheet fall from my naked body. His eyes turned animalistic, ready to attack his prey, and even though our night was cut short with everything happening with Sofia and Joaquin, I wanted to make up for the loss with him between my legs. Many people would say I was crazy for even thinking about dating a mobster, but becoming his fiancée was entirely another story. The biggest reason for our fights lately was me hiding our relationship. My job was to keep all eyes on Sofia and secretly, I feared dealing with the same problems that she was going through now.

"Breakfast in bed." Hugo kissed me on the forehead and placed the tray in front of me.

The food looked delicious, and I was starving for something to eat. When Sofia called me last night about Alessandra, my main goal was to make sure the family was good and worrying about Hugo's safety.

"You don't cook."

"Delivery."

"Have some. I can't eat all of this by myself."

"I like to watch you eat." Hugo reached over and rubbed my nipple.

"Mmmmm…"

"Eat."

"I'll eat afterwards. I want something else." I pointed to his boxers, and he chuckled.

"No time for that. I need to get over to the house with Sofia and Joaquin."

"How is Alessandra?" I cut into the pancakes and fed it to him.

"Quiet, playing the silent treatment with her brother."

"She thinks Joaquin is going to send her back?"

"He already made the call."

"Just like that?"

Hugo slid out of bed, and I admired his wide shoulders and muscular back with tattoos of his family and friends.

"Joaquin has enemies, and Alessandra is being foolish."

"She's young like me."

"But you're not acting dumb."

"Well, only for you."

He winked at me.

"I want to come."

"No, you need to stay here out of trouble."

"I can help."

"Cassi." He called me by a nickname whenever he was serious about something. I poked my lip out, moved the tray to the side, and crawled close to the edge of the bed. He stopped and narrowed his eyes at me.

"Sofia needs my help just as much as Alessandra."

"You're going to tell her about our ring."

He pointed at the jewelry box sitting in the nightstand.

"It's too early, Hugo," I whined.

"I'm not your little secret, Cassi."

"When have I ever made you feel like you're a secret?" I rose out of the bed, closed the distance between us, and wrapped my arms around his waist. Hugo sighed, extended his arms to my lower back, and cuffed my butt cheeks. He peppered my shoulder with kisses, and I groaned, wanting to feel his thick shaft.

"Busy first," Hugo muttered and pressed a kiss to my lips.

I dropped my hands from around his waist, stomped to the bathroom, and slammed the door.

"Withholding sex from me won't work!" I shouted from the other side of the bathroom.

"Cassi."

"What!"

"Wear your ring."

The feeling of making it known to the world that I was getting married to someone my parents had only met a few times, that I half-lied about his occupation being a businessman. If they knew he was a trained killer, I'd probably be shipped out to a convent.

* * *

LATER IN THE AFTERNOON, I arrived at Sofia and Joaquin's home to a barrage of cars and men outside like it was Fort Knox. Once Hugo left earlier, I had some work to do, getting Sofia back on set and approved for flying to Texas for an upcoming film shoot. I parked my car, grabbed my laptop and purse, and knocked on the front door.

"Hi, Cassidy," Martha answered and stepped to the side, allowing me to enter.

I removed my glasses and followed Sofia's voice in the living room.

"How is she?"

"Which one?"

"Both, I guess."

"Alessandra is sulking in her bedroom, and Sofia is in the living room with the kids," Martha explained.

"Thanks."

When Pamela threw that question, I was pissed and ready to kick her ass, but I had to maintain my composure, or we'd be in more trouble. I stepped in the living room and chuckled at JJ trying to keep his food away from Jianna. That little girl was still in the body-feeding stage and thought she was grown and could have solid foods.

"He's so big." I ran my palm through his black, curly hair. He took after his father so much, even with that crinkle in the middle of his forehead that popped up when he was angry.

"Remind me to lock him and my sister up so they can't grow up any more."

Sofia stood and reached out for a hug. I rubbed her back and took a seat next to her on the couch.

"Where is everybody?"

"Joaquin is in his office with Hugo and Gael."

"Alessandra."

"Upstairs, refusing to come out."

"When is she leaving to go back home?"

"I think tomorrow."

"How are you handling all this?"

Sofia waved her hand in the air.

"I worked hard to have a career without any scandals, and now all that is being washed away."

"You can't think like that."

"Easy for you to say."

"What does that mean?"

"Nothing."

"No, tell me."

"Hugo."

"What about Hugo?"

"You see what I'm going through with Joaquin. Why would you do the same thing?" she whispered.

I opened, then closed my mouth in surprise that she knew we were an item.

"You two are more obvious than you think."

"I thought I was hiding it well."

"No, you're not."

"He wants to tell everybody."

"What do you want?"

"Honestly?"

"Yes."

"Don't take this the wrong way."

"Depends."

"I can't worry what happens to him every minute and if people are trying to kill him by going through me."

"Like my life."

I nodded, hating to have these thoughts.

"It's not easy. Sometimes I wish I could go back."

"Any other surprises pop up?"

"The studio called me."

"Huh... Why? I'm your manager."

"They're thinking of recasting my part."

"What!" I jumped off the couch, startling the kids. Sofia grasped my arm and yanked me back down.

"Sshhh."

"They can't do that. We have a contract."

"I know, and I threatened to sue if they tried."

"What did they say?"

"Talked about the bad publicity with my marriage and shootout."

"That's bull crap." I had to catch myself when JJ treaded over to me with his toy car.

"Baby, go finish your food," Sofia said.

"Are you still going to Texas?"

"Joaquin said something about us needing to be on lockdown, but I have no choice but to go for work or lose out on this opportunity."

"I think you should go. We can get extra protection."

Buzz! Buzz!

"Who is that?" I questioned.

"My notifications have been going off all day."

"I'm sorry this is happening to you. I tried to get a statement out, but Joaquin—"

"Stubborn, I know. Today, I was planning on talking to him about some things we need to change."

"If he plans on staying married to me, he's going to make some changes."

"Are you thinking about divorcing him?"

"Divorce!" Alessandra shouted.

Sofia rolled her eyes, and I groaned, turned at her disheveled attire of gray sweatpants and large white T-shirts with her hair unkempt. This wasn't the normal Alessandra we were used to seeing. The bags under her eyes told a story she wanted to hide.

"You're married to the Fuertes family; we don't believe in divorce," Alessandra preached.

"Alessandra." I tried to calm her down.

She shoved her hand in my face, and I could tell Sofia was embarrassed about her sister-in-law.

"Alessandra, my marriage is none of your concern. You've done enough," Sofia replied.

"Does Joaquin know you're trying to divorce him? Take his bambina and son away." Alessandra pointed at the kids.

"What's with all the yelling?" Joaquin, Gael, and Hugo stood at the door, and all I wanted to do was escape before everything blew up.

"She's talking about divorcing you. I'm more loyal to you than your wife, and you want to ship me off!" Alessandra pouted and crossed her arms over her chest.

Joaquin narrowed his eyes at Sofia and gazed over at his kids. My mouth went dry in nervousness. The anticipation of World War III in front of my face was something I hadn't planned on doing.

Boom!

"Arghhh!!!"

Everything happened in slow motion, and I prayed the kids' lives would be spared. Joaquin leapt over like Superman and covered the children, Gael reached out for Alessandra and tugged her down. I watched Sofia crawl to the kids, and Hugo went into attack mode and shot back. I couldn't believe what I was in the middle of. I knew right there that my life would be forever changed.

Pop! Pop!

"Arghhhh!!" I screamed, watching Joaquin grab both babies. Sofia stood as the bullets stopped.

"We need to go to the basement," Joaquin commanded.

"Where's Martha and the rest of the staff?" Sofia called out, and we ran out of the living room and through the hallway to the basement door. We saw Martha holding the door open.

"Mr. Fuertes! We saw at least five or six men," Martha explained.

"Gael, where are you going?" Alessandra pleaded, holding on to his jacket. He kissed the side of her face as the tears pooled into her eyes.

"Go with Martha. I'm right behind you," Gael told her.

"No!" Alessandra screamed.

"Alessandra! Ti amore." Gael gripped her palm and kissed her on the lips.

We ran through the basement and down to another door underground. I felt like I was in a movie. Sofia never told me about the basement or any of these compartments underneath the house.

"Let's go!" Joaquin shouted and held tight on to both crying babies as they screamed for their mom.

"Joaquin, how much further?" Sofia reached for Jianna, and Joaquin nudged her along, not breaking his stride.

"Right here." He typed in the keypad on the wall, and the door opened to the outside. We stepped out to a helicopter, and I looked back over my shoulder and saw we were miles away from the house.

"What about Hugo?" I asked.

"He knows the rules."

Joaquin buckled the kids into the plane. Another guy got in the front seat. Sofia climbed in the helicopter, and I looked back for Hugo and hesitated.

"Cassidy, come on," Sofia muttered.

"I can't leave him."

"He's fine. They're securing the house and will meet us at our location," Joaquin explained.

"How do you know?" I questioned.

"I know my men," Joaquin said.

"Cassidy, he's fine."

"We have to go!" During her sobs, Alessandra covered her face with her hands.

"Joaquin." As Sofia reached for his hands, he raised them to his mouth and kissed her palm.

"Martha, I thought you were a cook," I inquired.

"I am a cook and house manager," Martha replied.

"She's trained on how to handle things in case I'm not home," Joaquin explained, and I saw her in a different way. The woman had to be damn near in her late sixties.

"What about the rest of your staff?" I watched as the helicopter flew in the opposite direction of the house. I prayed Hugo and Gael came out of this alive.

"I have safety measures in place," Joaquin responded, and I stared at the houses as they got smaller the higher we flew up.

SOFIA

$\mathcal{A}$ few hours later, we occupied the second home Joaquin owned under his parents' name, and I showered, fed the kids, and stood in his office, watching him pace back and forth and yell on his phone. I couldn't understand all of what he was saying since he was possibly cursing, but he seemed angrier than usual. The last scare of my kidnapping set him on a rampage, and now for his kids to almost be killed, my husband wasn't the same man standing in front of me anymore. He'd changed, and I needed to understand that getting him back to the guy I fell in love with would be a struggle. The front door chirped, and I looked over and saw Gael and Hugo stalking in with dirty, angry faces. I reached to hug them both, and Cassidy practically leaped into Hugo's arms.

"You're alive!" Cassidy shouted.

"Cassi, everything is okay." Hugo held her close, and something tugged at my heart to see Hugo so vulnerable and open in front of me. Usually, it was me being a big baby, but he let his guard down with Cassidy.

"You okay?" Gael questioned.

"I'm fine."

"Where's Alessandra?"

"In the kitchen with the kids."

"Don't worry, he's going to be fine," Gael said.

"I hope so."

"Let me check on the kids and Alessandra," Gael said, and I nodded.

"Sofia, you can't get rid of me that easy." Hugo chuckled, and I slapped him on the chest.

"I'm glad you're safe."

"Me too." He kissed me on the forehead.

"How did you get out?" I questioned.

"Prayer, but it was just a warning message."

"A bomb was a warning message?" Cassidy probed.

"I need to discuss some things with Joaquin." Hugo gripped his chin and kissed her on the lips.

"How do you live like this?" Cassidy questioned.

"I love him."

"What are we going to do about Texas?"

"Joaquin won't let me leave the grounds, let alone finish filming."

"This is not good."

"Maybe they can figure out how to get the people behind this sooner."

"I think I'm going to be sick." Cassidy held her hands to her stomach and mouth.

She ran off to the bathroom, and I chased behind her and held her hair as she threw up in the toilet.

"Have you eaten?" I asked.

`She shook her head, flushed the toilet, and went to the sink to brush her teeth and rinse her mouth out.

"Have you and Hugo been careful?" I asked.

Her eyes bugged out. She groaned and covered her face in shame.

"My life can't be this crazy right now."

"It might seem like it's crazy, but you're only making it worse. Calm down, I have a test you can take."

"How do you go day to day in this lifestyle and not freak out?"

"You make it work." I opened the cabinet, grabbed a pregnancy test, and handed it to her.

"You have these just randomly around here?"

"Joaquin told me about the home a few months back after having Jianna, and I made sure to get everything we would need in case of emergencies."

"A pregnancy test is an emergency?"

"He wanted more kids, and I didn't know what I wanted, so we compromised."

"What do you mean compromised?"

"After Jianna, I said let me have a career for a little while. If we still wanted another child in two years, we could try."

"And."

I waved the tears away before they fell.

"After today, I can't do this again."

`Cassidy dropped the test on the counter and held me in her arms for a tight hug.

"Talk to him."

"I will, but first you need to take a test."

"Hugo and I as parents is nuts."

I laughed and shrugged.

"I said the same thing about Joaquin, but he's the most supportive when I'm pregnant and with the kids."

"Let me get this over with."

Bang! Bang!

"Sofia!" Alessandra yelled.

"My other child is knocking." I groaned and opened the door to Alessandra in tears.

"Don't make me go back." Alessandra dropped to her knees.

"What's happened now?"

"She's friends with my enemy." Joaquin's tone dropped low and deadly.

"Huh?"

"I didn't know!" Alessandra cried out. Gael reached down to pick her up.

"Get her out of here!" Joaquin shouted.

"Joaquin, tell me what's going on. She's your sister."

"She betrayed me." He glared at her.

"Joaquin, you know Alessandra would never do anything to betray the family." Gael calmly held her in his arms and brushed a hand up and down her back.

"Get her out of my face," Joaquin spat.

"Someone tell me what is going on."

"Alessandra's report from the drugs found in her system were traced back to a woman named Odessa," Gael explained.

"So?"

"Odessa Lusting is the sister of Emile Lusting, the man who blew up our home!" Joaquin shouted.

"I didn't know!" Alessandra begged.

I covered my mouth in shock.

"Alessandra."

She reached for my hand, and I took a step back.

"Get her out of my sight!" Joaquin yelled.

"We met in class, and she approached me. We became friends with Sofia." Gael held Alessandra.

"We've been set up all along. Alessandra brought her friend to our house." The right vein on the side of Joaquin's neck popped.

"I remember her being at the house," I recalled, closing my eyes.

Flashback.

A month prior.

I was out by the pool, lounging with the kids and running through my lines with Madelyn. Cassidy was there to finalize details of my upcoming schedule.

"Sofia! Sofia! You look amazing." Alessandra held a mimosa in her hand and stood in front of the canopy lounge chair.

"What are you two doing today?" I dropped the script on the ground and stood to hug her.

"Sofia, this is my friend Odessa. We met in class." Alessandra introduced me, and I shook her hand. She was a tall woman, with a sharp jawline, heart-shaped lips, and long blond hair.

"Nice to meet you, Sofia. I'm a big fan," Odessa said.

"Thank you."

"I told her about your pool, and she suggested we come hang out. Plus, you have the best food," Alessandra joked.

"Help yourselves, please. Odessa, this is Cassidy."

"Hi," Cassidy said.

She ignored Cassidy.

"Those are your two kids?" Odessa asked.

"Yes."

"Beautiful, they look just like their father," Odessa hinted, and I didn't know if I should be offended or thankful.

"Uhm... thanks."

"Odessa's just joking," Alessandra said.

"How did you meet again?" I probed.

"In class, I cheated off her design!" Odessa cackled and clinked glasses with Alessandra.

I pursed my lips and glanced at Cassidy.

"She's joking. We met in class and became friends."

"Are you the one who keeps her out at all hours of the night?"

She pressed her index finger to her lips.

"Shush... you're not going to snitch on us, are you?"

"Mommy! Look at me!" JJ called out, and I looked away from Odessa.

"Can I use your restroom?" Odessa perked up, and I nodded.

"Sure, I can show you." I stood.

"Oh, no need. Just point me in the direction," Odessa said.

"Right through the doors you came from and around the corner," I responded and motioned to the house.

"Thanks! Be right back," Odessa replied, placing her mimosa on the ground.

"How long have you known her, Alessandra?"

She shrugged her shoulders.

"A few weeks, why?" Alessandra sipped on her drink.

"I don't know. Just feel a weird vibe from her."

"Odessa's really funny and sweet. Give her a chance," Alessandra responded.

"Food is ready!" Martha called out.

"Where's my brother?" Alessandra strolled next to me to the kitchen.

I grabbed a plate of hot dogs and burgers for JJ and a bottle for Jianna as Alessandra fixed a plate for herself. Cassidy came behind and took JJ's plate out of my hand.

"Thanks, I'll make you a plate," I told her.

"No worries, I'm stuffed from the snacks," Cassidy mentioned.

"Alessandra, I'm sorry I can't stay." Odessa stepped into the kitchen with a harsh grimace on her face.

"Why? What's wrong?"

"My guy needs me, and I have to run home to help him get in my apartment."

"How old are you, Odessa?"

"Why?" Her eyes darkened with her sharp response.

"Just asking. I know Alessandra is twenty-two, and her parents would go crazy if she lived with a man." I chuckled.

"Well, I'm not Alessandra." She slid her shades on, and I hugged Alessandra, turning to leave the kitchen.

"Maybe you should do a background check on her?" Cassidy mentioned.

"You two are being silly," Alessandra blurted out.

"Is she the reason you've been out all night and missing classes?"

"Sofia, can we have a peaceful day without all the questions?"

"Does Joaquin know your little friend?" I investigated.

"No, and I don't want him to know."

"She seems rude," Cassidy said.

"Odessa is nice, and I'm done talking about my personal life," Alessandra said as she dropped the spoon into the salad and marched out of the kitchen to the backyard.

ALESSANDRA

*P*resent Day.

The look in my brother's eyes was like a sharp dagger to his heart. I didn't know how we could come back from this betrayal. The rising and falling of his chest, the darkening of his eyes, and the pain in his tone meant I'd done more than disappoint him this time. I was the cause of an enemy getting close and almost killing his family.

"Get the fuck out of my house!" Joaquin shouted, stalking out of the living room. I tried to run after him, but Gael held me back.

"No! You don't understand. He has to listen to me."

"Gael, take her away," Sofia said, and my heart broke at her words, I looked around the room at Hugo's Cassidy's sad eyes.

"Hugo, you have to believe me. I didn't know."

He shook his head.

"We should go." Gael gripped my elbow and angled me toward the door.

"Wait! Can I say goodbye to JJ and Jianna? Please, Sofia?" I begged.

She waved me off.

"I love them and would never hurt them."

"You should have thought of that before!" Sofia screamed, and I nodded, understanding my decisions affected the family in a way I couldn't undo.

"Come on," Gael repeated, and I let him walk me out of the house. I stopped and glanced at the family as tears pooled in my eyes.

"I am sorry."

* * *

I PACKED up my things and loaded them in the car, while Gael continued to talk to Joaquin on my behalf. This was not only hard on me but him as well. I swallowed the lump in my throat and closed my eyes. As I sat in the back of the car, I thought of how Odessa had made it her mission to be my friend. All of my life was planned for me, and I thought if I could come to America and make my own decisions and make friends, I would feel normal. My family could see I could handle my life without being constantly watched by guards and hounding me about the people coming in and out of my place. Odessa was friendly and flirty, but fun and outgoing. She never gave off a sign that she was a part of the mafia world. The door opened, and Gael scooted in and covered my hand, lifting it to his lips.

"Give him time."

"When can I come back?"

"Let's not think about that right now."

"Do you hate me?"

Gael turned toward me and raised his right hand to my cheek. He caressed it and leaned over to press a kiss on my lips.

"Love you, baby, but disappointed."

"How much damage is done?"

He sighed and ran a hand through his dark, short, wavy hair.

"A lot we have to clean up."

"Are you coming with me?"

"To help you get settled in, but I can't stay long." He released my hand and grabbed his phone to scroll through messages.

"Did he tell my parents?"

"No way to keep this from them."

"That bitch needs to die."

I glanced out the window as the car drove down the street.

"You said you met her in class?"

"Yeah, she came in one day while we were designing and sat next to me."

"How did she come across?"

"Nice, Gael. I'm not Joaquin; I don't go around thinking everyone is out to get me."

"Alessandra!" He slammed his hand against the window. I jumped in shock, and tears welled up again.

"You hate me too."

"No, I want you to go back home and rethink your decision. You're trying to run away from this life, and there's no running, bella." He slid his hand on my thigh and squeezed. When we arrived at the airstrip, the door opened, and I hopped out in a somber mood, followed him toward the stairs, and climbed in to take a seat near the window. I buckled my seatbelt, and Gael sat across from me and watched me.

"Give him time," Gael said.

I nodded and blew out a breath.

"Hello, Miss Fuertes. Do you need anything to drink?" the flight attendant asked.

"A glass of wine please."

"Bring her water."

"Gael."

"You've had enough."

"Sure, water it is. And you, sir?" she questioned.

"Water please," Gael answered.

The stewardess walked off and left us alone.

"I didn't know I had drugs in my system," I whispered.

"Obviously she was drugging you," Gael told me, and I bit on my bottom lip, thinking of the night with Rich and Odessa.

"Now that I'm thinking about it, she always ordered the drinks for us."

"Alessandra, you're smarter than you give yourself credit for, and the woman I know wouldn't fall for the bullshit."

I started to speak and closed my mouth and stared out of the window.

"My father is going to kill me."

"Take it one day at a time."

"Here's your water. We'll be taking off shortly." Gael removed the seatbelt, switched to the seat next to me, and placed his arm around my shoulder. I leaned my head down on his chest and closed my eyes, taking in his clean, crisp cologne.

"She was plotting on me this whole time."

"Did she ever introduce you to Emile?"

"No, I only met a few guys around her. One guy was Rich."

He grunted in disapproval, and I pushed off his chest.

"I never cheated on you, Gael. He did kiss me, but I pushed him away."

"I trust you, baby."

The pilot came on and let us know he was about to take off. I leaned back on his chest and closed my eyes to sleep the last few hours away. We had a long flight, and I needed to be prepared for when I saw my parents again.

"Hi, I'm Odessa, your designs are gorgeous." She pointed at my open sketchbook.

"Thanks. I'm Alessandra."

"How long have you been designing?"

"All my life honestly."

"Everyone in here seems stuck up, except you." Odessa looked around the room.

I chuckled and pressed my index finger to my lips to be quiet.

"What? It's true. You're the only one who has talked to me since being here."

"I felt the same way when I first started here and getting my family to agree with me living here and designing clothes."

"Same, my family is very old fashioned."

"Seriously, they want you to marry rich and not have a career," I complained.

"Class, make sure you have the red cocktail dress sketch for next week." Our professor dismissed us for the day. I started to pack up my things to eat and meet Gael for dinner.

"Where are you off to now?"

I checked my watch.

"Grab something to eat and then meet my boyfriend."

"We should have lunch together."

"Uhmmm."

"Come on, you're too pretty to eat alone. Besides, I need to know who does your hair."

"Your hair is longer than mine and prettier."

"These blondie locks aren't real," she whispered in my ear and giggled.

"Lips are zipped. Come on, let's go for lunch."

Odessa locked her arm in mine, and we talked about everything as we went out for lunch that day and became fast friends.

* * *

A FEW DAYS later in Spain.

I could hear through the walls the loud shouts from my father and mother, going back and forth about me. We lived in a massive compound on acres of land, and I couldn't avoid the conversations that would happen once he saw me. When we arrived, I unpacked my clothes and went straight to bed. Gael was at his family home and would see me soon, but he had a few meetings he needed to handle before he could spend any time together. Without even knocking, my father forced his way into my room.

"Get downstairs now!" Father shouted in Portuguese.

"Papa."

"Joaquin Sr., leave her alone," Mother called out.

"Alba, stay out of this," he demanded.

"I'm coming."

I slipped on my flat sandals, grabbed my shawl, and followed behind him out of my room and toward his office.

"Are you hungry, sweetie?" Mother asked.

"No, I'm fine, Mommy."

"Do you know how this family runs?"

My head stayed down as he berated me.

"Yes, Papa."

"This makes us look weak! Stupid little girl," Father shouted.

"Stop it! You will not talk to our daughter like that. She made a mistake." Mother stepped in front of his face.

"Momma, it's okay."

"No, I will handle Alessandra. You made these problems before she was even born," Mother remarked.

"Alba, you will not interfere with me disciplining my children."

"She is not a little kid, Joaquin."

"Alessandra will be getting married."

My body trembled in shock as I gasped.

"No, I will not!"

"You've been making a lot of stupid mistakes; you can't handle the world on your own."

"Alessandra, go to your room," Mother said.

"I love Gael, and he loves me!" I yelled and stomped out of his office. I ran up to my bedroom, locked the door, and fell on my bed, crying over how my life had spiraled out of control and my father was going to force me to follow his rules.

JOAQUIN

$\mathcal{M}$y sister was back in my father's home country. I'd kept in touch with my father and explained how we were attacked. The conversation didn't go well, and he wondered if I needed to come back and start my business over. But I never ran from a fight. I sat on the back patio of our second home in thought, smoking on a cigarette to clear my head. Emile had made the first move on my territory, and then he blew up my home to bring me to my knees to sell a piece of what we had. Fuertes never got intimidated. When I killed my enemies, I went for the last bloodline. Our tech guy sent Odessa's address, and I made plans to visit her today.

"How long have you been out here?" Sofia asked.

I felt her warm hands massage my shoulders.

"An hour."

"Are you coming to bed?"

"Not anytime soon."

We'd finished dinner and put the kids to bed. It was still early, only nine p.m. I didn't have Gael, but Hugo would follow me on my mission.

"Come to bed, Joaquin." She ran a hand down the back of my

neck. I closed my eyes, reached up for her hand, and pulled her in front of me.

"I'll be up to bed soon."

"I need to talk to you about something."

She sat in my lap, and I rubbed her back.

"I have to fly out to Texas."

"Not now, sweetheart."

"It's important."

"I said no."

"I understand your business is complicated, but you can send more men with me and the kids."

"My kids aren't going anywhere."

"Are you fighting me on this? I've always done my work."

"I'm not stopping you."

"What do you call making us stay in an undisclosed location and away from my family and friends?"

"Your parents can visit, and Cassidy is here all the time."

"You sent your sister away, and now you're trying to lock me up."

"Sofia, you know you're important to me."

"Sometimes it doesn't feel that way when you're demanding me to follow your rules."

I rubbed her cheek and down to her chin.

"Only want you safe."

"How were we able to get so close to our house?"

"Odessa had to have given the address."

"Are you going to kill her?"

"Go to bed." I gripped her chin, captured her lips, and slid my tongue through her full lips.

"Hmmmm… stay out here," she moaned, and I picked her up. She wrapped her legs around my waist, and I walked her in the house through the kitchen and down the hall to the guest bedroom. I locked the door and placed her on her back. I kissed the back of her ankle, and my dick jumped when she rubbed her left foot up my stomach and down to my balls.

"I can't deny you anything," I whispered. Hovering over her

body, I buried my face in the crook of her neck. She wrapped her legs around my waist, slipped her hand in my pants, and gripped my shaft.

"Ohhh... Make love to me," she croaked out.

She kissed down my shoulder and up to my jaw as I squeezed her right breast in my hand.

"You ready for me, mi amore?"

"Yes... please."

Her nectar dripped onto the sheets, and I slipped her panties to the side under her robe, lined up my thick girth to her tight walls, and plunged deep. I couldn't speak for a second as she gripped me on both sides of my ass and arched her back.

"Ughh... Sofia."

"Oh... God!" she begged. I paced slowly, widened her legs, and watched her arousal overshadow her beautiful face. Her breath hitched, and that was my cue to take her over the edge. I slid my finger to her clit, grabbed both legs, and closed them together, straight up in the air. Raising my hips, I pounded her against the bedpost as our combined moans filled the room. I became aggressive, feeling that I had lost her. My chest rose and fell, and my vision became blurred as I thought about what we had just gone through and how I could have lost her. Taking her into my arms, I sucked on her neck as my hands roamed over every inch of her body.

"Sweetheart, I need you."

"You have me, Joaquin."

"Never leave me." My hand went to her throat, and I stared into her eyes.

"You have me forever."

"Do you promise?"

"I promise... baby!"

"Baby, I'm coming."

"Come for me, my love."

"Shit!"

* * *

THIRTY MINUTES LATER, I cocked the gun, checked our surrounding area, and pulled the ski mask over my head.

"Is she alone?" I asked Steven.

"She was."

"If she isn't, it's lost there." I opened the door, put the gun in my back, and headed into the apartment building. Surprisingly, it was near my sister's condo. They'd thought about everything when they planned to take over, except my retaliation wouldn't be a normal one and done. I planned to have his business destroyed within a few minutes of me taking his sister from this earth. Hugo followed me to the back entrance of the building, and we slipped through the doors that were left open by the security guard we had paid off. I opened the side stair doors and quietly went up to her third floor. Peeking out the window, I confirmed it was clear, and I grabbed the gun from behind my back and removed the safety.

"If she's not alone, take out whoever is with her."

"Ready to go," Hugo said, cocking his gun. Thinking about the noise my gun would make, I passed it to Hugo and removed my knife from my ankle. I pressed my head to the door and didn't hear anything, so I slid my hand in my pants pocket and took out the key to her apartment and pushed in to quietly open her door. I saw the living room was dark, so I waved Hugo to follow and look at the other side of the apartment. Her kitchen was open floor with a balcony attached. I went down the hall and saw three doors. I figured one was a bathroom. Hugo eased the door open and saw it was empty.

He mouthed, *Clear.*

I pointed for him to check the other room in the corner, and I'd take the main room on the count of three. Holding my hand up, on three, I pushed it open and saw Odessa lying in bed alone with the window open. I grinned, pulling on my black leather gloves, stalked to her bed, and pressed my hand over her mouth. Her eyes popped open.

"Arghhhh!" she screamed.

"Sshhh… Odessa, correct?"

Her eyes widened in surprise. I removed my ski mask so she could see my face.

"You've been a very bad girl, Odessa."

She shook her head and tried to claw my hands down.

"You listen, and I speak."

Odessa nodded.

"Your brother Emile, where is he?"

"Mmhmm…"

"I'm going to remove my hand so you can talk, but the second you scream, I'll kill you." I held the knife up to her jaw. "Understand?"

"Mmmmm."

"Where is your brother?"

"He gets in contact with me."

"I don't believe you."

"Please, he made me do that."

"I think you're right that he planned to take my family down."

"I swear I'm innocent," she pleaded as tears welled up in her eyes.

I chuckled, and Hugo came in the room next to me. Odessa tried to crawl out of the bed, and I caught the back of her head and yanked her back.

"Please! I don't know anything."

"Normally, I leave the killing to my friends, but you've made the biggest mistake, so I have to handle this alone."

"If you let me go, I can get my brother for you."

I laughed.

"Alessandra was foolish, but I am not. You can't manipulate me."

"If you kill me, this will be a war!" she shouted and tried to kick me in the balls. I smacked her across the face, lifted the knife, and held it up to her face.

"One move, and you die."

Odessa grinned.

"My brother will avenge me. The Lusting family doesn't fall to your kind," she spat.

"Too bad you won't be here to see it fail." I slid the knife across her throat. She tried to catch the blood but choked on it and died.

"Any signs of her brother's address?"

"Nothing."

"We need to go to the club."

We texted Gabriella to clean up the scene while we left to handle the next location Emile was seen. Steven was at the wheel of the car and jumped in the passenger side and waved for me to drive.

"She gave up the address?" Steven questioned.

"No, try the club now."

"They hit some of his men," Steven said.

"He'll show his face soon." I removed the ski mask, wiped off the knife, and grabbed the gun back from Hugo.

"If he's not there?"

"Keep looking. Sofia has to go to Texas, and I'm not taking any chances."

"Are you going with her?"

"That would be ideal, but until this is handled, I can't."

"The kids?"

"I want them protected at all times, but they're staying here with me."

He sped down the street, and we made it to the club of the shootout and parked two blocks away.

SOFIA

*T*wo days later.

I'd been out in Texas for two days, working with Shamar and doing press, while Joaquin was back home, doing what he did. The director was doing a shoot on location with a few of us, and I'd been trying to get in touch with Joaquin for the longest time. Madelyn kept me updated about the kids, but Joaquin hadn't come up late at night and left early in the morning. Some women would think he was cheating, but I knew my husband. Dating another woman would never enter his mind.

"All right, we're almost losing the light. Get this shot!" the director called out.

The makeup artist touched up my lipstick and held the small fan up to get air while we were outside the trailers, preparing to film. I read over my lines one more time, passed them back to the assistant, and stepped on the gravel near Shamar.

"So this scene is you stopping him from leaving," the director said.

"Should I be on the side of him, or do you want more of his face?"

"We can try both angles."

Shamar leaned back on the car door, and I placed my hands on my hips, moving my head left to right. I closed my eyes to drown out the noise of the world.

"Action!"

"Listen to me, if you leave now, our relationship won't mean a thing."

"Stop lying to yourself!" he shouted.

"So that's it… just forget about the nights we've spent together." I pushed my hand on his chest.

"Sorry, I need to go." He turned and went to open the driver's side.

"Cut!" the director shouted.

"Should we do one more take?"

"We can break for five and then come back."

Shamar grabbed the robe from the assistants, and we walked to our trailers. Cassidy passed me a bottle of water and the fan as I turned the knob of the trailer, stepping up the stairs to sit under the air.

"Have you heard from Hugo?"

"Yeah, anything from Joaquin?" Cassidy questioned.

I shook my head.

"No."

"He's probably doing what he does."

"That's what I fear."

"Give him time, Sofia."

"I miss my babies."

"We won't be much longer, and you'll fly back soon."

"Can you get the interviews in one day?"

"Let me see, and I'll talk to them about doing something closer to the premiere."

"I just have a bad feeling with everything going on."

"Any word from Alessandra?"

"Her mother called and told us she made it all right, and Gael should be on his way back."

"I'm still surprised so much has gone down, and we're alive to speak."

"No fear in marrying Hugo."

"A lot of fear, but I love him too much."

"I understand, and the only advice I can give is to be intentional with every moment."

"We have too much going good to be down right now."

"How are the numbers looking?"

Cassidy turned the computer around.

"Well, after the uproar with the studio trying to cut you from the movie, your social presence has increased."

"Really?"

"Yes, women especially are rooting for you."

"The magazine."

"The sales are through the roof, and they're even thinking of a second shoot."

"No more photos of my kids though."

"Understandable, but they want to know more about Joaquin."

"Because of the photos and sex tape?"

"Yes."

"I knew it. All these gossip bloggers think about is getting into people's private lives."

"Just let me know what you want to do."

"I'll finish up this shoot and do the interviews tomorrow."

"Do we want to have dinner tonight?"

"The hotel would be fine."

"Okay."

A knock on my trailer door came.

"Back on set!" someone yelled out.

"Be right there."

I checked myself out in the mirror and went to open the door, strolling back to set to finish the scene of the day.

* * *

THE NIGHT BREEZE in the restaurant of the hotel was exquisite, and I felt my cheeks blush in thinking of me and Joaquin here on our honeymoon. We hadn't been accosted by any fans, for the most part, but a few cameras did go off. I asked the wait staff to ask people to keep them at a minimum. Cassidy couldn't make the dinner, so Shamar was here, and we'd so far caught up on everything in our lives.

"What do you have planned after this movie?" I cut into my vegetables and rice.

"A film I'm looking forward to producing, maybe some TV."

"Can you believe the mess Pamela tried to pull?"

I lifted my glass of wine.

"She's relentless."

"She acts like I want my private life in the public."

His hand brushed over my palm.

"People like Pamela are only out for themselves."

"That's what I hate about this celebrity life."

"Mrs. Fuertes," the smooth voice interrupted, and I glanced up to a tall man with a bald head and a thin mustache and wearing a black suit.

"Yes."

"I'm a friend of your husband." He reached out for a shake.

I gulped down the wine.

"Joaquin."

"Yes, he'd informed me that you were here in town and asked that I make myself known."

"What's your name?" My emotions were high on alert, and I was ready to bolt out of the restaurant if he was an enemy of Joaquin's.

"Ezequiel Mota." He winked, and I gazed over at Shamar.

"Uhm, Mr. Mota, it's nice to meet you. This is my friend Shamar."

"You have to forgive me, I'm not really big on movie actors." Ezequiel removed his hat and held it to his chest.

"No, problem at all," Shamar replied.

"What can I help you with, Mr. Mota?"

"It's more of what I can do for you."

"I'm sorry?"

"Have you spoken to your husband?"

I didn't know if this was a setup, or he really worked with my husband; the last time I trusted one of his people, I'd ended in trouble.

"I have," I lied.

"Then you know I'm here on good faith. Protection," he hinted and placed his hat back on his head.

"Shamar and I are having dinner. Besides, I have protection." I pointed to the guards sitting at the table behind us that Joaquin had demanded I have.

"I understand, but my protection is at the level of your husband's. I have connections here so if you come up with any issues—"

"I doubt anything will happen while I'm in Texas." I chuckled.

"You can never be too careful." He slid a right hand in his pocket, pulled out a business card, and left on the table.

"I'll remember that, Mr. Mota."

I stared at the name and number on the card and put it in my clutch.

"That was strange." Shamar lifted his wine glass to his lips.

I nodded and glanced at the door of the restaurant again.

"Anything else you two need?" The waitress stepped over, removed the check, and put it on the table.

"No, we're great. Thank you." I started to remove my wallet, but Shamar put his card down.

"It's my treat," Shamar said.

"Thanks, Shamar." I stood, and the guards approached me, ready to leave.

"Tomorrow, we have interviews," Shamar said.

"Cassidy should be lining up flights for me to fly back home."

"Did they say anything about the explosion at your place?"

We walked out of the restaurant and stopped at the valet. The guard passed my ticket to get the keys to our car.

"No, the press is crazy and throwing so many lies out there."

"Glad the studio didn't cut you out of the movie." He leaned over and gave me a hug when a flash went off.

"Shamar and Sofia! Are you in love?" a photographer yelled out.

I blocked my eyes from the bulb flashes, jogged to the car, and climbed in when more reporters gathered around it.

"Can we go!" I shouted and held my head down.

* * *

BANG! Bang!

I groaned and tightened the covers around my head to block out the loud noise.

Bang! Bang!

"Cassidy!" I shouted.

I heard loud noises and whispers.

"You can't go in there." Cassidy's raised voice.

The bedroom door was pushed open, and I jumped in surprise.

"Mrs. Fuertes?"

I pulled the blanket close to my body.

"Yes."

My heart raced at the police standing in my room with guns drawn.

"You're wanted for questioning."

"I'm sorry. What is this about?"

"Don't say anything, Sofia. Let me call Joaquin," Cassidy stated.

The slimy smirk on the cop in front of me with eyes narrowed in slits, tall with a wide gut, dark hair, and front gold tooth creeped me out. He stepped closer to my bed and tossed down a piece of paper.

"This can't be true." I flipped the paper back and forth in disbelief, seeing Shamar was dead.

"You're an actress, no?"

"Who are you?"

"I'm the captain of police."

"I'm not going anywhere until I speak to my lawyer."

"Your money won't buy you freedom."

Cassidy tried to approach the bed, but one of the cops blocked her from coming farther.

"I've done nothing wrong, so this is a lie." I dropped the paper on the floor.

"Get dressed. You need to answer some questions since you're the last one to see him alive."

"Do you know who I am?"

He smirked.

"Like I said, you have five minutes, or my men will drag you out." He turned and motioned for his men to follow him.

The door shut, and Cassidy reached for her phone. I jumped out of bed to get dressed.

"What the hell is going on?" I whispered, opened the door slightly, and looked in the living room at them talking amongst themselves, touching our things.

"Why would I kill someone?"

"The studio sent out a public statement and said everything is on hold." Cassidy scrolled through her phone.

I grabbed a shirt and pants from my luggage.

"Where is my phone?" I tossed clothes out of my bag and remembered my phone was left in my clutch out in the living room.

"Shit!" I hissed.

"What?" Cassidy bit her nail, holding the phone up to her ear.

"My phone is out there in my purse."

"I'm trying to get a hold of production."

"I need to get Joaquin on the phone."

Knock! Knock!

"Mrs. Fuertes, your time is up!"

"Give me a second."

"No one is answering the phone." Cassidy ended the call.

"You don't think something happened to them?"

"Whoever is behind this wants you and Joaquin to suffer," Cassidy remarked, and I slid a hand through my disheveled hair and nodded in agreement.

"The same person who set the explosion at our house."

"No more waiting. Time to go!" He barged into my room and startled us.

"All right, let me grab my shoes."

"I'm coming with her," Cassidy said.

"No."

"She's my manager, and I don't even know if you're a real cop," I spat, and he stalked over and closed the distance between us.

"Your husband may have pull in New York but not here." He gripped my arm tight and dragged me out of the bedroom.

"You're hurting my arm!" I shouted.

"All you spoiled American women make me sick." He pushed me toward the other guard, and I noticed my purse was in his hand.

"I have a right to call a lawyer," I demanded.

He shrugged.

"We'll think about it."

Cassidy followed behind us as he walked me out of the room and onto the elevator. I didn't even get a chance to clean myself up. I felt like a prisoner all over again like the last time. Somehow, this was much worse. The elevator opened, and crowds of people from reporters and guests took photos of me while he paraded me out like a criminal.

"Sofia Fuertes, do you have anything to say to Shamar's family?" A reporter stuck a mic in front of my face.

"Sofia, over here!" another photographer yelled.

SOFIA

The dingy room was dark, dusty, and smelled of rotten food and blood everywhere. Our time in Texas should have been a way for me to become more than a pretty face, and I was now in handcuffs at the police station about my costar. The door opened, and the same cop from earlier walked in with a smile on his face. He sat in the chair in front of me, crossed his legs, and lit a cigarette.

"You smoke?"

"No," I muttered.

"Terrible habit." He chortled.

"When can I go?"

He flipped the file open and pushed a photo across the table. I leaned over and saw a picture of Shamar dead in the backseat of a car.

"What happened to him?"

He laughed, took the photo back, and shoved the photo of me and Shamar hugging at the valet station in my face.

"Come on, do us both a favor and tell the truth."

"Captain Herrera."

"Speak."

I cleared my throat.

"I don't know what happened to Shamar. I went to my hotel room after dinner. Plenty of people saw me walk into the hotel."

"That might be true, but you could have slipped out."

My heart was racing, and I shifted in my seat. This was a game to him, but my life was on the line, and obviously, he was looking for something.

"How much?"

Captain Herrera's eyes went wide.

"Excuse me?"

"You're not talking to some weak woman, Captain."

He put the cigarette out and leaned on the table with his hands clasped together.

"Money won't help you."

The door suddenly opened, and we both turned to see Ezequiel with Cassidy.

"Herrera... I thought we talked about this before." Ezequiel stepped in the room and picked up the picture of Shamar.

"She's not free to go."

"I have friends in high places, Herrera. You don't want to challenge me."

"Did he hurt you?" Cassidy asked.

"No."

"Release her now." Herrera pointed at my cuffed hands.

"A worthless scum like you doesn't give orders," Herrera fussed.

"As soon as I saw you go in the hotel this morning, I figured you'd pull something like this."

My head spun toward Mota.

"Hold up, you've watched my hotel?"

Mota nodded.

"My men and I kept tabs on you as soon as you came into town. Then, after the dinner, we followed you back."

"Do you know what happened to Shamar?" I asked.

"Herrera, Lusting can't keep you safe," Mota threatened.

Herrera jumped out of the chair, and it fell back.

"Are you threatening me?" Herrera pointed a finger at Mota.

"Everyone knows Lusting is behind you setting up Mrs. Fuertes."

"Captain! She's made bail, sir." Another cop walked in the room.

Captain Herrera's face grew heated, turning red in anger.

"This isn't over." Captain Herrera stood in Mota's face.

"I didn't kill anyone, Mr. Herrera."

"No need to explain to him, Mrs. Fuertes."

I rose from the chair and rubbed my wrists to relieve the pain.

"We'll be in contact about follow-up questions, Mrs. Fuertes," Herrera mentioned as we headed out of the interrogation room. I pushed through the crowds and kept my head down as Cassidy and Mota escorted me to a black van. I didn't know if we could trust him, but at this moment, I needed someone on my side to get me out of Texas.

The door shut, and Mota spoke to his men to drive off. He turned to look at me in the backseat and passed me my clutch.

"How did you get this back?" I questioned.

"Associate of mine."

I blew out a breath, opened it up, and removed my dead cell phone.

"Cassidy, what have you heard? My phone is dead."

"The entire situation is crazy. Shamar's car was found in a ditch."

"How is that possible!"

"It was set up by Lusting."

"The same man who tried to kill us?"

Mota nodded.

"He has reach, and after his sister was killed, it raised the stakes."

"His sister." I made eye contact with Cassidy.

"Odessa was found with her throat slit in bed," Mota replied.

"This is payback."

"I'm afraid your friend was caught in the middle."

"Framing me for his murder."

"They wanted to kill you as well, but you left before him."

The van drove back to the hotel, and I prayed I could get on the first flight out of here because if Herrera had his way he'd make me disappear to Mexico.

"Can you get us a flight out of here?"

"I will do my best." Mota reached in his pocket and removed his cell.

"Thank you."

"Hugo isn't answering his phone." Cassidy bit her bottom lip, staring out the window.

"Did Joaquin have something to do with Odessa dying?"

"I can't answer that question, Mrs. Fuertes."

"But you think it's payback, so more than likely, Joaquin sent a message."

* * *

As soon as the van dropped us off a few hours ago, I went to shower and change my clothes. Cassidy was calling the airlines to get us a flight out immediately, but everyone was booked for another two days. I didn't want to stay here and wait for Herrera to come back. I packed up my last bag and set it near the bedroom door. My stomach growled, and I remembered I hadn't eaten all day today. The press had a field day with the news of my arrest and made it seem like we were having an affair. On top of that, the studio and production team ignored my calls and acted like I was some piranha, putting out a blanket statement that they wished to wait until all the evidence had come out before determining any judgment. Cassidy sat on the couch next to me as Mota was on the phone yelling at someone.

"Any luck with Hugo?"

"Nothing."

"Do you think something happened to them?"

"We can't think like that."

"Joaquin has never gone a day without talking to me."

"We'll be home soon."

"I need to talk to my kids."

"Is your phone charged?"

"I couldn't get a signal."

"You think they did something to your phone?" Cassidy lowered her eyes, her breathing heightened.

"Something is going on, and we can't trust anyone."

Our eyes locked on Mota.

"Mrs. Fuertes, I have a private jet ready for you."

I jumped up in shock.

"Really... I can leave now?"

"Yes, I have word that some of Lusting's men are at the airport, so it's easier if we send you privately."

"Why are you doing this, Mota?"

"Your husband is a friend of mine."

"Have you spoken with him?"

"Not directly."

"So it's true... a war has started."

"Let me get you to the airport. Come, we have very little time." He looked at his watch.

"What about Shamar's body?"

"I'm afraid I can't help with that situation."

"But if we leave his body here, all of his family will think I'm guilty." My heart pounded in my chest

"Sofia, we need to leave, and I think Mota is right," Cassidy remarked.

"This is bad." My hands felt clammy.

"Let's just get out of here." Cassidy stood, grabbing her things.

As though my life were getting better, it all started to crash down again because of who I'd chosen to marry. I closed my eyes and said a little prayer for Shamar, then went to pick up my coat and bags to follow Cassidy out of the room. Ezequiel had a car waiting for us downstairs, and we locked the door, hopped on the elevator before it closed, and saw a couple of guys and one girl standing with drinks in their hands.

"Oh my God! Aren't you that actress who's accused of murder?" the redhead blurted out.

I swallowed the lump in my throat and covered my face with my hair.

"Shut up, Claire." The guy poked her in the arm. I was grateful he had a little more tact than his girlfriend. The elevator stopped in the lobby, and it was pretty quiet besides a few people checking in at this time of night. I followed behind Ezequiel, and his men were in the same black van as earlier. He took my bags as I jumped in and fastened my seatbelt.

"What about us checking out?"

"No worries. That was taken care of already."

"Thank God."

Ezequiel shut the door and jumped in the passenger side of the van. He waved for his man to drive off. My stomach growled, and I rubbed my belly, thinking of how my entire life had turned into a circus once again.

"How long do we have to get to the airport?"

"We're going through a shortcut," Ezequiel replied.

"Boss, we have company," the driver mentioned to Ezequiel. I turned to look out the window and saw a black SUV driving close behind us.

"Lose them," Ezequiel said, opening the glove compartment and taking out his gun.

"This can't happen."

"Stay calm. They would be stupid to do anything right now." Cassidy reached for my hand and squeezed it tight.

"We're going to be okay," Cassidy reassured me, and I nodded.

"Joaquin," I mumbled to myself.

Pop! Pop!

"Arghhh!" The car swerved, and my stomach dropped as I clambered to get low on the floor.

"Stay down!"

The driver cut into another lane, honked, and yelled about getting cut off. Ezequiel sent shots back, and the van sped up down the street.

"Take the back roads!" Ezequiel shouted.

Everything was quiet for another five minutes, and I sat up and looked out of the window, but I didn't see the car anymore. My hands shook, and my nerves were on edge as we continued to drive up on an abandoned dirt road.

"Where are we?" I asked, looking at the no trespassing sign and a dingy house with a broken-down car out front.

"Your private plane," Ezequiel replied, and the car stopped. My eyes rose in surprise at the helicopter sitting behind the house.

"You have to be kidding me."

"Mrs. Fuertes, the only way you're getting home is with that plane."

"Come on, Sofia. It doesn't draw any attention." Cassidy unfastened her seatbelt.

"Who is flying the plane?"

"Me," Ezequiel stated.

"What!"

He chuckled.

"Your husband and I go way back. We've done business off and on."

"That doesn't mean I trust you to fly."

"I'm certified to fly, don't worry." Ezequiel held the door open and helped me out.

"What about the men shooting at us?"

"They'll be taken care of once you're gone."

"Joaquin knows about this plan?"

"Joaquin created the plan."

My stomach tightened at those words. So he knew what had taken place all this time, but he had ignored my calls and kept me in the dark. Ezequiel grabbed my bags, and I followed behind him to the helicopter. I placed the things in the corner, slid in the seat near the door, and sent a prayer up that I'd make it home in peace. The driver of the car got in on the other side, buckled his seatbelt, and started pushing buttons.

"Relax, Sofia; we're safe."

"How can you be so relaxed?"

"I know we wouldn't make it this far without Hugo and Joaquin protecting us."

I shook my head and wiped the tears that pooled in my eyes.

"Glad you have that much trust."

Ezequiel started the plane and threw a thumbs-up at us. I sat back with my hands clasped together in my lap and held on tight as I thought of ways to breathe without freaking out that something could happen. Five minutes later, the plane rose from the ground, and I shut my eyes tight. When I opened them, we were in the air. When I scanned the ground, I noticed two or three SUVs drive up and open the doors with guns in their hands.

JOAQUIN

*S*mack!

"I was arrested!" she shouted and raised her hand to smack me again, but I blocked her and tightened my grip. When we got to the house, I pulled Sofia into my office, and she yanked out of my hold and smacked me across the face. The hateful glare in her eyes broke my heart, and I wanted to kiss away the pain, but I couldn't be soft with her right now. She needed to understand where we were and what was next with Lusting.

Ezequiel had done as I asked and brought her home safely. It was going on eleven at night, and the kids were asleep in their beds. Cassidy stayed in the guestroom with Hugo, and Sofia was finally speaking to me, after ignoring me when we did the exchange at the small airport I owned. The look in her eyes was disappointment, and I promised I would never hurt her again, but the only way it would have worked was if I kept my contact to a minimum. I still hadn't gotten a hold of Lusting. When we went to the club, he wasn't there. We set it on fire, and that caused another ripple because he came back and reached Sofia in Texas. When I got word she was going no matter if I agreed or not, I had Ezequiel in place to watch over her. Keeping her from talking to the kids was another issue, but I couldn't let anyone tap into my lines or get wind of where we lived. I was foolish in thinking my family home couldn't be touched, but no longer would I rely on just my men. I called Carlo to send me some backup to watch over our home, and it was all on lockdown unless it was an emergency.

"Baby, I know, and I have my men taking care of the captain."

"What does that mean?"

The scowl on her face made me hesitant before I answered. I reached for her hand, and she jerked back.

"Captain Herrera works for Lusting."

"I know."

"It was a setup. I don't have all the evidence, but we think he killed Shamar as soon as you left."

"Odessa, did you kill her?"

"Yes."

She groaned and threw her hand up in the air.

"When will this stop, Joaquin? My God." She sat on the couch near the window.

I walked over and dropped to my knees in front of her.

"Sweetheart."

"Don't."

I tried to kiss her on the lips.

"I need to shower."

"Lusting is trying to come into my territory. I didn't agree, so he sent Odessa."

"I want you to leave this life alone."

"Listen to me."

"No." She jumped up to leave. I grabbed her arm, spun her around, and pulled her into my chest.

"You're my wife. I love you, but you will never dictate my business."

"I finally see what Sabrina was talking about."

"We're not them."

"No, you're worse." She shoved me away.

"Sofia." I ran up behind her and picked her up in a bear hug. She kicked and yelled.

"Stop it!"

"Let me go."

"You'll wake the kids."

"He's dead, Joaquin."

"I know, sweetheart, and I apologize. We'll make Lusting pay."

"I'm going to be sick."

I walked her to the bathroom near my office, let her down, and held her hair back. She gagged, threw up, and sat on the floor for a few minutes.

"Tell me everything."

"Lusting has a cartel from France that wants to take over here."

"You said no."

"Not just me. Antonio, Carlo, and some friends have New York locked. We can't let anyone come in and take over."

"They used Alessandra, now me."

"It'll be over soon."

"Have you talked to your sister?" She stood to wash her face and brush her teeth.

"Not yet."

"What about your parents?"

"My father knows what's going on."

"I need to talk to my parents."

I shook my head. "Not right now."

She dropped the brush and turned to look at me.

"You think he'll go after my parents?"

"Safer to keep them out of this for right now."

"I don't like it when you ignore me, Joaquin."

She turned and finished brushing her teeth. I walked up and wrapped my arms around her waist, nuzzling my face in her neck.

"It wasn't on purpose."

Sofia spat out the toothpaste and rinsed her mouth out. I stood back as she wiped her hands and turned to face me.

"My career is over."

"We can fix that."

"How? More threats?" she hissed as she pushed me back, stormed out, and ran up the stairs to our bedroom.

"Sofia."

"Joaquin." I looked over at Cassidy.

"You should be asleep."

"Give her space," Cassidy said, crossing her hands over her chest.

"We never argued like this before."

"She's scared and upset, and I don't blame her."

"Herrera's going to get what's coming to him."

"He's a vile man. It was like he was having fun seeing her suffer."

My jaw clenched at her words.

"Did he touch her?"

"No… well, I don't know. He wouldn't let me see her."

"We couldn't make a move earlier, but I'll have some things in place for him."

"I think she should do an interview."

"No."

"Joaquin, what you're not getting is that her life has always been music and acting. Since she married you—"

"What are you saying?" My brows dipped in anger, forming a crease in my forehead.

"You might be a big-time mafia god, but when she married you, it didn't look like a good thing in the public's eyes."

"My life with Sofia isn't for the public."

"I get that, but they don't. Everything she does is picked apart and watched."

I waved off her comment.

"Listen, just let me set up an interview with you both, to clear the air and maybe savage her career."

"Not right now, Cassidy."

"Soon, it needs to happen soon if she has a chance of keeping her career stable." Cassidy turned and went back to the guest room. I sighed, ran a palm down my face, and went to our bedroom. Slipping my clothes off, I hopped in the shower and let the hot steam sprinkle down on my body to relax my muscles and take the stress away. I was making the wrong steps, and somehow Emile took me for a fool for giving in to his threats. Odessa didn't think she could be touched, and I needed to make a bigger statement than burning his club. I turned the water off, wrapped the towel around my waist, and walked out of the bathroom. Dropping the towel, I climbed in bed behind her and wrapped her in my arms. She tried to scoot out of my arms, and I tightened my grip.

"Joaquin, no," she mumbled.

"Sofia, please, sweetheart." I kissed her cheek and the side of her neck.

I rubbed a hand up and down her stomach.

"Just let me sleep."

"I love you, sweetheart. I would never put you in danger."

"You promise?"

She turned around in my arms.

"He will pay for what he tried to do to you."

"After that, you have to let it go."

I gritted my teeth.

"Go to sleep, baby." She caressed my cheek, and I lifted her hand to my mouth and kissed her wedding ring.

* * *

A FEW DAYS LATER, I agreed with Cassidy to let Sofia do an interview solo, as long as we had a chance to look at the questions first. I had Carlo's men follow her and Cassidy to the studio, while I was with Gabriella and Gael. Hugo was with us today and drove us to the warehouse. I held my cell and texted my father to check in on Alessandra.

Me: How is she?

Father: She's adjusting.

Me: How is Mother?

Father: She's pissed at me and you.

I smirked at his comment. Alba was a strong woman like Sofia and hated when certain decisions were made that would put the family in dangerous positions. Alessandra had betrayed our family, and I was too pissed to see she was a naïve girl who had been taken advantage of by Lusting's sister. After the hospital showed us the traces of drugs in her system, it sent me in a rage, and I felt Sofia was next on the list with the video being leaked. She'd suffered enough because of me, and I needed to realize that my choices weren't making things better.

Me: Tell her I'm sorry, and I love her.

Father: How are you moving with Lusting?

Me: I have dinner plans set up.

Father: Make sure the decision you make is the final one.

I sent him word in code that the final decision was dinner, and no one would leave the table alive now that I had the backing of Mota and the De Luca Cartel. They arrived at Antonio's. I stepped out, followed Gabriella and Gael once I ended my text message, and put my phone away.

Gael and I shook hands with Carlo and glared at Emile as he sat with a smile on his face.

"What's this?" I waved my hand around, feeling betrayed by my friends.

"It's not what you think," Carlo said.

I slid my hand behind me to reach for my gun. On cue, his men pulled their guns and pointed at my men.

"No blood today, boys." Carlo stepped in front of my gun.

"Carlo, I respect you and Antonio, but this is something I can't forgive."

"He seems unhappy to see me." Emile chuckled, and I growled, starting to charge at him. Gael pulled me back and whispered in my ear, "Not here."

"I called you both here to come up with an agreement," Carlo explained, picking up the shot glass and pushing it in my hand.

"I'm not drinking with him."

The smile dropped from his face.

"You killed my sister, and now you think I'm dirt on your shoes!" Emile smacked the table and jumped up.

"Fuck you and your sister!" I spoke in Italian.

"Gentleman, the only way we can settle this is by talking," Carlo demanded.

"I'm done talking. He made the first move, and I'll make the last."

"Joaquin."

I turned and saw Antonio standing at the entrance of the hallway.

"You knew about this?"

"We have certain things that could benefit Emile, and I think you should hear him out."

I cracked my knuckles and spoke in my native Portuguese.

"I see your friend doesn't want to make money." Emile lit a cigar.

"Emile, the way you approached him was wrong. We don't work like that in New York," Carlo explained. I was getting anxious and needed to see his blood spilled.

"How is your wife? She's a beautiful woman," Emile blurted out, his last words before I lifted my gun and shot two of his men in the head.

Pop! Pop!

He pushed the table up and sent gunshots back. Carlo and Antonio moved out of the way, shouting at us.

"Motherfucker! I'll kill you!" I yelled.

"She's a sexy woman, you should be proud," Emile continued to taunt, until he slipped out of the room as his men sent shots at us. Gabriella shot one of his guys in the leg, and Gael followed me toward the front entrance. We ran to the alley and saw him climb in a car. It backed up fast, coming at us as we sent bullets toward them. It was bulletproof and didn't make a dent. I jumped out of the way before they hit us. I dropped the gun and stood up as the car drove off and clenched my fist.

"We need to go before it gets hot," Gael said.

"I need to see Antonio and Carlo."

"Hurry, let's go."

We jogged back in and saw bullet holes in the walls. Carlo held his arm, hurt from broken glass, while it was getting wrapped up.

"How deep is the wound?" I questioned.

"Just a graze," Carlo responded, taking the shot straight.

"You won't have to worry about Emile killing you," Antonio replied.

"What do you mean?"

"Soon as Janice hears he got shot because of you..." Antonio mentioned, and I grunted, not ready for that conversation. Sofia had taken on a lot of their traits, and I'd hate for her to be the gun-toting donna like Janice and Sabrina had become.

"I'll send her flowers."

"'You'll need to do more than that." Carlo chuckled.

"You both played it well."

They slapped hands with me, and I pulled out money to pay for the damages.

"This is for the repairs."

"No need to pay us, we knew this could happen," Antonio told me and poured another shot for me and Carlo. The team we had on call to dispose of bodies came in and wrapped up Emile's men.

"You think he believed your plan of betraying me?"

"I think he was buying it until you got pissed off about Sofia," Carlo said.

"What if that was Sabrina or Janice?"

"We understand, but you can't let your enemy see you sweat," Antonio remarked.

"I need him dead."

"We put a tracer on him, so we'll have his location in a few minutes."

"I'll end this tonight."

"How is your sister doing?" Carlo asked.

"Better." I didn't want to talk about her business, especially with Gael here. Getting him worked up again would only cause us to fight and bicker. He hated that I'd sent her away but understood as my right hand, I needed to make a decision that would benefit the whole family.

"Tonight, you ended Emile Lusting for good." Antonio held his glass up to toast, and I chucked my head and took the shot down my throat, closing my eyes for a brief second to feel the strong liquor pour into my veins.

SOFIA

*S*itting under the lights I was used to doing as an actress, but having to tell my personal business was something I hated. Now I was one of many other celebrities who needed to let the world know how my life changed based on a lie.

"Sofia, thank you for being with us today." Robin Anders from Morning News Life smiled at me, and I thanked her.

"I appreciate you giving me the opportunity."

"Of course, we're all fans of yours here at Morning News."

"Thank you."

"We've had you here many times to talk about your movies and music, but today is different."

I nodded, picked up the glass of water, and took a sip. The audience was gone, and it was just me and Robin sitting together, one on one. She'd been a great reporter for many years. She was respectful with me and understood I wanted to tell my side of things. The media ran any lies they got ahold of, and Cassidy was able to talk them into an exclusive interview.

"Yes, unfortunately."

"You're here because explicit photos and videos were leaked of you and your husband."

"Yes."

"Also, you are currently being accused of murder."

"That's true, but my lawyer is handling that as we speak."

"Tell me what happened."

"My life has been turned upside down by some people who are jealous of me and my family."

"Explain, because there was an explosion at your home."

"Yes, we've been hit from all angles."

"Your husband is not in the business."

"No, he's a businessman."

"He's not here today, correct?"

"No, we thought it would be best if I came alone."

"How did Shamar end up getting killed?"

"Honestly, if I could go back to that day, I would have never left him."

"I know you can't speak about all the details."

"No, because of legal reasons, but I'm innocent, and I want the killers brought to justice."

"The studio states that they're waiting on the investigation before deciding what to do."

"I understand how the business runs."

"Do you remember anyone following you guys?"

I shifted in my seat. I couldn't talk about Mota or Lusting and have more blood spilled, so I lied.

"No."

"What about pictures and photos?"

"Someone planted a camera in our bedroom."

"Was it a fan or a stalker?"

"An investigation is happening right now."

"How are you moving forward?"

"Working with my lawyer to clear everything up and spending time with my children."

"We know you'll bounce back from this, and we hope you'll come back and talk with us again."

"Thank you, and I will for sure."

"I'm Robin Anders from Morning News Life, and you'll find more talk with Sofia Fuertes in an online exclusive." Robin signed off and reached to shake my hand.

"Thank you for being so brave."

"I just want things to get cleared up."

I stood, and we hugged as Cassidy approached me.

"How did it look?" I asked.

"I think you did good. Not too much, but let the audience see your vulnerable side," Cassidy explained.

"Thanks again, Robin." I let the sound guy remove my mic.

She waved and continued talking to her team for the next segment.

"What else is happening?" I walked to the dressing room to remove my makeup.

"Our endorsements aren't happy right now, so we need to handle that."

"I knew it was a matter of time."

"Yeah, they need reassurance."

"Joaquin and me."

"You don't need to say anything. I heard you last night."

I dropped the makeup wipe and turned to look at her.

"You think I was wrong?"

"No, I think you're afraid and have every right to be." Cassidy reached out to hug me.

"I keep having doubts about us."

"That's normal, Sofia, but that man loves you."

"I know, and I love him, but my life is spiraling out of control, and I've never been so emotional."

"You're not pregnant, are you?"

"No."

"Are you sure?"

"Positive." I reached to grab my bag of clothes and walked in the bathroom to change into my sweats.

"The guys are waiting, so we can go back to the house and make calls."

When I stepped out of the bathroom, I placed my hair in a high bun on top of my head and checked to make sure I had everything in my bag. Cassidy opened the door, and I followed her out to meet our bodyguards. We left Times Square and headed home.

* * *

CASSIDY AND I sat in Joaquin's office and made calls to talk about the magazine, clothing, and makeup brands I did business with to convince them nothing had changed. Jianna smiled up at me as I fed her a bottle.

"Sofia, we have a brand to protect," Heather, director of *Fashion Times Magazine*, spoke over the phone. I'd recently done two spreads for them, and it was supposed to come out soon, but Cassidy had received an email that it was on hold pending the current situation.

"Everything will be cleared up soon."

"It's not a good look for us," Heather replied.

"Heather, you've known me for years. This will blow over."

I lifted Jianna and took the bottle out and positioned her over my shoulder when the door opened and Joaquin, Gael, and Gabriella came in. I waved for Cassidy to mute the call, and I stood to burp Jianna and approach Joaquin.

"I'm on a call. Can you wait outside?" I whispered.

"We need to talk." He rubbed the back of Jianna's head.

I looked down at his clothes.

"What happened to you?"

"That's what we need to talk about."

"Can this wait?"

"I'll take Jianna. Hurry up and finish." Joaquin kissed me on the lips and walked off.

"Cassidy, we have investors, and if anything comes back on us..." Heather complained.

"Heather, either yes or no. I've been a long-time model of your magazine, and I bring in numbers."

"That's not what we—"

I cut her off.

"As the director, you make the decisions, so either the magazine will release as planned, or you'll lose a large demographic." I hung up the phone and plopped down in the chair.

"One down, ten more to go." Cassidy started to call the next person on our list.

"Let me talk to Joaquin first."

"Have you spoken to your lawyer?"

"He should be calling me tomorrow."

"We can hold off if you want."

I stood, wiped the tears away, and composed myself.

"Give me a second, and I'll be back." I left the office, walked to the kitchen, and only saw Martha, JJ, and Madelyn.

"Have you seen Joaquin?" I asked.

"They're in the living room," Martha replied. I bent down to kiss JJ's forehead.

"Mommy, want some!" He held a strawberry out for me to take.

I smiled and kissed his cheek.

"No, baby, you have it. Mommy's full."

"Dinner will be ready soon," Martha said.

"Thanks, Martha."

They continued laughing at JJ, and I went to find Joaquin standing with Jianna in his arms as Gabriella and Gael talked on their phones. I cleared my throat, strolled to Joaquin, and watched the stress in his eyes fade as my hand caressed his cheek.

"How was the interview?" he asked.

I tried to grab Jianna, but he pulled her back.

"She's fine with her poppa." He kissed her on the cheek, and she giggled.

"It was fine."

"We'll have everything fixed soon, my love."

"I trust you."

"Do you?" He lifted my chin and stared into my eyes.

"Yes."

He leaned down to peck my lips.

"We met with Emile today."

"Lusting?"

"Yeah, at Antonio's."

"What happened?"

"He's still alive."

"Joaquin, not in front of Jianna." I covered her ears.

"Baby girl is okay." He snuggled her neck, and she laughed loudly.

"What's the plan?"

"We're going in tonight," Gabriella blurted out.

"Alone?" My brows rose.

"With Carlo and Antonio's men."

"Is that safe?"

Jianna smacked the side of Joaquin's face, and he frowned as she laughed.

"Nothing will keep me from coming home, mi amore."

"So, after tonight, we'll be finished with him."

"I promise, Emile Lusting will no longer bother our family."

"What about Alessandra?" I saw out of the corner of my eye, Gael tensed at my question.

"My father says she's doing fine."

"Maybe it's time she comes home."

"Not now, Sofia."

He pushed Jianna into my arms.

"When are you leaving?"

"After dinner. Stop worrying, and you did good today."

Joaquin pressed a kiss on my lips.

"I invited my parents to come for a few days."

"We talked about this already, Sofia."

"With the extra protection surrounding us, my parents are worried."

"I won't argue. When are they coming?"

"In a week."

He rubbed my back and walked me out of the living room with Jianna.

"Call me when dinner is ready," Joaquin said, and I kissed him again before heading back to the office.

* * *

BESIDES THE KIDS TALKING, the table was quiet as we ate dinner. Cassidy and Hugo sat together at the end of the table, while I sat next to Joaquin at the head of the family. Martha and Madelyn kept the kids occupied with conversation, but my nerves were all over the place, wondering how tonight would go and if Joaquin should stay home and wait before another attack happened. I pushed the potatoes around on my plate and stared off when I felt his hand caress my palm.

"I don't like it when you worry." Joaquin picked up the napkins and wiped his mouth.

"Hard to mask my feelings about what you're doing tonight."

"I'm protecting our family."

I started to reply and caught myself before raising my voice. The kids never really saw us arguing in front of them, and avoiding glances from his people was one reason I never talked about business out in the open.

"The lawyer should be contacting us soon with updates." Joaquin drank from his glass of water.

"Just be careful."

"Always, sweetheart." He winked, and we continued the conversation about the kids and when my parents would visit. After dinner, we gave the kids a bath and put them to bed. I followed Joaquin outside as he loaded up the car, wearing all black. Cassidy already spoke with Hugo about him leaving tonight and what that meant for them. Joaquin directed his men and then stalked over to me, wrapping his arms around my waist.

"Go to bed."

"I won't be able to sleep until I know you're next to me." I pulled him into a longing kiss.

"Mmmmm…"

"Long as you and the kids are safe, Emile has to pay."

"I understand; I just wish someone else could handle things."

"I'm Ghost for a reason, sweetheart." He kissed my forehead.

I tightened my arms around him.

"Soon as I finish this, we'll be free of him."

"Okay."

"I apologize for bringing this to our home."

"I know."

"Good. Now go inside, and my men will make sure the house is secure." Joaquin released me, and I turned to go back in and shut the front door, watching as he slid down in the front seat and pulled a black skull cap down his face.

"Please be safe." I closed my eyes and sent up a prayer.

JOAQUIN

*G*ael ended the call and pulled off from the front of the driveway of my home as I checked the bullets in my gun. It was going on midnight, and Antonio's men were ready at every entry point of Emile's stash houses. Carlo texted me the address of Emile and his family near New Jersey. He kept them hidden well from us. He was married with four kids of his own, and I thought they would be in France away from here, but he was bold like me. I never let my enemies see me back down. After making my kids and wife suffer for so long, it was time I gave him payback.

"Carlo has men outside his house." Gael sped up and jumped on the freeway.

"Is the neighborhood crowded?"

Gael passed me the phone, and I saw a text message photo of the home.

"If we do this, it could blow back."

"I want it in the news, show people not to fuck with me."

"Joaquin, as your brother, we need to be clean with this kill."

Twenty minutes late getting off the freeway, he turned down the street of the address texted and saw more cars of our men a few blocks from the home. I slipped the silencer on my gun.

"You can be clean, I want blood."

As soon as he stopped, I jumped out and walked up to Carlo sitting in the van.

"I saw them go in a few hours ago, and he's there."

"He has them in an open area, a plain one-story brick home that we wouldn't suspect."

"Perfect distraction," Carlo said, pushing the door open to hop out.

"I thought you wanted to stay back after the restaurant."

"Janice already yelled at me, might as well get more fun before I'm grounded." He chuckled.

"Same, Sofia didn't want me to leave."

"She'll learn some things we need to do ourselves."

"You ready?" Gael closed in on us.

"I'll take the back, and you cover me, Gael."

"My guys have kids and a woman."

"How many guards?" I questioned.

"Surprisingly, only two."

"He didn't think we'd ever come to his home."

"Which means we need to be careful; there could be traps," Carlo explained, and I agreed.

"Let's go." I looked from my left to right. Checked to make sure most of the homes had their lights out.

"I have a backup plan if we can't take him out," Carlo said.

"What?"

"We call him out."

"It could save us from making a big splash."

"He's inside, probably waiting for us to make a move."

"Did you check the area for any traps?"

"Our men did a check, but that was yesterday. We couldn't get back here until it was dark out."

"Give me his number." I pulled out my cell, and Carlo held up his phone with Emile's number. I glanced up from where we parked and stared at his home that was a few houses down from us as the phone rang.

"Carlo, this isn't the hour to do business," Emile said.

I heard a woman in the background complain.

"This is Joaquin."

The phone went silent.

"I assume you've agreed to my offer."

I gripped the phone.

"To make it easy on you and your family, you should come outside alone."

"I don't know what you're talking about."

"7569 Middletown Ave."

The phone went silent again.

"My family is here."

"Where are you?"

"If you touch them—"

"I suggest you make your way out to me now."

"If you kill—"

I hung the phone up before he could finish and headed toward his home. All the guys stood up with their guns drawn as the door opened. I pulled mine out and held it up, ready to kill him where he stood.

"I'm unarmed," Emile told me.

I motioned for my men to grab him.

"Torch the place."

Emile's eyes rose in shock, and I watched them charge toward the stairs and grab him.

"Wait! My family is inside," he yelled.

Carlo and Gael jogged over to the van as Emile was knocked over the head and pushed inside.

"Tie him up." I started toward the stairs. Carlo stepped in front of me.

"We have him; no need to make any more noise."

"He's right, Joaquin. We don't kill children and women."

I removed the skull cap and ran a hand down my face.

"Think about Sofia."

"The motherfucker wasn't thinking about her when they set that bomb off!" I spat, pushing him away.

"Let's go. We've done enough." Carlo walked off and went to the other van. Gael waited for my call, and I blew out a breath and nodded.

"Leave them."

My heart pounded out of my chest, and rage filled me with leaving behind any witnesses. I would need to put more people in his family for a while and make it seem as though it was a bad deal gone wrong, or he cheated.

* * *

"Arghhh!" Emile screamed as I sliced him on the side of his back. I put him upside down, hanging on chains, and pulled out all my favorite tools that I liked to torture my prey. After I knocked him around a few times, I wanted his death to be slow and painful, the way he slowly tried to kill my family, one by one.

"You tried to kill my wife and children." I pushed the knife against his heart gently, without cutting him.

Blood dripped down his face, stomach, and back.

"I'll leave the country," he muttered slowly.

"Leave the country?" I chuckled, and my men smirked at him trying to buy some time.

I squatted down in front of him.

"I gave you a choice to leave my city alone and my family."

"Please, I'll go and won't be back." He groaned.

"Too late." I held the knife against his arm and sliced up to his armpit.

"Ahhhhh... Mmmmm." He shook, about to go into shock. I splashed him with hot water and burned his skin.

"Give me the gas can." I stood and diced his whole body.

"Fuck you!" Emile shouted.

"Have fun in hell." I flicked the match on him and stood back as he screamed and cried in pain. I smiled and watched my work end. I could now move on and know that he was no longer a threat.

***.

The next day after having breakfast with my family, I had Ezequiel meet me at Antonio's restaurant, now that everything was cleaned up. We parked, and I got out of the car and checked my surroundings. Gabriella stayed out front with Hugo. Gael followed me in, and we spotted Ezequiel laughing with Antonio and Carlo.

"The man of the hour." Ezequiel stood to extend a hand to me.

"Thank you for staying another day."

Everyone sat.

"Drink?" Antonio asked.

"Not today."

Ezequiel leaned forward on the table.

"I take it Mrs. Fuertes is still concerned."

"She is, and I'd like to give her some good news."

The left corner of his lip rose.

"Tell her the case is being dismissed."

"How?"

"We caught one of Emile's men, and he confessed."

"Voluntarily?"

"A little persuasion." Ezequiel chuckled.

"Explain."

"The cops found the car that caused it to go over the embankment."

"The bullets to his head?"

"Traced to Emile's gun ring."

"Is a lawyer on top of everything?"

"Everything should be emailed over, and Captain Herrera is retiring."

"What assurances do we have that it's clearly Mota?"

"Herrera doesn't want any problems with De Luca or anyone else."

390

"I need a formal statement made to the public clearing her name."

"I'll make that happen."

"For your support, I want to give you a twenty percent stake in Texas."

"Very generous." Ezequiel took a sip of the Hennessy.

"Anything else you might want?" I sat back and made eye contact, letting him know I wouldn't be taken advantage of even if he helped me out.

"I want Emile's stash."

"We have no authority on that," Carlo said.

"There's a reason you gentlemen run New York. I wouldn't think you'd have a problem."

Carlo and I glanced at each other, then Antonio.

"My father might be able to put in a good word," I replied.

He smiled and extended his hand, and I gripped it tightly, leaning forward.

"I appreciate your help, but don't think to try what Emiel has done—"

"Never, my friend."

"Then we understand each other."

"Drinks on me!" Ezequiel held the bottle up in the air.

"The girls want to get together with Sofia," Carlo said.

"Sofia would like that."

"Great, because Janice is driving me crazy."

We chuckled at his statement when a bartender brought a bottle for us with glasses. The rest of the afternoon, we talked more about business and what next jobs I had lined up. I looked at my watch and noted it was almost an hour late. I wanted to get home to have dinner with the family before we prepared for her family to come into town.

"Gentleman, I need to go."

"The wife put you on curfew?" Ezequiel joked.

"That's Janice, not Sofia." I chortled as Carlo glared at me.

"Just remind your wife about the ladies' lunch," Carlo said.

I slapped Carlo on the shoulder and shook hands with Antonio and Ezequiel. I shifted to the exit and put my shades back on to block out the sun. I felt my cell phone vibrate, pulled it out of my pocket, and saw a text from Sofia.

My Heart: Babe, the lawyer called!

Me: What did he say?

My Heart: The charges are dropped.

Me: I told you I'd handle everything.

My Heart: I know, but I figured it'll take a while.

Me: I'm heading home now.

My Heart: I got word from the studio.

Me: What did they say?

My Heart: The film will be released since we filmed ninety-five percent.

Me: I am sorry about your friend.

My Heart: I believe you. See you soon.

Me: Ti amore.

SOFIA

A week later.

"Oh... Joaquin!"

As his tongue brushed against my swollen clit, his hands grabbed my hips, keeping me immobilized. My wetness only intensified as I saw the lust in his eyes for me. After one more swipe of his tongue, he circled his index finger around my core and crawled up my body. Then I grabbed both sides of his face, pressing our foreheads together.

"I never want to be away from you."

Joaquin brushed his lips against mine and released a long-held sigh.

"Forgive me, baby."

"Always." I deepened the kiss, reached between us, and guided his thick member at my opening. He grunted, slamming into me.

"Perfect."

My body was tense, and I felt like I was riding a roller coaster as his shaft hit my spot and pulled back. As his hand wrapped around my waist, I turned on top of him in bed. I took off his shirt, exposing my breasts. When I tipped my head back a bit, I squeezed my legs around his dick, grabbed both hands, and pressed them to my breasts, rocking back and forth.

"You're mine forever, Sofia!" he groaned.

The sweat clung to the sheets as the ringing in my ears and the blurry vision started. I felt my chest rising, ready to climax.

"I'll never leave you!"

Our cries and grunts grew louder. Our lips touched in the middle, our tongues became familiar, and his hands grabbed my ass.

"Right there!" I screamed as my body convulsed, trembling in his arms.

"Shit!" His seed was released, and I prayed we didn't make another baby. I wanted another year before having another child since Jianna was still small.

"Come here." He pushed my wet, sweaty hair away from my face and kissed me on my lips, chin, and nose.

* * *

EARLY THE NEXT MORNING, we were still in bed, and he gripped me around the neck, breathing heavily in my ear as he lifted my leg on the side and slipped his thick member in slowly to play with my clit. I held my hand as he steadily moved in and out of me.

"When are your parents getting here?" he moaned. With my eyes rolled in the back of my head, I gripped his thigh and arched my back a little more, listening to his breathing increase. I felt kisses down my back.

"In about an hour!" I cried out.

"We need to shower and get the kids up." His strokes grew faster, and I pushed back on him to meet his strokes. My ass slapped against his pelvis, and I felt his nectar run down my legs.

"Joaquin!" I screamed and felt him release a load of his cum.

"You're going to be pregnant soon." He kissed the back of my neck. I pushed him away and sat up to stretch and get out of the bed.

"I have to see what the studio and sponsors will do."

"I do want more kids, Sofia."

"Can we not talk about this right now?"

I went to his side of the bed, kissed him on the lips, and pulled back. He grabbed my arm and pulled me down.

"When?"

"Not right now. We just dealt with a murder charge."

"I'll let you rest for a few months." He grinned, and I rolled my eyes and pushed him back to stand.

"Can you change the sheets!" I yelled from the bathroom.

"Yes, my love."

My parents would be here for a few days, and I planned on making the most of our time together. I wanted to see if Joaquin would be interested in them staying for good. In the shower, I felt strong arms around me, and I jumped in surprise.

"No hanky panky."

"I promise."

"Yeah, right." I stepped up closer to the water and passed him a towel and soap.

Facing him, I washed him across his chest.

"What do you think of my parents moving in with us?"

"Why?"

"I want to take a little time off and spend time with them."

"There won't be any more problems."

"I know, but time is short, and I want to make memories."

"Whatever you need." He wrapped an arm around my shoulder, closing the distance.

"Still not having sex, baby."

He dropped his arms, and I chuckled at the harsh glare across his face. I stood on my tippy toes and kissed him on the mouth and laughed.

* * *

TWO HOURS LATER, my parents sat around the living room with JJ and Jianna, playing with their presents they'd brought them.

"Mom, I didn't think you'd bring this many toys."

She waved me off. "These are my babies; we get to spoil them."

"Are you guys hungry? Martha's in the kitchen making lunch."

"We ate on the plane," Dad replied.

"Where's Joaquin?" Mom asked.

"In his office." I sat on the couch and watched Jianna try to eat the toy doll.

"So tell us how everything is going. The news has been running with lies."

"Everything was a misunderstanding. My lawyer got the charges dismissed."

"Did this have anything to do with Joaquin?" Dad questioned.

"I won't lie, it had to do with some business associates."

"You were caught in the middle?" Dad asked.

"Yeah."

"I'm not happy about this, Sofia."

"I know, but he fixed it and made sure the people who hurt Shamar got what they deserved."

"Your career?"

"I'm going to take some time off."

"For how long?" Mom inquired.

"A few months at least. I need to spend time with the kids."

"I think that's a good idea," Mom responded, lifting JJ in the air.

"What do you think about living with us?"

"Here?"

"It won't be our permanent home, but at least for a few months."

They looked at each other briefly.

"What does Joaquin say?" Dad inquired.

"He's fine with whatever I want."

"If you need us, baby, we're here." Mom stood with JJ and came to sit next to me on the couch.

"Thank you."

"Mommy, look what Poppa got me." JJ showed off the fire truck.

"I see, baby." I rubbed his back.

"What do you have to do today?"

"Nothing, I wanted to see if you want to go shopping."

"How about we pick up some food and have friends come over."

"We can take the kids to the pool out back while Martha gets the groceries."

"You still can't go out?" Dad questioned.

"I can go, but it's safer to keep it under wraps until the news cycle finds a new story."

"That's fine. Come on, JJ." Mom jumped up with JJ in her arms. I laughed at him giggling when she covered his entire face with kisses. Dad followed us with Jianna as she slept in his arms.

"I'll meet you out there. Get Martha a list of what we need."

I headed to the kitchen and saw Martha talking with Madelyn.

"My mom wants to make dinner."

"What do you need?" Martha asked.

"At least enough for fifteen people. I'm going to invite Cassidy and Gael over."

"Sounds fine to me." Martha grabbed the notepad and started taking notes.

Fifteen minutes later, I came outside to the backyard and saw my parents playing with JJ in the pool. Jianna sat on the edge with her feet in the pool.

"Martha's going to grab some groceries."

"Do you need to pick up anything special?"

"We can pick up some clothes at the mall."

"I'll have Cassidy get a personal shopper."

"We're regular people, Sofia. We don't need a personal shopper," Mom fussed.

"I agree, but for right now, just work with me please."

I slipped my sandals off and put my feet in the water. The kids had fun and laughed with their grandparents for about an hour. I stood and helped to take Jianna back in and feed her a new bottle. I stepped into the office to see Joaquin on the phone.

"Let me call you back." Joaquin ended the call and put the phone down.

"I miss you." I went around his desk and placed Jianna in his arms.

"How are your parents?"

"Good, waiting to see you."

"I'm done working. You got me for the rest of the day."

"Martha is back from grabbing groceries."

"You see this?" Joaquin turned his computer toward me, and I read the headlines.

Actress and Singer Sofia Fuertes Found Innocent.

"I know Cassidy probably had back-to-back calls."

"Are you sure you want to take a break?"

"Positive." I slid on top of his desk and crossed my legs.

"What do you think of traveling?"

"Where?"

"To visit my family."

"Does this mean you'll think of allowing Alessandra to come back?"

"Maybe, but not right now."

"I was upset with her, just like you. But you have to forgive her, baby."

"Jianna, tell Mommy you want another sibling." Joaquin coached Jianna, and she dropped her head, laughing.

"No, sir."

"Jianna, move your head if you agree." Joaquin joked, and I smacked my teeth and jumped off his desk to leave him in his office with her.

"Sweetheart!"

"Leave me alone, Joaquin."

CASSIDY

Two days later.

Most of the past few weeks and months kept me super busy with work and less time with Hugo. I knew he was busy with Joaquin, while I was held up handling meetings. The day was going by slowly, and I was headed to lunch with Sofia. We'd just left a final advance screening of the movie she'd done with Shamar. Plus, the girls wanted to catch up, so we said it would be perfect to spend time together and see how the families were doing. I laughed as soon as we walked into Demot's and saw Janice holding a champagne glass in the air, swiveling her hips.

"Please tell me what the occasion is." Sofia stood next to her and planted her hand on her hip.

"Sofia! Finally, you got here." Janice gulped the champagne down.

"What's the champagne for?"

"I'm not pregnant!" Janice announced, and my mouth dropped. Sabrina and Liz laughed at my expression.

"Cassidy, right?" Sabrina waved at me, and I waved back.

"Yes."

"She's my manager now," Sofia said.

"The glow up is nice," Janice replied.

"She's had at least three glasses," Liz complained, taking the bottle out of her hands.

"Hello, ladies. Can I get you anything?" the waitress asked.

"Can I get a glass of water?" I asked.

"You guys don't understand." Janice grabbed a piece of bread.

"Joaquin asked me about another baby," Sofia brought up.

"Hugo and I haven't talked about kids yet."

All eyes looked at me.

"Give it time," all the girls said at the same moment.

"Did Joaquin tell you my husband got shot?" Janice mentioned.

"I thought it was a graze," Sabrina responded and took a sip of her champagne.

"Graze, yeah, right. He thought I didn't have the wound," Janice grumbled.

"I am sorry it got that far." Sofia put her purse on the back of her chair.

"No apology needed; we've been in just as many situations," Sabrina explained.

"Hearing your stories, I'm still surprised I want to marry Hugo."

"We can't tell you not to; we'd be hypocrites." Janice clicked the knife against her glass.

"The situation was crazy, and for Shamar to get in the crossfire..." Sofia closed her eyes and reminisced about Texas.

"We've lost a lot of good people throughout the years," Liz said.

"I'm taking a break from filming and recording," Sofia blurted out.

"How does Joaquin feel about that?" Janice questioned.

"He was surprised but understands."

"You and Hugo." Sabrina pointed at me.

"Unexpected, but I'm happy."

"To be a wife of a soldier takes a lot of strength," Liz said. The waitress came back out and placed our glasses of water down.

"Can we get the pizza and salad?" Sofia ordered.

"Coming right up." The waitress picked up our menus and went back to the kitchen.

"What about going out to the club and celebrating?" Janice suggested.

"The guys won't agree to that," Sofia said.

"Who says they have to know?" Janice winked and sipped on the wine.

"I'm down for a night out."

"If you can handle Hugo's lifestyle, you're fine with us," Sabrina toasted, and I smiled.

"We call ourselves mommy mafia," Janice teased and chortled.

"A full-on text message group," Sofia explained.

"I'm ready for the group chat, but hopefully I can keep my career," I said.

"Just remember what they do keeps them in a headspace you sometimes can't reach," Sabrina explained.

"What do you mean?"

"She means blowjobs go a long way," Janice replied, and I choked on my water.

"She's telling the truth," Liz responded and cut into her tuna casserole.

"Sofia said you girls were funny."

"Welcome to the crew, Cassidy." Sofia raised a glass, and I joined in as we talked about the kids and going out tonight without the men.

* * *

JANICE SHIFTED her hips in the VIP section of Antonio's club as the DJs played all the old school music from Donna Summer to current Mariah Carey. I laughed when she climbed on top of the table and pretended to be the singer. The guys thought we were having a girls' night in at Sabrina's, and we'd snuck out to the club. I told Hugo I would meet him tomorrow for breakfast, but he insisted on picking me up, so I needed to make sure I was back at her place before the morning.

"Come on, Cassidy!" Janice extended a hand for me to get on top of the table.

"I think you're doing fine without me." I chuckled and watched her flip me off.

"How are your parents?" I asked Sofia.

"Good, watching the kids. I told them we came out tonight."

"You don't think they'll tell the guys?"

"We're surrounded by Antonio's people."

"You guys are boring. Get up and dance," Janice complained.

"How many drinks have you had?"

"Not enough. You guys are bringing my high down." Janice climbed off the table and sat on the couch.

"I guess you thought sneaking out was okay." Hugo stood with Carlo, Antonio, and Joaquin.

"Uhm."

"Baby!" Janice jumped up and held her arms out for Carlo.

All the girls looked at Janice and rolled our eyes.

"I thought you were in charge, Janice?" Sofia questioned.

"She runs her mouth," Carlo teased and grabbed her waist.

"Excuse you, don't give me too much now. That other arm can get a graze too," Janice huffed, crossing her arms over her chest.

I giggled at the two of them.

"None of you told us you'd be here." Antonio walked over to Sabrina and lifted her chin.

"I'm sorry, baby." Sabrina softened and kissed me on the lips.

"I thought the mommy mafia was hard core," I whispered in Sofia's ear.

"They talk a good game," Carlo said.

"Sweetheart..." Joaquin started to approach Sofia.

Janice stepped in front of him, tilting her head to the left.

"The next time you put my husband in the middle of a shootout, think twice," Janice said.

Joaquin held a smirk. "I do apologize, Janice," he said.

"You might be able to get that pretty smile over on Sofia, but I don't play," Janice fussed.

Joaquin looked back at Carlo, and he held his hands up in surrender.

"He has nothing to do with me and you right now." Janice poked him in the chest.

"Janice, you've gotten Sabrina in a lot of mess," Antonio complained.

"Sabrina, remind your husband it's because of me you two even met," Janice spat.

I walked over to Hugo and wrapped my arms around his shoulders.

"I missed you," I said.

"You want to go back to my place?" Hugo wrapped his hands around my waist.

"Love to."

"Cassidy! Cassidy!" Janice yelled my name.

"Huh."

"You give in too quickly, girl."

I chortled and nodded my head.

"I promise to work on that." I winked and turned to grab his hand. We walked out of the club with a few guards beside us. He held the door of his car open, and I slid in and went to open the driver's side and buckled my seatbelt.

"I love you," Hugo said.

"I love you more."

He held my hand up with my engagement ring, and I smiled, leaned over the seat, and grabbed his chin to tongue him down.

"Come on, hurry to your place." I kissed him again.

JOAQUIN

I laughed at JJ as he pushed the plate of vegetables away from him and went for the snack I had on my desk. I'd brought him and Jianna in my office with me while Sofia got dressed for her friend's funeral. Her parents were unpacking and settling in, and I didn't need them thinking I was a terrible father on top of crappy husband. News outlets did enough of trying to break up our marriage.

"Daddy, look at Jianna!" JJ yelled, bringing me out of my daze. I groaned, picking up the napkin to wipe her face and hands free of the chocolate pudding.

"Jianna, you made a big mess on Daddy's desk."

Jianna smiled, and the aggravation left me immediately as her full dimples and piercing eyes filled my heart. I placed her down in the baby seat and helped JJ finish eating when a small knock came to my door.

"Come in!" JJ shouted.

"What are you doing here, JJ?" Sofia grinned to mask her sadness of what today was and approached the desk and kissed the kids.

"Your car out front?" I questioned.

"Yeah, Cassidy is coming with me."

"Are you sure you want to go?"

"I need to go."

"When you come back, we can have dinner with just the two of us." I helped JJ down to play with his toys. I reached out for Sofia and pulled her in my lap, running a hand up her arm. She leaned over and pushed her tongue in my mouth.

"Mmmmm…" She twirled, flicking her tongue.

"When you get back, we can have dinner and dessert." I pulled back and stared into her eyes.

"I'd like that very much."

"Remember, my men will be with you at all times."

"I know, even though everything is done with Lusting."

"Our lives are never simple, sweetheart."

Her hands fell on my chest, and I picked up the back of her hand and kissed her palm.

Sofia stood and rubbed the kids' faces and walked out of my office. I reached for my phone while the kids played.

"I'm surprised to hear from you," Dante said.

"When are you coming into town?" I asked.

"I wasn't planning a trip for a few months."

From Philadelphia, Dante Achille was a friend who like me, was in the business. His family's roots were from Italy.

"Make a trip soon."

"Is this business or pleasure?"

Dante was a trained killer and bastard who no one wanted to do business with. If you owed him, then you were already marked for death. I'd done a few jobs for him that he couldn't reach, and we'd been friendly ever since.

"I hear you're thinking of expanding, and I wanted to make sure of the details."

He chuckled.

"Don't worry, friend. New York is all yours."

"Oh, I'm not worried."

"I'll see what I can do, but business here has ramped up."

"If you find yourself needing to get away, I have a few places."

"I might take you up on that offer."

"Then we have an understanding."

"Clear understanding."

I finished the call, sat back in my seat, and closed my eyes. The next call I needed to make would hopefully make our family whole again. I punched in the number and waited for someone to pick up.

"Fuertes residence."

"How are you?"

"Joaquin!"

"Yes, Mother."

"Oh! I'm so happy to hear from you," Alba said.

"How is the family?"

"Everyone is lovely. Do you want to talk to your father?"

"I spoke with him a few days ago. How is Alessandra?"

"She's adjusting."

"Did Father make her go through with the engagement?"

"No, and thank God he didn't."

I tensed up at her words.

"Why? What happened?"

"I can't say, but I know she's better."

"Should I come out there?"

"We'd love for you, Sofia, and the kids to visit."

"I'll check with Sofia and her schedule. Her parents are here."

"That's lovely. You need family around you."

"Mother."

"No, Joaquin, let Alessandra rest. You've done enough."

"Tell her I'm sorry."

"I will."

"Love you," I said and ended the call.

"Daddy!" JJ squealed, clapping his hands in excitement.

I smiled and went to pick up him and Jianna, and we walked out to the hallway and down toward the kitchen.

"Do you need anything, sir?" Martha asked.

"Did Sofia leave?"

"Yes, about ten minutes ago."

"I'm going to put the kids down for a nap and head out to my office," I explained and turned to head upstairs to their rooms.

* * *

ANTONIO POURED another shot of Hennessy in my glass, and I gulped it down as the monitor on the TV in the bar replayed the funeral of Sofia's friend. The camera panned to her briefly as she hugged his parents.

"I spoke with Dante today."

Carlo and Antonio looked at each other.

"How did that go?" Carlo questioned.

"Normal for us."

"You're both hotheads, so I'm surprised." Antonio stepped around the bar and sat at the end.

"Do you ever think about giving it all up?" I waved my hand around the room.

"This life can never be given up unless it's death," Antonio replied.

"I invited him to visit."

"What are you thinking?"

"He has connections with Russians and the Lusting family."

"Thinking of taking over?" Carlo questioned.

"You don't need the money," Antonio reminded me, and I nodded.

"I would say the same thing to you, but you built clubs and bars all over the world."

"Legit businesses."

My left brow rose in question.

"We can't discuss who is more legit or not," Carlo joked.

"He's right, but I need to make sure I have no more snakes lurking."

"Dante is friendly but deadly if he feels cheated."

"I know."

"How did your night end with Sofia after the club?"

"You mean after your wife tried to put me in my place."

He slapped me on the shoulder and stood.

"Janice is harmless." Carlo walked around the bar and grabbed another Hennessy bottle.

Antonio and I stared at him in disbelief.

"What?"

"Carlo, that woman is nuts," I said.

Carlo flipped me off, and I chuckled.

"Leave my woman out of this," Carlo replied.

"Hugo is next," Antonio mentioned.

"Gael and Hugo," I growled, still not overly happy about my sister being with my best friend.

"You of all people know love can't be stopped." Carlo pointed at my ring finger.

Sofia had our names and wedding date engraved on the inside of the wedding bands.

"I need to get home." I took the last of my shots.

"Where are you off so fast?"

"I promised Sofia a dinner just for the two of us."

"The doting husband," Antonio teased me, and I cursed him out in Italian.

I slid my hand in my pocket, pulled out fifty dollars, and left it on the counter before walking out of the bar to my awaiting car.

"Home?" Gabriella questioned.

"Yeah." My head fell back on the seat and closed my eyes briefly as the soothing alcohol raced through my body. Thirty minutes later, the car arrived at home, and I stepped out clumsily and went to slide my key in the door when it opened automatically, revealing Sofia wearing a long black silk gown. I licked my lips, ready to take her upstairs and undress her down to nothing.

"Wipe that thought out of your head," Sofia said, reaching for her coat.

"Wait, let's go upstairs for a second." I reached for her hand.

She chortled, and I frowned.

"We have dinner plans, Joaquin."

"Dinner will be there. I'll have a hot meal waiting." I licked the left side of her face. She trembled in my hold, and I planted both hands on her hips and squeezed her ass.

"Dinner first and then dessert."

I groaned, pulled back, smirking, and pecked her on the lips.

"I'm going to make you pay."

"Really, how so?"

"You have to wait and see."

"You remember the last time you tried to play this game?"

Sofia tapped me on my nose, and I shook my head, thinking of when I kept her from having an orgasm.

"Sweetheart."

"Dinner first, Mr. Fuertes, and then I might let you have dessert." She rubbed my chin and walked around me toward the car.

"She drives a hard bargain."

I hopped in next to her and snuggled up close as Gabriella drove us to Demot's for dinner, since it was still early in the night. The kids were fine with her parents, and I had planned on staying at a hotel tonight and never leaving the room unless it was an emergency. She wrapped her hand around mine, and we kissed non-stop as our mouths synced passionately.

I had her favorite foods pre-ordered, so all we'd need to do was sit and have an evening with just the two of us, since I'd rented the entire restaurant for us.

"I like this dress."

"Thank you."

"I'll like it better when you're out of it though." I slipped my hand underneath her strap and caressed the top of her breast. Her breath hitched, and her head tipped onto my shoulder.

"Dinner."

"We will. Afterwards, I have a hotel."

"What about the kids?"

"Your parents are there."

"I know, but I hate to leave them all night."

"They'll be fine."

"All right."

"How are you feeling after today?"

"It was sad, but I'm glad I went."

"Anyone say anything to you?"

"A few photographers tried to get interviews, but I ignored them."

"Long as no one did anything to touch you."

"Everyone knows I belong to Joaquin Fuertes." Sofia put her hand on my chest.

"Have to remind anyone that a problem can become a solution."

"You're a wonderful husband and father."

"The second I put that ring on your finger, I vowed to love you forever."

"You have."

"Even if it hurts?"

She ran a finger across my lips.

"The love pushed through the pain. I will always be yours."

The car pulled up to the restaurant, and Gabriella started to open the door.

"I got it." I climbed out and helped Sofia, wrapping my arm around her, and kept her close. I shook hands with the hostess, and the guard held the door open as we walked through. A banner hung with our names displayed.

"When did you do this?"

SOFIA

The words *Joaquin and Sofia* took me by surprise. My husband wasn't one for the most public displays of affection. For him to rent out a restaurant and show our love in this manner was new, but exciting.

"I had Cassidy help."

"Thank you."

"Come, let's sit down." He headed to the table in the middle of the restaurant and pulled my chair out, and I sat.

"Did the kids get to bed all right?" he asked.

"Yes, my mom gave them a bath and read to them."

The waitress filled our glasses with white wine.

"Thank you."

"Your food will be out shortly," she replied.

"We talked about visiting my family, and I think it's time."

"Okay."

"I want to make amends with Alessandra."

"You should."

"Even Gael has kept his distance unless it's work."

"She's your sister. It hurts, and we all know what that caused."

"At least you still love me."

411

"That will never change, even when you get into your caveman mode."

"Caveman?" he asked.

"You know that I'm king. I run the house, and you do what I say." I chuckled.

He smirked and shrugged his shoulders. I threw my napkins at him.

"Anyway, I'm happy you're going to make things right."

"When do you go back to work?"

"I'm going to take some time out, but we have the premiere in a week."

"Do you need me there?"

"No, baby, I'd rather not answer questions because all the attention would be gone."

The waitress arrived with plates of baked ziti and baked fish, and we thanked her.

"What do you think of another baby?"

"We have enough with the two we got now," I joked.

"I want another little baby that looks like you."

"Jianna's spoiled enough."

"We can practice at least." He winked his left eye.

"That's the best part."

"How about we leave and get this food to go?"

"Nope, we're going to have a nice dinner as a normal couple." I held my hand up and stopped him from calling the waitress over.

"You've been hanging around Janice too much," he mumbled, and I cackled in disbelief at the frown on his face.

* * *

A WEEK LATER, I pushed the stroller with JJ and Jianna inside through the mall surrounded by five or six guards like I was the First Lady, and they were the Secret Service in their shades. Cassidy and I wanted to pick up a few outfits for the trip that Joaquin had planned for the family. I hadn't seen his parents in so long. This would be interesting since Alessandra and I still hadn't talked.

"What about this dress for Jianna?" Cassidy held up a red and white polka dot dress with matching hat.

"She loves purple." I reached for the other dress in a maroon and purple color.

"Did you have a chance to look at the dresses for the premiere?"

I leaned down to help JJ with the chips in his hand, stood, and continued searching the dress rack.

"I have it picked out."

"We won't need to ask any questions on the red carpet."

"I'd like to avoid that at all costs."

"Already put out a notice that you're not answering anything."

"How are things with you?"

"Hugo and I are good."

"Happy for you, Cassidy. You've come a long way."

"Strange to be getting married, let alone to someone in the mob," she whispered, and I chuckled.

"Just wait until you have kids with them."

"Do we need anything else out here before we head home?"

"No, I think we have enough bags, and the crowd is noticing us."

I looked out the window of Neiman's and saw flashes of light from phones.

"Let me pay for these, and then we can go." Cassidy took the dress out of my hands and walked to the counter to pay.

Twenty minutes later, we loaded the car up with our bags, and I placed Jianna next to me in the SUV and JJ next to Cassidy as the car drove into traffic. I picked up the doll she was holding and played with it as she laughed.

"You come across as vibrant and fresh in this role," Cassidy read off a headline.

"Love how they try to build you up after tearing you down." I shook my head in annoyance.

"Hollywood for you."

The traffic was light heading back to our home, and we decided to come straight back home after the premiere. As long as I showed my face tonight and did a few interviews online, I should be good to step away from fully promoting.

The car arrived back home twenty minutes later, and I stepped out and carried Jianna inside. Cassidy held onto JJ when the door opened to Madelyn.

"She needs a nap," I told her.

"She looks tired," Madelyn replied, patting her back.

"I have the premiere tonight, and then I'm home for a break."

"Sounds good." Madelyn held out her hand for JJ, and they walked into the playroom.

I sauntered to the kitchen, opened the fridge, and grabbed a bottle of water.

"Hey, baby," Dad said.

He leaned over to give me a hug.

"Hey, Dad."

"Where are you coming from?"

"Shopping with the kids."

"Your mom is outside by the pool."

"I have the premiere tonight. Do you guys want to go?" I asked.

"You know I don't do movie mess." He sat on the chair in front of the island.

"This will be fun."

"Talk to your mother and see if she wants to go."

"Okay, old man. Don't be grumpy when she makes you come." I hugged him from behind, walked down the hall, and saw Joaquin's office door closed.

Shrugging my shoulders, I headed to the back door, pushed it open, and saw my mother and Joaquin talking.

"I thought you'd be in your office." I bent over and kissed him on the lips.

"He's keeping me company."

"How were the kids?" he asked.

"Good for once." I chortled.

"Are they sleeping?" Mom questioned.

"Madelyn has them in the playroom."

"I'll go check on them soon."

"I asked Dad and wanted to see if you wanted to go to my premiere."

"Oh, I'd like that, honey."

"Tell your husband he has to go." I pointed at the house.

"Marriage is a compromise. I see you and Joaquin seem to be doing better."

We looked at each other, and I grinned.

"Better than ever."

"Happy for you, baby."

"Thanks, Mom. So we need to get dressed because we leave in two hours."

"Glam squad doing my makeup?" she questioned.

"Yes, ma'am."

My mom stood, and I grasped her hand and walked with her back into the house. I saw the team coming in with our attire for tonight, along with hair and makeup. Mom was right about the compromise in our marriage and being able to show honesty in ourselves. Before, I was at a point of giving this all up, but I knew this man would fight tooth and nail to keep me and our kids protected. I giggled at JJ trying to put his feet in the shoes my dad picked out for his tuxedo. My boy had no clue what would be expected of him when the time came. Would I be ready to let him go out into the world and learn from his father, or would I keep him sheltered from the Fuertes family business?

JOAQUIN

a month later.

"Dante, glad you called."

It was therefore suggested that I travel out to Philadelphia to meet with Dante, which I agreed to do. Carlo, Gael, and Gabriella would accompany me. The trip back home was still getting worked out once Sofia finished her press tour that had gained considerable notice. A stunning parade of naked women appeared at Achille's club SSO. As I took a closer look, I wasn't interested in meeting him this way, but he wouldn't meet me anywhere else for business.

"We can talk in the back."

The women approached him as he escorted us down the dark hall of his club, and he smiled at them or smacked them on the butt.

"How many have you slept with?" I questioned when he opened the door of his office.

He waved me off and walked toward the bar in the corner.

"Only two this month," Dante replied, pouring a shot of tequila.

"My girl would say your dick might fall off," Carlo joked.

In response, he grunted and held up a glass for each of us.

"How long are you here in my hometown?" Dante questioned.

"I flew in just for today." I unbuckled my coat and relaxed.

"So you want me to broker a deal." Dante came over and sat on the edge of his desk. "Between my connections in New York, Spain, and Italy, we can do big things in Russia."

"I love money."

"The only thing we need to be careful of is blowback from Lusting."

"I heard his people are investigating what happened."

"His wife put out a missing person's report."

"We can make that go away." Dante cocked his head to the right.

"No killing children and women," Carlo said.

"That's the De Luca rules," Dante replied, slid off his desk, and went to take a seat.

"What are the Achille rules?"

"Money and family."

"Our names are too hot right now," I explained.

"So I'll talk to the Russians and Lusting to end the investigation."

"We'll cut you in on the deal."

"Sounds interesting." Dante rubbed his chin, lifting his feet on top of the desk.

"Twenty percent."

"Mota?" Dante inquired.

"Won't be a problem."

"Maybe I should visit New York a little more. I hear your women are exquisite."

"Our women, but you'll have to find your own," Carlo argued, sliding back in the chair.

"We go way back, Joaquin."

"I agree."

"Might get dirty?"

"I'm fine with that, are you?"

He grinned.

"Red is my favorite color." He extended his hand for a shake. I stood and grasped his palm.

"Then we'll do some business."

"You stay and get a dance from my girls."

"We have wives and kids at home," Carlo said.

"Forgot you're on leashes now," he joked, Carlo flipped him off.

"Call me when it's set up," I replied, heading out of his office to the front entrance and our waiting limo.

* * *

TWO DAYS LATER.

Right on schedule, Dante made the connection with the Russians, and Lusting's people were put on warning to keep my family's name out of their mouths. Currently standing at a loading dock to get a shipment of guns from France in crates to unload, Gael and Hugo were with me, and we had the trucks waiting to place everything up to send out to our customers.

"How much are we paying Dante?"

"Twenty percent."

"How many shipments are coming?"

"Two a month."

"We might need to hire more soldiers."

"Have Hugo take over handling the hiring." Hugo looked shocked, but I knew he was loyal. Giving him more responsibility showed that I trusted him outside of taking care of my wife and kids.

"We still need to get someone to replace him."

"He's the only one I trust with Sofia."

"Are you cool with that, Hugo?"

"More than ready," Hugo replied.

"Bigger things are happening." Gael shook his hand.

"Is Cassidy going to be a problem?"

"She's onboard," Hugo answered.

"Then you have my approval and gratitude. When's the wedding?"

"No clue; she's keeping me out of all the planning."

"Reminds me of Sofia."

We watched them pack up the crates and sign off.

"All the women are crazy."

"How's Alessandra?" I asked, and he went silent.

"She wants to come back."

"That's your choice."

"I told her to give it a little more time."

"Whatever you think is best."

"She's special to me," Gael responded.

"The second you have them, never let them go."

"Sofia said you're trying to get her pregnant?"

She'd been acting weird lately, refusing to take a test.

"She wants to wait another year or two."

"What do you want?"

"If it was my choice, she'd be pregnant with twins."

They chuckled as our security of the loading dock signed off and gave me the go ahead to leave. I paid him a hefty amount to keep our stash safe near the waterfront.

"Dante told me how you two met." Gael turned and got inside the driver's side of the car. I climbed in the passenger seat and read over the manifest for the shipment.

"What lie did he tell?"

"He didn't give me all the details and said that's the whole story."

"His life's a book that he refuses to tell."

"Maybe he needs a woman to calm him down."

"We have women; have we calmed down?"

He looked around at the surrounding area, and I chuckled.

"Point taken."

"Exactly: The Fuertes Mafia will never stop."

EPILOGUE: SOFIA

Six months later

The entire house was loud and in an uproar as our families came together to celebrate Jianna's first birthday. Joaquin flew the entire family to Spain to his family's home and hired an event planner to set up the inside and outside with beautiful decorations with Jianna's name across the banner. She was walking now and saying little words that we couldn't understand, but the enjoyment of her learning and growing was something I couldn't wait to see. I'd arranged for Cassidy to hold off on me taking any new film roles, because we planned on staying in Spain for a few months. Even Alessandra was back to her old self and being helpful and supportive. She was staying and getting her design classes transferred, so she could be closer to her parents now that she was pregnant. Gael made it his number-one mission to wait on her hand and foot. Even Joaquin was surprised by how attentive he was being to his sister. The eight hundred thousand-acre land held everything you could need from the main house to a private landing strip. With the kids here, they'd added a little swing set for Jianna and race car area for JJ, which I refused to let him play with since he was too young.

JJ was handsome in the same outfit as his father. I stood on the side, admiring JJ talking with Joaquin's mother. Jianna wobbled behind them to keep up. Her hair was up in little pigtails with ribbons my mother had from when I was a baby.

"Mi amore." His strong hands enveloped my waist, and I sighed, leaning my head on his shoulder. He kissed the side of my neck, squeezing me close.

"She's getting big."

"Mi manchi."

"What are we going to do when they grow up?"

"Have another one." He kissed me on the side of my neck.

I paused and frowned.

"I thought you wanted it to be just us after the kids get older?" I grabbed him around the neck.

He wrapped a hand around my waist, pulling me in close.

"I've thought about that, but something about seeing you with a belly."

"And making the baby doesn't hurt."

JJ ran over to Alessandra and reached for her to pick him up. His parents held on to Jianna, and I laughed at her trying to run away.

"What do you think about renewing our vows?"

"Just us?"

"With the kids, you, and me."

"Whatever you want, sweetheart."

"I guess those nights coming to see me paid off."

"I told you a long time ago, your beauty and voice drew me to you."

"This family has been the strongest when we're together."

"Fuertes is all about family."

"Then let's go home."

* * *

Thank you for reading Joaquin and Sofia's story. Check out the bonus scenes.

BONUS SCENE: GAEL

"Congrats!" JJ yelled, and I held him up close to Alessandra, so he could kiss the baby's forehead. He was officially four months old today, and I couldn't be happier in life than I was right now. I put JJ back down to run off and play with his toys as Sofia reached for Alexander Gael Velez. We named him with a mixture of both our names, but he looked exactly like me. I was ready to get her pregnant again, but she wanted to wait for when she finished school.

"He looks just like you, Gael," Sofia said.

"I think I helped a little." Alessandra pouted.

Joaquin bent down to hug her, then stood.

"When are you going to make another one?" Alessandra questioned.

Sofia and Joaquin looked at each other.

"We might have something brewing."

"I knew it!" Alessandra excitedly clapped her hands.

"Story will be told later," Joaquin said.

"How did your parents take it about the marriage?"

"They were fine with us eloping."

"How was the delivery?"

"Stressful, and he didn't help." Alessandra pointed at me.

"She was crazy!" I waved my hand in the air.

"Sofia, you had to have seen him. This big, burly mafia guy, running around nervous." Alessandra laughed, and I pursed my lips.

"Ahh, poor baby." Alessandra giggled.

"I get what you mean, Joaquin," I said.

"What?" Sofia and Alessandra spoke at the same time.

"Women hangin' with Janice too long."

They all burst into laughter, but I was serious. Alessandra showed me the text thread for the mommy mafia, and I was disturbed by some of the messages. I even called Carlo to ask if he was safe by living with her because she was nuts.

"Janice isn't that bad," Sofia replied.

"I told Carlo if he needs an alibi, to call me."

Sofia chuckled, and Alessandra got up from the bed.

"We can go out to the patio and eat lunch," she said.

Sofia handed Alexander to Joaquin, and I felt proud to see me and my best friend come to terms and be joined as real brothers and family.

"Maybe you two should create a daddy daycare cartel," Alessandra joked.

"That's enough American TV for you." I pressed a kiss on her lips.

BONUS SCENE: SOFIA

Everyone stood and clapped hands as the happy couple kissed and walked down the aisle. It was a beautiful thing to see Cassidy and Hugo married and in love after denying their feelings for so long. Reminded me a little of myself and Joaquin in the early beginnings and how I'd tried to block out what became a great blessing in my life. The church was full of friends and family on both sides, along with Alessandra, Gael, and the De Luca Cartel. Cassidy wanted to continue managing my career, but I told her it was on hold until she got back from her honeymoon and settled in as a wife. I mean we both found out we were pregnant at the same time, so it was nice to take a break and enjoy life without the headaches of trying to get the latest role or finish an album. I waved at Alessandra as she held her little boy in her arms. He looked exactly like Gael. His long, auburn hair, icy blue eyes, and chubby cheeks made him look like a doll. I was happy they'd stuck it out and became a family even throughout the hardships we'd endured over the past year. I gripped JJ's hand, and Joaquin carried Jianna's little feisty butt while I rubbed my small belly in my maid of honor dress.

"Mommy, can we have cake now?" JJ looked up at me, and I smiled. My son was four now and reminded me of his father every day with his dark, bushy brows and how he demanded attention from all the ladies, especially me.

"Not right now, JJ. We have to take pictures and then go to the reception."

"I want cake now," he fussed, crossing his arms and stomping his feet.

"You see your son." I pointed down at JJ, and Joaquin smirked.

"He's fine."

"No, he's spoiled, and it's your fault."

"That reminds of you when I'm devouring you at night," Joaquin whispered in my ear, and I blushed, fanning myself. He put a hand on my lower back and tapped me on my butt.

"I can't believe Hugo is married, and Alessandra and Gael are parents."

"My parents can't either."

"Your father has come around, though."

"Thank Alba for that."

Cassidy and Hugo finished with photos, and the planner directed us toward the limos outside. Joaquin gripped my hand and walked down the stairs with JJ next to him and our parents behind us. Joaquin wanted to rent out Antonio's, but I told him it was too small for the amount of people who'd RSVP'd. We'd rented the Waldorf for two hundred and fifty people, but what made it even more crazy was the amount of cartel families who showed up from De Lucas to Carringtons. It was a who's who of cartel life. The driver shut our limo door, and I helped fasten the kids' seatbelts as we followed Cassidy and Hugo to the reception. Joaquin gripped my hand, moved toward my belly, and rubbed the top before leaning over to kiss me on the lips.

"This is our last one." I pointed at my stomach.

He glared, and I chuckled.

"Mommy, I want a brother," JJ said.

"Well, you'll be happy to know that soon I will find out."

I was only two and a half months along and wanted to keep it a surprise at first, but Joaquin hated surprises, so we decided to find out. While in the States, we decided that living back in Spain for some time would work out best until I was ready to get back into acting and singing. Living in his family's home permanently was not an option, so he bought land and decided to build our own compound on twenty-thousand acres.

"We're here!" JJ yelled excitedly.

"Wait, JJ." I helped him unbuckle his seat. Our son was fast and loved to take off without us, no matter where we went. Joaquin grabbed my hand, helped me step out of the limo, and went to grab Jianna. I walked over to Cassidy talking with the girls and gave her and Hugo a hug.

"How does it feel?" I asked.

"Like I'm somebody's wife." Cassidy giggled and covered her mouth.

"You're a part of the club now," Janice joked.

"As long as she doesn't have to initiate like you two did."

"That comes with the territory," Janice replied and slid her shades down her nose.

"Thank you again, Sofia, for renting out this hotel," Cassidy said.

"My pleasure. Well, Joaquin actually."

"Hugo, let's go inside." Cassidy grasped his hand.

"Only one left is Alessandra and Gael," Janice blurted out.

"I think we'll get an update from them soon."

* * *

Thank you for reading Joaquin and Sofia book 3. If you love dark mafia romance, check out Antonio and Sabrina Struck In Love here.

ORDER OF SERIES: A&S DARK MAFIA UNIVERSE

Order of Reading

The Early Years-A Prequel Short Story
https://books2read.com/u/49Zjnw
Antonio and Sabrina Struck In Love Book 1
https://books2read.com/u/4AxKLo
Antonio and Sabrina Struck In Love Book 2
https://books2read.com/u/bpED6g
Antonio and Sabrina Struck In Love Book 3
https://books2read.com/u/3LpgdJ
Janice and Carlo Captivated By His Love
https://books2read.com/u/b6je6M
Antonio and Sabrina Struck In Love Book 4
https://books2read.com/u/4NQyE9
Joaquin Fuertes-The Fuertes Cartel Book 1
https://books2read.com/u/mvZlgV
Joaquin Fuertes-The Fuertes Cartel Book 2
https://books2read.com/u/4DWwLd
Antonio and Sabrina Struck In Love Book 5
https://books2read.com/u/b5kZ8O

Joaquin Fuertes-The Fuertes Cartel Book 3
https://books2read.com/u/4A5LGp
The Carrington Cartel

SNEAK PEEK - THE CARRINGTON CARTEL-2022

Gigi's future has always been known. She's to marry into the Ramini family. Nothing matters more than that to her family.

As the daughter of the renowned Laurent Carrington, long-time gun and drug runner for the cartel, nothing about her life is ambiguous. She does what her father says or suffers the consequences.

Axel is good at his job. As lead enforcer for a notorious cartel associate, he's entrusted to monitor Gigi's every move. What he doesn't expect is to fall in love with her. Now he's faced with a tough choice—one that could cost him his life if he's not careful.

Will Gigi's plan to keep her arranged marriage at bay and keep her budding relationship with Axel sunder wraps shield her from her father's wrath, or will she go down an ugly path?

ACKNOWLEDGMENTS

I want to thank my team, who helps me behind the scenes, from my editors to my test readers and graphic designers, and the list goes on. I truly appreciate each of you for keeping me on my toes.

CATALOG OF RELEASES

The Early Years-A Prequel Short Story

Antonio and Sabrina: Struck in Love 1, 2, 3,4,5

Heart of Stone, Book 1 (Emery & Jackson)

Heart Of Stone Book 1.5 Emery &Jackson A Valentine's Day Short

Janice and Carlo: Captivated By His Love

Heart of Stone, Book 2 (Jordan and Damon)

Temptation

Heart of Stone, Book 3 (Angela and Brent)

Cocky Catcher

Bossy Billionaire

Bottoms Up Heart of Stone, Book 3.5(Jessica and Joseph Short

Love Shorts: A Collection of Short Stories

Joaquin Fuertes (The Fuertes Cartel Book 1)

Exposed (Salvation Society Novel)

Joaquin Fuertes (The Fuertes Cartel Book 2)

Refuel (A Driven World Novel)

Pressure (A Driven World Novel)

Until Serena (HEA World Novel)

Antonio and Sabrina: Struck in Love 5
Heart of Stone, Book 4 (Jessica and Joseph)
She's All I Need
Red Light District (A Fantasy Romance Short)

PLAYLIST: JOAQUIN FUERTES: THE FUERTES CARTEL

1.Monica-Without You
   2.Missy Elliot -Hot Boyz
   3.Jazmine Sullivan-Need U Bad
   4.Rihanna-Love The Way You Lie
   5.Jonas Bros-Sucker
   6.India.Arie-Steady Love
   7.Maroon Five-Girls Like You
   8.Jason Mraz-Better With You
   9.Thomas Rhett-Playing With Fire
   10.Kendrick Lamar-Love

WHAT'S NEXT?

Want to know what happens next? Follow me at the links below to catch the next release.

Thank you so much for reading, and if you enjoyed the crazy ride and decided to leave a review, we'd truly appreciate the support. Reviews are the lifeblood of the publishing world. They're read, appreciated, and needed. Please consider taking the time to leave a few words on Goodreads or Bookbub.

Sign up for updates and sneak peeks at the sites below:
www.chiquitadennie.com
www.bookbub.com/chiquitadennie
www.goodreads.com/author/chiquitadennie
Facebook.com/chiquitassteamyreadinggroup
www.Twitter.com/304_publishing
www.Instagram.com/304publishing
www.Facebook.com/authorchiquitadennie
www.304publishing.tumblr.com

ABOUT THE AUTHOR

Chiquita Dennie is an author of Contemporary, Romantic Suspense, Women's Fiction, and Erotic Romance. She lives in Los Angeles, CA. Originally from TN and before she started writing contemporary romance, she worked in the entertainment industry on notable TV shows including the Dr. Phil show, Tyra Banks show, American Idol, and Deal or No Deal. But her favorite job is the one she's now doing full time – writing romance.

A Best-Selling Author and Award-winning Filmmaker, her first short film, "Invisible," released in Summer 2017 and screened in multiple festivals and won for Best Short Film. She also hosts a podcast that showcases the latest in Beauty, Business, and Community called "Moscato and Tea." Her debut release of Antonio and Sabrina Struck In Love has opened a new avenue of writing that she loves.

If you want to know when the next book will come out, please visit my website at http://www.chiquitadennie.com, where you can sign up to receive an email for my next release.

www.ingramcontent.com/pod-product-compliance
Lightning Source LLC
Chambersburg PA
CBHW030749030726
47497CB00001B/196